Her mouth was lush and warm, as full of golden promise as the heart of summer.

Their tongues tangled, and Dev groaned and deepened the kiss.

"I knew it." Arta released him. Her eyes were alight. "You do want me!"

"Good God, woman," Dev said, "You've had me turned inside out since we met."

That morning—had it only been that morning she'd appeared, disrupting his life and the investigation, not to mention his peace of mind? It seemed a lifetime ago.

"I confess 'twas the same with me," she said. "Why, then, did you send me away?"

"I didn't send you away. Winnie invited you to stay with her."

"Be that as it may, 'tis lowering." She focused her gaze on his bare chest. "A huntress is not accustomed to indifference."

"A huntress is gorgeous and damn well knows it." Dev took her by the waist and tugged her firmly against his groin. "Does this seem indifferent to you?"

"Nay, I find you impressive, in this as in all things." A saucy smile played about her lips, and she set aside all pretense of coyness. "I think we shall deal extremely well together, you and I, in work... and in play."

Also by Lexi George

Demon Hunting in Dixie
Demon Hunting in the Deep South
Demon Hunting in a Dive Bar
Demon Hunting with a Dixie Deb

And read more Lexi George in
So I Married a Demon Hunter

Demon Hunting with a Southern Sheriff

Lexi George

LYRICAL PRESS
Kensington Publishing Corp.
www.kensingtonbooks.com

LYRICAL PRESS BOOKS are published by

Kensington Publishing Corp.
119 West 40th Street
New York, NY 10018

First Electronic Edition: April 2022
ISBN: 978-1-60183-181-1 (ebook)

First Print Edition: April 2022
ISBN: 978-1-60183-182-8

Printed in the United States of America

Chapter One

Behr County High School, nineteen years ago

"Fight, fight, fight."

The bell rang for first period, shrill and insistent, but the circle of excited students lingered around the two boys squared off in front of the school. Hooting and jeering, the group egged them on.

At the edge of the crowd, Livy Freeman drew her gray bomber jacket around her thin shoulders. "Dev, please. Let it go."

Dev shook his head and glared at his adversary. Russ Barber was a senior and a star athlete at BCH. His dad owned R&B Transport, a major contributor to the Booster Club, but Dev was too angry to care.

"No," he said, clenching his fists. "He hurt you."

Russ took a menacing step toward Dev. "What did you say?"

"You heard me." Dev widened his stance. "You hurt Livy. Don't do it again."

"Back off, twerp, and mind your own business."

"Livy's my friend. That makes it my business."

"Yeah? Well, I don't take orders from ninth graders."

"Nah, you just smack 'em around." Dev sneered. "You're the man, picking on a girl half your size. Whadda you do for kicks in your spare time, beat up toddlers?"

With a snarl, Russ shoved Dev to the sidewalk and jumped on top of him. The air exited Dev's lungs with an audible *whoosh*. Russ outweighed him by at least sixty pounds.

"Shut up, you little shit," Russ said, and punched Dev in the face.

The blow broke Dev's nose and busted his upper lip, filling his mouth and the back of his throat with the coppery taste of blood. Black spots danced in front of his eyes. The simmering rage he had struggled to control since reaching puberty surged to the surface. With a roar, he shoved Russ, and the muscular football player sailed into the air. Russ's expression of surprise as he shot high above the flagpole was comical and supremely satisfying...until gravity kicked in and the bully hurtled back to earth.

Dev rolled out of the way, and Russ hit the pavement with a sickening crunch.

"My leg," Russ bawled. "My *leg*."

Shaking with adrenaline, Dev got to his feet. Russ's left foot was twisted at an unnatural angle, and the bones of his lower leg protruded through the skin. It was an ugly break, and Russ screamed in agony, a horrible, keening sound that went on and on.

Dev stared at the other boy in horror. *A man in a passion rides a wild horse*, Aunt Weoka had often cautioned him.

She'd warned him to control his temper, that things would happen if he did not.

"Oh, my God." Terri Osborne, a pretty junior girl Dev had secretly admired from afar, clapped her hand over her mouth. "I think I'm going to be sick."

"Dev, you've ruined *everything*," Livy wailed. "Russ and I were supposed to go out Friday night after the ball game."

Dev stared at her in disbelief. "Livy, you aren't... Please tell me you aren't still seeing him."

She tossed her head, her tight black curls dancing around her temples. "Of course, I'm still seeing him."

"Are you nuts? He tried to *choke* you."

"He was drunk. It was an accident."

"You don't 'accidentally' try to wring someone's neck. The guy's a douche."

"He said he was sorry. See?" Livy pushed back the cuff of her jacket sleeve, displaying a charm bracelet on her brown wrist. "It's Juicy Couture. It's official. Russ and I are dating."

"I'm sorry to hear that. You deserve better."

"Better?" Livy stamped her foot. "I'm a freshman, and he's a senior football player."

"So? He's still a douche."

"I think you're jealous, Dev Whitsun." She glared at him belligerently. "You're jealous because *I'm* popular, and you're not."

Whirling, she pushed her way through the crowd and fell to her knees beside Russ.

"It's okay, baby," Livy said, taking his hand. "It's going to be okay."

"What are you, stupid? My leg's broken." Russ writhed in pain. "It hurts." A metal door crashed open, and a redheaded man sprinted out of the building. It was Noble Brock, the freshman English teacher. Dev liked Mr. Brock. Most of his teachers were older than dirt, but Mr. Brock was young and cool.

Mr. Brock pulled Livy to her feet. "Go inside, Livy," he said. "I've got this."

"But—" Livy protested.

"Now, young lady."

Pushing Livy toward the building, Mr. Brock pulled his flip phone from his pocket and punched in a number.

"Hello, Dispatch?" he said. "Send an ambulance to Behr County High School right away. A student has been hurt." He slid the cell phone back into his pocket and laid a hand on Russ's forehead. "Easy, now, son. Help is on the way."

Russ went stiff as a board, then his eyes rolled back in his head and he went limp.

"Ohmygodohmygod," Terri said, bursting into tears. "He's dead."

"Hush, he's not dead. He's unconscious." Mr. Brock removed his jacket and tucked it around Russ. "Stop carrying on and tell me what happened."

"He threw Russ into the air and broke his leg." Terri sniffed and pointed a shaking finger at Dev. "I don't know his name. He's a ninth grader, I think."

"Don't exaggerate, Terri," Mr. Brock said. "Don't you mean Dev *pushed* Russ?"

"No, I don't." Terri stamped her foot. "I know what I saw, and that boy threw Russ into the air. *Way* up. Russ hit the concrete and—" Her face crumpled. "It was awful."

"Thank you," Mr. Brock said. "Run down to the principal's office and tell them there has been an accident. Please inform Miss Martha that I've already called 911." Terri scurried away, and he turned to the crowd of gawking students. "Show's over. Get to class."

Reluctantly, the bystanders shuffled away.

"Not you, Whitsun," Mr. Brock said when Dev started toward the building. "You stay put."

Shit. Dev halted. He was in trouble, big trouble. Why, oh, why, had he let Russ goad him? He recalled the bruises on Livy's slender throat and felt a surge of anger. He wasn't sorry, not one little bit. Russ had gotten what was coming to him.

Mr. Brock walked over to examine Dev's face. "You're bleeding. Broken nose?"

"Yes, sir. I think so."

"Does it hurt?"

"No, sir, not anymore."

Mr. Brock grunted. "Fast healer, huh? What the hell were you thinking, picking on a norm?"

"S-sir?" Dev spluttered. He didn't know which shocked him more, hearing a teacher cuss or Mr. Brock's casual use of the term "norm."

"Don't play innocent. You know better, or you damn well ought to." Mr. Brock studied him. "You aren't kith. Don't have the purple eyes. What kind of super are you?"

"I—I—" Dev's shocked brain went blank. Norm. Super. Mr. Brock knew who he was, *what* he was.

"Forget it. We've got company," Mr. Brock said as the high school principal and the school secretary hurried toward them. In the distance, there was the strident wail of an approaching ambulance. "You and Russ were fighting, and Russ tripped and fell," Mr. Brock said under his breath. "Got it?"

"But I—"

"Russ's father is going to raise almighty hell about this, so you'd better have your story straight. Rule number one, son. You never, *ever* out yourself to norms."

"I don't like lies."

"Then don't lie. Act like you're in shock. Cry. Throw up. Piss your pants. Do whatever you have to, but do *not* tell the truth—that a hundred-and-thirty-five-pound freshman tossed an all-state football player around like a sack of dried beans and broke his leg."

"A hundred and forty pounds," Dev muttered. "Like anyone would believe it, anyway."

"Terri's not the only witness," Mr. Brock said. "Luckily, adults don't listen to kids. That's the good news, but if you come clean, people— Russ's parents and the other teachers, for starters—will think you're delusional or on drugs."

"Drugs? No way."

"Drugs." Mr. Brock's voice was firm. "Either that, or they'll dub you the biggest liar between here and the Mississippi line. You want to wind up in Behr-Cap?"

Dev stared at him in horror. "No, sir."

The Behr County Alternative Program, or Behr-Cap, was a school for disruptive students. He did not want to go there.

"Then keep your mouth shut and let Principal Hart and Weoka handle things."

Dev gaped at the teacher. "Y-you know my aunt?"

"Everybody in these parts who's not a norm knows Weoka Waters." Mr. Brock gripped Dev by the shoulder. "Take my advice and learn to control that temper of yours. The Council has a way of dealing with reckless supers." He heaved a sigh of relief as a vehicle with flashing lights screamed up the school drive. "The ambulance is here, thank God. Let's get out of the way."

* * * *

"And I'm telling *you*, suspension ain't enough." Roger Barber slammed his fist on the principal's desk. He was an intimidating man with a barrel chest, thick neck, and a perpetual scowl. "I want that thug expelled."

"Dev ain't a thug," Aunt Weoka said, "and Russ attacked him first. Punched him in the face and broke his nose." She pointed to Dev. "Look at that shiner. You can see for yourself."

"The kids who saw the fight say your nephew threw Russ into the air."

"Threw him into the air? Take a gander at my boy, Mr. Barber. Dev is three years younger than Russ and skinny as a beanpole, besides."

"Aunt Weoka, please," Dev muttered, slouching in his chair. "I'm not a total wimp."

"Hush," Weoka said. "I know Russ plays ball, but—"

Roger Barber sprang to his feet. "Plays ball? *Plays ball*? Russ is the star receiver for the Wildcats, woman. Going to Bama this fall. On *scholarship*."

"Calm down, Roger, and stop yelling in my office," Principal Hart said. "We do everything we can to keep our students safe at BCH, but accidents happen. I'm sorry Russ got hurt, but—"

"Hurt?" Barber's eyes bulged. "Russ is out for the season. The Wildcats play the Hannah Blue Devils Friday night—our biggest rival—but will Russ be playing? Hell no, thanks to that little creep." He jabbed a fat finger at Dev. "I want him *gone*, and what I say goes. R&B money keeps this football program afloat."

"Thank you for the reminder, Roger." Principal Hart folded his hands on the desktop. "The school appreciates your support, but Dev is a straight-A student, and he's never been in trouble before." He gazed sternly at Dev. "There is zero tolerance for fighting at BCH, young man. You're suspended for a week."

"A week?" Dev sat up. "What about my classes? I don't—"

"Thank you, Principal Hart. Dev has learned his lesson," Aunt Weoka said, flashing him a warning look. "Right, boy?"

Dev flushed and looked away. "Yessum. It won't happen again."

"Good. Now, tell Mr. Barber you're sorry Russ got hurt."

"But Aunt Wee—"

"You heard me, boy." There was steel in her voice. "Tell him."

"I didn't mean to break Russ's leg, but I'm not sorry it happened," Dev added quickly. "Russ is a world-class jerk."

"Why, you—"

Roger Barber lunged at Dev. Aunt Weoka's hand shot up, palm out, and the burly man froze in his tracks. For a moment, he struggled to break free, face purpling with the effort, then gave up.

"Damn woman's a witch," he grumbled, slumping back into his chair. "Put the whammy on me. You seen it."

"A witch, Roger, really?" Principal Hart said. "More likely, you're overwrought. I suggest you calm down before you have another heart attack."

"That boy assaulted my son." Barber scowled at Dev. "And he ain't sorry. You heard him."

"Dev don't cotton to lying," Aunt Weoka said. "If he says Russ is a jerk, then you can bet your bottom dollar it's true." Ignoring Barber's spluttering, Aunt Weoka rose and slung the strap of her worn purse over one shoulder. "Sorry for the stir, Jimbo," she said to the principal. "I'll see the boy causes no more trouble. Give Myrna and the twins my regards."

"Thank you, Weoka, I will." Principal Hart gave her a significant look. "Don't be too hard on Dev. These things happen, and we both know it."

Weoka gave him a jerky nod and led Dev out to her truck, a faded blue Chevy 4x4. "Get in, boy. Brought you a clean shirt."

Dev obeyed. Dumping his books on the floorboard, he pulled off his bloodstained garment and slipped the clean one his aunt had provided over his head. He didn't bother to ask how she had known he needed a change of clothes.

Aunt Weoka knew. She always knew.

"There's a bottle of water and a washcloth at your feet," she said, angling her body behind the wheel. "Give your face a scrub. You're a mess."

Dev obediently wiped the blood from his face and set the soiled cloth aside.

"Feel better?"

"Yessum."

Dev peeked at his aunt's weathered profile. By rights, she should be mad as fire, but she didn't seem angry. Her calm acceptance made him feel worse. Aunt Wee was family, all the family he had, and he loved her. She'd raised him, cared for him, and given him a home, and how had he repaid her?

By breaking a norm, for Pete's sake.

"Sorry about the ruckus." The words crowded his throat. "Russ hurt Livy."

"Never could abide a bully."

"Me, either." Dev balled his hands into fists. "I lost it. Told him not to do it again or else."

"Reckon that got his dander up. Used to getting his way, I'd imagine."

"Yeah." Dev scowled. "He's a wanker."

"Takes after his daddy, then."

"I don't get it," Dev said. "Livy still plans to date him."

"There's no accounting for taste." She gave him a hard look. "Something else bothering you, boy?"

"Terri Osborne doesn't know me from a hole in the ground."

"Who?"

Dev sighed. "An eleventh grader. Mr. Brock was asking her questions about the…the fight, and she called me 'that boy.' Terri Osborne doesn't even know my name."

"Reckon she'll know who you are from now on. Reckon everybody at school will." She clucked in disapproval. "Fighting with a senior boy." She gave him a sideways look. "Pretty, is she, this Terri?"

"Yeah." Heat prickled the back of Dev's neck. "She's a cheerleader."

"Oh, a *cheerleader*. That explains it. Is she norm or kith?"

"Norm." He shrugged. "Most of the kids at school are."

"Yep. See you remember it."

"Yessum." Dev swallowed. "My teacher…Mr. Brock said…" He looked down at his hands. "A-am I in trouble with the Kith Council?"

"If the Council has a problem with anybody, it'll be me. I raised you." She shook her head. "I knew the sap was rising. Should've given you The Talk long ago."

"Gah, Aunt Weoka. I know about sex."

"That so? Well, this ain't about sex. It's about what you are."

"Which is what? I mean, exactly. I'm not a norm, but I'm not kith, either."

"Ain't no exact to it. You've got a little of this and that, a smidge of demon blood…" Her voice trailed off. "And something more. Something a whole lot more powerful."

"Like what?"

"It's complicated."

"You mean, I'm a freak." Dev slammed his fists against his thighs. "I hate being different. It stinks."

"No need to get your bowels in an uproar." Weoka reached over and patted his cheek. "After supper, we'll talk, and you can ask me anything you want." She winked at him. "You can even ask me about s-e-x, if you wanna." She chuckled when he groaned and slid down in the seat. "What say we stop by McCullough's on the way home? Got me a hankering for salmon patties and pork and beans."

Dev eagerly lifted his head. "With creamed taters?"

"What else?"

Much cheered, Dev sat up and looked out the window at the rolling farmland. The two-lane highway ended in a T at Devil's Fork Road. Aunt Weoka stopped at the intersection and let the truck engine idle. The country store across the road was covered in metal signs advertising everything from chewing tobacco to Pepsi-Cola. Double screen doors at the front were decorated with red and yellow plates proclaiming MALBIS ENRICHED BREAD in chipped blue letters. The dirt lot beside the square wooden building was empty, but for a gleaming sedan sitting beside one of Sloan McCullough's old-timey red gas pumps.

"Well, well," Weoka said. "If that ain't four kinds of trouble."

"What?" Dev demanded. "Something wrong?"

"So, I'm a-thinking." She pointed to the car in the lot. "You know anybody 'round here drives a fancy car like that?"

"No, ma'am."

"Me, neither." She eased across the road and parked the truck next to the store. "That car has a Mobile County tag. What in tarnation brings rich city folk way out here?"

She was already exiting the truck as she spoke, striding for the door with the agility and energy of a woman half her age. Dev jumped out and caught a whiff of something sweet and metallic.

Blood.

Fresh blood.

"Aunt Weoka, wait," he yelled, tripping over his size-eleven feet in his haste to reach her.

He raced inside and skidded to a halt. The store had been ransacked. The antique brass cash register stood open, and the drawers were empty. Goods had been pulled off the shelves, racks overturned, and the glass case at the front was shattered. A gallon jar of pickled eggs lay smashed on the floor, the pungent scent of vinegar mingling with the smell of congealing blood.

Sloan McCullough, the gray-haired proprietor, lay sprawled on the floor, his eyes open and unseeing. Dev stared at the hole in the dead man's chest. The cloth around the bullet wound was charred. A large round of hoop cheese sat next to the old man's head. Many an afternoon, Mr. McCullough had sold Dev a slice from that very same wheel. Now, the buttery cheese inside the red wax rind was spattered with blood.

Dev's stomach lurched, and he dragged his gaze from the old man. To the right of the counter were three more bodies, two men and a woman. The corpses had been decapitated. Blood congealed in sticky pools on the wooden boards. Beside each body was a puddle of black sludge. *The robbers*, a detached, analytical part of Dev's brain informed him. He stared at the woman's severed head, that same dispassionate part of his mind noting the female's lank, greasy hair and hollow cheeks, and the oozing sores that dotted the corners of her mouth. Horrible, but her eyes were the worst, like liquified pitch. Dev half-expected them to spill out of the sockets and run down her face and onto the floor. He dragged his gaze from the abandoned skull to her body. She was wearing a filthy skirt and sweater, and her thin legs were covered in scratches and dirt. The worn loafers on her feet had holes in the bottoms. In one grimy hand, she clutched a wad of money. He turned his attention to her accomplices. They were equally shabby and disreputable looking. The trio stank of body odor and something rancid like spoiled meat.

There was a pitiful moan from the other side of the store. Winnie McCullough, Sloan's ten-year-old granddaughter, lay a few feet away from him with a gaping hole in her belly. A huge warrior in leather clothing knelt beside her, a sword strapped across his broad back. His head was bent, his features obscured by his long chestnut-brown hair. A golden nimbus of light surrounded him. Murmuring in a strange language, he moved his hands above Winnie's body.

The ugly wound in her belly closed, and she sat up with a gasp. *"Pawpaw."*

"Shh, little one." The man's tone was soothing, almost tender. "All will be well."

He touched her on the shoulder, and she slumped back to the floor. Rising, he turned to face them, and Dev took an instinctive step back, staring at him in awe. Jeez, the guy was built like a superhero, big and tall and muscular, with gray-green eyes, a straight nose and strong jaw.

Aunt Weoka waved a hand at the unconscious girl. "You healed her."

"Aye." The warrior seemed puzzled. "I could not bear to see her suffer. Surpassing strange, is it not?"

"I've seen stranger. You got a name, mister?"

"I am called Eamon." He hesitated and added, "You are one of the elder?"

"Yup, though I ain't been called that in a spell. Name's Weoka."

He bowed. "Greetings, Old One. You sensed the presence of the djegrali and sought to take them to task?"

"Nah, just stopped in for a can of salmon." Weoka jerked her thumb at what was left of the robbers. "Not that you needed my help. A bit messy, but you got the job done."

"I strive." Eamon's gaze moved to Dev. "And the youngling?"

"My nephew, Devlin. Goes by Dev for short."

The warrior inclined his head. "Well met, Devlin."

"Uh...hi." Dev cleared his throat. "What's a juhgrobby?"

"Djegrali," Aunt Weoka said. "Fancy word for demons. Parasites, really. Catch a human and use 'em up, then move on to the next one."

"That's horrible." Dev stared at the headless corpses. "Couldn't the humans be saved?"

"I commanded the demons to quit their mortal shells, but they refused," Eamon said, "leaving me no recourse but to slay the hosts. When the human dies, the demon in possession dies as well. These poor souls were done for, I fear. E'en had I freed them from the demons, they would have died. Consumed from within, as it were." His gaze moved to the old man's body. "Alas, I arrived too late to save this one. The girl I found near death."

"The gal's name is Winnie," Aunt Weoka said. "The old man was Sloan McCullough, her grandpa. He owned the store."

"Ah. You are acquainted?"

"It's a small community, and this is the only store between here and Hannah." She cocked her head at Eamon. "What are your plans for the gal?"

"Plans? I do not take your meaning."

"You saved her. She's your responsibility."

Eamon looked incredulous. "Mine?"

"Yup," Weoka said. "I'm sure you meant it as a kindness, but Winnie is a norm." She paused. "Reckon I should say *was* a norm—ain't no more. Look at her. Glowing like a power plant."

"You have the right of it, I fear. I failed to consider..." Eamon's mouth tightened. "Changing a human is forbidden."

"Fat's in the fire, for sure. Reckon you'll be hanging around to see to the gal."

"Nay, I cannot," Eamon protested. "I am Dalvahni, pledged to seek the djegrali through space and time. We do not tire. We do not fail. We hunt."

Dev whistled. "You're a demon hunter? Cool."

Weoka shot him a quelling glare. "Gal's a mutant now, thanks to you. Got a duty to her, too."

"I am a warrior, not a wet nurse."

"Should've thought of that before you healed her."

Eamon frowned. "Pursuit of the enemy leads me afar, but I suppose I could spare the occasional visit."

"Mighty big of you, but an occasional visit won't do," Weoka said. "Somebody has to see to the gal, regular like."

"We could do it," Dev blurted. "Keep an eye on her, I mean."

"Hush, boy. Last thing I need is another young'un to raise." Weoka straightened. "'Sides, the gal has family of her own."

"A *norm* family, Aunt Wee. Winnie's a...a Dalvahni-oid, now. She needs us."

"Not my doing. *I* didn't change her."

"I would be most grateful, an' you would care for the girl." Eamon's voice was coaxing.

"You're a handsome devil, but you can play your tricks someplace else," Weoka said. "I'm too old and wise by half to be taken in by the likes of you."

"Too wise, I doubt not, but too old?" Eamon laid a hand over his heart. "Nay, I protest. Yours is the kind of beauty unaffected by time."

"Flatterer."

"You would be doing me a great service, milady," Eamon said. "'Strewth, I cannot abandon my duties to care for the child."

"Too bad. Should've thought of that sooner."

"'Twould not be forever," Eamon said. "I will return for her. On my word as a Dalvahni."

"Humph." Aunt Weoka looked unconvinced. "See that you do."

He flashed her a dazzling grin. "Many thanks. I depart with my heart at ease, knowing her fate is in your capable hands."

His brawny form wavered, and he disappeared.

"He's gone," Dev said, gaping at the spot where the warrior had been. "Fled the coop and left us holding the bag."

"He'll be back. He said so."

"Demon hunters have a one-track mind. Could be a hundred years before that fellow remembers Winnie and thinks to check on her. Meantime, she's our problem."

"Aunt Weoka, are there more of the djegrali?"

"More'n you can shake a stick at."

"Around here, I mean."

"Yup. A long time ago, a meteorite landed smack-dab where the town of Hannah is built. The impact thinned the veil, and things have a way of leaking in."

"What kind of things?"

"Supernatural things, good and bad."

"Like demons?"

"For starters."

"Do the norms know about the leak?"

She shook her head. "By and large, norms are clueless, and a good thing." She gave him an odd look. "Since when are you worried about norms?"

"They're helpless. Somebody has to protect them."

"That would be a full-time job." Aunt Weoka looked around the bloody shop. "Guess we'd better call this in," she said with a frown. "When the authorities arrive, keep your mouth shut and let me do the talking." She went behind the counter to check the phone. "Line's out. They must've cut it before they robbed the place."

"If I had a cell phone, I could call the sheriff from here," Dev said.

He held his breath and waited. Aunt Weoka was dead set against technology. She didn't own a television or a radio, and her only telephone was a rotary model, but that didn't mean Dev hadn't tried to change her mind.

"You on about that again?" she said, dashing his hopes. "Tarnation, half the time, them things don't work in Hannah."

"We don't live in Hannah. We live in the county."

"Same difference."

"Aunt Weoka, please. All the kids at school have them."

"*You* don't have one, so I reckon that ain't so."

"But—"

"No buts, boy, and no cell phones. Techno gadgets are for norms. The old ways are the best. Now, run down to the Bibb farm and call the sheriff. I'll wait here with Winnie."

Dev sighed. "Yes, Aunt Wee."

Chapter Two

Present day, in the woods outside Hannah.

Shifter stew, Dev thought, grimly surveying the carnage.

The smell of decomp was nauseating, a pungent reek reminiscent of rotting pork and Porta Potty. The odor assaulted Dev's sensitive nose and clung to the back of his throat. He could *taste* the funk. Forcing himself to ignore the stench, he took stock of the crime scene. Someone had turned a pack of weres inside out.

Or some*thing.*

More than a dozen mangled corpses were scattered around the once-peaceful forest glade. Blood and body parts spattered the ground and vegetation, but the murderer had not been satisfied with mere slaughter. The clearing in the woods was a smoking ruination of splintered trees, upended boulders that had been tossed about like so much chaff, and deep runnels gouged in the earth.

The one responsible for this butchery was not a norm. Dev was certain of that much. After more than ten years in law enforcement, he knew supers, but this was something new. The nightmarish wasteland thrummed with residual power, a magical fingerprint left behind by the killer. Behr County was a magnet for the weird and uncanny, but the kith and those Dev privately referred to as "others" generally avoided the limelight, careful not to expose themselves to ordinary humans.

Whoever had done this had been too angry or too arrogant to care.

A curvy brunette in a khaki shirt and brown pants slipped soundlessly from the woods. "Sheriff," she said, leaping lightly over a fallen log.

Speaking of others, Dev thought, watching her land in the leaves without so much as a rustle. Compared to Winnie McCullough, Legolas Greenleaf was a klutz.

"Deputy," Dev said. "'Bout time you arrived. I notified Dispatch more than an hour ago."

"Parks and I were up in Caldwell responding to a domestic."

"Caldwell?" Dev raised his brows. "Thrashers at it again?"

"Yep. Lula went after Herman with a frying pan. Neighbors heard the ruckus and called it in. She was chasing him around the yard when we got there." Winnie paused for effect. "Naked. I'm thinking of putting in for hazard pay."

Dev chuckled. "On our budget? I doubt seeing Lula in her birthday suit qualifies."

"Well, it should. Ain't enough brain bleach in the world to unsee that." She took in the grisly scene. "What happened here, somebody blow up a cow?"

"A herd of cows, maybe."

Jim Parks, a graying deputy in his fifties and Winnie's partner, stamped out of the woods. He got one whiff of the decay and retched.

"You going to puke, Jim, do it someplace else," Dev said. "You'll taint the evidence."

Deputy Parks nodded and staggered off.

"Man has the gag reflex of a mama bird," Winnie said, listening as Parks noisily emptied his stomach behind a clump of bushes. "Who found this?"

"A dove hunter stumbled across the bodies early this morning," Dev said. "He was pretty shaken up."

Winnie nodded curtly and crouched beside a mutilated carcass. "Male, mid-thirties," she said, assessing the victim. "Brown hair with red streaks. Left arm is missing. Ripped out of the socket. Right upper arm has a tattoo. Animals have been at him, but it looks like a wolf's paw inscribed with the letter *R*." She cast a swift glance in Parks's direction and said in a low voice, "This the Randall pack?"

"What's left of them." Dev rubbed his jaw. "My guess, they've been dead a couple days." He ran a finger under the edge of his damp shirt collar. "'Course, this is Alabama in September. Given the heat and humidity, I could be wrong."

"Werewolf feud, maybe?" Winnie asked. "Pack Randall and Pack Lyall have been at it for years."

Dev shook his head. "The Lyalls didn't do this. This was something else."

"Like what?"

"No clue, but I mean to find out."

The air shimmered, and a tall, lithe woman dressed in form-fitting gray doeskin and boots appeared. She carried a bow and quiver on one slim shoulder, and she was astonishingly lovely, a silvery blonde with long legs; a slim waist; high, round breasts; and eyes the vivid green of new leaves. A bell rang in Dev's head when he saw her, a single, pure note that sent a ping of awareness through every cell of his body.

At last, he thought, staring at the newcomer. At last, what? Annoyed, he dismissed the whimsical notion.

"What the—" Winnie got to her feet. "Stay back, lady. You can't be here."

"An inane remark and erroneous." The huntress's voice, cool and crisp as April rain, sent another shiver of recognition down Dev's spine. "As you can plainly see, I *am* here."

Winnie's brows lowered. "Now, just a darn—"

"I've got this, deputy." Shaking off his momentary daze, Dev strode up to the stranger. "You're Kirvahni?"

"Indeed." She raised her brows. "You are familiar with the Kir?"

"I wouldn't go that far, but I've met one of your sisters. Her name is Taryn."

"I see." Her assessing gaze roamed Dev's tall frame. "I am Arta, the High Huntress of the Kir. And you, sir?"

"I'm Devlin Whitsun, the sheriff of Behr County."

"The shire reeve? I have heard of you."

"I'm in the middle of an investigation. What brings you here?"

"Like you, the Kirvahni are also tasked with keeping the peace."

"You're a demon hunter. Demons didn't do this."

Arta's troubled gaze moved over the bloody crime scene. "Of a certainty, the djegrali are not responsible. I received word of Pratt's atrocity but did not credit it. I came to see for myself."

"Pratt?" Winnie walked over to them. "Who's Pratt?"

"Pratt is—" Arta whirled at a slight sound from the underbrush. In a blur of motion, she nocked an arrow in her bow and released it. The missile whined through the air and hit a tree with a solid *thwunk*.

"*Shit*." Deputy Parks burst out of the bushes, wild-eyed. "Some damn fool just took a shot at me. Missed me by an inch." He saw Arta and checked. "Who the hell are you?"

"My name is mine own to give or withhold as I like," Arta said in a dampening tone. "And I did not miss. 'Twas a warning shot. Someone should caution you not to skulk in the woods."

"I wasn't skulking. I was—" Parks faltered and turned red. "I wasn't skulking, all right?"

Dev heard the distant squelch of tires on dirt. "Never mind, Parks," he said. "Wendall just pulled up. You and Deputy McCullough go bring him back here."

"The coroner's arrived?" Parks blinked. "How do you—"

"That old clunker he drives rattles," Winnie said. "Bad valves. Can't you hear it?"

"No, I can't, and neither can you." Parks gave his gun belt a belligerent hitch. "We must be three miles from the road. Maybe more."

"Tell you what," Winnie said. "If I'm right, lunch is on you." She glanced at the puréed body on the ground next to her boot. "I'm thinking barbecue from the Sweet Shop."

Parks made a strangled sound and beat a hasty retreat.

Dev sighed. "Winnie, I assigned you to Jim Parks for a reason. He's a good officer, steady and reliable, and you're still new to the job."

"I've been with the department eighteen months, and I've seen Lula Thrasher naked." She grinned. "In deputy years, that's like ten." She raised her hands in defeat at a look from Dev. "Okay, okay. I'll go after him." She glanced at the huntress. "Though I don't think it's a good idea to leave you alone with Lara Croft."

"I'll be fine."

Winnie shrugged. "Your funeral."

"Who is Lara Croft?" Arta asked when Winnie had gone.

"A fictional character and a badass."

She stiffened. "My rump is not deficient."

No, it most certainly is not. The High Huntress's rump was perfection, like the rest of her.

"It's an expression," Dev said. "It means formidable."

"Oh. That is different." Arta eyed him thoughtfully. "The female constable is lovely. You are lovers?"

"What? *No.* Winnie and I work together."

"Comrades in arms?"

"Yeah."

"This I understand." She motioned to what was left of the Randall pack. "Do you often encounter such grotesqueries in your work?"

"No, this is unusual, even for Hannah. What can you tell me about this Pratt fellow?"

"Pratt is not a 'fellow.' He is a god and the brother of Blessed Kehvahn, the creator of the Kirvahni."

Lifting her hands to the sky, Arta burst into song. Her voice was agile and bright, the haunting melody drifting through the trees like birdsong or a murmured prayer.

"Where can I find Pratt?" he asked when she had finished. "I'd like to bring him in for questioning."

"Bring him in?" She stared at him, aghast. "Pratt is a god, not a common outlaw."

"Tell me where he is and let me worry about that."

"I applaud your spirit, Devlin Whitsun," she said. "Duty, I understand. The Kirvahni have pursued the djegrali for millennia."

"Millennia, huh? That's a long time."

"You doubt my veracity?"

"Nope. I can tell when someone is lying."

"A useful skill when dealing with miscreants."

"It has its merits."

Arta tilted her head, studying him. "I like you, shire reeve. How many cycles have you seen?"

"Thirty-four."

"Centuries?"

"Years."

Arta's eyes widened. "I am astonished. You have the mien and bearing of a seasoned warrior."

"I've been at it for a while. Started working for the sheriff's department as a dispatcher when I was a senior in high school."

"High school?"

"It's…uh…an institute of learning for teenagers."

"Striplings?"

"Exactly."

"Shackled by grim duty e'er you were fully formed. It seems unfair."

"It kept me out of trouble. About Pratt—"

He broke off as the trees on the far side of the kill zone parted and a bronze giant in a rough-rider uniform and a wide-brim slouch hat clomped into view. A trumpet hung from a loop on the giant's belt, and he carried an enormous metal peanut like a club. He paused at the edge of the clearing.

"A mechanical man?" Arta's eyes brightened with interest. "Does a race of such titans dwell here?"

"Good God, no." Dev was horrified by the thought. "He's the only one, and I've been chasing him for days."

"To what end, pray?"

"To keep some norm from seeing him and having a conniption fit."

"Norm?" Her gaze grew distant. "Ah, you refer to humans without supernatural ability. The creature is conspicuous, is he not?"

"Yep. Hard to ignore an animated three-ton statue." He pointed to the hesitant goliath. "His name is Jeb Hannah. Jeb was a Spanish American war hero and founder of the town by the same name. Until a few days ago, this statue was a monument in a park."

Arta seemed to digest this. "And the impetus behind his change of address?"

"Some fool brought him to life."

"Powerful magic, but to what purpose?"

"Who knows?" Dev said. "But I'm fairly certain Cassie Ferguson is responsible, although I can't prove it."

"She is a sorcerer?"

"Nah, kith."

"Kith?"

"Demonoid."

"The offspring of a demon-possessed human and another?"

"Yep."

"The captain of the Dalvahni is wed to a demonoid named Beck." Arta regarded him. "What of you, Devlin Whitsun? You are no norm."

"It's complicated." The ready admission surprised Dev. He rarely talked about his background, even with Winnie. His mother had run off when he was born, and he had never met his father. "Wee says I'm a mutt."

"Wee?"

"My aunt Weoka, my great-aunt. She raised me. Now, if you'll excuse me, I need to speak to Jeb."

"I will accompany you."

He shook his head. "Stay here. Jeb is skittish. Wouldn't want you to get accidentally squished."

Making a wide circuit around the edge of the slaughter field, he strode up to the creaking giant. "Jeb," he said, gazing up at the goliath. "I've been looking for you."

Jeb regarded him warily.

I don't want to play in your yard, he sang in a hollow baritone.

I don't like you anymore.

You'll be sorry when you see me,

Sliding down your cellar door.

Arta materialized at Dev's side. "The creature converses through song? How droll."

"Yeah, he's a regular hit parade," Dev said with a touch of annoyance. "I told you to stay put."

"I fear you labor under a misapprehension. The Kirvahni answer to no one."

Dev closed his eyes. *Temper is the tool of a foolish man*, he murmured silently. He had not lost his cool since high school, but something about Arta got under his skin.

"Shire reeve? You seem perturbed."

Mister Burns and his wife, Jeb sang.
Together had strife,
And to loggerheads with him went she.

"Very funny," Dev said. "I've been looking for you. What brings you to this crime scene?"

The giant's gleaming face grew mournful.

I'm dreaming now of Hally, he sang.
For the thought of her is one that never dies:
She's sleeping in the valley, the valley, the valley,
And the mockingbird sings where she lies.

Arta frowned. "'Strewth, the creature is trying to warn us, but of what?"

"No idea," Dev said. "You know anyone named Hally?"

"Nay."

"Me, either."

Jeb stamped his foot, booming with a touch of impatience,
Where the broken sunbeams fall,
And soft shadows are her pall,
Have we laid our darling Nell.

"Bah, first Hally and now Nell," Arta said in disgust. "'Tis useless. Liefer would I converse with a stump."

Twigs snapped, and a girl with a cap of blond hair bounded out of the woods at incredible speed. Her feet were bare, and her cotton shorts and T-shirt were torn and dirty.

"What ho, 'tis a wood nymph?" Arta said. "She courses like a hare."

"Not a nymph, kith," Dev said, "and her name's Verbena." He held up his hand. "That's far enough, Miss Skinner. This is a crime scene."

Verbena halted, flushing. "I ain't no Skinner. My mama took up with a traveling man. I go by Van Pelt now." Her watchful gaze moved to Arta. "Who are you?"

"I am Arta, the High Huntress of the Kirvahni."

"Miz Taryn's boss? Jeb tell you she's hurt?"

"You are mistaken, child. The Kir are impervious to lasting injury, save for decollation."

"She means—" Dev began.

"Fancy word for 'beheaded,' I know," Verbena said. "Read it oncet in a book. Jeb's trying to tell you about Miz Taryn. She ain't lost her head, but she's in a bad way. That fellow with the tattoos—the one they call the rogue." She colored. "He come up on me and Jeb in the woods. Jumpy as a raccoon in a dog run, that one, but he stopped long enough to tell us Miz Taryn was hurt afore he took off."

"'Rogue'?" Dev asked, trying to keep up.

"A Dalvahni warrior corrupted by Pratt." Arta's brows drew together. "Gryffin, he was called, ere he fell into perfidy."

Verbena's eyes flashed. "He ain't fell into nothing. He's *good.*"

"An he attacked my sister and fled, he is a dastard."

"You got wax in yo' ears?" Verbena shot back. "I never said it was the rogue. The scary fellow done it."

"'Scary fellow'?" asked Arta.

"The one what makes the air thick and smothery, like when a storm's a-brewing."

"Do you, perchance, mean a god?"

"Yup. Saw him oncet at the Skinner camp," Verbena said. "He was after the rogue—I mean, Gryffin." She looked away, her blush deepening. "Gryff told us about Miz Taryn and took off. Led the scary fellow away from us." She slid Arta a resentful look. "Don't reckon he'd 'uv done that if 'n he was no count."

"Does this scary fellow have a name?" Dev asked.

"Methinks she means Pratt." Arta's voice was flat. "He seeks the orb, depend upon it."

"The orb?"

"A powerful object, shire reeve. Anonce, 'tis in Gryffin's keeping, but should Pratt gain dominion over it—" A shiver of dread shook Arta's slender form. "'Tis too dreadful to contemplate." She turned to Verbena. "You will take me to Taryn at once."

Verbena nodded and scampered away, her feet skimming the ground. The huntress followed without a backward glance.

Jeb gave Dev an inquiring look.

Time to move on, brother, he warbled.

Time to move on.

Your sweetheart has left you,

She's already gone.

"She's not my—" Dev began, but the giant had already trundled away.

Dev hesitated, torn between his obligation to process the murder scene and his desire to go after Pratt. Winnie and Parks could process the scene without him, he reasoned. After all, Taryn was hurt, and the living took precedence over the dead.

His mind made up, Dev pushed a button on his radio. "McCullough?" he said, speaking into the device. "I've got a lead on the suspect. You and Parks secure the scene."

"Copy," Winnie said.

Dev stepped into the shadow of the trees. He was doing the right thing, he assured himself. His decision had nothing to do with a certain haughty blond huntress who had captured his interest.

The forest smelled of growing things and the dry, dusty scent of moldering leaves. Eagerly, he inhaled, cleansing the charnel smell of death from his nostrils, and set out through the woods. He had not gone far when a bigfoot rose out of a thick bed of ferns. Wooly boogers, the locals sometimes called them. They were shy creatures and rarely seen, but Dev was well-acquainted with this one. It was huge, nine or ten feet tall and four feet wide, and white as a Jet-Puffed marshmallow.

"Pretty?" the massive thing said in a chirping trill.

The snowy beast held out a large furry hand. Nestled on its leathery palm was an ugly brown stone with a yellow streak, like a cat's eye. Dev looked closer and changed his mind. It was not ugly, he decided. It was lovely, exceptionally lovely.

"Pretty." The wooly booger offered his treasure to Dev, his wide blue eyes innocent. "Want pretty?"

"Yes," Dev whispered, reaching for the stone. "Mine. Give it to me."

The forest hushed, and the air grew heavy and thick. "Nay. Touch it not," a sonorous voice said, shattering the stillness.

Dev blinked as a naked man bounded out of the trees. The interloper's skin was silver, and he had the smoothly muscled body of a gymnast. His muscular legs ended in hooves, a pair of antlers sprang from his shining brow, and his luminous eyes were large and brown.

"Sugar," the silver man said to the wooly booger. "You have the orb, I see."

"Sid." The bigfoot held out the stone with a chortle of delight. "Sid want pretty?"

The shining man took a step back. "No, 'tis yours for now. Keep it safe and tell no one."

"Sugar hide pretty," the bigfoot said, loping away with surprising speed.

Dev stirred. "That stone... Was that the orb?"

"The very same," the stranger said. "'Twas fashioned by He-Who-Made-All-Things, and its power is vast. Only the pure of heart may touch it without injury."

"Who are you?" Dev shook off the remnants of his daze. "Scratch that. *What* are you?"

"I am Sildhjort, one of the *unluath*."

"*Unluath?*"

"A god and, as it happens, your sire."

This radioactive, antlered nudist was his *father?* Dev struggled to wrap his head around the revelation.

"Your mother, Brenna, was a lovely thing," Sildhjort mused. "Alas, our time together was all too brief. She is well?"

"No idea," Dev said. "She ran off when I was a baby."

"She was e'er a flighty thing. Water seeks the easiest course, does it not?"

"If you say so."

"Who cared for you upon your mother's flight?"

"My aunt Weoka."

"She abides by the river, still?"

"Wouldn't live anywhere else. You know Aunt Wee?"

"All paths cross an you wander long enough. Beware Pratt, my son. He is cruel, and his lust for the orb is boundless."

Sildhjort sprang away, bounding like a stag over the leaf-strewn duff. Pausing at the top of a hillock, he looked back. "Oh, and have a care for your sister, an you will."

"My sister?" Dev said. "You're mistaken, mister. I don't have a sister."

"Ah, but you do." Sildhjort smiled gently. "Have you not guessed? I am the traveling man."

"The traveling man?" Dev's brain whirled. "But that means Verbena and I—That you—"

"Consorted with Verbena's mother and yours. I rejoice in your acuity, my son."

Sildhjort loped into the forest and was gone.

Chapter Three

Arta sped after Verbena. A tingling sensation between her shoulder blades warned her that the shire reeve watched. The man was a mystery, and she adored puzzles. She had a knack for seeing to the heart of a coil and unraveling it. His Seneschal of Order, Kehvahn called her. Conall, the captain of the Dalvahni, was renowned for ferocity and implacability, but Arta took pride in efficiency and shrewd management. Delegation was the key to good leadership, in her estimation. She knew each of her sisters' strengths and weaknesses and assigned them to their respective tasks accordingly. Under her direction, the Kir performed their duty with unsurpassed skill, meticulous care, and rarely a blunder.

Which is more than can be said of the Dalvahni, she thought with a smirk of satisfaction.

Her mind circled back to the shire reeve. The man was a conundrum, still water with hidden depths and dangerous currents beneath, power cloaked in restraint. He reminded her of a Dalvahni warrior, save for the glint of humor in his gray eyes. She liked the way he moved, spine straight and shoulders back, each languid, graceful step measured and deliberate, as though he balanced upon some invisible rope or beam. Tall, with dark hair and the uncanny gaze of a wolf, he had a slow, sensual voice that made her shiver with delight.

His attempt to shield her from the metal man had been a surprise. She was the High Huntress, not a damsel in need of rescue. The welfare of the Kirvahni was in her keeping. She cared for her sisters, protected and guided them, but her position and the weight of her concerns denied her their easy camaraderie.

So be it.

She accepted the charge and gladly, but Dev Whitsun's solicitude for her well-being had been unexpected...and secretly pleasing.

You desire him, and small wonder, she admitted. *'Tis an age since last you availed yourself of a thrall.*

Thralls—succubi created to service the Kir and the Dalvahni—dwelt in the House of Pleasure. Beautiful and insatiable, thralls fed upon emotion. *A quiet mind lends a steady hand to the bow,* the Great Book taught. By joining with a thrall in coitus, a huntress emptied herself, preserving her equanimity and keeping her focus upon her duty—the pursuit of the djegrali.

How long had it been since she had lain with Korth, her favorite thrall? A strapping blond male with wide shoulders, Korth had a disinclination for idle chatter that appealed to Arta. She frowned. But not *too* appealing, 'twould seem. When had she last enjoyed a session with him? Faith, she could not remember. Were her sisters so lax, she would take them to task.

She returned her attention to the waifish girl flitting through the woods. Verbena darted up and down the gently rolling hills, her slender feet flying over the forest floor. Arta sprinted faster. Behind them, the metal statue thumped in their wake, humming a wordless tune. They ran for leagues without slacking, startling rabbits from the brush as they sped and, once, a bevy of quail. Arta's spirits soared. Her duties as High Huntress had kept her confined to the Temple of Calm far too long. 'Twas a joy to hunt again. She lifted her face, reveling in the kiss of the wind, and breathed in the scents of loam, damp mulch, and vegetation. Intoxicating.

Fie, you are a selfish creature, she thought with a stab of guilt, *thinking of your own pleasure while Taryn lies ahead, alone and injured.*

"Whither dost my sister lie?" she called to Verbena.

The slim girl paused. Despite their exertion, she did not seem winded, Arta noted with admiration. Indeed, the chit seemed indefatigable.

"Not far, now," Verbena said. "You tuckered?"

Arta processed the strange term. "Nay, a Kirvahni huntress can run for days on end."

"Me, too. That's why old Charlie made me run the dawgs."

"Dawgs?"

"Dogs." Verbena pronounced the word with exquisite care. "I got learning. I can speak proper, if 'n I wants."

"Then why do you not?"

"Who am I gon' impress in the woods, a raccoon? Jeb's forever sanging, but he ain't much for conversation."

"You abide in the wild with the behemoth? Have you no home?"

"Nothing permanent-like. Not since I left them no-count Skinners."

"The Skinners?"

"Family what raised me. Made me sleep outside with the dawgs and eat scraps, until Old Charlie give me to the demons to kill."

"They offered you as a sacrifice?"

"Yep. Got away and never went back."

"I should say not." Arta was outraged. "Show me this Charlie, and I shall dispatch the cur."

"Can't. He's dead. Drowned in his own moonshine. Serves him right, the no-good peckerwood."

"After the peckerwood's demise, you returned to the Skinners?"

"Nah, I'm done with that trash. I stayed with Miz Beck for a while."

"Rebekah Damian, the Dalvahni captain's life mate?" Arta asked.

"Yep. Miz Beck helped me get away from them Skinners. Give me a new life. She and Mr. Conall have been awful nice to me."

Arta absorbed this startling information. Conall Dalvahni had a reputation for many things, but "nice" was not among them.

"Had to leave, though," Verbena continued. "Skinners started poking around, and I got to worrying they'd cause Miz Beck trouble. Took off and wound up staying with Miz C—you know Cassie Ferguson?"

"By name only."

"She's nice, too. Offered me a place to live permanent-like, but I don't like to be beholden."

Jeb stomped up and took a swing at a wayward sapling with his cudgel.

Once when I was but a lad, I sailed the River Grande, he sang. *Good times we had, my friends and I, that I remember fondly.*

"Faith, he has a merry aspect, but he is odd," Arta observed.

"Gets things mixed up sometimes." Verbena looked up at the giant. "Jeb, I done tole you before. Miz Taryn's in the *Devil* River, not the Grande."

"What is this?" Arta said in alarm. "You abandoned my sister in the drink?"

"'Course not," Verbena said. "She's on a sandbar. River's up, and me and Jeb couldn't get to her. I don't swim so good, and old Jeb would sink. Come on. It ain't far, now."

She scampered away, and Arta followed her up a bluff overlooking a rushing brown watercourse.

Verbena pointed. "There."

Far below them was a pebbled sliver of land amid the foaming torrent. Taryn lay crumpled on the damp sand, her flaming hair spread out like a bloody banner.

"That Pratt fellow walloped her good and left her fer dead." Arta made a sound of dismay, and Verbena hastily added, "Ain't dead, though. Saw her stir. That's when me and Jeb hightailed it fer help."

Murmuring a fervent prayer, Arta dematerialized and reappeared on the jut of land beside her sister. Dropping to her knees, she examined the injured huntress. Taryn's face and lips were colorless, her pulse a feeble thread.

"Merciful gods." Arta frantically patted Taryn's icy cheek. "Awake, sister. I command you."

Taryn moaned but did not open her eyes. Placing her hands a few inches above Taryn's limp form, Arta bathed her sister in healing light. She did not respond.

Arta leapt to her feet. "Master, I need you," she cried in great distress. "This wound is beyond me."

She held her breath, but there was no answer. A flicker of movement made her stiffen. Something prowled within the trees, something dangerous and powerful that was not her master.

"Pratt," she whispered, "returned to finish his foul work." Drawing her bow, she stood over the injured huntress. "Keep back, villain. You shall not have her."

"Lower your bow—it's me." The shire reeve stepped into view, moving with his peculiar, deliberate grace. Despite the noise of the river, his deep drawl easily carried across the water.

"Have a care," Arta said. "We are not alone. Some dread thing lurks in the wood. I felt its presence."

"Pratt?"

"So I surmise, though I cannot be certain."

"Hold on. I'll have a look."

"Nay, shire reeve, 'tis too perilous. Do not—" Arta protested, but he was already gone.

Arta gritted her teeth and waited with an arrow nocked. The river gurgled and chuckled, indifferent to the danger. Long minutes ticked past. Each seemed a small eternity, and Arta's nerves tightened.

To her fury, her hands began to shake on the bow. "By the gods, when he returns, I shall bend his ear," she muttered.

If he returns.

She brushed the worrisome thought aside. At last, the shire reeve emerged from the woods and strode to the edge of the river.

"Nobody around, far as I can tell," he said with maddening calm.

Arta glared at him in mingled wrath and relief. "Fool, did you think to challenge a god? Had you met Pratt, you would be worm meat."

"Didn't meet him, though. Didn't meet anybody." He waved a hand at her bow. "Mind putting that thing away? You're making me nervous."

"I misdoubt you possess the wits to be nervous," Arta said, lowering her weapon, nonetheless. "How came such a dolt to be shire reeve?"

"Long hours, the pay sucks, and nobody else wanted the job. How's Taryn?"

"In truth, I cannot say. Her body is unmarked, but my healing gifts are of no avail." She raised a trembling hand to her brow. "Kehvahn could heal her, but he does not answer."

"Can't take her to a norm doctor. Cause too much of a stir. Looks like we're on our own."

"I thank you, shire reeve, but 'tis not your affair."

"I'm the sheriff. That makes it my affair."

"As you will," Arta said. "Howe'er, I fail to see in what way you can be of assistance. I shall take her home to the Temple of Calm."

"Is there someone there who can heal her?"

"I fear not. This mischief is beyond our skill."

"Better take her to my aunt, then. She's a healer." He removed his communication device and gun belt and dropped them on the ground. Bending, he began to remove his boots. "Stay there. I'll swim over and lend you a hand."

"There is no need," Arta said.

Hoisting Taryn's body over one shoulder, she dematerialized, reappearing beside the shire reeve on the far bank.

"Well, damn." He gave her a slow smile. "I was hoping to be a hero."

His imperturbability irked Arta. "You have the advantage of me, sir," she said with a touch of asperity. "Plainly, you are accustomed to our ways, but I know aught of you."

"You're not my first demon hunter."

"You speak of the Dalvahni?"

"Yep."

"We prefer to ignore the connection."

"Sibling rivalry?"

"Patent dislike."

His gray eyes twinkled. "Tough family." He jerked his chin at Taryn's body. "I can take her, if you like."

"There is no need. The Kir are surpassing strong."

"What's the matter, don't trust me?"

"I do not know you, as we have already established."

"Fair enough." He lifted his head at a noise. "We've got company."

The bronze statue clunked out of the woods with Verbena perched on one shoulder. The girl jumped lightly to the ground.

"Goody, you got her," she said. "Is she hurt bad?"

"So I fear." Gently, Arta lowered Taryn to the ground. "'Twould seem Pratt has dealt her an evil blow."

"Lordy, Mr. Evan's gon' be shook."

"Who?" Straightening, Arta stared at the girl.

"Evan Beck, Miz Taryn's beau. They snarl like a couple o' badgers in a sack, but they's sweet on one another, fer sure."

"You are mistaken," Arta said. "The Kir do not consort with humans. Such a thing is forbidden."

"Evan Beck's not human," Dev said. "He's kith."

"Yup," Verbena said, "and you'd best get Miz Taryn fixed up double quick. Mr. Evan finds out she's hurt, he'll snap his twig." She shook her head. "Then thangs gon' get ugly."

A petite blonde materialized in a burst of citrus perfume. She wore a navy and pink mini-dress and thigh-high transparent white boots.

"Wuz up, losers, trying to figure out whether bears really do shit in the woods?" She propped one hand on a narrow hip, her blue eyes glittering with malice. "Well, well, if it isn't that scrumptious sheriff," she said, admiring Dev's lean, masculine beauty. "You can strip-search me any old time."

"Meredith Peterson." Dev eyed the newcomer. "What brings you here?"

"Ooh, he knows my name." Meredith batted her lashes at him. "You don't seem surprised to see me."

"Oh, I'm surprised," Dev said. "You're dead."

"'Tis a shade?" Arta said. "I thought her a succubus."

Meredith's eyes narrowed. "Suck a what?"

"A demon," Arta said, "though I see now that I was in error. Your garb is surpassing odd. Were you, perchance, a mummer in life?"

"Odd?" Meredith's thin bosom swelled. "I'm wearing Chanel, you Middle Earth reject. Trey Peterson was my hubby muffin, one of *the* Petersons."

Arta raised her brows. "Am I supposed to be impressed?"

"She's swole on account o' the Petersons got money," Verbena said. "Not that money done Meredith much good. She was kilt."

"Murdered, and just when I'd finally gotten an appointment with Jerome to have my hair done," Meredith said in tragic accents. "I died a week before my first session. Isn't that *awful?*"

"Missing a hair appointment," Dev said. "That's your biggest regret?"

"Jerome is très exclusive. I was on the waiting list for a *year.*"

"Tragic. Why are you here?"

"Heard on the deadnet something was kicking. Business was slow, so I decided to investigate."

"What kind of business are you running, Mrs. Peterson?"

"I thought you'd never ask, Sheriff." She produced a card from thin air and handed it to him. "Bitchin' Banshee Services, that's me. Frights and hauntings, paranormal investigations—the usual spectral bunk, but with style and for a reasonable fee. Satisfied?"

He slid the card in his pocket. "Not in the least. I can't have you frightening the norms."

"I'm a ghost, Dudley Do-Right. Try and stop me." She jabbed a long, pink fingernail at Taryn. "Is it true? Has Fire Crotch punched her ticket?"

"Fire Crotch?" Arta frowned. "I do not—" She stiffened. "You are offensive, shade. Also, you are misinformed. My sister abides."

"Sweetie, if there's one thing I know, it's dead, and Tomato Twat's three parts gone. If she's not dead yet, she soon will be." Meredith sniggered. "Oh, this is rich."

She vanished with a lemony poof.

"Egad, what a dreadful creature," Arta said, wrinkling her nose. "Was she such a harridan in life?"

"From what I hear," Dev said. "We don't run in the same circles." He turned to Verbena. "We're taking Taryn to my aunt's house. I'd like you and Jeb to come along. It's not safe in the woods with Pratt on the loose."

She looked suspicious. "You ain't jes a-saying that so's you can lock Jeb up, is you? I done lost Bobo. I ain't losing Jeb, too."

"Bobo?"

"My dawg," Verbena said. "That low-down snake Joby Ray Skinner kilt him jes fer spite."

Poor dog, Jeb sang mournfully, *he was faithful and kind, to be sure, And he constantly loved her, although she was poor.*

When the Skinners sent her heartless away, She had always a friend in her poor dog Tray.

"He does the best he can do, but he don't know any songs about Bobos, and 'Tray' rhymes with 'away,'" Verbena confided. "See?"

"I understand, and I'm sorry as I can be about Bobo." The shire reeve's voice was gentle.

"Thankee." Verbena wiped her eyes with the back of a grubby hand. "Joby Ray's a mean 'un, and no lie."

"Don't worry." His jaw tightened, and his gray eyes glinted with anger. "He'll pay for killing Bobo."

"Good luck finding the lousy frog turd," Verbena said. "Since them Skinners lost the moonshine trade, they don't stay put."

"They trade in spell craft?" Arta asked.

"Huh?" Verbena gave her a blank stare and then chuckled. "No, illegal liquor."

"Spirits?" Arta's burgeoning interest vanished. "The Kirvahni are unaffected."

"The kith aren't so lucky," Dev said. "The Skinners cooked up a bad batch of 'shine and poisoned a bunch of them. Charlie Skinner, the head of the clan, added a 'secret' ingredient that turned out to be a hallucinogen. Big mistake. Someone drowned him in his own still."

"I have heard of this Charlie Skinner," Arta said. "Verbena has told me of him. In truth, the peckerwood's death seems to me a small loss."

"Pecker—" Dev was overcome by a sudden spasm of coughing.

Arta glared at him. "Are you laughing at me?"

"No, no. I—" He gasped and wiped his eyes. "Okay, maybe I am laughing a little. I didn't expect to hear you say 'peckerwood.'"

"'Tis a word, is it not? Did I not use it correctly?"

"Just right," Dev said. "If ever there was a peckerwood, Charlie Skinner was one." He turned to Verbena. "I know you don't trust me, but I insist that you and Jeb come with me."

"But—" Verbena protested.

He held up his hand. "I won't lock Jeb up, but I can't let him keep wandering around, either. If the norms see him, the Kith Council will get involved, and they'll turn Jeb into scrap."

Jeb moaned and swayed in alarm.

Mother, sweet mother, your child is in need,
His life would be blighted,
By hard men and greed.

"Don't fret none, Jeb," Verbena said. "I won't let 'em hurt you. Drained that no-count Joby Ray. Do the same to the Council if 'n they messes with you."

"You are a lamia?" Arta asked.

"Enhancer," Verbena said with a touch of pride. "I can make a super stronger, or I can bleed 'em dry."

"No one is going to hurt Jeb," Dev said. "I promise."

"This aunt o' yourn, ain't you a-feared old Jeb will give her a spasm?"

"My aunt is a hard one to rattle."

"Huh." Verbena clearly had doubts. "She got vittles? Jeb don't get peckish, being metal and all, but I do. Ain't had nothing to eat the past few days but a few berries and some cattails."

"Aunt Wee always has something warming on the stove."

"She ever make fish cakes?" The girl's expression grew wistful. "I'm terrible partial to fish cakes."

Dev's serious face creased in a smile that made Arta blink. Faith, 'twas like the sun coming from behind the clouds.

"You mean salmon patties?" His voice was a smoky drawl. "She makes them all the time. They're my favorite."

Verbena gazed up at Jeb. "Whadda you think? Should we go with the sheriff?"

We're going to my auntie's, Jeb sang.

In a cart and horses three,
And we'll dine on fish and crumpets
In her cottage by the sea.

"I declare, Jeb, sometimes you don't make a lick o' sense," Verbena said. "We ain't nowheres near the sea, and she don't— Oh, never mind." She turned to Dev. "Jeb says yes, but no funny business. Got it?"

"No funny business," Dev promised with utmost gravity. "Got it."

Chapter Four

Their destination decided, Dev considered the best way to get to Aunt Wee's. "We could take my Jeep," he said. "It's parked on Dark Corners Road, but I'm worried Jeb might follow us out of the woods and be seen."

"You's right," Verbena said. "He follows me around like a dawg. Where 'bouts do this aunt of yourn live?"

"On the river between Hannah and Paulsberg. There's a logging trail that will take us close."

"I knows the one," she said. "Been down it many a time with the dawgs." She stole a glance at Arta. "You'd be doing me a favor if you'd let Jeb tote Miz Taryn. He likes to be useful."

"Very well," Arta said, though she was obviously reluctant.

"Hear that, Jeb?" Verbena said. "You's carrying Miz Taryn. You be careful, now, and don't drop 'er."

Jeb saluted smartly and hung his giant peanut on a belt loop beside his trumpet. Creaking like a windlass, he lifted Taryn and tucked her in the crook of one arm, then trundled off at a rollicking gait. Verbena darted ahead of him, quick as shadow. Dev watched her flit away in bemusement. Hard to believe this feral woman-child was his sister.

Arta raced after Verbena and Jeb.

"Damn," Dev muttered, sprinting in pursuit. He caught up with Arta. "You keep running off, you're going to give me a complex. Makes a fellow wonder what he's done wrong."

"Your sensibilities are not my concern. My only care is my sister."

"There, that's put me in my place, hasn't it?"

"I misdoubt I could." She spared him a considering glance. "You run well, shire reeve, but can you stay the course?"

Dev grinned. "Try me."

She settled into a ground-eating lope, and Dev kept pace. Arta was light on her feet and graceful as a cat. Quite the beauty, the High Huntress, and sexy as hell. Her mouth alone was a work of art, pink and lush and softly curved. He found himself watching her when she talked. She had a way of pressing her lips together when annoyed that drove him nuts.

He glanced at her. She was doing the lip thing now.

"Worried about Taryn?" he asked.

"Of a certainty, but my thoughts were on Verbena." She bounded over a shallow gully, and Dev followed suit. "She is a wild thing. Given the reprobates who fostered her, I suppose 'tis no surprise. Far better had she been raised by wolves. Indeed, wolves would have been kinder. The Skinners forced Verbena to abide with the hounds and eat their leavings."

"Well, now," Dev said. "That makes me sorry old Charlie's dead. Real sorry."

"The man was a scoundrel. When he wearied of his abuse, he gave Verbena to the djegrali for sport." Arta sprang over a downed tree. "She spoke of her father, the traveling man. Perhaps this Charlie suspected she was not his get."

"Son of a bitch." Dev cleared the tree without breaking stride. Arta's account of his sister's life was grim. "The Skinners should be horsewhipped. How did she escape?"

"With the aid of Conall's wife."

"Beck? I owe her one, then."

"Why? Verbena is not your responsibility."

"Yes, she is." Arta gave him a curious look, and he quickly amended, "I'm the sheriff."

"Your devotion to your duty behooves you, shire reeve."

"I do my best," he said.

And she's my sister, he wanted to add, but refrained. He barely knew Arta, and he was still trying to process Sildhjort's astonishing revelations. Somehow, he would have to break the news to Verbena. Talk about awkward.

Hey, Verbena, guess what? I met your father, the traveling man. He was running bare ass through the woods, naked as a newborn baby. His name is Sildhjort, and he's silver—all over. Shiny as the hubcaps on a pimped-out caddy, and he has antlers that grow right out the top of his head. You think that's weird? Hold on. It gets better. He's a GOD...and get this. You and I share the same gene pool. Turns out the traveling man is my daddy, too.

Welcome to the Addams Family, baby sister.

Yeah, he was really looking forward to that conversation.

They reached the logging road and found Verbena lounging on a broad oak limb twenty feet above the ground.

"'Bout time you got here." She dropped out of the tree and landed in a crouch. "I'd 'bout give up."

"Where is the behemoth?" Arta demanded, catching her breath.

"Up ahead," Verbena said. "He ain't gone far."

They found Jeb waiting for them farther down the dirt road. Woods surrounded them, a thick maze of sycamores, scrub oaks, pines, bamboo, oak leaf hydrangea, kudzu, honeysuckle, and vicious bull vines.

"My aunt's place lies just over there." Dev pointed northeast. "The underbrush is thick. It'll be slow going from here."

Pursing his mobile lips, Jeb whistled a quick, mournful dirge and gently laid the injured huntress on the leafy ground beside the road. The huntress's face was waxen, and her cheeks were pocked with pale, gray squiggles.

"Jeb says we need to hurry," Verbena said. "He says Miz Taryn ain't doing so good."

"What?" Arta rushed to the injured huntress's side. "Dear gods, the behemoth is right. I fear my sister is dying."

Dev swore under his breath. "We need to get her to my aunt in a hurry. Jeb, can you blaze a trail?"

Jeb nodded. Turning, he crashed into the woods, knocking over trees and kicking scrub and brushwood aside with the ease of a bulldozer. Slinging her sister over her shoulder like a sack of wheat, Arta plunged after the bronze wrecking ball.

"And she's off again," Dev muttered, setting out after her.

"Reminds me o' Miz Beck," Verbena said, trotting along beside him. "She ain't a-feared of nothing. Took on them demons was after me single-handed and a passel of Skinners besides. Got me a notion Miz Arta's a lot like 'at."

"You don't strike me as a wimp, either."

"Me? I'm afraid of everything—least ways, I used to be."

"Yeah?" Dev gave her a curious glance. "What were you afraid of?"

"Skinners, mostly." Verbena leapt over a pile of bracken and downed limbs. "They thought I was a dud, but they was wrong. Oncet they figured out I got power, they tried to wheedle me into coming back, but I'm done with them varmints."

The green tunnel Jeb had smashed through the overgrown copse ended abruptly, and Dev and Verbena trotted into a sunlit clearing. Wild purple asters dotted a gentle hill sloping down to the river. Below them,

Jeb hovered beside Arta and a gray-haired woman in jeans, scuffed work boots, a baggy cotton shirt, and a straw hat that had seen better days. Taryn was on the ground, and the old woman knelt on the grass beside her, a Remington 870 within easy reach.

Dev strode up to her. "I see you brought your shotgun. You plan to shoot us?"

Aunt Weoka frowned beneath the brim of her battered hat. Time had ravaged her countenance, but she was still strikingly handsome, and her hazel eyes were sharp.

"Planned to shoot something," she said in her husky drawl. "Thought maybe a T-Rex was in them woods. Grabbed old Bessie and come a-running."

"No big lizards," Dev said, grinning at a mental picture of his aunt facing down a huge dinosaur armed with nothing but a shotgun. "Just us."

Weoka grunted. "Should have guessed it was you. You were always bringing something home for me to mend, but this poor child is suffering from more than a broken wing. Who did this?"

"His name is Pratt," Dev said. "He's a god."

"That would explain it." Weoka rose to her feet. "Bring—" Pausing, she looked at Arta. "This here demon hunter got a name?"

"Taryn." Arta's eyes were clouded with worry. "Her name is Taryn."

"Bring Taryn to the house, Dev. We'll put her in your old room." Weoka gazed up at Jeb. "I see you finally caught this gad about. Whadda you mean to do with him?"

"Thought I'd plant him in your garden to keep the deer away."

That earned him a chuckle. "Jeb Hannah guarding my okra and tomatoes," his aunt said. "Wouldn't that be something?"

Verbena scowled at Dev. "You'd better not lock him up. You *promised*."

"Draw in your stinger, child," Weoka said. "What's your name?"

"Verbena Van Pelt."

"Pleased to meetcha. I'm Weoka."

Verbena's mulish expression melted into astonishment. "Weoka Waters?" She rounded on Dev. "Yo' aunt is Weoka Waters?"

"You have heard of her?" Arta asked.

Verbena made a noise. "Everybody in these parts knows Weoka Waters, 'specially the kith. She's always patching up this one and that one."

Arta's shoulders sagged. "Praise the gods."

"Can't make any promises," Weoka said, "but I'll do what I can." She gave Verbena a measuring look. "Good thing you tagged along, booster. I'm going to need your help."

Verbena started. "How did you—"

"Power has a shine, child."

Picking up her shotgun, Weoka tossed her long, gray braid over her shoulder and strode toward the house.

Verbena glanced at Jeb and hesitated.

"Jeb will be fine," Dev assured her. He looked at the metal giant. "We could use someone to stand guard. That all right with you?"

Jeb tipped his hat and stomped off, whistling a merry tune.

"Thankee." Verbena gave Dev a shy smile that transformed her thin face. "Jeb ain't one fer sitting around. Giving him sumpin to do was a kindness." Looking down at her feet, she wiggled her toes in the grass. "Sorry I was snappish before. I was a-feared you'd changed your mind and meant to lock Jeb up."

"I told you I wouldn't."

She flushed. "I know, but folks lie."

"I don't. Not unless it's necessary. I've got a thing about lies."

"Me, too."

"Well, there you go," Dev said. "That's something else we have in common."

"Sumpin else?" Her brow furrowed and then cleared. "Oh, you mean fish cakes." She gave a deep chuckle. "You's pokin' fun at me."

"Not at all," Dev said. "Salmon patties are important."

Verbena grinned and scampered after Weoka.

Arta started to lift Taryn, but Dev moved her aside. "My turn," he said.

Taking Taryn in his arms, he strode down the hill with Arta. His aunt's home, a sprawling cabin of weathered pine with a rusted tin roof, was situated on a bend in the river. The HVAC unit Dev had purchased his aunt at twenty-one with his deputy salary hummed softly in the side yard. He and Arta climbed the back stoop and stepped into the kitchen. The house was blessedly cool after the sticky heat of the day, and a supper of roast chicken, corn bread, and sweet potatoes sat warming on the ancient green and white Magic Chef stove.

"Aunt Wee's room is that way." He jerked his chin at a door that stood ajar. "There are three more bedrooms and a bath on the second floor."

Arta followed him up the stairs and down the hall to the left, where they found Weoka waiting in Dev's old room. It was a spacious chamber, with an arched beamed ceiling, whitewashed walls, and two large windows with a lovely view of the river. The space had not changed a jot since Dev had moved out: same sturdy oak bed and chest of drawers, same apple crate bedside table, same pictures on the walls. A purple and gold pennant with a snarling feline and *BCH Wildcats* hung next to the bureau.

Aunt Weoka stood beside the bed. The covers were turned down, and the crisp, white linens smelled faintly of lavender, a soothing fragrance that knocked Dev straight back to childhood. Aunt Wee's house was a miscellany of comforting smells, from the yeasty aroma of homemade bread to the fresh scent of sun-dried towels. He compared his upbringing with Verbena's nightmarish life and felt shitty as hell.

He was lucky. He had never known abuse, or hunger, or fear. Thanks to Aunt Wee, he'd been loved and nurtured and valued.

"Dev Whitsun, be you a man or a stump?" Aunt Weoka barked, startling him from his musings. "Put that poor child on the bed."

"Yessum," Dev said, hastening to do her bidding.

He settled Taryn on the bed and stepped back. The wriggling lines on the huntress's face had turned black.

"She's been blighted." Weoka sounded grim. "Nasty business. Magic of the darkest kind." She glanced at Arta. "You were there?"

"Nay." Arta's voice was thick with misery. "The girl witnessed Pratt's savagery. Would that I had been present."

"If you'd been there, I'd be treating both of you." Weoka rolled up her sleeves and motioned to Verbena. "All right, gal. Time to show your stuff."

Verbena eased over to the bed.

"What of me?" Arta protested. "Give me something to do, I beg you."

Weoka ran her hands along Taryn's extremities. "I could use some herbs from the garden. Sticklewort for spell reversal and rosemary and thyme for healing and protection." She straightened with a frown. "Oh, and bamboo. It's handy for breaking hexes. There's a canebrake down by the river."

Arta nodded. "I will fetch them at once. What else?"

"Nothing. Just clear out." Weoka flapped a hand at Dev and Arta. "Scat, both of you."

She turned her back on Arta in dismissal. The huntress stared at her with a stricken expression and fled the room with a muffled cry.

"Arta, wait," Dev said, going after her.

She did not slow. Stumbling headlong down the stairs, Arta rushed out of the house and down to the river. Pausing on the grassy bluff, she looked out at the rolling water, her spine rigid. She seemed fragile, breakable as old glass.

Dev's heart twisted with the sudden urge to comfort her. "You okay?" he asked, standing back to give her space.

"Aye, it is well with me." Her voice was bitter. "Would that I could say the same of my sister."

"What happened to Taryn is not your fault."

Arta whirled to face him, and Dev sucked in a breath. Fragile? Like hell. She was incandescent with wrath. Energy crackled around her. Her green eyes blazed, and her hair, pale as moonlit frost, shone with an unearthly light.

She was the most splendid, breathtakingly beautiful creature Dev had ever seen.

"Is it not?" Her bosom heaved. "'Twas I who ordered her to free the rogue. *I* who put her in harm's way."

"She was doing her job," Dev heard himself say, unable to look away. "Besides, you couldn't have known this would happen."

"But it did happen, and I am to blame." Quick as a flash, she drew a knife from her boot. "Pratt shall answer for this." She raised her shining face to the sky. "This I swear by the Vessel and the blood."

In a flash, she sliced the blade across her palm and let the blood drip onto the ground. The earth trembled, and there was a distant rumble, as though the heavens had heard and answered.

"What the—" Dev grabbed her wrist, but the cut on her palm was already healing. "That was a stupid thing to do."

She jerked away. "I will have my vengeance. I have sworn it."

"Taryn isn't Pratt's only victim. A lot of people are dead because of him."

"That is your concern. Taryn is mine."

"The attack on Taryn is part of a murder investigation. Stay out of my way."

"And I would advise *you* to stay out of mine."

"Don't interfere, Arta."

"Or what? You will toss me in gaol?"

"If it comes to that." He folded his arms on his chest. "You wouldn't be the first super I've put behind bars."

She threw back her head and laughed. "I am Kirvahni. You are welcome to try."

Dev felt a flash of anger. The unexpected emotion shook him to the core. Jesus, this woman got under his skin.

There was a soft *whoosh* from the direction of the house, and the windows in his old room exploded outward in a shower of wood and glass. With a muffled oath, Dev threw himself on top of Arta, shielding her from the raining debris.

"What the hell?" he said, getting to his feet. Thick puffs of blue and green smoke poured from the gaping holes in the loft bedroom. "Oh my God, Aunt *Wee*."

He raced back to the house and burst into the upstairs bedroom with Arta at his heels. Acrid smoke filled the room, and there were jagged holes where the windows had been. Dev coughed and looked around. Verbena was huddled in a corner, her thin arms wrapped around her knees. Dev's horrified gaze found his aunt. Weoka was sprawled on the floor, her face gray and blank.

"What happened?" Dev demanded, dropping to his knees beside her.

"She laid hands on Miz Taryn." Verbena rocked back and forth. "A-glowing like the sun, she was, so bright it hurt to look at her, but the curse was too much. I gives her a little nudge, and that's when..." She moaned. "Lordy, I done kilt the river lady."

Dev checked his aunt's pulse. His shoulders sagged with relief. "She's not dead."

Verbena lifted her head. "She ain't?"

Her face crumpled, and she burst into tears. An inarticulate sound drew Dev's gaze to the bed. Arta stood looking down at her sister.

"Taryn?" Dev asked, his stomach clenching with dread.

Lifting her head, Arta met Dev's gaze, her eyes bright with unshed tears. "Restored," she said in a shaking voice. "I know not how, but your aunt has done the thing."

Dev thought "restored" an exaggeration. Taryn's breathing was even, and the hideous marks were gone, but her skin was the color of old parchment, and there were dark circles under her eyes.

Arta crossed the room to Weoka's side. "She had no need of herbs from the garden, did she? 'Twas a ruse. She sent us away a-purpose."

"Probably," Dev said. "She's hardheaded that way."

"I have some skill in the healing arts. An you will permit, I would lend her mine aid."

Weoka opened her eyes. "Not on your life." She tried to sit up and fell back with a gasp. "Dadflabit, I'm weak as a kitten. Help me to my room, boy."

Ignoring her sputtering, Dev lifted his aunt and carried her downstairs.

"I said help me, not carry me," she said when they reached her room. "Put me down. I can make it on my own from here."

"Nope." He carried her to the bed and lowered her onto the mattress. "Are you sure you're all right?"

"Fine, fine," she said, collapsing against the bank of pillows with a scowl. "A little rest and I'll be right as rain."

Dev frowned down at her. "You really are wiped out. I've never seen you like this. I'll get Verbena to help you undress."

"You'll do no such thing," she snapped. "I ain't decrepit." She flapped a hand at the door. "Stop fussing and see to our guests. Verbena's too scrawny by half. Feed her and see that she bathes. Where has she been living, a sty?"

"In the woods with Jeb."

"That ain't right. Where's her family?"

We're her family, Dev wanted to say but refrained. "She was raised by the Skinners," he said.

"Them no-counts? No wonder she lives in the woods." She motioned weakly toward the door. "There are clean towels in the upstairs bathroom and some of Winnie's clothes in the closet. Find that poor child something to wear."

"Yessum."

Weoka sighed. "You're a good boy. I'll lie here for a spell. Food's on the stove. I made extra. Dropped a knife and two forks when I was putting away the dishes—told me company was coming. You know where everything is."

She closed her eyes.

"I'll check on you later," Dev said. "Would you like a bite to eat?"

"Not now." Her voice was gruff with weariness. "Leave be. Let me rest for a spell. That's all I need."

Disquieted by his aunt's weak condition, Dev slipped out and closed the door behind him. He found Arta upstairs. She was sitting in a chair by the bed watching her sister sleep. Dev looked around. To his surprise, the damaged wall and windows had been repaired and the room returned to its former order, down to the smallest detail.

"She done it."

Verbena sat cross-legged on the floor in the far corner of the room, facing the bed. She had dried her tears and seemed calm. No, it was more than that. There was a stillness about the girl, a determined placidity that enabled her to escape notice when she desired. With a flash of insight, Dev realized this was how Verbena had survived the Skinners. She had made herself invisible.

"Arta?" he asked.

"Yup," Verbena said. "She waved her hands and fixed everything."

"Thank you," Dev said to the huntress. "My aunt will be relieved."

"'Twas nothing, the merest trifle."

"You magicked the house back together. That's hardly nothing."

Arta rose from her chair. "The Kirvahni are often called upon to restore order. The Dalvahni are inveterate bunglers."

"You're equalizers?" Dev said with some amusement.

"I do not take your meaning."

"Fixers. Someone who comes in and cleans up."

She waved a hand. "Acquit me of marvels. The small restoration you perceive is of no moment." She turned to Verbena. "Your talent, howe'er... That is something quite out of the ordinary. My sister was in extremis, and you saved her. I am in your debt."

Verbena shook her head. "You don't owe me diddly squat. I give Miz Weoka a little push, but she's the one who removed the curse."

"What manner of being is your aunt, shire reeve?" Arta gave Dev a stern look. "And be plain about it."

"Plainly speaking, she's what you might call a keeper."

"A keeper of what, pray?"

"The Devil River. Been at it a long time." Dev paused. "Like always."

"Shire reeve, are you saying that your aunt is a *goddess*?"

Dev shrugged. "Yeah, but it's no big deal. It's just who she is."

"Why did you not tell me? My sister was near death, and I was frantic with worry."

"I told you she's a healer."

"That is not—" Arta paused. A look of unease flitted across her face. "Are you a keeper, as well?"

"Me? Nah, I'm no river god."

"You's the sheriff," Verbena said. "That's a kind o' keeper."

"Thank you. I like to think so." Dev strode to the door. "Verbena, I'm under strict orders from Aunt Wee to find you some clean clothes."

She gave him a pugnacious frown. "I ain't no charity case."

"Of course not, but supper's ready and you can't come to the table wearing that dirt. You need a bath and some clean clothes."

"I suppose you's right." She looked down at her grubby apparel and wrinkled her nose. "I do smell like I been playing with the Goat Man."

She followed Dev down the hall to another bedroom.

"Help yourself." Opening the closet door, he motioned to a shelf of neatly folded garments. "They belong to Winnie McCullough. She stays here most weekends and is forever forgetting things. Aunt Wee says she's like a drippy faucet, only with clothes."

"This Winnie gal family?"

"Practically speaking. Aunt Weoka raised us both."

"Is she pretty?" Verbena asked.

"Winnie? Lord, yes. Has a trail of admirers from here to Namath Springs."

"Miz Arta's pretty, too, doncha think?"

"Miz Arta is a royal pain."

Verbena's eyes danced. "You like her. I can tell."

"Good God, you're a better interrogator than half my deputies." Dev tugged at his shirt collar in mock discomfort. "I'm starting to sweat." He handed her a stack of clothing. "The bathroom is down the hall. You'll find everything you need in the cabinets—towels, toiletries, extra toothbrushes—that sort of thing. Make yourself to home."

"Thankee." Verbena clutched the bundle to her bosom. "Thankee ever so much."

"Don't thank me, thank Aunt Wee and Winnie." He jerked a thumb toward the door. "Get a move on. Supper's ready. I'm so hungry I could eat my belt buckle."

Verbena ducked her head and scurried from the room. A moment later, he heard the bathroom door close behind her. Dev silently marveled at the strange girl. She was a curious mixture of boldness and timidity. Shaking his head, he left the bedroom and found Arta waiting at the head of the stairs.

"Taryn?" he asked.

"Sleeping peacefully." She studied him solemnly, one hand on the railing. "'Twas my thought to lend a hand with the victuals."

She glided ahead of him downstairs and into the kitchen. Dev followed, admiring the seductive sway of her hips. They washed up at the sink, using a bar of sweet-smelling soap he found on the windowsill. Under Arta's watchful eye, he took down three polka-dot tumblers from the cabinet, filled them with ice and sweet tea from the fridge, and placed them on the embroidered place mats his aunt kept on the table. Arta helped him put the food out: two roast chickens on a green Fiestaware platter surrounded by baked sweet potatoes, field peas cooked with bacon and okra, oven-fried corn, and hot corn muffins served in colorful ringed bowls. Last came a Depression-glass dish of sliced cucumbers and tomatoes from the garden.

A door opened somewhere above them, and Verbena padded downstairs in a cloud of shampoo and soap scent. Her short strawberry-blond hair was damp, her skin rosy from a vigorous scrubbing.

Dev paused in the act of placing plates and silverware on the oak table. "Good God," he said with an exaggerated start. "There was a girl under all that dirt."

Verbena grinned and fidgeted with the waistband of her shorts. "They's a mite big. A stick insect, that's what Leaberta called me."

"Leaberta?" Arta asked, raising her brows.

"Leaberta Skinner." Verbena's hand crept to her damp curls. "She was fond o' tying me to a chair and doing stuff to me."

Arta gasped. "She tortured you?"

"Nah, less'n you count pinching the stew out of a body and kicking 'em."

"I most certainly do," Arta said, her expression indignant.

"She weren't so bad, not as bad as some of 'em." Verbena's face clouded. "'Ceptin' fer m' hair. Leaberta had a thang about my hair. She was forever 'sperimenting on it."

"Why?" Arta asked.

"Dunno. Maybe she hates blondes." Verbena studied the huntress's silvery locks. "Reckon she'd bust wide open if 'n she seen you." She sighed. "But you probably wouldn't let nobody tie you to a chair, being a demon hunter and all."

"No, indeed." Arta raised her hand. "I can alter your raiment to fit you, an you like."

"No, thankee. I like these jes fine."

Arta shrugged. "Suit yourself."

Dev drew back two chairs and motioned to the table. "Dinner is served."

They sat down and passed the food around. Verbena filled her plate. Eating with the single-minded devotion of a person who has known hunger, she put away an astonishing amount of food for one so slight.

Dev bit into a corn muffin. The crust was slightly crunchy, and the buttery insides crumbled on his tongue. Arta was seated across from him, and she ate slowly, as though committing the different flavors and textures to memory.

"The peas are excellent," she said, touching a slimy green strand with her fork. "'Tis the snails that lend them their hearty flavor?"

"That's not a snail," Dev said. "That's okra from Aunt Wee's garden." He added when Arta looked blank, "It's a vegetable."

"No, it ain't." Verbena looked up from her plate. "Okra is a fruit. So is a bunch o' other plants folks call veggies, like 'maters and cucumbers and green beans, and even olives and pumpkins." She blushed when Dev looked surprised. "Read it in a book. Ladyfingers—that's what okra is called in some parts."

"Bookworm, huh?" Dev smiled. "You must have done well in school."

"Never went to school. Charlie didn't hold with learnin.' Said we'd get above our raising, and he didn't like us mixing with norms."

This didn't surprise Dev. The kith were wary of norms and generally homeschooled, for obvious reasons.

"Who taught you to read?" he asked.

"My ma," Verbena said. "Learnt my letters off the back of a flour sack. I'd draw my letters in the dirt and erase 'em, so's Charlie wouldn't see. Charlie didn't hold with books, either." She helped herself to another serving of fried corn. "Learnt about okra at the library. Mr. Toby took me."

"Toby?"

"Used to be the bouncer at Beck's Bar," she said. "Friends with Miz Cassie, too. He took me to the library in Hannah. Read all the books they had. The ones I liked, I read twicet. Went through the stacks in a couple o' days."

Dev set down his fork. "You read an entire library in a couple of *days*?"

"Yup. Started with the children's section." She wagged a finger at Arta. "Don't never read *Where the Red Fern Grows* or *Old Yeller*, if 'n you knows what's good fer you."

"Why not?"

"'Cause they's *sad*. Bawled my eyes out. Oncet I finished the children's books, the librarian give me some pointers." Verbena turned back to Dev. "You ever heared of a feller named Shakespeare?"

"The name is vaguely familiar," Dev said, trying not to smile.

"Miz Bunny—she's the librarian—says folks call him the Bard. Alls you got to say is 'The Bard,' and people know who you's talking about."

"Like Elvis."

"Who?"

"He was a singer."

"On the radio?"

"Yep. Television, too."

"We didn't have neither. When I'd read all the books they had at the library, Mr. Toby took me to his house. Read his *World Book Encyclopedia* and a bunch o' biographies, too. Oh, and *Popular Mechanics*. You ever have a ping or a rattle in your car or need your refrigerator fixed, I'm your gal."

"I'll keep that in mind." Dev rose and began to clear the table. "We have pie for dessert."

A trumpet blared on the hill.

Dev froze with a stack of plates in one hand. "What now?"

Verbena jumped up, knocking over her chair. "It's Jeb. Something's wrong."

They rushed from the house and onto the back porch. Jeb stood at the top of the hill, his horn raised to his lips. *Ta-tummm*, he blared in warning. *Ta-tummm.*

There was a bloodcurdling growl from the forest at his back, followed by the sound of trees snapping and breaking. Something was in the woods. Something large and seriously pissed.

"Red." An agonized rumble came from deep within the copse. "*Red.*"

With a shuddering groan, a large oak crashed to the ground, and a monster stepped into view. Hulking and gray-skinned, with arms and legs like tree trunks and thick, square-toed feet, the thing was ludicrously clad in a pair of harlequin knee breeches. The enraged creature dragged a huge pine behind him like a huge, enraged toddler with a pull toy.

"'Tis a colossus," Arta said, drawing her bow.

Verbena pushed the weapon aside. "That ain't no colossus. That there's Mr. Evan."

"Red," the ogre bellowed again. He slammed the pine into the turf, and a shower of bark and splinters erupted. "*Red.*"

Dev stared at the monstrous being in astonishment. "That's Evan Beck?"

"Yup." Verbena nodded. "Told you he was gon' snap his twig if he heared Miz Taryn was hurt."

Chapter Five

The ogre yanked a large maple up by the roots. He broke the tree in half and tossed it aside. "*Red.*"

"Good God," Dev said. "Is that his shifter form? The Kith Council discourages exotics."

Easy to dismiss a were sighting as the product of an overactive imagination, alcohol, or drugs, but an ogre? Straight out of *Grimm's Fairy Tales*. Hard to explain, and the norms would panic.

"Nah, it's a curse," Verbena said. "Happens when he gets riled."

Dev glanced at her in surprise. "You've seen the ogre before?"

"Sure. The ogre put a beatdown on some demons at Miz Cassie's. First time I seen the rog—" Her cheeks pinkened. "I mean, Gryffin. You remember Miz Cassie, doncha, Sheriff?"

"Cassandra Ferguson, the Witch of Devil River? Yeah, I know her. Did she curse Evan?"

Verbena gasped. "Ain't never. She's *nice*. It was the other one."

"What other one?"

"The other witch. Little old lady what lived across the river from Miz Beck's bar."

"Are you talking about Ora Mae Luker?"

"That's her. She took Mr. Evan prisoner and spiked his food with some sort o' growth potion. That's what brung on the ogre."

"There is a BOLO out on Ora Mae," Dev said. "She's a suspect in Charlie Skinner's murder."

"You can quit looking. Mr. Evan tole me she's dead."

"Did Evan—"

Dev was interrupted by a frantic bawl from the ogre.

"Red." Abandoning the woods, the ogre stomped down the hill, his eyes glowing like embers. *"Reddd."*

"Damn," Dev muttered. "We really should do something about that. Suggestions?"

"Leave him to me," a weary voice said from the doorway behind them. "He can be quite unreasonable when in this state."

Arta whirled about. "Sister," she cried. "You should be abed."

"And leave you to deal with this irksome creature? I think not." Gray-faced and trembling with exhaustion, Taryn made her way down the steps and staggered up to the ogre. "What ho, lumpkin?"

The ogre grunted in surprise and focused his gooey black eyes on Taryn. "Red?" With a howl of joy, he snatched her into his arms and held her close. "Red not dead? Red *alibe?*"

"Yes, yes, Red is alive." Taryn winced. "Have done, oaf, ere you crack my ribs."

"Alibe." Ignoring her admonition, the ogre cradled her and rocked back and forth. "Red alibe. Ebban 'fraid..."

The monster's huge form shimmered, and Evan Beck stood on the lawn, naked from the waist up.

"Meredith said..." His chest heaved as if he had run a race. "S-she told me you were dead."

"The shade lied."

"Thank God." Evan's knees buckled and he sat down in the grass with Taryn in his arms. Raising a trembling hand to her cheek, he said, "I thought you were a goner."

"So you keep saying." Taryn plucked at a fold of his garish britches. "You wear the jester's garb still?"

"Yeah." He gave her a crooked grin. "I can't seem to shake the stupid outfit when I shift."

"Why ever not?"

"Maybe because it was some snooty ginger bitch's idea of a joke?" Placing two fingers beneath her chin, Evan examined her face. "Damn, Red. You look like warmed-over shit in a two-bit pot."

"I thank you, sir. Allow me to return the compliment. I find you vulgar, improper, and rude in the extreme."

"Sure, babe, anything you like. Whatever lifts your skirt."

"Impossible creature," Taryn said. "Why do I put up with you?"

"Easy. You're madly in love with me."

"Absurd," she said, and went limp in his arms.

"Red?" Evan gave her a frantic little shake. "Talk to me. Damn it, Red, don't you bug out on me."

The screen door flew open, and Aunt Weoka stomped out of the house. "Stop it. Rattling the gal's teeth around in her head ain't gonna help." Her gaze swept over the destruction on her lawn. "What in tarnation's been going on around here?"

Evan got to his feet with Taryn in his arms. "Sorry. I...um... lost my temper."

"Huh," Weoka said. "You Jason Damian's boy?"

His eyes narrowed. "What if I am?"

"I ain't accusing you of nothing. You look like your sister is all." She motioned. "Bring the gal back into the house. She needs rest after taking on Pratt."

"Pratt did this?" Evan's brows lowered. "Son of a bitch. He's *mine*."

"Nay," Arta protested. "Taryn was acting on my orders when she was attacked. By rights, Pratt is my quarry."

Evan's eyes glittered dangerously. "You sent Red after a god? Congratulations. You're an idiot."

Arta stiffened. "I am the High Huntress."

"You sent Red into harm's way while you lounged around Chateau La Bimbo eating bon-bons? Nice job, High *fricking* Huntress."

"I do not 'lounge,' and I know not what a bon-bon may be."

"It's candy for spoiled little bitches. If you wanted the rogue freed so damn bad, you should have gone after Pratt yourself."

Arta was white around the mouth. "Agreed, which makes Pratt my affair, not yours."

Dev put his fingers to his mouth and let out a shrill whistle. "Time-out. Listen up, both of you. I'm the sheriff, and you will leave Pratt to me."

Aunt Weoka chuckled. "Snarling like a pack of dogs over a soup bone." She gave Evan a motherly look. "You're grumpy and out of sorts, and no wonder. Low blood sugar—shifting will do that to you. A good meal will set you to rights."

"Thanks, but no thanks," Evan said. "I'm a picky eater."

"Skittish, huh? Ora Mae did a number on you, but don't worry. My food ain't tainted."

"How do you—"

"The river talks, and I listen."

"The river talks," Evan muttered as Weoka went back into the house. "Weird old broad."

"You don't know the half of it," Dev said, "but she's right. You need to eat. Come on to the house and I'll feed you supper." He glanced wryly at Verbena. "If there's anything left."

"Har," Verbena said. "The sheriff's poking fun, Mr. Evan, but you can trust him. He's gon' help me and Jeb."

"Jeb?" Evan said. "Don't tell me that walking beehive is here."

"Sho' is. Went into the woods when you started flinging stuff around. 'Spect he didn't want to get dented." Verbena pointed. "Here he comes now."

Jeb tromped down the hill, flourishing his trumpet.

Over in the meadow,
In the sand, in the sun, he sang in his hollow voice.
Lived an old mother toadie
And her little toadie one.
"Jump," said the mama toad.
"I jump," said the one.

Jeb executed an awkward little hop and landed with a *clank.*

So, they jumped and they jumped,
In the sand, in the sun.

"Jesus," Evan said, shaking his head. "That is fucked up."

* * * *

Skulking at the edge of the wood, the gaunt figure fixed his unblinking gaze on the cabin below. The bindings on his skin writhed, leaving burning trails in their wake, but he paid little heed to the discomfort. Pain had been his constant companion lo these many years, and the girl's lure was stronger. She was there, inside the dwelling, a soft, pulsing beacon irresistible as a siren song. She was clarity and respite. He was a stranger to himself save in her presence, his mind mired in delirium, but when he was near the girl, the haze that gripped his fevered brain briefly lifted, and he knew himself.

Outcast.

Betrayer.

Rogue.

Apostate.

The knowledge filled him with horror, but anything, even self-loathing, was preferable to darkness and confusion. Pratt had taken everything from him—honor, his brothers and his god, his very calling—but it was the loss of self that rankled the most.

The air hummed, and an ugly little man appeared. The rogue grunted in surprise. Less than an arrow's length in height, with florid cheeks and bright eyes set in a cunning face, the imp had a nose like a parsnip and a droll, rubbery mouth. He was clad in a yellow tunic belted at the waist, patched stockings, and wool slippers of cerulean blue with curling toes and leaf-shaped uppers. An orange skullcap completed this ensemble, worn at a jaunty angle upon his misshapen head.

"Greetings." The strange creature sketched him a bow. "I am Irilmoskamoseril."

"Why?" The word scritched past the rogue's dry lips.

"Why am I here?" The imp cocked his head. "I work for Sildhjort. A holiday every other century and the pay blows, but what's a nibilanth to do? We can't all weave straw into gold. At any rate, it beats living under a bridge. Not that the trolls would share." He scowled. "Clutch-fisted cheeseparers, trolls." He jabbed a gnarled finger at the rogue's charred hands. "That looks like it smarts."

"Orb." The rogue stared at his ruined flesh. "Burns."

"Aye, but leastways you're still here. Anyone else would be dust. That's why old Thunder Mug impressed you, ain't it, to carry the orb?" The imp chuckled. "Gryffin Fairheart, you were once called, the best and brightest of the Dalvahni. Your brothers thought you dead and wept in their ale at word of your passing. They never guessed you were Pratt's stooge." He tilted his ugly head. "Slipped your leash, did you? Gave the orb to the one creature who could hold it and not perish—besides you, of course."

"Pratt want orb. Sugar…not bound."

"True enough," Irilmoskamoseril said, "and you were a sitting duck. The markings Pratt gave you make you easy to find."

Gryffin gave him a blank stare. "Bound. Gave Sugar…orb."

"Jings, Pratt's curse has softened your brains." The little man tapped one foot. "Where is Sugar, by the by? Sildhjort ordered me to keep an eye on the nincompoop. Never mind Pratt is a raving fiend. That's the gods for you—issuing orders left and right without a thought for anyone else."

"Sugar gone."

"I can see that. Any idea where he is?"

"Gone."

"Brilliant," the imp said in disgust. "Fecking brilliant. How am I to watch over Sugar if I can't—" He paused as something stirred in a nearby thicket, and a pair of large blue eyes peeped at them from the brush. "That you, looby? No need to hide. Come out, where we can see you."

The branches parted, and a shaggy creature stepped forth, white as new-fallen snow and enormous.

"Pretty?" the ape man trilled.

Holding out a paw, he offered the orb to Gryffin, who shook his head and backed away.

"No, no, Sugar." Plucking the orange cap from his head, Irilmoskamoseril threw it on the ground and stomped on it. "You're supposed to hide the cursed thing."

Sugar's gaze was on Gryffin's burnt hands. "Owie?"

Gryffin nodded. The orb had scorched him terribly. A mortal man would have died of his wounds, but he was Dalvahni and healed in an instant...only to burn again.

And again.

He had quickly learned to switch hands and often, allowing one palm to heal while he carried the orb in the other. For more than three thousand years, he had endured the smell of his roasting flesh in his nostrils.

The orb did not burn Sugar. Gryffin Fairheart had been a nonpareil among warriors—faithful, strong, valiant, and true—but the ape man was pure and innocent as a child.

Sugar's lips trembled, and his woolly face creased in concern. "Hurt?" He indicated Gryffin's squirming tattoos.

"Curse," Gryffin managed to rasp. "Burns."

Sugar trilled in distress. "Sugar heal owie."

Before Gryffin could guess his intention, the ape man bounded up to him with the orb and clasped him on the shoulder. The world went white, and Gryffin was falling, falling, through fire and pain. His very bones burned. The skin sloughed off his body, and his flesh melted like wax.

Ah, death.

He welcomed it and gladly, had longed for its release for years past counting. Unbidden, the girl's piquant face flitted before him, and he felt a pang of sorrow that he would never see her again. Then the blackness gripped him, and he knew no more.

* * * *

Dev surveyed the scene in his old room from the doorway. Arta pulled down the covers, and Evan tenderly lowered Taryn onto the mattress and covered her with a blanket.

"She is very pale." Arta's brow was creased with worry. "Has she done herself an injury?"

"She's fine. Tuckered, is all." Weoka sat in a chair by the window, a quilt in her lap. "Nothing a little bedrest won't cure." Her tone sharpened as Evan eased himself onto the edge of the mattress beside Taryn. "Stop mooning, boy, and get yourself something to eat. Arta and I will sit with Taryn."

"Of a certainty," said Arta, "though I will happily bide with her an you are not recovered, milady."

"Pshaw," said Aunt Wee. "I'm fine. Right as rain. Just needed to shut my eyes for a spell."

Evan frowned at them. "I won't leave her," he said. "I'm not hungry."

Weoka gave Dev a look, and he responded with a nod of understanding.

"Food," he said. Striding over to Evan, he took the shifter by the arm. "Now. After you eat, we'll find you something to wear."

"Lands, yes," Weoka said. "You look a fool in them belled britches."

"What if Red wakes up?" Evan fretted, following Dev down the stairs and into the kitchen. "What if she needs me?"

"Aunt Weoka will see to her. She knows what she's doing."

Dev glanced out the window over the sink. Hat a-tilt, Jeb Hannah was strolling the grounds, loudly singing "Row, Row, Row Your Boat." Verbena sat in a rocking chair on the porch watching him, one bare foot wagging in time to the jaunty tune.

Dev turned away from the window. "I know you're worried about Taryn, but I expect you to show my aunt a little respect. She saved Taryn's life today."

To his surprise, Evan flushed.

"Sorry." He shoved his hands in the pockets of his jester britches. "It made me nuts when I thought Red was—" He broke off, shaking his head. "Chick has me turned inside out. The worst of it is, I don't know if she feels the same way. Hell, maybe I'm nothing but another thrall to her."

"A what?"

"Thralls are sexual companions, compliments of dear old Kevin. Thralls feed on emotion. Need it to survive, and demon hunters are their food source. Neat little job perk, huh?"

An image of Arta in the arms of another flashed through Dev's mind, and something hot and ugly stirred inside him.

"These thralls," he said, a pulse throbbing in his temple. "Are they sex slaves?"

"Nah, more of a symbiotic thing." Evan's mouth twisted. "Apparently, a horny demon hunter is an inefficient demon hunter. They're supposed to get frequent tune-ups, according to some manual, but Red's done with that shit, if I have anything to say about it." He laughed wildly. "Jesus, listen to me. I'm jealous. Told you. The chick makes me nuts."

"What are you going to do about it?"

Evan ran a hand through his dark hair. "Damned if I know."

"You might try marrying her."

"Yeah?" Evan's expression brightened, but only for a moment. "What if she says no, and I never see her again?"

He looked so miserable that Dev felt sorry for him.

"Have a seat," Dev said, waving him toward the old farm table. "Leftovers are in the oven. I'd nuke them for you, but Aunt Wee doesn't believe in microwaves."

Evan slumped into a chair and dropped his head into his hands. "There are two demon hunters upstairs, a magical amplifier on the porch, and a singing statue on her lawn, but your aunt doesn't believe in microwaves?"

"Oh, she believes they *exist*, she just won't use 'em. Says they take up too much counter space. Same goes for the electric coffeepot I bought her two Christmases ago. Still in the box. She uses the metal percolator she bought in the 1930s."

Evan looked up. "How old *is* your aunt?"

"Old."

"What is she, demon, shifter, witch, or vampire?"

"Deity," Dev said.

Evan sat back. "No shit? Just when I think it can't get any freakier around here, the Universe bitch-slaps me." He swayed. "Say, I don't feel so hot."

"You need to eat." Dev plunked a loaded plate in front of him. "Sweet tea, water, or milk?"

"Tea." Evan tore into the chicken. Ripping it apart with his bare hands, he shoved the meat into his mouth. "This is good. Real good."

Dev handed Evan a glass of tea, along with a napkin. The shifter took a long gulp from the tumbler and finished off the chicken. He wiped his greasy hands on the napkin, picked up the fork beside his plate, and dug into the vegetables. His devotion to the task of eating forcibly reminded Dev of Verbena.

Dev sliced Evan a slab of buttermilk pie and handed it to him. "I'd heat it for you, but Aunt Wee—"

"Doesn't believe in microwaves. Got it." Evan took a bite of the creamy custard. "Oh, man," he said with a moan of appreciation. "That's good."

"Aunt Wee can cook," Dev said. "Some of my best memories involve this kitchen and food." He studied the demonoid. "What about you?"

"No warm fuzzies for me, if that's what you're asking. I went hungry a lot as a kid."

"Sorry to hear that. Where you from?"

"All over—Mobile, New Orleans, and half a dozen other cities." He sat back in his chair. "What's it to you? I'm not in the habit of confiding in cops." Dev leaned against the counter and folded his arms. "You hang around my family, I want to know something about you."

"Seems to me, your aunt can take care of herself." Evan finished the last of his pie. "Being a god and all."

"Humor me."

"You going to read me my rights, Officer?"

"You're not in custody. You got something to confess?"

"Nope." Evan pushed the empty plate aside. "You want the goods? Here they are. I was born in a flophouse. My mom left me for dead, and a couple of demons snagged me. I was raised by them. Elgdrek and Hagilth were their names."

"That doesn't sound like fun."

"It was a shitfest." Evan's purple gaze went unfocused. "Their favorite games were punch-the-demon-boy, starve-the-squirt, and burn-the-brat. They enjoyed…other amusements, too." His expression grew hard. "Things I'm not going to talk about and would rather forget."

"Child Services didn't step in?"

"Child Services didn't know I existed. The 'rents moved from one crappy dump to another—rat-infested trailers, abandoned buildings, and apartments with no hot water and leaky roofs. Sometimes we lived in an old car."

"That's tough," Dev said. "You ever run away?"

"Once, when I was six. They caught me." Evan absently rubbed the tattoo on his upper arm. "I was their errand boy, see? Drugs, booze, whatever they wanted, I was expected to produce it. If I didn't…" He shrugged and looked out the window. "Things got…interesting."

Arta swept into the room. "You should have denied them. 'Twas your duty to resist the djegrali."

Evan swiveled around in his chair. "Resist them, how? I was a kid. Besides, after I ran away, they bound me with demon runes so I couldn't leave. Tattoos from head to toe. *Ilgrith unduth*, the demons called it, or some such shit."

Arta looked thoughtful. "'Bound unto death'—so it means in the demon tongue. 'Tis magic of the foulest kind. The rogue is bound by similar markings, Taryn tells me."

"Then I feel sorry for the poor bastard, because that shit hurts," Evan said. "Like being wrapped head to toe in hot wire."

"But you eventually escaped," Arta said. "How?"

"I didn't escape. Cookie freed me. She specializes in demon removal."

"Cookie?" Dev asked.

"My sister, Rebekah."

"Beck Damian?" Dev said. "I know her."

"Cookie's a nickname." Evan made a twisting motion with one hand. "She sucked old Haggy out of the girl she was possessing at the time and trapped her in a bottle." His lips curved in an unholy smile. "A bottle of *hot* sauce. Turns out, demons are allergic."

"Good to know," Dev said. "And Elgdrek?"

"Cookie took care of him, too." Evan got to his feet. "That's my sad little story, or as much as I'm going to tell."

"One more question," Dev said. "I've heard a rumor that Ora Mae Luker is dead. You know anything about that?"

"If you're asking whether I killed her, the answer is no. Gilbert ate her."

"Gilbert?"

"Giant catfish. Ora Mae raised him from a guppy."

Dev frowned. "I found Charlie Skinner's boots on Ora Mae's stoop. They were covered in gunk and fish whiskers."

"I'm guessing the boots didn't agree with Gilbert," Evan said. "He swallowed her whole."

"'Strewth," Arta said, "'tis an unpleasant demise."

"Not unpleasant enough." Evan's eyes glittered. "The Hag deserved worse. Much worse."

"Hag?" Dev straightened. "Hold on. Are you telling me that Ora Mae and the Hag are one and the same?"

"*Were* the same. Jekyll and Hyde. Sweet little granny and flesh-eating monster rolled into one. Ask Grim Dalvahni if you don't believe me. He was there."

"I will," Dev said. "Why didn't you report this? There's a BOLO on Ora Mae."

Evan gave him a look. "Please. Who's gonna believe that shit?"

"Me," said Dev.

"Yeah, but, see, I thought you were a norm."

"And I thought you were an asshole."

Evan grinned. "Leastways, one of us was right. What are you, anyway, besides the law?"

"Yes, shire reeve." Arta practically quivered with interest. "This I would know, an we are to work together."

"Are we working together? That's news to me."

"'Twas your lady aunt's notion. She thinks we shall deal well together." Arta shrugged. "There is some merit in the notion. You know this province, and I know Pratt."

"Okay," Dev said, "but I want access to your reports on the djegrali and Pratt, and anything else pertaining to Behr County, including the rogue and the orb. I'm tired of working in the dark."

He had not known about Monster Evan, or that Ora Mae and the Hag were one and the same. He *hated* being out of the loop.

"Done," Arta said.

"Yeah, yeah, whatever," Evan said. "'Fess up, Sheriff. What kind of super are you?"

Why not? Dev thought. It had been a day of revelations. What was one more?

He opened his mouth to tell them, and the bomb dropped.

Chapter Six

A ball of light exploded at the top of the slope, bleaching the woods ghostly white.

"What the—" Dev grabbed the kitchen counter and held on as the house rattled and shook.

Glancing out the window, he saw Jeb stagger to one knee. Verbena leapt to her feet with a startled cry and darted off the porch, taking the steps two at a time.

"Verbena." Dev lunged out the back door. "*Wait.*"

She scampered up the hill and disappeared into the trees. He sprinted after her. The girl was running headlong into danger. Baby sister needed a come-to-Jesus that big brother would happily deliver.

He found Verbena hunkered beside an unconscious man. Quickly, Dev assessed the scene. There was no smoke or fire, no burning trees or telltale signs of the explosion that had rocked the house. The forest appeared untouched. He inhaled, his nose twitching. A sharp, slightly citrus tang hung in the air.

Not a bomb. *Magic.*

"That was a damn fool thing to do," Dev said to Verbena. "You had me worried."

"Why?"

Because you're my sister and life has dealt you a crap hand, Dev wanted to say. *Because I had Aunt Wee and you had the Skinners. Because I want to make it up to you, and I can't do that if you get yourself killed.*

"Because it's my job to protect people," he said aloud. "You could have been hurt or worse."

"Weren't in no danger. Knowed it was Gryffin."

"How?"

"Just knowed." Her chin trembled. "He looks terrible bad. Is he...is he dead?"

Dev knelt beside him. The poor schmuck certainly looked dead. Gryffin Dalvahni was a big man, with wide shoulders and the promise of impressive musculature if he hadn't been half-starved. He wore a pair of ragged leather breeches and nothing else. Intricate black tattoos ran down one cheek, along his neck, and the length of one arm.

Dev checked his pulse and sat back. "He's still breathing, but he's skin and bones." He studied Verbena. "You seem awfully concerned about him. What's the rogue to you?"

"Don't call him that." She flushed. "I hate when people call him that. Gryffin rescued me and Miz Cassie from that low-down weasel Joby Ray. Don't reckon he'd 'uv done that if he was bad as folks say."

"Take it easy. I didn't mean anything by it."

"Whatever." She stuck out her chin. "You gon' help him, or not?"

"Of course, I'll help him."

"Thankee. I'll pay you back, somehow."

"I don't want you to pay me back," Dev said. "Verbena, we're—"

Arta appeared without warning. "Faith, 'tis Gryffin. He looks ghastly."

"The sheriff's gon' help him." Verbena's eyes were wide and trusting. "Right, Sheriff?"

Dev got to his feet. "Right."

"What of the orb?" Arta asked. "'Twas in his keeping."

"Not anymore," Dev said. "Sugar has it."

"Who," the huntress said with deliberate care, "may Sugar be?"

"An albino sasquatch."

"Sasquatch?" Her gaze clouded briefly and cleared. "You refer to a skellring?"

"If a skellring is big and furry and ten feet tall, then yeah."

Verbena cradled the rogue's head in her lap. "Skellring is what the Vikings called bigfoot. They's lots o' names for 'em. Woolly booger, tree man, skunk ape, yeti. Yowie, they calls 'em in Australia."

"Wild guess," Dev said. "You read that in a book?"

A dimple peeped in her cheek. "Yep."

Ding! A hideous little man appeared. "Here's a to-do." He jabbed a twiggy digit at the insensate warrior. "Sugar used the orb on that useless lump of shite."

Dev grunted. "Knew I smelled magic."

"Magic? It was a thaumaturgic tumult." The little man's long nose quivered in indignation. "The deuced thing went off and sent me flying." He brushed dirt and leaves from his mustard-colored tunic. "Tumbled into a badger's den and suffered a nasty bite."

"You or the badger?" Arta asked.

"You're hilarious." The little man goggled her. "Arta, ain't it? I've been wanting to meet you a thousand years and more."

"Alack, the feeling is not mutual."

"Saucy." The little man smacked his lips. "You're a tasty dish, tall and leggy. Nice diddeys to boot."

"Observe me basking in the glow of your approval."

"Enough," Dev said. "Who are you, and what do you want?"

"Hoo." The creature winked at Arta. "Careful, me darling, it's a testy buck."

"Peace, scamp," Arta said. "Shire reeve, this rapscallion is a nibilanth. Lesslings, some call them. Half fairy and half imp, and trouble by any name." She gave the little man a stern look. "Out with it. Why were you with Gryffin?"

"Wasn't." He tucked his thumbs in the folds of his tunic and puffed out his chest. "Name's Irilmoskamoseril. I work for Sildhjort."

"The god?" Dev asked. "We've met. Ran into him this morning."

Arta stared at him. "You did not tell me."

"We've been busy, and the subject never came up."

Arta's mouth thinned. "Out with it, scamp," she said, turning her ire on the imp. "If 'tis true you work for Sildhjort—which I misdoubt—what are you about?"

"Whist, 'tis a suspicious lass." Irilmoskameseril's long ears twitched. "Ask him yourself."

A white stag with silver antlers floated out of the trees on diamond hooves.

"That's not Sildhjort," Dev said. "Or, at least, that's not the way he looked this morning."

The imp made a helpless gesture. "The gods take many forms."

Verbena lifted her head. "He's right, Sheriff. Read a book on mythology, and there was this Greek feller name o' Zeus, had a roving eye. Disguised himself as a satyr and a swan, and a golden shower to have his way with women." Her nose wrinkled. "Even turnt himself into an *ant* oncet. Lucky somebody didn't squish 'im flat."

The stag loped up to the imp with a loud snort.

"Here now, your worship, that's hardly fair," Irilmoskameseril protested. "How was I to guess the hairy nodkin would set it off?"

The stag grunted and trotted over to Verbena. Lowering his antlered head, the deer exhaled in her astonished face, setting wisps of her blond hair aflutter.

Verbena blinked at the huge ruminant. Timidly, she laid her hand on the stag's velvet nose. "Oh," she breathed, her eyes round with wonder. "Really?" The stag wheeled and pawed the ground.

Snapping to attention, the nibilanth gave a sharp salute. "Aye, your lordship. At once."

"What is afoot?" Arta demanded.

The imp's black eyes gleamed with excitement. "Pratt has seen the orb fire and is headed this way."

"Excellent." Her luscious mouth curved in an exultant smile. "Now we have him."

Irilmoskamoseril smirked. "Nay, sweetling. Sildhjort says you are to abide here."

"What?" Arta protested. "But I—"

"Sildhjort says the lump of shi—I mean, *Gryffin*—needs care. Sildhjort says leave Pratt to him."

"Sildhjort says an awful lot for a giant deer," Dev drawled. "He and Pratt are acquainted?"

"Aye, and there's no love lost between them." Springing onto the stag's broad back, the imp showed Dev a set of sharp, pointy teeth. "Sildhjort says not to worry—Papa's got this."

The imp blew a ringing note on a curved horn, and the stag bounded away, leaving whorls of light in his wake.

"Papa?" Arta's voice was sharp. "Shire reeve, is Sildhjort... Is the god of the wood your sire?"

"Claims to be."

"You lied. You said you were not a god."

Dev held up a forefinger. "I said, if you will recall, that I'm not a *river* god."

"Do not mince words with me, sirrah." Her eyes were bright with outrage. "If Sildhjort is your father, then that makes you—"

"The sheriff," Dev said.

In the distance, there was an ominous rumbling. A foul wind tossed the trees, and the air grew heavy.

"Wuzzat?" Verbena said, her face pale with alarm.

"'Tis Pratt." Arta pointed at an angry cloud looming to the west. Red streaks of lightning crackled within the purple mass. "And he is wroth."

The thunderhead bore down on them with alarming speed and came to an abrupt halt. The pulsing blob pulsed forward and stopped, as though encountering an invisible wall.

"Foiled," Arta cried, pumping her fist into the air. "See how he presses onward but cannot proceed? Sildhjort has blocked his way."

In the east, there was a bright flare of light.

"Like a dawg to the scent," said Verbena as the cloud surged in pursuit.

"I would shadow them, an I could." Arta's mouth was set. "But I daresay Sildhjort's invisible shield would prevent my leaving."

"Daresay it would." Dev hoisted the senseless warrior over his shoulder. "Let's get Gryffin back to the house."

* * * *

An hour later, Dev was seated at the kitchen table nursing a cup of coffee when his Aunt Weoka came into the room. "How's Gryffin?" he asked.

"Malnourished, but he'll live. Demon hunters are hard to kill—a curse in Gryffin's case. Death would have been easier. He's suffered, Dev, and not just in body."

"All the more reason to bring Pratt in."

"It won't be easy," Aunt Weoka said. "He's not your run-of-the-mill super."

"I know."

"I'll help you any way I can," she said.

"Know that, too. If he's awake, I'd like a word with Gryffin."

"Have fun with that. His brains are scrambled."

"Is Verbena with him?"

"Yep, refuses to leave him."

"How is Taryn?"

"Full of pepper and raring to have another go at Pratt." Weoka chuckled. "Evan nipped that foolishness in the bud. Threatened to bust out the ogre if she put so much as a toe out of bed. That got her attention." She shook her head. "Different as a duck from a dandelion, those two, but the heart pays no toll."

Dev recalled his visceral reaction to Arta and silently agreed. The High Huntress was achingly lovely, with her pale, silvery hair and green eyes, but he had met beautiful women before. Dated his share of them, too. His attraction to Arta went beyond the physical. She somehow penetrated his carefully constructed defenses.

Not good. Pratt was a nasty customer, and he needed his wits about him. All of them. Nothing and no one could distract him from the job, including the oh-so delectable Arta.

Yeah, he thought with a rueful grimace. *You keep telling yourself that.* The High Huntress was impossible to ignore.

"Something bothering you?" Weoka asked, drawing him from his thoughts. "You haven't touched your pie."

"Well, let's see, now." Dev leaned back in the chair. "I've got a dozen dead shifters on my plate, an injured huntress, and a man upstairs recovering from years of systematic torture and abuse." He snapped his fingers. "Oh, and there's a crooning statue in your garden, and my lead suspect is a god."

"In other words, a normal day. You knew what you were signing up for when you became sheriff." Her lined face softened. "Out with it, boy. What's got you blue deviled?"

Dev poked the piece of pie with his fork. "I met my father today."

"*What?* Where?"

"In the woods. This morning."

Weoka sank into the chair beside him. "Well, I declare. This has been a long time coming. Was he what you expected?"

"He was a silver naked dude with hooves and antlers. Who expects that?" Dev added after a moment's thought, "But at least he wasn't an ant."

"Eh?"

"Nothing. Something Verbena said." He traced the pattern on the edge of the plate. "Are you and Sildhjort related?"

She shook her head. "Different planes. Sildhjort is not from Earth. He came through the rift."

He considered his words. "Do you know if he has any other children here?"

"Not that I—" She looked at him more closely. "Why do you ask?"

He took a deep breath, but before he could tell her about Verbena, a blast from Jeb's horn drew him to the window. He looked out. The trees were white with frost, and a foot of ice rimed the ground, stopping at the edge of the tree line.

"What now?" he muttered.

Stalking into the kitchen, Evan announced, "Captain Ice Dick is here."

Dev looked back at him. "Captain who?"

"Conall Dalvahni." Evan's expression was sour. "The winter wonderland routine is his calling card. He goes nuclear winter whenever he's pissed...which is pretty much all the time. Guy has the personality of a constipated porcupine."

Arta materialized. "I bear little love for the Dal. Even so, you should not speak of Conall with such disrespect. He is a renowned warrior."

"A renowned pain in the ass, you mean." Evan jumped at a crack of thunder. "Damn it, he keeps that up, he'll wake Red. I won't have it, I tell you. I won't have it."

"Settle down, mother hen." Weoka winced at another loud rumble. "All the same, Dev, you'd best lower your shield before Conall flattens the house."

"Your shield?" Arta rounded on Dev. "Dissembler! You led me to believe 'twas Sildhjort's doing."

"I didn't lie. It's not my fault you assumed it was Sildhjort."

"You did naught to rectify my misapprehension, and you know it."

"I had my hands full with Gryffin," Dev said. "I wasn't about to let you go tearing after Pratt alone."

"You overstep, sir." Arta's voice was cold. "I forge my own path, and I do not run from danger."

"Neither did Taryn, and look how that turned out."

"You would taunt me with my sister's plight?"

"I'm trying to get you to see reason. You wanted us to work together? Okay, I'm in, but you can't go running off on your own."

Thunder blasted, rattling the cabinets.

"The shield, Dev," Aunt Weoka, "before he breaks every dish in the house."

"Yessum." Dev held Arta's gaze. "Are we agreed?"

The huntress's lips tightened. "Agreed."

"Good."

Dev breathed a sigh of relief. Focusing his will, he dissolved the protective invisible wall he had placed around his aunt's property. No sooner were the wards dispelled than a cyclone of ice and snow rumbled down the slope toward the house. Within the spinning flume, a dark shape moved. The twister dissolved in a flurry of ice crystals, and a powerfully built man stalked up the back steps.

"Show-off," Evan said. "He could ring the bell, like anyone else, but *noooo*. He has to make an entrance."

Dev started for the door. "I'll let him in."

Weoka stopped him in his tracks. "Last time I checked, this was still my house," she said. "I'll handle it."

Rising from the table, she stomped across the room and flung open the door. "Well?" she demanded of the man on the threshold. "Don't just stand there. You're letting out the bought air."

Brushing past Weoka, Conall stepped into the kitchen. A force field of energy crackled around him, and the temperature dropped when he entered the room. The captain of the Dalvahni was a tall man and superbly built, with broad shoulders and an autocratic manner. Unlike his men, Conall wore his blue-black hair cut short. His mouth and jaw were unyielding, his black eyes hard and merciless.

"Conall, ain't it?" Weoka said. "I'm Weoka."

"Greetings." Conall scanned the room, nodding at Arta. "High Huntress."

"Captain," Arta said. "What brings you here?"

"I received a visit from an imp," he said, "an odd little fellow who claimed to be in Sildhjort's employ. He tells me a skellring has freed Gryffin from bondage. He is here, I am told. I would see him at once."

"He's upstairs, but you can't move him," Weoka said. "He's in a bad way."

"I am the captain of the Dalvahni, madam, and Gryffin is my brother," Conall said. "'Tis not for you to tell me nay."

"She's a god," Evan said with a smirk. "I'm pretty sure that means she outranks you, asshat."

"What is this?" Conall met Weoka's gaze, and he inhaled sharply. "Forgive me, Old One," he said with a bow. "I did not realize."

"We are both in the Lady Weoka's debt," Arta said. "Pratt blighted Taryn and left her for dead. But for Weoka, I fear she would be no more."

"Happy to do it," Weoka said, "but I couldn't have managed without Verbena. She's a comfort to your brother, too."

"I am not surprised," Conall said. "Verbena is a delight." He turned to look at Dev, standing by the sink. "Shire reeve, what is your interest in this affair?"

"Pratt murdered a family of weres," Dev said, "and Weoka is my aunt."

"Your aunt?" Conall's eyes narrowed. "Tobias had the right of it, then. You are no norm."

"Tobias?" Dev said. "You mean Toby Littleton?"

"The very same. My wife loves him like a father. Cunning as a fox, Tobias." He bowed again to Weoka. "Milady, with your permission, I would speak to my brother. Long have we been parted, and there is much I would ask him."

"You'll get dick-all," Evan said. "The Gryffster is fried."

"Fried?"

"Crazy-pants, whacked in the head." Evan tapped his temple. "Out to lunch with no plans to return."

"Hush. It's early days yet," Weoka said. "Dev, see to the captain while I step outside. Want to make sure that overgrown spittoon ain't squashed my tomatoes."

"But a moment, an you please." Conall's flinty gaze was on Evan. "First, I would have a word with this one."

"Me?" Evan's smarmy expression dissolved into wariness. "Whatever you're cheesed about, I didn't do it."

"Ah, but you did," Conall said. "You distressed your sister."

"You're raving," Evan said. "I haven't seen Cookie in months, and that's on you. In case you have forgotten, I wasn't invited to the wedding."

"You tried to kill your sister. That much I have *not* forgotten."

"That was Hagilth and Elgdrek, and you know it." Evan pointed to the ceiling above. "Ask that brain-dead scarecrow upstairs what it's like to be bound if you don't believe me. I'm done trying to explain myself."

He turned and stalked away.

"You loosed the ogre today." Conall's quiet words stopped Evan. "Rebekah sensed your pain and was distraught."

Evan's back and shoulders were ramrod stiff. "We're twins," he said without turning. "Twins know things about one another."

"The breach between you grieves her." Conall hesitated, then grated out, "After much contemplation, I have decided to allow you to see her."

"Allow? *Allow?*" Evan wheeled around. The earth shifted, rocking the house. "Listen, asshole. I don't need your permission to see my frigging sister. If Cookie wants to see me, she knows where to find me."

Turning on his heel, he plunged up the stairs.

"That boy has anger issues," Weoka remarked. "Me, I would have handled things differently, but maybe you know better."

"In truth, Evan and I gall one another," Conall admitted.

"Reckon you two had better learn to get along then, for Beck's sake." Weoka jerked her head at Arta. "Come with me, gal."

"Nay." Arta was glaring at Dev. "The shire reeve and I have matters to discuss."

"You can discuss them later," Weoka said. "You and I need to talk."

"But I would—"

"Now."

"Very well." Arta threw Dev such a look of scorching fury that he felt his insides shrivel. "Mark me well, sirrah. You and I are not done."

She stalked from the house and slammed the door. Dev went to the window, watching as Arta crossed the lawn with Weoka, her head high.

"The High Huntress seems distempered," Conall observed. "More so than usual."

Dev turned away from the window. "Yeah, she's not happy with me."

"What dread offense have you committed?"

"I stopped her from going after Pratt alone."

Conall's brows rose. "You gainsaid Arta? How?"

Dev looked him in the eye. "That shield you encountered was my work, not my aunt's."

"Indeed?" Conall said. "I had no notion demonoids were adept at shield work."

"I'm not a demonoid."

"That is not what you told Ansgar. You told my brother that you are kith."

"Last summer," Dev said. "He mentioned it?"

"Naturally. I am captain of the Dalvahni. 'Tis my job to be informed."

"I lied. I've got a job to do, and I didn't know Ansgar at the time."

"Caution I understand, but I would have the truth now." Conall lifted a black brow. "Unless you do not trust me, either?"

"I trust you," Dev said. "Ansgar, too, now that I know him. Are you familiar with Sildhjort?"

"He is *unluath*, a lesser god of Gorth."

"He is my father."

"Your sire?" Conall's harsh face creased in amusement. "At last, I begin to understand. Arta did not know, I take it?"

"Not until a short while ago." Dev made a face. "She's not happy with me."

"Arta prides herself on her perception. The discovery that she misjudged you must surely rankle."

"Yeah, that's the vibe I'm getting. How long do you think she'll stay ticked?"

Conall shook his head. "That I cannot say. A Kirvahni huntress neither forgives nor forgets."

"Great. If a fellow wanted to get out of the doghouse in the next millennium, what would he have to do?"

Conall looked thoughtful. "You could try self-immolation."

"Very funny." Dev crossed the room to the kitchen door. "Gryffin is upstairs."

He led Conall to the upstairs bedroom where the rogue was ensconced. Verbena was sitting quietly by the bed. She turned pale when she saw the captain.

"Don't hurt him, Mr. Conall," she cried, springing to her feet and throwing her slim body across the injured warrior. "It weren't his fault. None of it were. It was that Pratt feller."

"Peace, child," Conall said. "I mean Gryffin no harm."

"You promise?"

"On my word as a Dalvahni warrior."

She nodded and wiped her eyes. Climbing off the bed, she stepped aside, giving Conall a clear view of the ailing warrior. It was not a pretty sight. Gryffin lay on his back with the sheets tucked around him and his emaciated arms carefully arranged at his sides. He had been washed, and his tangled locks had been combed and smoothed. He was very thin; his cheekbones jutted sharply in his gaunt face, and his eyes were sunken hollows.

Conall inhaled sharply. "Merciful gods, he is a veritable ghoul." He leaned closer to examine the warrior's inky tattoos. "Why do his marks linger when Evan's are no more?"

"I'm not sure," Dev said. "Maybe because the demons that bound Evan are dead, and Pratt is still alive?"

"A good supposition." Conall's expression was brooding. "By the sword, Pratt has much to answer for."

"He will," Dev said. "I mean to bring him in."

"'Tis not your place." Conall's jaw hardened. "'Tis the right of the Dalvahni to avenge our brother. We will destroy Pratt or perish in the attempt."

"Pratt's a suspect in a mass homicide. Interfere, and you and your men will be cooling your heels in lockup."

Conall laughed. "We are Dalvahni. The prison does not exist that can hold us."

"We'll see about that," Dev said. "Let me try. If I fail, then you can go after Pratt. Deal?"

"We will not seek him for now. This much I can promise you, but no more." Conall's gaze was on Gryffin. "Our brother is returned. I must away to deliver the glad news."

He vanished in a blast of cold air. In the kitchen below, the landline rang, shrill and insistent.

"What now?" Dev muttered, hurrying down the stairs. Aunt Weoka had one telephone in the house, a 1950s black rotary wall mount.

He untangled the curly cord. "Whitsun," he said, speaking into the clunky handset.

"Dev." Winnie McCullough exhaled thankfully in his ear. "I've been trying to reach you for hours. You aren't answering your radio."

Dev reached for the unit at his belt; it was gone. "Sorry," he said. "I must've left it in the woods. What's up?"

"We've got another DB."

"Kith or norm?"

"Norm."

The line fell silent.

"Winnie? You there?"

"Yeah. You went to school with a Freeman girl, didn't you? Livy?"

Dev clutched the receiver. "We were in the same class. What about her?"

"We think she's the vic."

"What do you mean, *think*?"

"We found some identification, but it's hard to tell, for sure." Winnie drew a deep breath. "You need to get here, Dev. It's bad. Real bad."

"What's your twenty?"

Winnie gave him the directions.

"On my way."

Dev hung up. Shoving a hand in his pocket, he fumbled for his keys and belatedly remembered.

His radio wasn't the only thing he'd left behind. His Jeep was sitting on Dark Corners Road, and Winnie was miles away.

"Damn," he muttered. "Damn, damn, damn."

He would have to borrow Aunt Wee's truck. He glanced out the window. It was still daylight. There was a faster way, but it was risky. If he were seen…

There had been panic in Winnie's voice and genuine horror. In more than a year on the job, she had seen a lot of nasty stuff, but this—whatever *this* was—had shaken her.

Screw it. He'd have to chance it.

Chapter Seven

Arta followed Weoka down the steps. Despite the old woman's earlier protestations of fatigue, she moved briskly across the lawn toward the garden on one side of the house. Jeb Hannah marched along the perimeter, a tin soldier guarding the lush vegetable patch. At his side, a slight goatish figure trotted upright on willowy legs.

"Your garden seems in good repair." Arta peered at the roving statue's companion. "Milady, is that a satyr I see with the behemoth?"

"Nope, Trevil's a pooka," Weoka said. "I toss him a hunk of meat once a week and he keeps the deer out of the garden. Chew my plants down to a nub, otherwise. Deer will eat most anything that grows, plaguey critters."

"A fairy?" In Arta's experience, fairies were capricious and ofttimes malicious. "Is that wise?"

"Trevil's not a bad sort. Taught Dev to swim when he was a young'un."

Arta halted. "Are you mad?" she said, staring at Weoka in astonishment. "Water demons delight in drowning humans."

"Dev ain't human. What's more, he swims like a fish—my sister Wedowee was a water nymph. Trevil's fond of the boy, but even if he weren't, he wouldn't cross me. It's my river, and I let Trevil live in it." She gave Arta a sharp look. "You thought Dev was a norm?"

"When first we met," Arta admitted. "I do not enjoy being made the fool."

"Ruffled your feathers, did he? Don't take it personally. Dev doesn't trust many people."

"He is close as an oyster."

"No choice. On account of the norms, you know."

"Demon hunters do not bide in one locale for long," Arta said, "or were not wont to. Recently, a number of the Dal have made their home here."

"Reckon Taryn will be hanging around, too, if Evan has anything to say about it."

"He is a boor. I cannot fathom the appeal."

"Different strokes for different folks. Love is like a butterfly. You never know where it may land."

"The Kirvahni do not fall in love, though I can readily believe the demonoid is smitten with my sister. The Kir were created for one purpose, the pursuit of the djegrali."

"Sounds a lot like them Dalvahni fellers."

"We share the same maker."

"Several of them have fallen in love."

Arta frowned. "So I am given to understand. A flaw in their makeup, perhaps. As for Taryn, I am certain the shifter is merely a diversion. A vigorous session with a thrall or two should soon set her to rights."

"Don't think Evan would much care for the notion."

"You speak of jealousy?"

"Yup."

"The Kir are immune, but, as it happens, the decision is not mine. Only Kehvahn may release us." She gave Weoka a curious look. "What of you? How long have you dwelt here?"

"Always. I'm bound to the river."

"And the shire reeve?"

"Dev could leave, but he won't. This is his home." She linked arms with Arta. "Let's go sit by the water."

Weoka waved farewell to Jeb and the pooka and led Arta down to the river. A huge tree spread its limbs on the riverbank, its heavy limbs sagging close to the earth. Laying a gnarled hand on the rough bark, Weoka murmured something in a strange language before taking a seat on a stone bench.

Arta sat down beside her and stretched out her long legs. The rich, earthy scent of the river perfumed the air, and the wind played a melancholy tune through the tree branches. Heat shimmered on the water, and the lowering sun scattered diamonds of light across the glistening surface. A fish jumped and landed with a splash. With a sharp call, a hawk winged overhead, its golden feathers glimmering in the sun. It was a peaceful spot, calming and serene, and Arta let the soothing energy wash over her.

"We need to talk about Dev," Weoka said, startling Arta from her reverie. "The Kirvahni may not fall in love"—her tone clearly indicated she had her doubts—"but I've seen the way you look at him."

"Nay, I—" Arta caught herself. In truth, she was hourly becoming more enamored of the oh-so-fascinating shire reeve. His easygoing façade disguised an iron will and determination equal to her own. "He is pleasing to the eye," she admitted, quickly adding, "but mine interest is purely practical, of course. We have agreed to work together. Naturally, I would know more of him."

"Of course," Weoka murmured.

"In truth, I do not understand him," Arta said. "'Tis obvious he has power. He raised a shield that thwarted the captain of the Dalvahni—no easy feat—but he chooses to remain in this backwater. Why?"

"Dev came face-to-face with pure evil at an impressionable age, and it changed him," Weoka said. "He swore right then and there to protect people, be they norm or kith."

"The Kir are also pledged to protect the weak. I would hear more of this evil the shire reeve encountered. Was it demons?"

"Yep. An old man by the name of Sloan McCullough was murdered by two men and a woman. Demon possessed, the three of them. Dev and I happened along not long after. Blood everywhere, the old man dead and Winnie hanging by a thread, poor child."

"You refer to the female constable?"

"Yup," Weoka said. "Sloan was Winnie's grandpa. She was at the store and saw Sloan killed. Would've died, too, if that Eamon feller hadn't happened along."

"Eamon?"

"Dalvahni warrior. Gave her a little Dalvahni pick-me-up."

Arta hissed in surprise. "He shared his essence with her? That is a violation of the Directive."

"Maybe so, but he healed her and took off." Weoka scowled. "Promised to come back, but we ain't seen hide nor hair of him since."

"He is bound by duty to pursue the djegrali. The Kir, as well."

"Be that as it may, he had a duty to Winnie, too. He turned the gal into a mutant and left. Her family are norms. Winnie was a child when Eamon changed her. She'd 'uv been a lost ball in high weeds if not for me and Dev. She and Dev are close. He's like a big brother to her."

"I see," Arta said. "The shire reeve...what manner of being is he?"

"Little of this and a little of that. He's a smidge demon and part human. Mostly, though, he's other."

"Other? You refer to his nymph blood?"

"That's the least of it," Weoka said. "My sister, Wedowee—"

"The nymph?"

"That's right. Wedowee fell in love with a fellow named Selvans. Big on boundaries, Sel. Dev takes after him. Me, I see things in shades of gray, but there's right and there's wrong in Dev's book and very little wiggle room."

Arta's thoughts chased one another like startled rabbits. "Selvans is a god. He is the shire reeve's grandsire?"

"Great-grandfather."

"And Sildhjort is his sire?"

"That's right. Dev told you?"

"Nay, we were visited by an imp, and he let it slip."

Weoka grunted. "Dev knew Sildhjort was his father. Told him so years ago, but they didn't meet until today. The hooves and antlers came as something of a shock."

"He should be proud. The blood of gods courses through his veins."

"Dev ain't the boastful kind."

"Indeed, he is not, and I like him the better for it. He was reared among norms?"

"Went to school with them. No other choice except to home-school him, and I didn't want that. We live with norms. Might as well learn to get along with 'em, to my way of thinking. Worked, for the most part, but Dev hated being different."

"He is different. He does not accept his nature?"

"Does now," Weoka said, "but it's hard enough being a teenager without supernatural growing pains, and hormones made it worse. He always was a little shy."

"What of his human and demon blood?" Arta asked. "Whence do they come?"

"His grandmother Deirdre—she was Wedowee's daughter by Selvans— lost her heart to a human named Doran." Weoka's gaze dimmed. "Lordy, that Doran was a handsome thing—dark hair and eyes gray as a winter sky. Dev is his spitting image." She stirred. "Not long after Deirdre and Doran became lovers, Doran caught a demon, and Deirdre got pregnant."

"The demon could not be extracted?"

"Maybe, but Doran took off. That old demon was driving him hard."

"What of Selvans and Wedowee? They could not help?"

"Both gone." Weoka's face creased with sadness. "Wedowee wandered away when Deirdre was a girl. My sister was a lovely thing, but nymphs are fickle. Any burbling brook or stream will catch their fancy."

"Doran perished?"

"Yes," Weoka said sadly. "Deirdre found him, but it was too late. "The demon had used him up. He died, and Deirdre grieved herself to death.

Left me to raise Brenna, Dev's mother. She was a wild thing. Took up with Sildhjort, had Dev, then ran off."

"Leaving you to care for her offspring."

"And a blessing he's been, too. Dev's a good son, and you won't find a better man. See you remember it."

"I am sure 'tis nothing to me."

"Uh-huh. You keep telling yourself that." A shrill sound pulled Weoka to her feet. She gazed up the hill toward the house. "Phone's ringing. River says it's ill tidings. Damn nuisances, phones, if you ask me." A door slammed, and a huge black shape loped up the slope toward the woods. "Dev's unleashed the wolf." She squinted after the gigantic animal. "Told you it was bad news."

"He is a shape-shifter?" A sudden thought made Arta stiffen. "He has received word of Pratt and has gone without me. By the gods, I shall put a flea in his ear."

Weoka chuckled. "Best hurry then. The wolf is fast."

"Wolves may be swift, but wings are faster."

Arta whistled sharply, and with a shrill *skree*, the golden hawk landed on her leather gauntlet.

"That the same bird we saw flying over the river?" Weoka asked.

"Aye. Her name is Merta, and she is my friend." Arta gently stroked the hawk's bright feathers. "Right, my love?"

The hawk clicked her beak in answer.

Arta laughed. "Follow the wolf, my sharp-eyed beauty, and keep me apprised."

The hawk spread its wings and flew away.

Arta's blood sang at the prospect of pursuit. With a murmured farewell to Weoka, she sprinted up the hill and into the forest. She reached the cool shadows of the trees and looked up. The hawk circled above her in a patch of blue sky. Opening her mind, Arta connected with the bird. The sensation of freedom was exhilarating. She felt the warm sun on Merta's feathers and the wind's welcoming caress. The world spread to the horizon, and Arta saw it through the bird's keen eyes. The landscape was magnified a thousandfold, colored in a dazzling array of shades. Far below, an ant crawled along the edge of a leaf and a squirrel darted up the trunk of a tree. In a clump of brush, a fawn huddled beside a doe.

These and a myriad other impressions Arta caught in the blink of an eye, but her mind was bent on the shire reeve.

There. She spotted the huge wolf with a rush of exultation. He bounded ahead of her in a southeasterly direction, his huge paws skimming the ground. Maintaining contact with Merta, Arta sprinted after him, her nimble feet skipping over leaves and branches. He would not escape her. Nay, not so easily.

* * * *

Loping through the forest, the wolf's nose twitched at the profusion of smells. The sharp tang of pine needles muddled with the darker smells of resin, rotting wood, damp earth, and moldering leaves. Wild mushrooms, pungent and musky, mingled with mint, the dusty scent of goldenrod, and the rich perfume of the nearby river. A whiff of smoke caught his notice, earning a growl of disapproval from deep in his chest. There was a county-wide burn ban in place—it had been a dry, hot summer—but some idiot was burning brush. *Later,* he thought, turning south. Ahead of him, a rabbit exploded from the brush, startled into flight. The wolf grinned. *Another day, little rabbit. Aunt Wee makes a mean rabbit stew with dumplings.*

He scanned his surroundings as he raced through the forest. Birds twittered in the trees and underbrush, and a startled chipmunk darted beneath a fallen log, the creature's stubby tail twitching in agitation. Squirrels scolded him from the safety of high branches, chucking in indignation. A skunk digging for insects lifted its head, bristling; the wolf gave it a wide berth.

He spied a hawk circling overhead. For a moment, he had the curious notion the bird was following him. Dismissing the idea, he lengthened his stride. Winnie had said on the phone that the body was in a quiet spinney outside Hannah. Three miles from the site, the wolf halted, alerted by the murmur of voices and the crunch of booted feet on the dry ground.

Noisy, the wolf thought, sniffing in disdain.

He closed the distance on silent paws, halting at a wash of sickly sweet odor. Beneath the stench, the wolf caught another scent, one he recognized from long ago. He snarled. A wolf's nose never forgot.

Slinking to the edge of the trees, the wolf gazed through a thicket of privet hedge. A creek chuckled nearby, a pleasant burble of water on rock. Golden asters and swamp sunflowers dotted the pleasant glen with bright splashes of yellow. A finch took flight with a harsh *zreeeeet.* Somewhere nearby a dog barked. The clearing appeared peaceful, a green bubble safe from the world, but Death had been here.

Winnie McCullough stood near the corpse with her back to the woods.

"'Bout time you got here," she said without turning her head. "You can come out. Coast is clear."

Dev shed his wolf form and strode from the trees. "You knew it was me?"

"Please." Winnie tapped one side of her elegant nose. "You smell like dog, a great big, *wet* dog."

"I'm a wolf, not a dog."

"Wet mutt is wet mutt. I sent Parks back to the truck to radio the coroner. He's pretty shook up."

"Who found the body?"

"Kid on a four-wheeler. He lives about a mile from here on Grumpkin Road. He hightailed it home and told his folks. They called it in." She motioned to the wizened form on the ground. "We found a driver's license and a wad of cash in her skirt pocket. The license belongs to a black female, age thirty-three. Name on the license is Olivia Jane Freeman, Six-Six-Eight Chindi Drive, Hannah."

Dev stared at the husk on the ground. The thing was barely recognizable as human, much less someone he'd known since elementary school. Wisps of hair clung to the fleshless skull. The dead woman wore a jean skirt and a cotton top. Her body was emaciated and shrunken, her brown skin waxy and wrinkled.

"Told you it was bad," Winnie said, noticing his expression. "I doubt her own mother would recognize her."

"Her mother is long gone." A vise closed around Dev's chest, making it hard to breathe. "She left when Livy was a kid."

"Father?"

"Dead. Drank himself to death years ago. Mr. Freeman was in the military, but he grew up on a farm outside Paulsberg. He moved the family back to Behr County when Livy was ten."

Dev recalled his first glimpse of Livy, a thin, timid girl with glossy braids and large, dark eyes standing hesitantly in the doorway of Mary Willie French's fourth grade classroom. The other girls had ruthlessly snubbed Livy that year, partly because she was new, but mostly because Livy was pretty.

Very pretty.

"I know you graduated with her," Winnie said, "but you seem to know a lot about her."

"We were friends when we were kids." Dev cleared his throat. "Though not at first. She was very shy."

"How'd you win her over?"

"I found her crying in the library one day," Dev said, remembering. "I asked her what was wrong, and she said 'nothing.' I called her a liar."

"Rude."

"It was the truth. Her nose was running like a faucet, and her eyes were swollen and puffy."

"Okay, Mr. Don't-Tell-Me-A-Lie. How did you smooth things over?"

"I shared my snack with her."

"Let me guess," Winnie said. "You had some of Aunt Wee's cookies."

"Yep. Three snickerdoodles later, I had Livy in the palm of my hand. Seems Bootsie Mullins was having a spend-the-night, and Livy wasn't invited."

"Bootsie Mullins?" Winnie opened her eyes wide. "You mean *Elizabeth Mullins Barber*, as in Mullins Pharmacy?"

"She went by Bootsie back then. She asked the other girls to her party at the lunch table. Right in front of Livy." Dev paused, adding, "On purpose."

"Girls can be mean."

"That sounds like the voice of experience."

"Oh, yeah," said Winnie. "I had my own Bootsie back in the day. Several, in fact."

"The boys liked you," Dev pointed out. "The girls were jealous. Prettiest girl in school. Everyone said so."

Winnie shifted uncomfortably. She never could abide a compliment. "Whatever. I was a misfit, like you. Not many supers at BCH."

She lapsed into brooding silence, and Dev's thoughts spun backward to his conversation with Livy.

"Bootsie Mullins?" he'd said when Livy had told him of Bootsie's slight. "Who cares? She's a butt wad." Emboldened by Livy's appreciative giggle, Dev added, "Come to my house instead."

Livy's eyes rounded. "I can't spend the night with a *boy*. My daddy would wallop me good."

"For the *afternoon*," Dev said. "I live on the river. We can go swimming."

"Swimming sounds like fun." Livy sounded wistful. She hesitated. "How...how will I get home?"

"Aunt Wee will take you home after supper."

"You live with your aunt? What happened to your parents?"

"Gone." Dev pushed the hurt away. "Both of 'em."

"My mom left us." Opening her purse, a rectangular macramé bag with a long strap, Livy produced a tissue and wiped her nose. "She ran off with another man and left me and my brother. Daddy says she's a whore." She tucked the Kleenex back in her purse. "You got any brothers or sisters?"

"Nope," Dev said. "It's just me and my aunt."

"You're lucky." Livy sighed. "My brother, Jax, is four, and I have to do *everything* for him."

"Like what?" Dev had been equal parts curious and envious.

"Like make him snacks and give him a bath and make sure he brushes his teeth." Livy heaved another sigh. "He's a ginormous pain."

"Dev? *Helloooo*. Where'd you go?"

Dev snapped back to the present. "Sorry...I was thinking about Livy. As I recall, she has a younger brother named Jax. Short for Ajax, I believe."

Removing a small notepad from her shirt pocket, Winnie scribbled the name down. "Any other kin?" she asked.

"Not that I know of."

"I'll get in touch with the brother." She slid the small notebook back into her shirt pocket. "Almost forgot. The victim was wearing a charm bracelet."

"What?" A chill of foreboding washed over Dev. "Gold bracelet with dessert charms? Ice cream sundae, slice of cake...that sort of thing?"

"Yeah, how'd you know?"

"Russ Barber gave it to Livy," Dev said. "They were a thing back in high school. He was a senior, and Livy and I were freshmen."

"That's a big age difference."

"Yeah. She and Russ dated for a while after he graduated."

"Huh." Winnie looked thoughtful. "That was a long time ago. Weird that she was still wearing it."

Winnie was right. It was weird. Downright suspicious, in fact. Dev's hands tightened into fists. Russ Barber was an asshole. If he had anything to do with Livy's death, he would pay.

Jim Parks tromped into the clearing. "Hello, boss." Averting his gaze from the wizened body, the deputy tossed Dev a roll of barricade tape. "How'd you get here?"

"I came through the woods. Left my Jeep at the other scene."

"Came through the woods?" Parks gaped at him in astonishment. "It must be fifteen miles from here to your aunt's place."

"More or less," Dev said.

"It's called exercise, Parks," Winnie said. "You should try it sometime." She gazed pointedly at her partner's generous belly. "You're getting fluffy."

"The wife likes a little cushion for the ride."

"Ew," Winnie said. "Thanks a bunch for that image."

"You're welcome." Parks jabbed a stubby finger at the body. "What happened to her, you think? She looks like a bog baby."

"Bog what?" Winnie said.

"A body that's been preserved in a peat bog. There are bunches of them in Europe. Thousands and thousands of years old, some of them. Saw it on *National Geographic*."

"There aren't any peat bogs in Behr County, Parks," Winnie said, "and the victim isn't thousands of years old. She's wearing denim and OTBT knockoffs."

Dev barely heard them. A picture of Livy, young, gap-toothed, and shy, rose in his mind's eye, and grief clogged his throat, bitter as unsweetened chocolate. He'd made it his job to keep people safe, particularly from things that went bump in the night, but he'd failed to protect Livy. She was dead. Someone or *something* had murdered her and in the most horrible fashion.

Helpless rage burned in his gut and spread. Job—he needed to focus on the job. He couldn't afford to lose it, not now.

Dragging his gaze from the pitiful body, Dev frowned at Winnie. "OT what?" he asked, latching on to the last thing she'd said.

Parks answered. "Off the Beaten Track," he said. "It's a kind of shoe."

"Parks, you are a man of hidden depths." Winnie stared at him in mock amazement. "I had no idea you were a fashionista."

He reddened. "Give me a break. My daughter wears them."

"Sure, sure. Got any tips for fall? I hear plaid's gonna be big."

"Much you know, McCullough," Parks said. "Plaid *never* goes out of style."

The rage bubbling inside of Dev spilled over. "Shut up," he said through his teeth. "Goddammit, shut the hell up. You're standing next to a dead woman. Show a little respect."

"Sorry, boss," Parks said. "It's just our way. We don't mean any harm."

Dev nodded and rubbed his aching sternum. Jesus, it felt like an Angus bull was sitting on his chest.

A car horn blew in the distance.

"That'll be Wendell." Winnie grabbed her partner by the arm. "Come on, Parks. Let's go get the coroner."

Chapter Eight

Dev stayed rooted to the spot after they'd gone, the crime scene tape clutched in one hand. Sweat beaded his forehead. He wanted to rend something, but that wouldn't bring Livy back. Slowly, he forced the lid back on his simmering rage.

"Who did this, Liv?" He squatted near the mummy, careful not to compromise the scene. "Who killed you?"

A whisper of jasmine and roses warned him that he was not alone. He leapt to his feet and spun around. Arta stood poised at the edge of the trees, an otherworldly vision with her pale hair aglow in the afternoon light and her cheeks flushed.

"Arta?" Dev blinked at her, half-expecting her to evaporate. "What are you doing here?"

"I followed you. I had no notion you could shape-shift." She regarded him curiously. "Are all the wolves of this demesne so large?"

Dev rubbed the back of his neck. "There aren't any wolves in Alabama that I know of. A couple of werewolf packs, but no wolves."

"You are discomfited. Why?"

"Not many people know that I can shift."

"For someone who dislikes subterfuge, you are a remarkably guarded man."

"Have to be," Dev said. "The norms would panic, and most of the kith assume I'm human. Don't have the purple eyes, see?" He shrugged. "The members of the Kith Council know I'm a super, but not what kind."

"'Tis no easy thing to be caught between the mundane and the uncanny. Why not walk away?"

"Because this is my home," Dev said. "Someone has to protect these people."

He was the man, all right, he thought bitterly. He'd done a jam-up job of protecting the Randalls and Livy.

"You have set yourself a thankless task." Her expression was grave. "Nonetheless, you strive and achieve, like a paladin of old."

"Me, in armor?" Dev laughed. "I'm more of a jeans and T-shirt guy."

"A true knight is judged by his deeds, not by his garb." She sighed. "I envy you the wolf. The Kir have many abilities, but we cannot shape-shift. Merta and I connect mind to mind, but 'tis not the same."

"Merta?"

"My hawk." Her gaze went to the bird circling overhead. "She followed you."

"So, that's how you found me." Dev exhaled in relief. "Thought I was slipping."

"Fear not. Your wolf moves as shadow, but little escapes Merta's keen notice." Arta pointed to the deformed lump on the ground. "I overheard you and the female constable conversing. This human was special to you?"

"It's not polite to eavesdrop."

"I did not spy on you a-purpose. The norm you call Parks was present, so I lingered within the spinney." Pausing, she added, "Though I misdoubt he would remember me. He does not seem a clever sort."

"Don't let the drawl fool you. Parks isn't stupid," Dev said. "Besides, you've showed up at a murder scene. Twice in one day. Dressed in medieval chic, I might add."

"'Medieval chic'?" Her gaze became unfocused. "Ah. My garb is outmoded?"

"Only by a thousand years or so."

"I am in violation of the Directive Against Conspicuousness. I shall remedy my mistake at once."

She smoothed her hands down the length of her body, and her deerskin leggings, tunic, and boots disappeared. In their stead was an exact copy of Winnie's deputy uniform, down to the gun she wore on one slim hip and the Bates Ultra-lite side zip tactical boots on her slender feet.

She twitched her shirt collar into place. "There. Am I more the thing?"

"Very official. You licensed to carry?" Dev pointed to the weapon at her side. "If not, you're carrying illegal. What's more, you're impersonating an officer of the law."

"I am a warden of the universe pledged to capture rogue demons. Pray, what am I if not an officer of the law?"

"You may be a demon hunter, but you're not a deputy. There are rules and training and—"

"Bah," she said. "I cannot be bothered with such trifles."

"Impersonating an officer of the law is not—" Dev drew a deep breath. "Why are you here, Arta?"

"To offer my assistance." She pointed to the body. "Have you remarked the body's putrid odor?"

"Yeah. It smells like burnt rubber."

"'Tis the stench of the djegrali. Note the wasted condition of the body. *Taaktha*, the djegrali call it."

"Tah-what?"

"'Tis a kind of sport with lesser demons. The victim is tossed into a swarm, and the djegrali go into a feeding frenzy, like a pack of wild dogs devouring a kill."

Dev swallowed convulsively. "You think... You think Livy was *eaten*?"

"Consumed, not eaten. Drained of her essence, bit by bit, leaving naught but the empty shell you see before us. 'Tis a slow death—the djegrali enjoy toying with their victims—and excruciating."

"God," Dev said, tasting bile.

"Shire reeve, your feet," Arta cried.

Dev glanced down and sprang back with an oath. He stood in the center of a rapidly spreading circle of charred leaves and blackened earth. He motioned, and the angry smoldering was extinguished.

"Sorry," he said, flushing. "Happens sometimes when I get upset."

"'Tis I who owe you an apology. I spoke without thought. Sometimes, my tongue runs on wheels."

"It's okay. I'm a big boy."

"Have you any notion how your friend fell into the clutches of the djegrali?"

"No clue." Dev gazed at Livy's withered form. "But I detected a strange scent when I first came up. Something besides demon."

Winnie strolled out of the woods. "Human, kith, or other?"

"Human." Dev frowned at her. "What are you doing here? You're supposed to be with Parks."

"You seemed upset," Winnie said. "I came back to check on you."

"I'm fine."

"Sure, tough guy. Whatever you say." She jerked her chin at Arta. "Blondie one of us, now?"

"Nah, she magicked herself into that getup."

"Too bad." Winnie hooked her thumbs in her belt. "I was hoping you'd decided to make her a reserve officer. We could use the help, what with Johnson in Baldwin County on a drug op and Ced out for surgery."

"Ced?" Arta raised her brows.

"Cedrica Davis," Winnie said. "Blew out her knee chasing a drunk and disorderly into a ditch."

Dev glared at Winnie in warning. "That's enough. What you're suggesting is impossible."

"Why? She already has the uni, and we know she's a good shot."

"Nay," Arta protested. "I am an *excellent* shot."

"With a bow," Dev said. "Guns are different."

"The Kir are skilled in weaponry." Arta caressed the gun on her hip. "I have no doubt I shall master this one in a trice."

"No," Dev said. "Absolutely not. You're headstrong and stubborn and used to being in charge."

"Pot meet kettle," Winnie muttered.

"Not helping, Deputy."

"I find you foolish in the extreme," Arta said. "Your friend died at the hands of the djegrali, and I am an experienced demon hunter. You need me."

"Like a hole in the head, maybe," Dev muttered.

But if Arta heard him, she gave no sign. "The djegrali have tortured and slain a helpless mortal. By my oath, I am sworn to their pursuit."

"See?" Winnie said. "She's going after the murderer with or without you."

"Of a certainty," Arta said. "I cannot allow this atrocity to pass. 'Tis a matter of honor."

"What about Pratt?" Dev was scrambling for an argument—any argument—to dissuade her.

"Pratt?" Winnie looked at them. "Who's Pratt?"

"Never mind, I'll tell you later," said Dev.

Arta shrugged. "'Tis my aim to bring Pratt to task, but duty lies along many paths."

"Okay," Dev said. "We'll give it a try. Consider yourself a reserve deputy—"

"I knew you would see reason."

"—but you're to follow my orders—"

"Naturally."

"No going off half-cocked on your own."

"But of course."

"—and you are not to take matters into your own hands. Got it? You work for me now."

"Fear not," Arta said. "I shall be all compliance."

Winnie's eyes twinkled. "Yeah, she'll be all compliance, 'cause everybody knows demon hunters roll that way."

"I like your attitude, Deputy McCullough," Dev said, "because I'm making you her FTO."

"*What?*" Winnie said. "But I'm not— She's—"

"You're the logical choice," Dev said. "Only other super in the department. I can't very well place her with a norm. Train her and teach her how to use a gun."

"No need," Arta said. "The Provider will direct me."

"The Provider?" Dev said.

"'Tis an information source employed by the Kir and the Dal. The Provider is our guide and translator."

"Like Google for demon hunters," Winnie said. "That must come in handy."

"With the Provider's wise counsel, we are able to traverse the various worlds."

"Be that as it may, you'll still read the manual," Dev said. "All of it. Front to back. Winnie will go over it with you and answer any questions."

"I do not need this child to tutor me."

"Hey," Winnie said. "I'll be twenty-nine next month."

"We'll sort out the paperwork later," Dev said. "It's a headache, but I don't want to get sideways with the county pencil pushers." He wheeled around at a low, shivering moan from the distant woods. "What was that?"

"'Tis a winding horn." Arta's bow appeared in her hands. It was an elegant weapon, but totally incongruous with her uniform. "I must away."

"Wait, Arta," Dev said. "I'll—"

She dematerialized with a sharp *ping*.

"Shit-hot, she disapparated." Winnie's eyes shone with excitement. "That is freaking awesome."

"It is not awesome," Dev said. "She's barely been deputized a hot second, and she's already disobeying orders."

"Yeah, but you have to admit she's cool."

"She's trouble and a powerful supernatural being, Winnie, not some inbred possum shifter. See that you remember it."

"Worried about me, big brother?"

"Always."

"Okay, I'll try. Pinkie swear."

"I wouldn't want you to sprain something. Just watch your tongue and try not to insult her."

Her eyes widened. "Me?"

"I mean it, Winnie."

"Sure, sure, whatever you say, boss."

The horn sounded again, followed by a high-pitched chittering and a shouted challenge.

"What the—" Winnie said.

"No idea, but I mean to find out," Dev said. "Wait here."

He sprinted in the direction of the noise, but he hadn't gone far when Winnie shot past him in a blur of motion. Startled, he skidded to a halt in a shower of leaves.

"Winnie, stop," he shouted after her.

She whirled to face him, and Dev sucked in his breath. Winnie was almost unrecognizable, her face shining with a terrible hunger.

"Sorry, Dev," she said. "No can do."

"Damn it, Winnie. You—"

She was already gone, flitting through the trees like a will-o'-the-wisp. Dev swore and ran after her. He was fast, but Winnie was quick as lightning. He plunged deeper into the woods. Ahead of him, there was a bloodcurdling bellow and a metallic clang. Dev burst out of the woods and into an area of downed pines, oaks, and maples. A nightmarish scene greeted him. Shattered tree trunks thrust wooden spears into the air, and patches of black ash rose in choking puffs from the forest floor. A throng of hideous, gigantic insects swarmed the blast site. The monsters were vaguely beetle-like in form, with hard exoskeletons, pincers, and cruel mouths, and they were as big as dump trucks.

Arta stood on the far side of the clearing, an ancient oak at her back. Her legs were slightly parted for balance as she fired a shining stream of arrows from her bow. An arrow pierced a charging insect, and the beast shrieked in pain and crumbled into dust. Three more arrows found their mark, and a trio of monsters disintegrated.

A huge warrior stood amidst the carnage, his lips drawn back in a defiant snarl. His long brown hair was tied back with a piece of leather, and he wielded a wicked-looking sword. Legs braced, he brought the weapon down on a rampaging beetle. The blade sank deep into the thing's armored thorax but did not penetrate the tough outer shell. With a shrill chitter, the beetle snapped at the warrior, pincers closing with bone-shattering force. The warrior yanked his weapon free and leapt aside. The thing darted at him. Rising from a crouch, the warrior drove his sword through the monster's lower jaw. The blade pierced the thing's head. With a squeal of anguish, the monster burst in a puff of smelly powder.

"Keep that up and you'll be bug food, mister." Winnie ran up the trunk of an elm like a squirrel, tucked her knees to her chest, and backflipped onto a monster's back. "You can't chop your way through 'em—the armor's too thick."

She shoved the muzzle of her Glock in the space between the monster's head and thorax and fired. The bullets entered the beetle with a meaty splat. Green ichor shot up, splashing Winnie's arms and face; the enormous insect staggered but did not dissolve.

"Bravely done, lass, but the djegrali cannot be slain with a mortal weapon." The warrior tossed Winnie a knife from the sheath at his thigh. "Try this and aim for the head."

"Thanks."

Plucking the spinning blade out of the air, Winnie drove the knife into one of the bug's compound eyes. The creature turned to ash beneath her, and she hit the ground with a *thump.*

She bounced lightly to her feet and wiped the goo from her eyes. "Was that the last of them? Darn it, I was just starting to have fun."

"Winnie, look out," Dev shouted as a hideous creature with a tricorn-shaped head crashed into the clearing.

The thing was at least twenty feet tall and walked upright. Four segmented arms sprouted from the monster's scaly torso. It lashed a powerful, tensile tail, and chunks of wood and debris flew into the air. Snatching Winnie up by one leg, the monster dangled her upside down.

"Put me down," Winnie shrieked, slashing at the thing with the knife.

With a horrible chuckle, the fiend lifted her toward its sharp, open beak.

"Nay, you shall not," the warrior roared, charging the towering horror.

Dev got there first. Shoving the warrior aside, he confronted the demon.

"Let her go." Dev held his hands out, palms facing one another. "Let her go now, and I'll let you live."

The demon laughed. "I am *morkyn*, human, the greatest and most powerful of my kind. You cannot gainsay me."

"Yeah? Well, guess what. I'm not human."

Dev pressed his hands together and jerked them apart. The demon exploded, showering him with foul-smelling dust.

Winnie landed on her back. Gasping, she struggled to draw breath into her deflated lungs.

Dev bent over her. Her hair was wild and disheveled, she smelled to high heaven, and she was covered in bug gunk and soot.

"You okay?" he asked, gazing down at her in concern.

Wiping her eyes, she glared up at him. "I'm fine. What the hell was that?"

"Demon, I think. Ugly sumbitches, aren't they?"

"Not that. *You*." She accepted his outstretched hand and got to her feet. "What was that freaky shit you did?"

"Oh, that." Dev coughed. "It's hard to explain, but you...sort of compress things together real tight, and then let go."

"You compress—" She stared at him. "Gee, thanks, science guy. That was clear as mud."

"I told you it was hard to explain."

She slapped at her ash-covered uniform. "Do me a solid. The next time I'm about to be eaten by a scaly, six-armed asshole, do *not* stop and ask the damn thing to give itself up."

"Four," Dev said. "The demon had four arms, not six."

"Don't nitpick. You know what I mean."

"Attention to details is good police work."

"Right." Winnie whacked at her sooty pants. "I'd like to see *you* take notes while a monster is trying to eat you like a French fry."

Dev turned at a deep groan. The big warrior was sprawled on the ground on the far side of the clearing. The tree behind him had been split in two.

"Bravely done, brother." Arta strode over and gave the tree a kick. "You have vanquished an oak."

"Spare me your levity, Kir." The warrior staggered to his feet. "I am in no mood to be mocked."

Dev and Winnie hurried over to them.

"Is he badly hurt?" Dev asked.

"Stunned, and small wonder," Arta said. "'Twas a mighty blow you dealt him, shire reeve. You tossed him fifty yards and more and slammed him into this unfortunate tree, but he is Dalvahni and will soon recover." She sighed. "Alas, I fear the same cannot be said of the oak."

"To the Pit with the oak and with you," the warrior said, giving her a look of dislike. He gave Dev a searching look. "Have we met?"

"Once," Dev said. "A long time ago."

"Indeed? You must be much changed, for I do not recall."

"Yeah, I grew up."

The warrior grunted and turned to Winnie. "Well fought, little sister. 'Twas your first demon kill?"

"Yeah." Winnie held out the knife. "Thanks for the loaner. It did the trick."

"Keep it. A Kirvahni huntress should never be without steel."

"You're mistaken, mister. I'm not Kirvahni."

"You are not?" The warrior gazed at her with a puzzled expression. "But—"

"She speaks the truth." There was a malicious twinkle in Arta's eyes. "As you should well know, *Eamon*."

Winnie went rigid. "You're Eamon Dalvahni?"

"I am." The warrior bowed. "We have met?"

"Yeah, we've met, you sorry son of a bitch," Winnie said and punched him in the face.

* * * *

Five hours later, the murder scene had been diagrammed and photographed, evidence had been collected and tagged, and Livy's body had been carefully bagged and removed. There was no blood at the scene—Livy had been killed someplace else and dumped—but a set of tire tracks was found and measured, and a plastic mold of the tracks made. Furthermore, Winnie had spotted some cloth fibers in a clump of sweet shrub.

"Good eyes." Parks strolled up to Winnie and gagged. "God almighty, McCullough, you take a dip in a septic tank?"

"Kiss my ass, Parks," Winnie said and stomped off.

"Jesus." Parks stared after her. "What's eating her?"

"Let it go," Dev said. "We're all on edge."

"Boss?"

"What is it?"

"You smell bad, too."

"Thanks, Parks. That's a big help."

Dev walked the scene several more times and scanned the area. The purple gloom of dusk deepened into night. Satisfied he hadn't missed anything, Dev sent everyone home.

"Arta, you can stay at my place," Winnie said. "I've got plenty of room."

"You are gracious, but I do not wish to impose."

"No imposition at all," Winnie said. "We can talk about your training."

Arta gave Dev an inscrutable look and followed Winnie into the darkness.

"Not from around here, is she?" Wendall Saxon asked.

"Nope," said Dev. "Just blew into town."

"Easy on the eyes. 'Course, so is Deputy McCullough."

"Yep," Dev said. "Mind if I bum a ride? I left my car at the other scene."

"Sure." The coroner led the way to his battered van and opened the driver's side door. "Terrible day," he said, his handsome brown face illuminated by the interior lights. "First those poor people in the woods and now the Freeman woman. I baled hay for her dad back in high school."

"You did?" Dev climbed in on the passenger side. "I didn't know that."

"He was a good farmer, but a hard man. Livy looked...dehydrated. Like a raisin. Never seen anything like it." Wendall glanced at Dev and cleared his throat. "Sorry. You two went to school together, didn't you?"

"Yeah, same class."

"Anybody told her brother? What's his name...Jed?"

"Jax. Not yet," Dev said. "We're trying to locate him."

Wendall rambled about this and that on the way to Dev's place. Dev listened with half an ear, too bone-tired to mumble more than the occasional response. At last, Wendall turned down the dirt road leading to Dev's property, 248 acres of heaven in the deep woods, and parked in front of the house, a tidy one-story bungalow with a deep front porch, pitched roof, and a screen porch off the back.

"Home sweet home," Wendall said. "Don't know about you, but I'm ready to hit the sack. It's been a long day."

"Eternal." Dev climbed wearily from the van. "Thanks, Wen. I owe you one."

"Any time."

The coroner rattled off into the darkness, and Dev made his way up the path and into the dark house. Stripping off his filthy clothes, he threw them in the washer and hit the shower, scrubbing the powdered demon from his skin. Visions of dead weres and Livy's desiccated body ran in a maddening loop in his head. He dried off and pulled on clean boxer briefs and jeans. Padding barefoot into the kitchen, he opened the refrigerator and stared, unseeing, at the contents on the shelves. There were eggs and cheese and cold cuts, beef vegetable soup compliments of Aunt Weoka, and leftover pizza, but he was too tired to eat.

A beer winked at him from the shelf, a lone soldier left behind by Winnie. Dev didn't drink, a fact that Winnie delighted in teasing him about.

"Know what your problem is, bro?" she'd say. "You're too uptight. A drink would do you a world of good."

Dev would grin and shrug it off. Let Winnie think what she liked. His abstention had nothing to do with scruples and everything to do with reality: He had the alcohol tolerance of a two-year-old.

He healed in an instant. He could see in the dark, outswim a water moccasin, and run for long distances at a speed of forty-five miles per hour. Hell, he could walk through fire unscathed, but he couldn't drink.

It was embarrassing, really.

The kiss of the cold air on his feet drew Dev from his thoughts. God, what a cluster of a day. The beer beckoned. *Why not?* he thought. *It's one beer. What can it hurt?*

He twisted the top off the bottle and took a swig. It was a local craft brew, Devil's Dew, aged in bourbon barrels with a hint of vanilla. He took another pull, and the knot of grief and tension inside him slowly uncoiled.

Still a wuss, Whitsun.

Grinning, Dev made his way to the couch. He was about to sit down when there was a knock on the front door. He glanced at the clock on the wall. After midnight. He swallowed a groan. In his experience, nothing good ever happened after midnight. Hopefully, it was something uncomplicated, like a kid with their truck stuck in a ditch. It happened sometimes, especially after a hard rain.

The visitor knocked again, insistent.

"Damn it, I am so done with this day."

There was a third knock, and Dev set the half-empty bottle on the end table.

"All right, all right, I'm coming," he said, swaying toward the door. "Keep your shirt on."

He opened the door, and the words dried on his tongue. Arta stood on his porch. She was dressed in her deerskins and boots, and her lovely form glowed as though lit from within.

"Arta." He blinked at her. "You're out of uniform."

"As are you, shire reeve." Her gaze trailed from his bare torso to the jeans that rode his hips. "We are both—how do you say?—off duty."

"So we are." Folding his arms, Dev leaned against the door frame. "What can I do for you?"

"Slumber eludes me."

"Demon hunters sleep? Figured you types were above that sort of thing."

"The Kir are indomitable, but even we require the occasional nap."

"Huh. Try a glass of warm milk. I've heard that helps insomnia."

She wrinkled her nose. "Thank you, no. I have a more palatable remedy in mind."

"And you came all this way to tell me? That's mighty thoughtful of you."

"I do what I can. Shall we discuss it inside?" Her eyes widened. "You *are* going to invite me in?"

"Sure." Recalling his manners, Dev stepped back. "Come in and welcome."

She sauntered past him into the living room. She wandered slowly about the space, pausing often to examine this or that, much like a visitor in a museum or a curiosity shop. Nothing escaped her perusal—the floating shelves along one wall, the brown leather sofa and matching overstuffed chairs, the large, riveted aluminum trunk Dev used for a coffee table.

She paused before the hearth. "The fireplace draws well?"

"Like a champ. Built it myself from river rock."

She nodded in approval and glided up to him. "My compliments. Your home is comfortable, but unassuming."

"It's nothing fancy, but I like it." Dev was finding it increasingly hard to think in her presence. Heat settled in his groin. She was close, too close. He could feel the warmth of her skin, and her ravishing scent filled his head. "Was there—" The words came out a croak. He tried again. "Was there something you wanted to discuss?"

"Ah, yes." Her graceful fingers traced the line of his collarbone, sending a shaft of longing down Dev's spine. "I have hit upon a clever notion, methinks."

"Yeah?" He was feeling light-headed and not from the beer. "What's that?"

"A cure for my lamentable inability to sleep, of course." She met his gaze squarely. "After giving the matter much consideration, I have decided we should couple."

Dev stared at her. "Couple?"

"Copulate, fornicate, fadoodle."

"Fadoodle?" Dev's lips twitched. "Arta, are you propositioning me?"

"Yes, shire reeve." She sighed. "Faith, but for a clever man you are sometimes provokingly slow."

Sliding her arms around his neck, Arta kissed him.

Chapter Nine

Her mouth was lush and warm, as full of golden promise as the heart of summer. Their tongues tangled, and Dev groaned and deepened the kiss.

"I knew it." Arta released him. Her eyes were alight. "You do want me!"

"Good God, woman," Dev said, "You've had me turned inside out since we met."

That morning—had it only been that morning she'd appeared, disrupting his life and the investigation, not to mention his peace of mind? It seemed a lifetime ago.

"I confess 'twas the same with me," she said. "Why, then, did you send me away?"

"I didn't send you away. Winnie invited you to stay with her."

"Be that as it may, 'tis lowering." She focused her gaze on his bare chest. "A huntress is not accustomed to indifference."

"A huntress is gorgeous and damn well knows it." Dev took her by the waist and tugged her firmly against his groin. "Does this seem indifferent to you?"

Sliding a hand between them, she cupped the hard ridge of his erection. "Nay, I find you impressive, in this as in all things." A saucy smile played about her lips, and she set aside all pretense of coyness. "I think we shall deal extremely well together, you and I, in work…and in play."

"Work?" The word sobered Dev. Swearing softly, he dropped his hands and stepped back. "I'm sorry, Arta. I can't do this."

"I do not understand."

"The department has a no-fraternization policy." He could have screamed with frustration. Arta was the most fascinating, maddening, desirable woman he'd ever met, and he had to walk away. "You work for me now. I can't be involved with someone on the job."

The sultry light in her eyes dimmed. "I do not work for you. I work *with* you. 'Tis but a temporary ruse, a convenience so we may pursue Pratt and the djegrali without drawing attention."

"I'm your boss. Sex complicates things. People lose their heads when they get involved."

"I am Kirvahni. We do not 'get involved.' We hunt. We fight. We seek release as needed. Sex merely satisfies a physical need."

"Sounds mighty cold and clinical."

"What else is there?"

"Love."

"Love is a human foible. Have you ever been in love?"

"No," Dev admitted. "Had a strong case of like a couple times, but I've never been in love."

"Nor have I," Arta said. "The Kir are a dispassionate race and ill-suited to emotion. Love is mercurial. Even were it not so, I misdoubt I am capable of such feelings, nor do I wish to be."

Dev's chest felt strangely tight, as if he'd just found out there was no such thing as Santa Claus.

"What about Taryn?" he said. "You seemed plenty upset about her today."

"Taryn is my sister and bound to the same course. Naturally, as her leader, I am concerned for my sister's welfare, but the folly humans call romantic love?" She shrugged. "Such a thing is unproductive and superfluous. Lust, we know, but the Kir and the Dal are encouraged by the Great Directive to engage in regular and vigorous bouts of swiving. 'Tis a purgative of sorts, and in this way, we rid ourselves of strong emotion."

"The Great Directive?"

"Our guide in all things, spiritual and temporal," Arta said. "The Provider is our information source, but the Directive is our most sacred authority. Coitus, it instructs, balances the humors and prevents an excess of spleen." She laid a hand on Dev's arm, a simple touch that set him on fire. "Take you, shire reeve. You have had a grievous day. You are weary and heartsick. A vigorous shagging would do you a world of good."

"No doubt." Sex with Arta would be a game changer. "Once we solve this case and bring Pratt in—"

"Once our mission is complete, I shall depart." She lifted her chin. "I, too, have responsibilities. The djegrali are a plague that infests many realms. If you wish to be with me, the time is now."

She was leaving? Once, a bear shifter high on Skinner moonshine had punched Dev in the gut. This was worse.

He drew a ragged breath. "Sorry. I can't be with you. Not like that. Not now. Not while you wear the badge."

"Who is to know?"

"I would."

Confusion and hurt flitted across her lovely face; then her expression hardened. "You are a stupid man, I think—a very stupid man, and I am done with you."

Turning on her heel, she blew the door off the hinges with a flick of her fingers and stalked outside. There was a flash of searing light from the woods, and a strong wind tossed the branches of the old oak beside the house. A gust of heavily scented air blew in through the hole that had once been Dev's front entrance. The perfume filled his lungs, making him cough.

"Arta." He lunged onto the porch after her. "Arta, *wait*."

He jumped down the steps and paused. Arta stood at the end of the flagged walkway, her back to the cabin.

"Are you okay?" Dev strode to her side. "What the hell was that?"

She flicked him a single cool glance before dismissing him with a shrug of her shoulder. "You, in the wood," she said in a ringing voice. "Show yourself at once."

Leaves rustled, and out of the shadows stepped a tall, muscular man, broad-chested, with brawny shoulders and thick biceps. His torso was bare, as were his powerful legs. He was dressed in a linen skirt, a simple garment belted at the waist that fell to his knees. Sturdy leather sandals covered his feet, and his long blond hair was braided at the temples and knotted at the crown.

"What has brought you from the House of Pleasure?" Arta demanded of the stranger. "Answer me, at once."

"You, my moonbeam." The newcomer's voice was deep and hypnotic, and Dev disliked him on the spot. "I sensed your distress and have come to offer you ease."

"Who is this guy, Arta?" Dev glared at the oversized slab of beefcake. For two cents, he'd knock his lights out. "Is he one of the Dalvahni?"

"Nay, his name is Korth, and he is my favorite thrall. A thrall is—"

"I know what a thrall is." Anger pulsed in Dev's temples, and flashes of red flickered at the edge of his vision. "Evan told me. Why is he here?"

"To service me, as you would not."

"No. Send him away."

"No? *No?*" Her lips tightened with fury. "You overstep, sirrah."

Korth drew closer. "The human is of no consequence, High Huntress. Dismiss him and allow me to serve you."

"He is not human." Arta's breasts rose and fell. "He is arrogant and capricious a-and tiresome in the extreme, but he is not human."

"And stupid," Dev added. "You forgot stupid."

"I forget nothing." Arta rounded on him. "You do not want me, yet you would deny me release. I find you incomprehensible and...and monstrously selfish."

"Noted." Dev crossed his arms on his chest. "Are you going to send him away?"

"No, and no," Arta cried, stamping her foot. "I tell you, I will not."

"Okay." Dev swept her into his arms and started back up the walk. "Have it your way."

"Release me," she said, struggling to free herself. "I am Kirvahni, not a bag of oats."

"No."

"Shire reeve, an you do not unhand me this instant, I shall—" She drew a deep breath. "I shall *smite* you."

"Smite away." Dev paused on the walk. She was vibrating with fury like a bee trapped in a jar. "You might as well give up. I'm not going to let you go."

"Not going to— I should like to see you try to stop me."

"Lord, woman, get a clue." He smiled down at her. "I already have."

Her eyes flared wide in shock. "What do you—"

Behind them, Korth cleared his throat. "My moonbeam, if you would but—"

"Not now, Korth."

"But Arta—"

"I said, not now." Arta's narrowed gaze was fixed on Dev. "Weoka tells me that Selvans is your great-grand sire. He is the god of boundaries."

"Is he?" Dev said. "Wouldn't know. Never met the fellow."

"Do you think me a fool? You hold me hostage with your shield."

"Yep."

She gasped. "You do not deny it?"

"Nope."

"*Why?* What are you about?"

"Breaking the rules," Dev said, and carried her up the steps and inside the house.

He lowered her feet to the floor, and she immediately spun out of reach.

"Gratifying, to be sure," she said, panting with fury, "but I would not want you to do so on my account."

Dev stalked after her, backing her against a wall. "You're worth it. I'd break 'em a thousand times for you."

"Only a thousand?" She straightened her shoulders and met his gaze squarely. "Fie, methinks you make a paltry gallant."

"A million, then," Dev said, "but that's my limit."

He jerked her into his arms and kissed her. She resisted for an instant, then wrapped her hands in his hair and kissed him back with a ferocity that made his head spin. He was an idiot, a pluperfect moron to think he could have resisted her.

"Arta," he murmured against her lips, tightening his embrace. "My God, you drive me insane."

"Wait," she said, pulling away and placing her hands on his chest. "What of Korth?"

He scowled. "What about him?"

"He is an incubus and cannot be allowed to wander." Slipping from his arms, she strode to the door and peered into the darkness. "He is gone."

"Good riddance."

"It is *not* good. What if he should happen upon some unsuspecting mortal?"

Mentally, Dev consigned Korth and all his kind to the devil. He sighed. "Is he dangerous? Will he kill someone?"

"I do not think so. Thralls feed on emotion."

"Then Korth's hit the jackpot because humans are all about the feels." Unable to resist her siren pull, Dev moved closer to her. "With any luck, your precious thrall will gorge himself and blow an artery."

"He is not my—" She broke off. "You wish him ill. I do not understand. Korth has done nothing to you."

"It's not about what he's done to me." He brushed the pad of his thumb across her full bottom lip. "It's about what he's done to you. I'm jealous, damn it."

"Jealous?" She gave him a strange look. "How odd. What is it like?"

"Damned unpleasant." Dev dropped his hand and stepped back. "Stay away from Korth and the rest of the thralls while you're with me. I don't share—understood?"

Her lips thinned. "I believe I have sufficient intellect to take your meaning. I am to lie with you and no one else whilst I am here. Is that the gist of it?"

"Yeah."

She stuck out her jaw. "And what of you? Am I to have your undivided attention, as well?"

"You don't have to worry about that."

Ignoring her startled protests, Dev picked her up and carried her down the hall to his room. He tossed her onto the bed, and she landed in an elegant sprawl.

"Why not?" she said, rolling to her knees. "Why should I not worry about it?"

"Because I don't want anyone but you, goddammit." Dev unzipped his jeans and fisted his jutting cock. "This is for you, and no one else, so long as we're together. Satisfied?"

She pushed his fingers aside and took the hard length of him in her hand. "Not even a little." She smiled up at him. "Judging from the evidence, howsoever, I am confident I soon shall be."

Dev's heart jerked, and a slow, exquisite pressure built inside him. He felt a flash of panic. Arta roused something primal in him, something dangerous and wild. She was not his first sexual partner, by any means, but he would not be able to hold back, not with her. He was going to lose control, something he'd never done before.

"Arta," he said, clenching his teeth. "I—"

"No more talk." She leapt up in a blur of motion. "I would have you and now."

She slung him on the bed as though he weighed no more than a cat and pounced, straddling him. Her breathing was rapid, her eyes bright, and she crackled with raw, pent-up energy. She was his equal in power and strength. With her, he could let go, lower his guard and to hell with the consequences.

The prospect was exhilarating, dizzying. He could smell her arousal, and it heightened his need. She wanted this, *needed* this, every bit as much as he did.

He fumbled eagerly with the laces of her tunic.

"Too slow," she said, knocking his hands aside.

Her clothes melted away, leaving her gloriously, deliciously naked. Dev drank in the sight of her, his gaze roaming from her slender waist to her plump breasts and curving hips. Her nipples were brownish-pink and puckered, and her pale hair fell in a shimmering curtain to her hips. He wanted to wrap his hands in it, to feel the silken strands on his belly and cock.

"Beautiful," he murmured. "So damn beautiful. One day, you must show me how— *Ahhh.*"

She took him inside her in one, fluid movement.

"Wait," Dev said, a flicker of sanity returning. "I'm not wearing a condom."

"The Kir are immune to disease."

"What about—" Dev clenched his teeth. Her channel was tight and warm, and wet, and it was all he could do not to come, right then and there. "What if you get pregnant?"

"Such a thing is not possible."

"Are you—"

Thought fled as she began to ride him. She was perfect, her breasts swaying as she took him. Her head was thrown back, her eyes closed. The pressure inside him ramped up another notch. It was torture—relentless, voracious, exquisite torture. The feel of her, the knowledge that they were joined, was an agony of delight. He wanted it to stop. He wanted it to never end. His muscles were trembling steel.

She did this to him. Arta, only Arta.

Open your eyes. Look at me, Dev wanted to plead, but the greedy, slick pull of her flesh rendered him incapable of speech. She quickened the pace, a delicate flush climbing from the slopes of her beautiful breasts, up the smooth column of her throat, and into her cheeks.

Dev groaned as the well of sensation inside him expanded, spiraling toward critical mass. "Dear God, I— Kiss me, Arta."

She made a throaty sound of impatience and leaned over, the tips of her breasts brushing his chest. She fastened her lips on his, and he opened his mouth. Her tongue met his, mimicking the hot, urgent thrust of his cock inside her. The coiling tightness inside Dev increased, a swelling pressure that moved from the bottoms of his feet and spread up his legs to the place where they were joined. The feeling was intense, beyond anything. They were one, joined in an exquisite primal dance. It was too much. He let go with a shout of relief, the pleasure-pain of his orgasm tearing through him and outward. The house rocked, and the bedroom windows shattered.

Dev collapsed with a grunt. "God." His eyes drifted shut as a deep, heavy lethargy crept over him. "That was…amazing."

"'Twas moderately enjoyable."

With a supreme effort, Dev opened one eye. "Excuse me? Did you say *moderately?*"

"Aye." Arta contracted her inner muscles in delicious invitation; his cock twitched in response. "I feel certain you can do better. I would do it again."

"What—now?"

"Yes, now." She tossed her silvery hair over one shoulder. "You were sired by a rutting stag, were you not? I should think you up to the task."

"Very well," Dev said, "but only if you do something for me."

She smiled and trailed her fingertips down his chest. "Faith, I thought I already had."

"Something else." Dev flipped her onto her back and knelt between her legs, opening her thighs. She was beautiful here, too. "Say my name. It's been 'shire reeve' this and 'shire reeve' that all day. I'm sick of it."

"Why?" She raised her brows. "'Tis your title."

"I have a name, and I want to hear you to say it."

She blinked at him, his uninhibited, splendid tigress. "I think you are very silly. Why does it matter what I call you?"

"It just does." Dev bent his head and licked her sweet flesh. "Say it, Arta. Say my name."

"Nay, I will not be bullied or badgered into—" She broke off with a gasp as Dev took the little nub in his mouth and suckled. "Shire reeve, that feels so...so..." She arched her back, offering herself to him. "Dev, please. I need you. I need you now."

Dev was so pleased and gratified by this display of enthusiasm that he gave himself wholly and utterly to the task of pleasuring her. Maybe it was nonsensical, he mused, as he rose to his knees and sheathed himself inside her, but a fellow had certain expectations.

He expected to hear his name on a lady's lips when they fadoodled.

Perhaps it wasn't much, in the vast scheme of things, inconsequential, even, but it would do.

For now.

* * * *

White-hot flames licked at Gryffin's flesh, bathing him in anguish. He screamed and covered his face with his hands; they burst into flame and turned to ash.

He awoke with a shout and bolted upright.

"Easy, mister," a soft, drawling voice said. "You's all right."

Gryffin's vision swam. Gradually, the clinging vestiges of the nightmare receded, and the speaker came into focus. It was the girl. She was thin, too thin, with pale, freckled skin, a mop of short reddish-blond hair, and huge violet eyes. The garments she wore were obviously borrowed, loose and ill-fitting. She hovered at the edge of the bed. Gryffin inhaled, breathing in her scent, a pleasing combination of soap and a light clean smell that was her own. The fiery anguish in his brain cooled, a relief so sweet that Gryffin nearly wept.

"You a-hurtin', mister?" Her brow puckered in concern. "Can I gitcha anything?"

The chamber door opened, and an old woman stomped in. "What in tarnation's going on?" She tied the sash of her worn robe around her lean waist and shoved her unbound gray hair over her shoulder with a leathery hand. "Somebody boiling a cat in here?"

"Bad dream, I'm a-thinking." The girl gazed worriedly at Gryffin. "You's aright now, though, aincha, mister?"

"Gryffin." His voice, harsh from disuse, came out a guttural croak. He tried again. "I...Gryffin."

"Glory be, he speaks," the old woman said. "Well, Gryffin, I'm Weoka Waters. Welcome to my home."

Home? There was no home for him, no safe harbor, only pain and recrimination and regret. He tried to rise and collapsed. The surface beneath him was soft and giving. He lay back on the mattress. There was a bank of plush pillows at his back. Clean linens smelling of lavender and sunshine covered his bare skin, and a brightly colored quilt had been spread over all for warmth.

Warmth, blessed, blessed warmth. How long had it been since he'd slept in a bed, with a pillow and clean sheets and blankets to ward off the cold? How long since he'd rested indoors?

Centuries, surely.

No matter. He struggled to his elbows. He could not stay. His very presence placed the girl and the old woman at risk.

"Go," he said, though the room spun in a sickening fashion. "Danger...must leave."

"You ain't going anywhere, not for a while," the old woman said. "Too weak."

"You listen to Miz Weoka, mister," the girl said. "You was three parts dead when they brung you in."

"Feeling more the thing, now, though, huh?" the old woman said. "Not surprised. Gal's hardly left your side. She's got a talent for making things better."

Gryffin was half-listening. He should leave—now, before it was too late. He willed himself to move, but he ached all over, and his brain was soggy and thick as three-day-old mush. Dimly, a sliver of memory surfaced. This old woman had taken him into her home, and the girl had tended to him. Civility required a certain response.

"Thank...you," he said, dredging the words from the distant past. "Obliged."

Remembering the simple courtesy gave him a twinge of pride, but his brief satisfaction vaporized when the girl scowled.

He stared at her in confusion. "Girl?"

"Girl is mad as fire," she said. "I don't want your thanks, not after you rescued me and Miz Cassie."

"Rescued you?" the old woman said. "What's this?"

"Joby Ray Skinner caught us and locked us up," the girl said. "Would've done bad things to us, too, if"—she peeped shyly at him—"if you hadn't come along and helped us. Even though it was dangerous. Even though that Pratt feller almost caught you."

"Pratt?" Gryffin jerked in alarm and stared wildly around the room. "Go…must leave."

"He ain't here," the girl said, hastening to soothe him. "Don't matter, anyway. You's free now."

Gryffin shook his head. "Pratt…bound."

Traitor. Apostate. The old, familiar shame ate at him like acid.

Changeable as quicksilver, the girl stamped her bare foot. "You ain't bound no more, I'm telling you. Sugar freed you with the orb." She waved a thin hand at him. "Take a gander at yerself, if 'n you don't believe me."

Gryffin glanced down and received a shock. The inky patterns on his skin remained, but they no longer writhed and slithered across his flesh like worms, and his flesh did not burn.

"Free," he murmured, recalling a pair of innocent blue eyes set in a white, furry face. "Sugar heal owie."

"'Owie,' is it?" The old woman chuckled. "That's a peculiar way to describe the darkest magic I've seen in an age."

Gryffin nodded absently, his gaze on the girl's pixie face.

"Girl…name?"

She had been a light in his darkness, his one respite from pain and despair, and he didn't even know what to call her.

"Verbena," she said, her thin cheeks turning pink. "Verbena Van Pelt."

An ebon-haired man stalked into the chamber. Muscular and fit, he was unclad but for a pair of rough trousers, unbuttoned at the waist. His purple eyes glinted with ill humor, and his expression was surly.

"What the hell?" he demanded. "How's Red supposed to sleep with people carrying on like their balls are on fire?"

The girl—*Verbena*, Gryffin corrected mentally—bristled.

"You be nice, Mr. Evan," she said, rushing to Gryffin's defense. "He had a bad dream. Ain't nobody done woke Miz Taryn a-purpose."

"Didn't say it was on purpose. Said Red needs her sleep. Peace and quiet, you feel me?" His glare shifted to Gryffin. "She's not going to get it around here, which is why I'm taking her home with me tomorrow."

"Huh," the old woman said. "Reckon the High Huntress will have something to say about that."

"The High Huntress can't say jack shit, 'cause I'm not going to ask her." He broke off with a disgruntled grunt as a giant of a man with russet hair and golden eyes appeared. "Big 'Un, you here, too? What's next, a frigging marching band?"

"Peace, scapegrace." The warrior stared at Gryffin. "Brother, I hied me here as soon as I heard the gladsome news."

"Yeah, yeah, the prodigal demon hunter is back, and everybody's tickled as shit," Evan said. "Tomorrow, we'll have cake and candles and all kinds of happy fuckery, but, right now, it's the middle of the night, and people are trying to sleep. *Red's* trying to sleep."

"What care I for slumber at such a time?" The big warrior's expression was tormented. "Lo, these many years I thought my brother dead, but he lives. He *lives*."

Evan stared at him in astonishment. "Well, of all the selfish— And people say *I'm* a dick? There are sick people in this house, Big 'Un, and sick people need rest, including this pathetic sack you call brother."

"No." Gryffin fisted the covers at his waist and turned his face to the wall. "Not...brother."

"Gryffin?" The warrior's voice was anguished. "You are my brother... my *twin*, created in the same moment by our maker, Kehvahn. Please. Eons have passed since last we met. I would make things right."

"Jesus, Big 'Un," Evan said, "give it a rest. The poor bastard's been tortured and starved, and God knows what-all. Do him a favor—do *us* a favor and go away."

"Evan's right," the old woman said. "Gryffin needs rest. Everybody out."

"Nay," the warrior protested. "I will not leave him."

"I insist." The old woman's voice held a palpable push of power. "You, too, Verbena. You're worn to a thread."

"Yessum," Verbena said, turning reluctantly for the door.

One by one, they shuffled from the room, and the door closed softly behind them. Gryffin kept his gaze averted until he was sure he was alone. 'Twas for the best, he supposed, brooding darkly. He had been too long without the company of others. Brother? Once he had been Dalvahni, but no more. He was the rogue, the oath-breaker.

Bitterness and self-loathing soured his mouth, and spots danced at the edge of his vision. A wave of sickness washed over him, and his heart began to thud as the hideous visions returned, flickering and solidifying to dance about the room. Rotting corpses and screaming children, their mouths agape in horror. The smell of burning flesh, his own and that of others, was a noxious stench in his nostrils.

Shaking, Gryffin clutched the covers around him for warmth and curled into a ball. He clenched his teeth, forcing back the scream that clawed its way up his throat. Free? He would never be free, not from the things he'd seen.

Not from the things he'd done. Not from what he'd become.

He whimpered in relief as a cool hand touched his brow.

"Shh, it's all right, mister," the soft voice said. "I'm here."

It was the girl. She had come back and stood beside the bed. Her large eyes were clouded with concern. "Girl…" His mouth twisted. "Verbena…stay?"

"Sure, mister. Long as you want me to."

"Gryffin." He reached out and dragged her slight form onto his chest. "Not…mister," he said, wrapping his arms around her. "Gryffin."

Trembling as if she had the ague, she laid her cheek on his chest. "Gryffin," she whispered.

Gryffin sighed. "Verbena…sleep?"

"I will, if 'n you will."

A smile tugged at Gryffin's cracked lips. Such a slight creature and yet, untamed and stubborn.

"Close your eyes," she murmured, her breath chuffing lightly against his skin. "I won't leave you. I promise."

Gryffin closed his eyes. Her calming scent soothed his fevered thoughts, quieting the chaos. Little by little, his muscles relaxed. His heartbeat slowed, and he slipped into nothingness. Drifting untethered in the gray mist, he slept for the first time in thousands of years, his slumber undisturbed by horror, recrimination, or pain.

Chapter Ten

"Dev, what the everlasting hell?"

Dev bolted upright in the bed. A dark-eyed fury glowered at him from the foot of the bed like it was Judgment Day and she was the Lord God almighty.

Quickly, he tucked the covers around his waist. "Winnie. What are you doing here?"

He glanced at the other side of the bed. Empty. His stomach did a peculiar flip-flop. Arta was gone. She'd screwed him senseless and left. *Wham-bam, thank you, man.* Services rendered; services no longer required.

"What am I doing?" Winnie's voice rose. "What are *you* doing?"

"Sleeping, until you barged in."

"Don't take that smarmy tone with me—"

"I wasn't—"

"Dammit to hell, Dev, I thought you were *dead*."

"Dead?" He stared at her. "Why would you think that?"

"I dunno." She glared at him. "Maybe because your front door is in the driveway, and your room looks like somebody took a wrecking ball to it."

Dev took in his surroundings. There was a yawning hole in the exterior wall where the windows had been; the jagged opening framed a patch of lawn and the dark green woods beyond. Shards of wood, glass, and Sheetrock littered the bedroom floor.

"Well?" Winnie said. "What happened? I nearly had a heart attack when I pulled up and saw this mess."

"Is that so?" Dev leaned back and folded his arms on his chest. "Maybe now you know how *I* felt yesterday when you took on a beetlesaurus, and you were this close"—he held his thumb and forefinger a fraction of an inch apart—"to becoming a demon snack."

"That's different."

"Yeah? How do you figure?"

"I don't *know*," she cried. "It just is."

Lowering his arms, Dev stared at her in surprise. Winnie wasn't angry. She was shaken, her face drained of color, and her brown eyes, usually warm and twinkling with mischief, so dilated they looked black.

"Calm down," he said. "I'm fine."

Except for being dumped. He was not fine with that. Arta had used him and discarded him like a candy wrapper. It was enough to give a fellow a complex. What's more, it didn't make sense. Yesterday, she'd been gung-ho about the investigation, and this morning—*poof*—gone without a word.

He racked his brain for an explanation. Had Kehvahn summoned her away on other business? If so, she could be anywhere, another planet, another dimension. His stomach did another slow roll. What if he never saw her again?

His mind balked. No, she'd come back. She had to—they were working together. Bad guys to catch, asses to whup.

"Dev?"

He looked up. "Yeah?"

"Are you going to tell me what's going on?"

"I told you. Nothing."

"Bullshit. The evidence says otherwise." She pointed a finger at the rumpled bed linens and the pillow beside him. "Someone has been here. Who have you been banging?"

"That, Winifred Rose, is none of your business."

Calling Winnie by her given name was a calculated move to get her dander up, but Winnie didn't so much as twitch.

"We're family," she said. "That makes it my business." Her eyes narrowed. "Arta didn't sleep in her bed last night."

"You don't say? Demon hunters are unpredictable."

"Devlin Theodulf Whitsun, you totally had sex with her, didn't you?" She braced her hands on her hips. "Then you did something to tick her off and she—"

"Me?" Dev said. "Now, hold on. What makes you think I—"

"—trashed your house to shit."

"Relax, Winnie. Arta didn't do this. I did."

"You did?" She looked aghast. "Why?"

"Rough night."

A rough, glorious night of life-altering, mind-blowing sex, but that subject wasn't open for discussion with Winnie or anyone else, except Arta.

If she came back and he got the chance.

He wrapped the sheet around his waist and rose from the bed. "It's after six thirty, and I need a shower and breakfast. See you at the SO."

"But, Dev—"

"For God's sake, Winnie, give it a rest."

He stalked into the bathroom and shut the door. Dropping the sheet, he stepped into the walk-in shower, a six-by-twelve miniature heaven of neutral tile, gleaming glass doors, stainless-steel finishes, multiple jets, and a large rain forest showerhead. There was even a wide marble bench at one end and a sauna feature.

He loved his shower. Fond as he was of Aunt Wee, he'd outgrown the clawfoot tubs at her house by the time he'd reached the tenth grade and his present height of six-feet-two. Taking pity on him, she'd added a shower enclosure and a watering can showerhead to the upstairs tub, but he was forever knocking the thing down or getting tangled up in the shower curtain. Consequently, a large walk-in shower had been at the top of his must-have list when he'd built his cabin in the woods, and he was especially pleased with the result. The shower doors had been custom-ordered due to their size, but he considered the extra expense well worth it. He had his dream shower with endless hot water and killer water pressure to boot, thanks to the water demon in the well.

Meg Fowler was her name. He'd caught her one evening trying to lure a small child into a pond off Cat Man Road. She was hideous, an emaciated horror with stick limbs, moldy-green hair, a face like a trout, and sharp, pointy teeth. He'd been repulsed, but reluctant to kill her. Meg couldn't help what she was any more than he could. He'd confined her to his well instead, with the understanding that she'd amp up his water pressure and keep the water hot. Deprived of human flesh, she subsisted largely on mice, possum, and sundry small creatures she lured into her lair. Dev threw her a pack of chicken legs now and then and the occasional sweet. Meg, he'd discovered quite by accident, *loved* sweets.

But nothing with peanuts. The hag was allergic. He'd made the mistake of tossing her a bag of PayDay bars once, and the house had reeked of rotten eggs for a week.

He twisted the valve on the wall and stood under the oversized showerhead. The water beat down on him with a ferocity just shy of a fireman's hose, but it did nothing to wash away his memories of Arta. She'd been amazing, at times playful and teasing, at others commanding and rough. She took what she wanted without hesitation or shyness, and she was insatiable. Dev liked that about her. His sex drive was strong, too.

But he was *not* his father, the roving stag, spreading his DNA willy-nilly. He'd been raised by his aunt, and Weoka had taught him constancy.

A river goddess did not abandon her sacred charge.

A river goddess was tenacious and loyal.

A river goddess was faithful and dedicated.

Other life lessons had shaped him, as well. The incident with Russ in high school had made a lasting impression on Dev. He was neither kith nor norm and different from both.

More powerful.

Less human.

Keenly aware of his abilities and the weight that came with them, he'd chosen the path of service, dedicating himself to the job and burying himself in work. His previous relationships had been casual, short-lived affairs, and he always, always used condoms. His *cojones* were a supernatural piñata—you never knew what you might get.

Until last night with Arta. He hadn't used protection with her.

Arta—sweet Jesus, she had rocked him to the core. His response to her had surprised and shocked him. Sex with her was intense and powerful. His previous experiences paled in comparison. His reaction to her had been like nuclear fusion, but she'd ditched him without so much as a good-bye. The memory of her still made him hard. He closed his eyes and stroked his rigid cock, imagining being inside her, his hands on her plump, lovely breasts, her inner muscles clasping him. He could still taste her. Could feel her smooth, luscious skin beneath his fingers as he explored her strong, sexy warrior's body. She was unlike any woman he'd known. Even her scent was unique, an enticing blend of rose and jasmine brightened with something spicy and the faintest hint of musk.

She was gone, yet her maddening, intoxicating perfume still lingered in his wolf's nose.

He inhaled, drawing the tantalizing essence further into his lungs, absorbing it. God, it was almost as though she were—

His hands were pushed aside, and he felt the slow, exquisite drag of a warm tongue on his erection. Startled, he opened his eyes. Arta knelt at his feet on the shower floor beneath the pulsing spray. His heart clenched at the sight of her. She was naked, and her wet hair streamed like pale silk down the graceful length of her back. Drops of water sparkled on her eyelashes and beaded her sleek skin. Her cheeks and lovely mouth were rosy, her eyes alight with sensual promise.

She smiled up at him. "Verily, I thought she would never leave," she said, giving his rock-hard erection another lick.

"Arta." Dev snatched her up and kissed her, a bruising, ravenous caress fueled by relief and longing and lust. Taking her head in his hands, he leaned his forehead on hers, his chest heaving. "I thought— Never mind. It doesn't matter."

She placed her hand on his chest. "You are shaking, and your heart is pounding nigh to bursting. What is amiss?"

"Nothing. You're here." He cupped her wet buttocks and pulled her close. "You came back."

"'Strewth, I never left. I heard Winnie approach and masked my presence."

The hollow feeling in Dev's stomach and chest melted away. She hadn't left. She'd been with him the whole time.

"You made yourself invisible?"

"Aye, 'tis a gift the Kir and the Dal share." She slid one knee up his hip, opening herself to him. "What, you thought me done with you so soon?"

"The thought crossed my mind when I woke up and you were gone."

"Given your scruples, I thought it best to hide from Winnie."

He gave her a slow grin. "I think my scruples went out the window the moment we met."

"I am glad." She rubbed her damp center against his erection. "Now that Winnie has gone, methinks a morning romp in order." She regarded him from beneath heavy lids. "For purely medicinal reasons, of course."

"Yes, ma'am," Dev said. "I'm sworn to serve."

Lifting her by the thighs, he pressed her against the shower wall and entered her in one, swift stroke. She sucked in her breath, her eyes widening.

"Shire reeve, you are impressive." She grasped him by the shoulders and gave a little wiggle that made Dev's eyes cross. "A veritable stallion."

"It's Dev, remember?" he managed to gasp before he forgot his name and everything else.

She was slick with desire and tight as a clenched fist. He drove into her, his hips thrusting. The world narrowed to the two of them and the place they were connected. The familiar pressure started at the base of his spine and expanded. Nuclear fusion, indeed. He would shatter, and Arta was at ground zero.

He tried to draw back, but she clung tight.

"Nay," she said. "Do not stop. Let it happen."

"No." He clenched his teeth. "I don't want to hurt you."

"I am Kirvahni. You cannot break me." The tile walls of the shower spun, and he found himself seated on the bench with Arta astride him. "This you should already know."

Dev clutched the edge of the bench as she slid up and down the aching length of him. His heart was pounding to beat the band, his breathing quickened, and his muscles drew tight. He was close, so close. "Arta, I—"

"Stop fighting it," she said. "Let go."

The exquisite pressure within him swelled. With a deep, shuddering groan, Dev orgasmed. Arta's body blazed with the shining light of a thousand candles as she absorbed the impact. She cried out, her slender form spasming with waves of delight.

She opened her eyes. Light surrounded her supple form, bright particles that danced around them in a shower of tiny stars.

"That was...remarkable." She swayed like a reed in the wind. "Quite...unexpected."

With a deep sigh of contentment, she closed her eyes and slumped against his chest.

Dev held her in his arms and floated in postcoital bliss. His body felt sluggish and heavy, and his mind was a pleasant blank. He doubted he could move if his life depended upon it. How long they sat beneath the pounding spray, he could not say, but he finally roused when the water began to cool.

Even Meg had her limits.

Arta lay limp in his arms, her head resting on his shoulder.

"Hey, there." Tenderly, he brushed his lips over her damp temple. "We're starting to prune, and I have work to do."

She lifted her head. "As do I. We are partners."

"We've been through this. I'm your boss, not your partner."

She chuckled. "An it pleases you to think so."

She was irrepressible. A wise man, Dev decided, picked his battles.

"I'm hungry," he said. "What say we finish this shower and have some breakfast?"

"Hmm, that sounds delightful," she said, nuzzling his neck. "Coitus always makes me ravenous." He tensed and she sat up. "But what is amiss? Your face is a thundercloud."

"Nothing, I—" Dev stopped himself. "That's a lie. I don't like to be reminded of your other lovers."

"But I am Kirvahni and the Directive—"

"I know, I know. It's in the rules. If I could get my hands on that damn book, I'd torch it."

"*Dev.* You speak of sacrilege."

"Can't help it. I'm jealous as hell." He rose. "Don't worry. I'll get over it."

They bathed quickly in silence and stepped out of the shower.

"Here." Dev threw her a clean bath sheet from the shelf and grabbed another for himself.

She stood, dripping water onto the bath mat, her expression troubled. "Dev, I would—"

"Forget it." He put his towel to vigorous use. "Look, we're adults. We've both been with other people. I get it. This is a hookup."

"A hookup? I do not—"

"Sex, Arta." He jerked the damp towel around his waist. "Getting laid and nothing more."

Very grown-up, Dev thought. *You sound like a sullen little boy.*

But a man had his pride, damn it, and he was gaga about her. Too bad the feeling wasn't mutual. Arta seemed unaffected, but he couldn't say that he hadn't been warned. Arta was incapable of love. She'd told him so herself. He was a momentary diversion, an amusing dalliance between thralls. She, on the other hand, was rapidly becoming an obsession with him.

He strode into the bedroom and screeched to a halt. Winnie lounged in a chair near the door, her legs crossed.

"Winnie," he said. "I thought you'd gone."

"And I thought you told the truth." She swung one booted foot. "Didn't have sex with her, huh? Liar, liar, pants on fire."

"I didn't lie," Dev said. "I avoided your questions."

"Obfuscation. Same difference, or at least that's what you've always preached. Guess the rules don't apply to you."

"What I do on my own time is my own affair."

"Affair—now, there's an interesting word." Winnie uncrossed her legs and sat up. "Here's another one—fraternization. Or maybe you prefer 'sexual harassment'?"

"She's Kirvahni. I hardly think that will be a—"

"Conflict of interest? Inappropriate behavior?" She arched a sardonic brow. "No boinking a coworker? Keep your schlong where it belongs and a lock on your box? Any of that ring a bell?"

"Why are you still here, Winnie? I told you to leave."

She held up a finger. "Actually, your exact words were 'give it a rest.' For your information, I couldn't leave, though I wanted to, believe you me."

"Then why didn't you?"

"Because I'm in your car, jackass."

"Oh," said Dev.

"I tried to tell you, but you wouldn't listen. You left your Jeep at the scene yesterday, remember? Parks dropped me off first thing this morning, and I drove it out here. Figured you'd need a ride to work."

"Oh, Lordy, I forgot." Dev groaned. "Winnie, I—"

"Save it." She made a face. "Never dreamed I'd have a front-row seat at the grand premier of *Dev and Arta Make a Porno*."

"You could've gone outside. You didn't have to stay in my room."

"I *did* go outside." She jumped to her feet. "Shot out of here like my ass was on fire and my tits were dynamite soon as I figured out what was going on. You think I want to hear that shit? Hell, no. Haven't heard howling like that since Mazie Bedsole caught her old man diddling her sister and threw lye water on his crotch."

"If you're so horrified, why'd you come back?"

She glared at him. "Because I was *worried* about you, for Pete's sake. The house lit up like the Fourth of July. I'm surprised the volunteer fire department didn't show up."

Arta padded out of the bathroom wearing nothing but a towel.

"Well," Winnie said with exquisite sarcasm, "if it isn't the wandering houseguest."

"Greetings, Winnie." Arta returned her perusal without a trace of embarrassment. "What brings you here?"

"Dev will fill you in. *Oops*," Winnie said. "He already has." She crossed the room to the hole in the wall, her boots crunching on debris. "I'll be in the car—with the radio on, in case you two decide to have another go." She leveled a look at Arta over her shoulder. "But, later, missy, you and I are going to have a talk. A *serious* talk."

She jumped lightly through the ragged opening and stalked out of sight.

Arta looked thoughtful. "Winnie seems out of sorts."

"Noticed that, did you?"

Dev went into the closet to dress, pulling on clean boxer briefs, a fresh uniform, and boots. When he came back out, Arta had done her Kirvahni woo-woo act and was fully dressed in her deputy's uniform. She'd also magically repaired the damage to his room. Everything was back in its place, framing, Sheetrock, windows, and paint, down to the last nail.

"Thanks," he said once he'd recovered from the shock. "I...er...don't know what to say."

She shrugged. "'Tis nothing. I replaced your front door, as well."

They ate a quick breakfast of scrambled eggs and toast and went outside. Dev's Jeep was in the driveway. On one side, the back passenger seat was a transport cage with a hard plastic seat, a Plexiglas shield, and bars on the window. The other half of the back seat was cushioned and comfortable with access to the front, in the event Dev was transporting a non-prisoner.

Winnie sat in the front passenger side of the Jeep Cherokee with the engine running. Arms folded, she stared straight ahead.

Dev opened the driver's door and was pummeled by a wave of music.

"Kind of loud, isn't it?" he shouted over the din.

"Depends on what you're trying to drown out."

Dev got in and pushed a button to lower the volume. "You're never going to let me live this down, are you?"

"Not in a million years."

"Is that TKX you're listening to?" he said. "We don't usually get Pensacola stations way out here."

"Tilt your left butt cheek and press your tongue to the roof of your mouth, and you can get a signal—for a little while, at least." Winnie glanced through the window. "Your girlfriend seems to be having trouble with the door handle."

"She's not my—"

"Never mind," Winnie said as the door behind Dev was ripped off the hinges and tossed aside. "She figured it out."

"The door to your carriage would not open," Arta announced, hopping in the back.

Winnie smirked. "That's because I locked it."

"You kept me out a-purpose? Why?"

"For fun."

"Damn it, Winnie," Dev said. "This is a county vehicle."

"Take it up with Wonder Woman. *I* didn't tear up your car."

"Do not fratch. All will be mended." Arta waved her hand, and the car door sailed off the ground and back into place. "See? No harm done." She rapped on the Plexiglas shield that separated her seat from the cage on the other side. "You imprison miscreants in this unit?"

"Transport space," Dev said. "Drunks and domestics, mostly. Thus, the plastic interior."

Winnie wrenched her head around, staring first at the perfectly repaired door and then at Arta. "You are such a freak."

"She repaired the house, too." Dev waved a hand in the direction of the cabin. "No more broken windows or busted wall. Nice, huh?"

"Shittastic." Winnie crossed her arms again. "I hate demon hunters. I really do."

"Then you hate yourself," Arta said, "for Eamon made you one of us."

"I'm not—"

"But you are. What is more, you need training."

"Are you volunteering for the job?"

"Nay, that task rightfully belongs to Eamon."

"Eamon is a jerk."

Dev glanced in the rearview mirror at Arta. Her gaze was vacant. Ten to one, she was checking with the Provider.

"The Dal are many things, but they are not cruel," she said after a moment. "Eamon is dauntless and driven by duty. No doubt the matter slipped his mind."

"I'm a *person*, not a matter. He turned me into a mutant freak and took off. Yesterday was the first time I've seen him since—" Winnie swallowed convulsively. "You know."

"I know." Dev shifted the Jeep into gear and rolled down the drive. "You still miss Pawpaw Sloan, don't you?"

"Every day."

"The Lady Weoka has told me of your loss," Arta said. "You and your grandsire were close?"

"We were pals."

"And you would spare others such pain?"

Winnie clenched her fists. "It's why I joined the department."

"Then you should accept direction."

"I did all right yesterday."

"Your powers are untapped. You could do more."

"I can run fast," Winnie protested. "Faster than Dev, even."

"Fleetness is but one ability," Arta said. "You have other gifts."

"Demon hunters aren't all the same?"

"There are certain things we can all do, but we are individuals."

"Yeah? So, what's my talent?"

"I do not know. Your essence is Dal, not Kir."

"Shoot." Winnie lapsed into silence. "Okay," she said at last. "I'll agree to this training thing, but not by Eamon. That shit wouldn't last five minutes."

"Methinks Eamon would be more amenable an you refrained from breaking his nose."

"Yeah, that's not going to happen."

"The Provider, then. 'Tis the obvious solution. The Kir and the Dal were trained by the Provider in all matters of warcraft and magic."

Dev glanced at Arta in the mirror in surprise. "What about the guy who created you?"

"Kehvahn was otherwise occupied."

"Absentee dad, huh? Too busy for his own kids." Winnie shook her head. "That stinks."

"We are not children, in the human concept of things," Arta said. "Do you wish to receive instruction in our ways or not?"

"I don't know," Winnie said. "This Provider dude creeps me out. What does he look like?"

"The Provider is formless," Arta said. "Moreover, the Provider is not, strictly speaking, a 'he.' The Provider assumes the gender you prefer or none atall."

"So, there's a Provider for each and every demon hunter?"

"In a manner of speaking."

"Like multiple users operating the same computer language?" Winnie asked.

"'Computer language'?" Arta paused. Again, she had that vacant look. "The analogy is not inaccurate."

"You were talking to the Provider just now, weren't you?"

"Yes."

"Can the Provider teach me to take the Ether Bus?"

"She means vanish," Dev said. "Winnie was impressed when you disappeared yesterday."

"Yeah," Winnie said. "I'm stoked about learning how to do that."

"The Provider can teach you to take this bus. The Void, we call it," Arta said.

"Awesome."

"Whoever trains you," Dev said to Winnie, "make sure the norms don't see, especially if magic is involved."

"Magic will most certainly be involved," Arta said, "but should the norms witness something untoward, their memories will be adjusted."

"The Provider can do that?" Winnie asked.

"Nay, but I can. The Provider will inform me should that be necessary."

"This memory thing," Dev said, "is it permanent?"

"Generally," Arta said, "although some humans retain brief flashes of recollection. These, however, they ascribe to fancy and soon disregard."

"Sweet." Winnie glanced at Dev in surprise when he turned south on the main road. "What's up? I thought we were headed to the station."

Dev eased the car around a curve. "I need to swing by Aunt Weoka's first."

"An excellent notion," Arta said. "I would see Taryn."

"Who?" Winnie asked.

"Her sister," Dev said. "We found her in the woods yesterday. She was injured, so I took her to Aunt Wee's."

"Oh, yeah, I forgot. Arta mentioned her on the way to my place yesterday." Winnie settled back in the front seat. "If we're going to Aunt

Wee's, I'm grabbing a bite to eat. *Some* of us didn't have breakfast, and Aunt Wee makes a mean biscuit."

"Truly? I should like a sample," Arta said.

"What are you, a hobbit?" Winnie demanded. "You already ate."

"The veriest morsel. The shire reeve's attentions have given me an appetite."

Winnie gagged. "'Attentions'? Gross, does she mean—"

"If you don't want to know, don't ask," said Dev.

Chapter Eleven

Dev drove slowly through the woods to Weoka's house, pausing at the mouth of the gravel drive. Septembers in Alabama were hot, and the early morning temperature was already nearing eighty. By midafternoon, it would be hotter than the seventh layer of hell. Wisps of mist rose from the river, humid ghosts skimming the water's surface. On the opposite bank, rough-barked pines, river birches, hackberry trees, and stately oaks squatted like sullen, green giants groggy from the heat. Some three hundred yards distant, Aunt Weoka tended her garden. Jeb Hannah was on patrol. He clomped the far perimeter like an automated watchdog, a slender hircine figure cavorting at his heels.

There's a long, long train a-winding, Jeb boomed.
Into the land of my dreams,
Where the nightingales are singing
And the white moon be-eeams.

Winnie bolted upright. "What the—"

"That's Trevil," Dev said, fully aware that she wasn't referring to the pooka.

"Gosh sakes, Dev, I know Trevil when I see him. He taught me to swim."

"You, as well?" Arta pursed her lips in disapproval. "'Strewth, the Lady Weoka is careless."

"I'm talking about the statue." Winnie's voice rose. "It's singing."

"No flies on you, Deputy," Dev said.

"It's *alive*, Dev."

"Noticed that, too, did you?"

"Be serious. What are you going to do about it?"

"I honestly have no idea, but I'm open to suggestions."

"You're a super. Break the spell."

"You're a super, Winnie," he retorted. "You break it."

"Me? I don't know how."

"Neither do I."

She muttered something under her breath and turned to Arta. "What about you?"

Arta arched a perfect brow. "What about me?"

"You can do magic and shit."

"'*Magic and shit*'?" Arta's tone would have frozen the gonads off a marble statue. "How am I to take that, I wonder?"

Winnie put up her hands in a defensive gesture. "Calm down. I wasn't trying to offend you."

"You have a natural talent for it, then."

"I meant," Winnie said, slogging on despite the glacial chill, "that you have powers."

"I could slay the behemoth," the huntress admitted, thawing ever so slightly, "but I cannot undo the spell that brought cold, unfeeling metal to life. Only the wielder can."

"No one's messing with Jeb, and that's final," Dev said. "I like him, and so does Verbena."

"Who?" Winnie asked.

"Verbena Van Pelt. She's staying with Aunt Wee. Helping out with Gryffin, you know. I'm sure I mentioned it."

"No, you didn't. Who is Gryffin?"

Arta answered from the back seat. "A Dalvahni warrior enslaved these three thousand years and more, until he was freed from dread bondage."

"'Enslaved'? I thought demon hunters were pretty much invincible."

"We are staunch, but even a demon hunter is no match for a god and forbidden magic."

"A 'god'?"

"Pratt," Dev said. "Arta mentioned him yesterday."

"Oh, yeah," said Winnie. "I remember."

"I'm pretty sure he murdered the Randall clan."

"All of them?"

"Yep."

"Holy shit," Winnie said. "How did this Gryffin fellow escape?"

"With the skellring's help," said Arta.

"The what?"

"Albino bigfoot," Dev said. "Snow white. Blue eyes. Chiclet teeth."

"You mean Sugar, Old Lady Hall's pet?"

"That's the one. Sugar freed Gryffin from Pratt."

"Sugar freed—" Winnie stared at him. "Are we talking about the same bigfoot?"

"Your confusion is understandable," Arta said kindly. "In truth, the skellring could not have done the thing without the orb."

"The 'orb'?"

"An ancient artifact," Dev said. "Like a superweapon."

"A superweapon." Winnie's expression was dumbfounded. "Whose bright idea was it to give Sugar a superweapon? He has the IQ of a dust mop."

"Doesn't matter who gave it to him." Dev took his foot off the brake, and the Jeep crunched on down the drive. "Sugar has the orb, and Pratt wants it. We have to make sure he doesn't get it."

Winnie shook her head. "That's more layers of messed up than I can count."

"I tried to get you to go to law school," Dev reminded her. "Offered to pay your way."

"And miss this cluster? No freaking way."

Dev parked near the back steps. Reaching the top of the slope, Jeb turned with a clatter of metal joints.

"You can't keep him here," Winnie said, observing the lumbering giant. "You know that, right? There's a BOLO on that statue."

"He's keeping an eye on things for me."

"He's already got a job, Dev. It's catching pigeon shit in the Hannah town square."

"Would *you* want to stand around on a block of stone all day, come wind, rain, or shine?"

"No, but—"

"Neither does Jeb," Dev said. "There's a broken cookie that won't go back in the box."

"'Cookie'?" Arta's voice was bright with interest. "I could eat a cookie."

Winnie shot her a look of disgust. "Don't you ever think of anything but your stomach?"

"I think of many things. At present, I think I am hungry."

There was a piercing blast from the top of the hill. Jeb had spotted them. *Giddy Giddap! Go on! Go on!* he boomed, careening toward them like an eighteen-wheeler with no brakes.

We're on our way to war,
We're goin' to tell 'em to go to–well!
That's what we're fighting for!

Winnie clutched the edge of her seat. "Holy crap, he's headed this way."

"Yeah, and he's putting ruts in Aunt Wee's grass. She's not going to be happy about that."

"He's got a bat, Dev."

"It's not a bat. It's a peanut."

"He looks pissed."

"He does seem excited. Probably doesn't recognize my vehicle."

"No kidding? Could you maybe do something about that, or do you plan to sit here and let him squash us?"

"You've got a point," Dev said, exiting the vehicle. He waved his arms at the stampeding giant. "Whoa, Jeb. It's me—Sheriff Whitsun."

Jeb clanked to a halt. Bending, he peered closely at Dev.

The captain has returned at last,

From battles far away? he rumbled.

"That's right, I'm back," Dev said. "Thanks for taking care of things in my absence."

Winnie eased out of the car. "Yeah," she said. "Good job."

Jeb started in surprise when he saw her and swept the hat from his head.

Hellooo, there, Red Hot Janie, he crooned.

If you ain't the prettiest thang I ever seen,

And when it comes to loving, honey,

I'll bet you is the sugar queen.

"Um…thanks," Winnie said. "I think."

"Well done, soldier," Dev said. "You may resume your duties."

Jeb saluted smartly and stomped away.

"Wow." Winnie stared after him. "Just wow."

The back door of the Jeep gave way with a grinding shriek, and Arta stepped out.

"Arta, you've busted the door again," Winnie said, whirling around. "What is it with you?"

Arta flicked a speck of automobile paint from her khaki shirt. "Naught that sustenance cannot cure."

"You can't go around tearing hell off the hinges every time you get in or out of a car."

"Why not?"

"Because." Winnie sputtered helplessly. "You just can't."

"A less-than-compelling argument, but so be it." With a flick of her fingers, Arta repaired the door. "There. All is restored. Shall we proceed?"

She sauntered past Dev and Winnie without waiting for an answer and glided up the back steps.

"You're sleeping with that nightmare," Winnie reminded Dev as Arta disappeared into the house. "When she breaks your dick, remember I warned you."

Aunt Weoka waved at them from her garden. "Morning, you two. Dev, I'd like a word with you."

"See you later," Winnie said, running lightly up the steps.

"Hey, get back here," Dev said. "You're supposed to be my backup." She winked down at him from the porch. "Sorry, bro. You're on your own. Gotta get in there before the High Hoglet eats all the biscuits."

The door slammed behind her. Aunt Weoka strolled up, a basket of tomatoes under one arm.

"Lucy Hall called," she said. "News about Olivia Freeman is all over the county."

"I'm sorry to hear that," Dev said. "I was hoping to keep it quiet until we find her brother."

"That kettle's boiled. Folks are saying Livy died at work. Fell into a vat at the papermill and was pickled."

"Folks are wrong. Livy's death wasn't an accident. She was murdered."

Weoka sucked in her breath. "Murdered? Lands, that's terrible."

"She was killed by demons, Aunt Wee. *Taaktha*, Arta called it."

"*Taaktha?*" Weoka rolled the word around in her mouth. "Don't know it. But I ain't a demon hunter like your mate."

"My—" Dev took an involuntary step back. "Arta's not my mate."

"Tell that to your wolf. Like flint on steel, the two of you. Noticed it yesterday."

"You're mistaken. We hardly know one another."

"That's the man talking. The wolf knows different." She shrugged. "You'll figure it out, sooner or later. Wanted to talk to you about Sugar. Lucy hasn't seen him in days, and she's in a taking. Worried about her baby."

"Her baby is ten feet tall, Aunt Wee, and a sasquatch."

"Love doesn't see color or shape."

"I saw Sugar yesterday morning, and he was fine."

"I'll let Lucy know. That'll give her some comfort. Not going to mention Pratt or the orb. Nothing she can do about it, and it'll just send her into a tizzy."

"You know about that?"

"Yup, Verbena told me." She chuckled. "Remember when Sugar was a cub?"

"I do."

"Cutest little fluffball you ever seed. Earl Skinner's dogs got at him. Would've killed him, too, if your wolf hadn't run 'em off."

Dev grunted. "That little fluffball weighed close to a hundred pounds. I carried him five miles to Lucy's place. Five miles, Aunt Wee."

"You could have easily carried a car the same distance, and you know it."

"A car wouldn't have squirmed like a greased eel. He wiggled and licked my face the whole way."

"You did a good thing," Weoka said. "Found Sugar a home and gave a lonely old woman someone to love."

"I couldn't let Earl kill him."

"Could have, but you didn't. You saw what Pratt did to that gal upstairs. Sugar's as helpless as a rabbit. Find him, Dev, before Pratt does."

"I'll do my best, Aunt Wee. I promise."

She gave him an approving smile. "That's my boy. Knew I could count on you. Come inside and have a bite to eat."

"Thanks, but I grabbed something at the house."

"You'll eat again. You look poorly. Burning the midnight oil?"

"You could say that." A vision of Arta, naked and glorious, kneeling over him as she took him in her mouth, flashed through Dev's mind.

"Huh." Weoka squinted at him, and for a horrifying moment, he wondered if she could read his thoughts. To his relief, she merely said, "Winnie took off like her drawers were on fire. What ails her?"

"Biscuits," he said. "Apparently, there's a dearth."

"Nonsense, I made extra. The river told me I'd have company."

"That river sure does love to talk."

"And I listen," said Aunt Wee.

Dev followed her up the steps and into the kitchen, where they found Winnie munching on a biscuit.

Removing his hat, Dev hung it by the door. "I see you triumphed over evil. Was it an ugly fight?"

"You laugh, but it was a near thing," Winnie said. "That Arta eats enough to make a pig squeal mercy."

"No need to brangle," Weoka said. "I made extra."

Stepping into the pantry, she emerged with a jar of golden liquid and set it on the table. She crossed to the oven and removed a pan of biscuits and set them aside. The tantalizing smell made Dev's mouth water.

Eagerly, he watched Weoka transfer several of the little golden cakes to a dish with her gnarled hands. "Eat." Handing him the plate, she twisted the cap off the honey jar. "Have some honey, too."

Dev obeyed. Slicing open the biscuits, he slathered butter and honey on them and took a bite; the sweet, creamy taste of butter mingled with the sweet, sunlit taste of the honey on his tongue. Biscuits were a Southern staple, and memories of Aunt Wee's biscuits were woven into the fabric of his life. Cold mornings before school; lazy summer breakfasts with Trevil and Winnie down by the river; holidays, birthdays, and graduations; his first day working dispatch at the SO; and the day he was sworn in as sheriff—good days and bad days and countless so-so in-betweens—all had begun in Weoka's kitchen with this simple breakfast. Aunt Wee's biscuits were more than flour and lard. They were magic, seasoned with otherworldly knowledge and some doughy secret known only to her.

"The honey tastes different," he remarked, trying to decipher the bright note hidden within the elixir. "Like flowers."

"Lavender." Aunt Wee smiled in approval. "Lucy's bees buzzed around my lavender in May."

"Lucy's place is more than five miles away," Winnie said. "Bees fly that far?"

"They will for the right nectar," Weoka said. "Besides, we have an understanding, Lucy's bees and I. Full of secrets, bees."

Winnie leaned back in her chair. "Bees. Have secrets."

"Sure do. They see and hear all kinds of things. When's the last time you paid attention to a bee?"

"Um…let me see. Never."

"There you go," Weoka said. "The sooner you figure out you don't know everything, young lady, the better off you'll be."

Dev set his plate in the sink. "You haven't lost your touch, Aunt Wee. Now, if you'll excuse me, I'd like a word with Verbena."

"She's not here. Lit out with Gryffin before daybreak."

"*What?* Why didn't you stop her?"

"Didn't know she was gone until I got up."

"Gryffin's unstable. Verbena could be in danger. If he hurts her—"

Dev broke off, shaking his head.

Weoka's eyes narrowed. "You're mighty worked up over a gal you hardly know."

"She's my—" He caught himself and coughed. "Responsibility."

"That right? Seems to me, the gal's got a mind of her own. Half wild, in case you ain't noticed. Not one to be roped or hemmed."

"Where did they go?"

"No telling. My guess is, Gryffin hightailed it to avoid them demon hunters. Don't blame him. Ought to leave him alone, if you ask me."

A door slammed, interrupting them, and Evan Beck stomped downstairs. His darkly handsome face was flushed, and his purple eyes glittered with anger. Chaotic energy burned around him.

Weoka met him at the foot of the stairs. "Take it easy, son. You're a cat's hair away from monstering out. What's got you so hot under the collar?"

"I'm not your—" Evan clenched his fists. "Whatever. Arta's ordered Taryn back to the Temple of Divine Hoo-has. *And she's going.*"

"Seems sensible. The gal needs peace and quiet to recover from the blight. Said so yourself."

"With me," Evan shouted, thumping his chest. "*I* was going to take care of her, goddammit, but no. Arta says jump, and Red says, 'Which hoop?'"

Dev stepped between his aunt and the furious demonoid. "Calm down. Taryn's Kirvahni. If Arta ordered her to leave, she has to obey."

"The hell she does," Evan said savagely. "We're a team. I thought that we—" He shook his head. "Forget it. I'm outta here."

He stormed out of the house.

A chair scraped in the kitchen, and Winnie sauntered into the hall. "Peach of a guy. Taryn's significant other, I presume?"

"Evan's got a temper, but he's not a bad sort," his aunt said. "Demonoid, you know."

"No, I didn't." Winnie's voice was dry. "Dev forgot to mention him. Dev's forgotten to mention a lot of things lately."

"I've been preoccupied," Dev said.

"Yeah." Winnie's lips curved in a sly smile. "I think we both know what you've been preoccupied with."

As if on cue, Arta appeared on the landing above them. "My sister will importune you no longer, Lady Weoka," she said in her clear, cool voice. "She has returned to the temple."

Watching her glide down the steps, Dev was aware of a jolt of lust and recognition, and a sense of absolute rightness.

Mine. Mine. Mine. The wolf's possessive snarl vibrated in his bones.

Down, boy, Dev told the wolf. *I think the lady might disagree.*

In fact, he knew she would, but that didn't mean he liked it.

"Evan told us," Weoka said to the huntress. "He's nuts about that sister of yourn. Pretty het up that she's gone."

"In truth, Taryn was reluctant to depart, but I insisted. 'Tis my duty to see to her care." Arta reached the bottom of the stairs. "In time, I daresay, she will forget her peculiar fascination with the demonoid."

"You trying to convince Taryn or yourself?"

Arta colored. "I–I do not take your meaning."

"Oh, I think you do." Weoka turned to Dev. "Meant to tell you, a young man stopped by this morning. Strapping blond fellow by the name of Kurt…" The wrinkles in her brow deepened. "Or maybe it was Kody?" She shrugged. "Said he knew you and Arta."

"Korth?" Arta grabbed Weoka by the arm. "Was his name, perchance, Korth?"

"Hmm," Weoka said, looking thoughtful. "Now I think on it, you may be right."

"Whither did he go?" Arta cried. "Please, milady. You must tell me at once."

"Dunno. He looked hungry, like he hadn't eaten in days, so I gave him some biscuits and sent him on his way."

The air hummed, and the captain of the Dalvahni appeared, along with Grim, a huge warrior with golden eyes.

Conall bowed to Weoka. "Greetings, Lady of the River. Grim and I have come to escort our brother Gryffin back to the Great Hall."

"Can't," Weoka said. "He's gone, and before you ask, no. I don't know where he went."

"My brother is weak and befuddled." Grim was visibly upset. "Should he encounter Pratt, I fear he will be undone."

"Come, Grim," Conall said. "We must find him at once."

"Gryffin's not alone," Dev said. "Verbena is—"

But the warriors had already disappeared.

"Great," Dev said. "Fantastic."

"Something bothering you, boy?" Aunt Wee asked. "You seem out of sorts."

"'Out of sorts'?" Dev said. "On top of a morgue full of dead shifters, a murder victim, and a lunatic god running around, I've got three missing persons."

"Four," Arta said. "Do not forget the missing thrall."

Winnie's brows shot up. "'Thrall'?"

"Sexual companions that serve the Kir and the Dal," Arta said. "This particular thrall is named Korth."

"Well, well," Winnie purred. "You have been busy."

"'Tis not what you think," Arta said, flushing. "Korth but appeared."

"*Appeared*'? What is your vagina, an interdimensional beacon?"

"Don't be crude, Winifred," Weoka said. "Dev's plate is full, and you're not helping." She turned to Dev. "What you need is a tracker who can sniff out supers. Do you know Toby Littleton?"

"Gray-haired shifter," Dev said. "Used to be the bouncer at Beck's before the bar burned down?"

Weoka nodded. "He's your man. The Great Snozzola, they call him."

"Do you trust him?"

"Absolutely. Known him these seventy-five years and more."

"That's good enough for me." Dev turned to Winnie. "Find Toby Littleton and bring him to me."

"Toby Littleton." Winnie scribbled a note on the pad she kept in her pocket. "Got it."

They were interrupted by a dissonant bray outside.

"What now?" Dev said.

He strode to the window and looked out. A horde of muscle-bound warriors had sprouted on Weoka's lawn like mushrooms after a rain. Raising a panpipe to his lips, a leather-clad warrior sounded a jarring note. The legion roared in response and stamped their feet.

"The Dal," Arta murmured, joining Dev at the window. "Come to welcome their long-lost brother back into the fold, no doubt."

"Gryffin's not here."

"Aye, but they do not know that. I fear Conall and Grim neglected to impart that information."

There was a bugle blast from the top of the slope. The army wheeled about, weapons drawn.

"Aw, hell." Dev jerked open the door and tore down the back steps. "Stand down, Jeb," he shouted. "Stand *down*."

Aunt Wee followed Dev out of the house. "Them boys look hungry, Dev," she called after him, flapping a dishrag. "Bring them to the house when you're done playing. I'll put another batch of biscuits in the oven."

Chapter Twelve

The motorized carriage prowled down the road with the satisfied purr of a contented cat. Cool air flowed from the molded surface Dev called the "dashboard," but Arta took no notice. The Kir and the Dal were seldom affected by heat or cold—she glanced at the man beside her—unless it came from a certain source. He stared straight ahead, his strong, lean hands gripping the wheel. Hands that had pleasured and delighted her. Clever hands with clever fingers that had stroked her body, as though memorizing every curve and hollow.

The place between her thighs clenched and throbbed at the thought of their joining. Coupling with the shire reeve had been exhilarating. Faith, but a few hours in the man's company had left her giddy as an unbreached maid.

She frowned. Her reaction to him was baffling. She was Kirvahni and immortal, not some green chit. Through the long ages of the hunt, she had enjoyed many thralls, emptying herself of desire and emotion as prescribed by the Directive. Afterward, she had departed without a backward glance. Not so with the shire reeve. Upon their first acquaintance, thoughts of him had nipped at her like gadflies, disturbing her tranquility and disrupting her focus. Mulling the matter over, she had concluded an imbalance of the humors was to blame. She had been too long without physical release, she reasoned, and a vigorous bedding was in order. Confident that a shake of the sheets would set things a-right, she'd tracked Dev to his lair. Alas, far from slaking her desire, sex with Dev had sharpened her appetite and left her hungry for more.

By the gods, if this endless, gnawing craving was the fate of the thralls, then she pitied them.

She stole another look at his strong, unyielding jaw. Devlin, a fierce name for a fierce man. Impossible to tell what he was thinking behind that calm, unyielding façade. Stoic as any demon hunter was the shire reeve, his mirrored spectacles a kind of armor that shielded him from others. How had he passed among mortals and kith alike without detection? She had known him for a super at once, though she had not guessed he was a demigod.

'Twas an error in discernment that chafed her still.

She assessed him through her lashes. Since lying with him, she could see his aura. Doubtless it had something to do with the strange and exhilarating energy they had exchanged during coitus. When the shire reeve had climaxed in the shower, her body had pulsed and shimmered with the light of a thousand stars, and she had tumbled after him into indescribable bliss. Since then, she could assess his mood at a glance. In the pleasant afterglow of coitus, his nimbus had been shimmering silver. Presently, his aura was bluish-green—the shire reeve was deep in thought, and his hunter instincts were fully engaged. It puzzled her, this odd new connection. It was startling and uncomfortable, too intimate and too much, and she was not at all sure what to do about it.

It was happening again, she realized with a stab of annoyance. She was obsessing over the provoking man. By the Vessel, she would conquer this fixation.

Forcing her gaze from his countenance, she stared out the window at the trees that formed a verdant tunnel. The earth magic here was strong. If she let her eyes go unfocused, she could see the dancing energy all around them.

"You're mighty quiet," Dev said. "Are you okay?"

The sound of his deep, masculine drawl sent a responsive hum through her. Faith, but she liked the way he talked. He had a way of lingering over certain words, as though caressing them, that pleased her.

Truth be told, *he* pleased her, this quiet, confident man of resolve.

"Arta?"

"I was but marking the green."

The words came out a husky rasp. *Have a care, Arta. He will guess his effect on you.*

Unthinkable. A huntress had her pride. A huntress had her duty.

A huntress would soon depart this realm and leave the shire reeve behind. Her stomach hollowed at the thought.

"Trees we got," Dev said, unaware of her inner turmoil. He guided the carriage over a hill and down the other side. "You seem distracted. Something on your mind?"

"Nothing, I assure you."

"Liar. I know when someone's buffaloing me."

"'Buffaloing' you?"

"Not telling the truth."

"I am not accustomed to having my veracity questioned," she said with a touch of asperity.

"Then don't tell whoppers."

"'Whoppers'?"

"Don't lie to me."

"I did not—" She bit her lip. "Tiresome man. Do you always know when someone is untruthful?"

"Pretty much, although I don't always know why." He glanced over at her. "Like now. I know something has upset you, but I don't know what." He let the words simmer between them. "Are you going to tell me, or not?"

Arta folded her hands in her lap. "I am not."

"Very well. What *do* you want to talk about?"

"The near fracas between the behemoth and the Dal. You managed the situation well, methinks."

"Nah, you did the hard part when you calmed down the Dalvahni. All I did was put a shield between them and Jeb."

The admiration in his tone warmed her. Alarming. She needed no man's approval.

Except, perhaps, this one's.

She shook off the thought. "I only had to remind them that the behemoth is under the Lady Weoka's protection," she said. "The Dal are hotheaded and feckless, but not wholly without reason. Your aunt's offer of sustenance helped. Her biscuits seemed to have a palliative effect."

"Yup. Aunt Wee's biscuits will fix whatever ails you."

"The Dal certainly seemed to enjoy them, and the ham and honey, too. She produced enough viands to feed an army in the twinkling of an eye."

He shot her a grin. "She *is* a goddess. I think we can safely assume magic was involved."

"But of course." Wedging her shoulders against the door, Arta studied him. "What was it like, being reared by so powerful a deity?"

"You tell me. You were raised by a god."

"*Trained* by a god. The Kir and the Dal were created, not born."

He gave her a glance of surprise. "You have a belly button. I've seen it."

Of a certainty, he had. Hot memories of their entwined bodies flashed through her head. His lips and tongue had traced the outline of the indention in her belly, nibbling, licking. Mercy, the man had an uncanny knack for disturbing her composure.

"Kehvahn is meticulous," she said. "Else we could not pass among mortals unremarked."

"You didn't have a childhood?"

"My earliest memory is of archery practice in the Temple of Calm. In Earth years, I would have been twelve."

"That doesn't seem fair."

"You cannot mourn what you ne'er had."

He was silent for a moment. "I had it good growing up," he said at last. "Not every kid has a pooka for a swim coach."

"Thank the gods," Arta said. "I esteem your lady aunt, but I marvel at her lenience."

"Trevil's all right. Supers are drawn to Aunt Wee. It was nothing for me to come home from school and find an alicorn in the garden shed, or a clutter of brownies in the pantry."

"She exudes a peculiar energy, to be sure."

"She's like a beacon."

Arta sighed. "Would that Korth had tarried in her company. The incubi are too powerful to wander unattended."

"We'll find him." His hands tightened on the wheel. "Remember our deal. You're mine for now."

For now. Temporarily, which was as it should be, given their disparate paths and lives. Why, then, did she feel utterly desolate at the notion of leaving him?

Shaking off her melancholy, she steered the conversation onto safer ground. "The elderly shifter with the extraordinary nose..."

"Littleton?"

"Yes, Littleton. Constable Parks will assist Winnie in locating him?"

Dev shook his head. "Parks is a norm. Winnie and I handle the 'special' details and leave the mundane stuff to the others." A corner of his mouth kicked up. "Though 'mundane' might not be the right word. You wouldn't believe some of the stuff norms get up to."

"Such as?"

"Tipping cows. Blowing up duck blinds. Pulling a beer keg couch behind a tractor."

"Beg pardon?"

"There was a party, and Verne Newton—the guy in question—was supposed to bring the booze. He didn't have a truck, so he borrowed his uncle's tractor and stacked a dozen kegs on his aunt's sofa. Her *favorite* sofa, one of those old-fashioned settees with velvet upholstery and cherry legs. Belonged to her grandmother, I think."

"I am filled with foreboding. What happened?"

Dev chuckled. "Couldn't resist sampling the beer. Said it was his duty to make sure it wasn't flat. He got sloppy drunk and wound up in a ditch."

"A man of principle. You detained him?"

"Yep. Wrote him up for driving under the influence and threw him in the county jail to sober up."

"And the divan?"

"Ruined, or at least the upholstery was," Dev said. "Verne forgot to close the tap, and it leaked—all over the sofa. His aunt was livid."

"Please," Arta said. "Tell me another."

"Well, let's see..." Dev drummed his fingers on the steering wheel. "Had a couple of rednecks steal a utility pole once. Thing must've been thirty feet long and weighed over five hundred pounds. How they got it on top of their car, I have no clue. They lost it on the highway. Caused a four-car pileup. It was a miracle no one was killed." He glanced at her. "They stole it for scrap, see? Felony theft of property."

Arta did not see, but she loved to hear him talk. "Go on," she said, giving him an encouraging nod.

"Then there was the drunk who decided his life was incomplete without a pet alligator."

Provider? Swiftly, Arta connected with the Kirvahni information source. *What is an alligator?*

An image of a large, armored reptile with a rounded snout and an alarming number of sharp teeth appeared in her mind.

"A fearsome beast," she said aloud. "What happened?"

"He tied a rope around a gator and tried to take it home," Dev said. "The gator objected. Bit the guy's arm off at the elbow. He nearly bled to death."

"Pain is a brutal tutor."

"Oh, he didn't learn a damn thing. Six months later, he tried it again. We found his body in the river—or what was left of it."

"The man was a dolt."

"Unfortunately, he's not unique," Dev said. "Had a burglar once who got himself pantsed."

Arta frowned. "I do not—"

"Lost his trousers on a fence."

"Ah," she said. "How?"

"It was a holiday weekend," Dev said. "He broke into the county health office outside Paulsberg. Thought there'd be drugs inside, I guess. The alarm was triggered, and he panicked. Caught his jeans on the metal fence on the way out." He paused. "He was commando."

"'Commando'?"

"Naked."

"His rudder and plums were exposed?"

"For all the world to see," Dev said, grinning. "The alarm company called the clinic director first, and that caused a delay. By the time we arrived on the scene, our would-be burglar was almost asphyxiated. A human's lungs are meant to sit on top of the other organs, not the reverse."

"'Twould seem between the kith and the norms, you are much occupied."

"Never a dull moment."

She gave him a curious glance. "You enjoy it?"

"Most of the time." He shrugged. "Wouldn't know what else to do."

The woods ended, and the carriage rolled through rumpled farmland dotted with bales of hay. The morning sun turned the stubbled fields to burnished gold. Cows grazed, heads down, or lazed in thickets of scrubby trees to avoid the humid heat. Arta found the landscape peaceful and idyllic.

"But you will have to, will you not, in due course?" she murmured, gazing out the window at the bucolic scene.

"Have to what?"

"Find another vocation." She turned her head to look at him. "You are a demigod and will not age. Sooner or later, the humans around you are bound to notice."

He groaned. "You're right. I never thought about that. Guess I'm not much brighter than Mr. Rudder and Plums."

You have dismayed him, curse your unruly tongue.

"You could take up arms with me in pursuit of the djegrali," she said without thinking. "Though, I daresay, you would not care for it."

Dev wheeled the carriage onto the grassy berm and killed the engine. Snatching his mirrored spectacles from his face, he tossed them aside. His eyes blazed.

"Arta, did you just ask me to come away with you?"

Her face grew hot. "Nay, I spoke in haste."

"Don't do that. Don't push me away." He reached across the seat and pulled her close. "Tell me you meant it."

"And bolster your overweening vanity?" Arta played with the top button of his shirt. "I think not."

"Vixen." Bending his head, he pressed his lips to hers. "Kiss me."

"Nay, why should I?"

"Because I need you. Because I want you." His arms tightened around her. "Because if you don't kiss me, right here and now, I'm lost."

Faith, but he was a prettily behaved devil when he wished to be. One kiss could surely do no harm.

Relaxing against him, she trailed her lips along his stern jawline and captured his firm mouth with hers. His aura flared red, and the heat of his body enveloped her. Recklessly, she pressed on. He smelled of sandalwood and soap and *male*, an altogether heady combination. She coaxed his mouth open. Their tongues danced, an exquisite slide of velvet on velvet that made her blood sing. Trailing her hand down his hard, muscled abdomen to his groin, she found his shaft straining against the fabric of his jeans. Triumph and relief surged through her. Praise the gods, she did not burn alone.

"Jesus." Dev arched against her hand. "Arta, you—"

"Sheriff Whitsun, what *are* you doing?" a sharp voice said from the back seat.

With a startled curse, Arta pushed Dev away and whirled around. Meredith Peterson sat in the back of the patrol car. The ghost wore a clingy, sleeveless red dress with a high neck and high-heeled silver and gold shoes. Her blond hair was scraped back from her pinched face, and her thin mouth was painted bright red.

Arta stared at the apparition in surprise. "'Tis the shade from the forest, she of the poisonous tongue."

"I'm a townie, stupid, not from the forest," Meredith said. "And tongues you should know about. You had yours shoved far enough down the sheriff's throat." Her malevolent gaze narrowed. "What *are* you wearing?"

Arta straightened her rumpled shirt. "'Tis called a uniform."

"It's hijus. I'm dead, and I have more fashion sense."

Dev picked up his mirrored spectacles and slid them back in place. "Mrs. Peterson," he said, the greeting measured and polite. "What can I do for you?"

"I'm here about your little friend." The ghost tittered. "The one who got herself freeze-dried."

Dev's mouth hardened. "I don't care for that term. Did you know Livy?"

"Of course not." Meredith smoothed her hands down her skinny form. "Livy Freeman worked in a papermill, and this dress is a Balmain. We didn't run in the same circles."

"Then why are you here?"

"As a concerned citizen, of course. Civic duty and all that." She twirled a finger. "Rah rah, vomit, puke."

"I doubt that very much," Dev said. "The truth, if you please."

"If you must know, I'm here about that twat maggot, Elizabeth Mullins Barber." Meredith made a face. "*Bootsie*, they call her."

"What about her?"

"I hate that freckled heifer."

"I'm afraid I don't see how—"

"She's the president-elect of the Lala Lavender League," Meredith snapped. "*I* was president-elect before I got offed and Trish and Blair nominated her."

"Trish and Blair?"

"My so-called BFFs. Those trash goblins ruined my club."

Dev's brows rose. "'Your club'?"

"You're damn straight it's my club. Bootsie Barber and her Neanderthal hubby aren't even from Hannah. They grew up in Paulsberg."

"Fascinating, but what does any of this have to do with Livy?"

"You want to find out who killed her, don't you?"

"Very much."

"Love, lust, loathing, and loot." Meredith ticked off the list on her fingers. "Those are the prime motives for murder. Even *I* know that, and I didn't go to cop school." She leaned closer. "Word has it, Russ Barber is hurting for money."

"And you know this how?"

"Ghosts talk, sweetie. Bull Barber conked from a heart attack five years ago. Two double cheeseburgers a day with fries and an extra side of stress will do that to a person." She admired her manicured nails. "It took Bull twenty years to make R&B Transport a success and less than three for Russ to run it into the ground. Big Daddy isn't happy with his baby boy."

"Livy wasn't rich," said Dev, "so loot doesn't fit."

"She was wearing Russ's bracelet when she died, wasn't she? Maybe they were having a thing. Maybe Livy was pressuring Russ to leave the heifer. *Maybe* he whacked her to keep her quiet."

Dev went still. "Funny. I don't recall mentioning a bracelet."

"Didn't you?" Meredith opened her eyes wide. "Goodness me, I must've heard it on the 'net."

"That's a lie. I don't like lies, Mrs. Peterson."

"Enough," Arta said, losing patience. "The truth, shade, and now."

"Watch your tone, Stork Legs," Meredith snapped. "I don't like—"

Arta curled her fingers into a fist, and the ghost's torso pinched sharply inward.

"Ow, *ow*," Meredith cried, struggling to escape Arta's crushing grip. "Stop!"

"The bracelet," Arta said. "How did you learn of it?"

"All right, all *right*," Meredith said. "I was at the scene yesterday when the body was found. I heard you talking. Satisfied?"

"More lies." Arta squeezed until the ghost's form narrowed to a thread. "Had you been there, I would have sensed your presence."

"Fat chance, slut waffle," Meredith shrieked. "You were too busy mooning over Hottie McTottie, the-sheriff-with-a-body, to notice your own tits."

Arta flushed and released the ghost. "I was not—"

Meredith regained her former shape with an audible *pop*. "The hell you weren't. What gives? You almost made me ectoplasm on my new dress."

"I care not a whit for your raiment." Arta flexed her fingers in warning. "What else did you hear?"

"Nothing, I swear," Meredith said, cringing. "Just that Livy was wearing some tacky bracelet Russ gave her in high school."

Arta turned to Dev. "Shire reeve?"

"She's telling the truth."

"Very well." Reluctantly, Arta lowered her hand.

"That hurt." Meredith glowered at Arta. "I should haunt your ass for that."

"You are welcome to try." Arta produced a small bottle with a flourish. "Methinks, however, you would not care for the consequences."

"Careful," the ghost said, drawing back in alarm. "Don't wave that thing around. It's dangerous."

"It's just a perfume bottle," Dev said.

Meredith shuddered. "No, it's not. Ask her."

"Arta?"

"'Tis a djeval flaske," she explained to Dev. "Such vessels are used by our kind to transport demons."

"Transport them where?"

"To the Pit, a prison for rogue demons." Arta waggled the bottle at the phantom. "Troublesome spirits, as well."

"Okay, I'll play nice, I promise," Meredith said, shrinking against the seat. "Just put that thing away."

Arta slid the flask back in her pocket. "I very much doubt you know how to behave."

Meredith gave her a baleful look and turned to Dev. "I'm right, aren't I? Russ Barber's a person of interest?"

"Maybe, maybe not. We're still gathering evidence."

"So discreet." The ghost batted her lashes at him. "Come on, Sheriff. You can trust little ole me."

"Sorry. I can't discuss the case."

"Oh, pooh." Meredith stuck out her bottom lip. "You're no fun."

"You wouldn't be the first person to say that about me." Dev regarded her curiously. "Do ghosts really talk to one another?"

"Oh my God, all the *time*. They never shut up, probably because eternity is boring AF."

"What sorts of things do you talk about?"

Meredith lifted a bare shoulder. "The usual—family dysfunction, things we wish we'd done. Things we wish we *hadn't* done. Like the time I borrowed my cousin Stacey's foundation. Stacey's an ivory gal, and I'm Totes McGoats porcelain. I was *orange*." The shade shivered. "Orange is not in my color wheel."

"Have you—" He hesitated. "Have you spoken to Livy?"

"Nope, haven't seen her. Probably still hanging around. It happens sometimes with fresh murks, you know. The shock, I guess."

"Murks?"

"Murder victims, like me." Meredith splayed one hand on her narrow chest. "There are tons of us. We compare deaths. The more gruesome the death, the more points you get. You should hear some of the saints." She rolled her eyes. "They go on and on, bunch of whiners." She leaned closer, sending a wave of scent into the front of the vehicle. "I've got the goods, Sheriff. You should totally ditch the stork and deputize me, though I refuse to wear that tacky uniform. I have a reputation for style, you know. I'm featured in *Corpse Couture*."

"Congratulations," Dev said, "but I'm afraid the uniform is part of the job."

"You're the sheriff. Make an exception."

"No."

"Fine, but you're making a big mistake," Meredith said, pouting. "I'm a ghost. I can go anywhere. Without a warrant." Her lips flattened. "Unless I've been banished. Banishment is the worst."

"Woe unto the unfortunate priest who performed the offices," Arta murmured.

"I said I was *banished*, not exorcised, Storky. It's the Fairy Fart's fault."

"Fairy Fart?"

"Try and keep up, dim bulb," Meredith said. "I'm talking about my sister-in-law, Sassy Peterson." Sparks of raw energy crackled around the irate ghost. "She got herself a fairy infusion."

"A fairy infusion?" Dev straightened. "I've met Sassy Peterson. I'm intrigued."

"You want to know how she got fairyified? The Goody Two-shoes stuck her nose where she shouldn't have, that's how," Meredith said.

"She got crossways with a hag who was trapping fairies and got a dose of fairy essence."

"A hag?" Dev's aura turned a shimmering indigo. "Was it Ora Mae Luker, by any chance?"

"How should I know?" Meredith said. "Do I look like I run around with creepy old crones? I'll tell you what I *do* know. Sassy booted me to the curb, the nasty little gumdrop, and now she and Butt Boy are living in *my* house."

"Butt Boy?" Arta said. "I fear I do not—"

"Grim Dalvahni, flea brain. A gorgeous hunk of manscape, if ever there was one. Golden eyes and ass for days. Gluteus to the maximus."

"Have a care, shade," Arta said. "You speak of a Dalvahni warrior."

"I may be dead, but I can still look," Meredith said, "and Butt Boy is hawt."

Arta eyed the ghost with dislike. "You say you hate the Barber woman, yet 'tis the husband you seek to destroy. Why?"

"Think about it, gee-nius. If Russ goes to prison for Livy's murder, the heifer will be disgraced. No more Bootsie Barber in my club." Meredith gave Dev an oozing smile. "Call me if you change your mind, Sheriff. And I do mean any old time. The number is on my card. I've got Spectre."

She disappeared in a wave of sickly sweet perfume.

Chapter Thirteen

Dev restarted the carriage and opened the windows. "Whew, what a smell. It's giving me a headache." He eased the vehicle back onto the road. "That devil flask thing, how does it work?"

"In their natural form, demons are incorporeal," Arta said. "Wraiths, humans call them. They are drawn into the flask."

"And taken to prison? Why not send them back where they came from?"

"We cannot. Pratt ripped the Veil eons ago and released the djegrali."

"Why the hell did he do that?"

"As a distraction, I suppose, to allow him to take the orb."

"Can the Veil be mended?"

"Nay, 'twas set into place by the Maker of All Things. Only He can restore it." She motioned to the road ahead. "You mean to question the Barber man?"

"Headed to R&B Transport to do that now. I want some answers."

His tone was brooding. Glancing at him, Arta saw that his handsome face was set.

"What ended your friendship with Livy?" she asked, spurred by a compulsion she did not understand. "Were you—" She swallowed. "Were you perchance jealous?"

"Yeah, a little, I guess."

Arta's throat and chest prickled. "You were in love with her?"

"No, we were buddies. Friends since the fourth grade." His face twisted. "Until I blew it, but you don't want to hear about that."

"To the contrary." Arta laced her fingers together and placed her hands in her lap. "I should very much like to hear it." She hesitated. "Perhaps, though, you do not wish to confide in me?"

"It's not that. I—" He exhaled. "Aw, hell. I was an asshat, okay?"

"Asshat?"

"An idiot."

He was silent, and Arta waited.

"It happened the end of the first week of school when Livy and I were in the ninth grade," he said at last, rewarding her patience. "We were feeling our oats, so we swiped a six-pack of Blue Ribbon out of the fridge in her dad's barn to celebrate."

"Blue Ribbon?"

"Beer."

"Ah," said Arta.

"Her dad was a farmer, and we sneaked into a cornfield behind Livy's house to drink," Dev continued. "I popped open a can of PBR"—he made a small explosive sound—"and took a swig. I didn't much care for the taste, but I wouldn't admit it. Teenage boys are all about being cool. 'No, like this,' Livy said, holding up her can. 'Russ showed me,' and then she chugged her beer."

"Russ Barber?"

"Yes," Dev said. "Livy and Russ met at Terri Osborne's back-to-school swim party. Terri Osborne was two years ahead of us in school. Juniors don't usually have anything to do with ninth graders, but Russ had a habit of checking out the new girls. Apparently, Livy caught his eye, and he wheedled Terri into inviting her. He and Livy hit if off at the party, and he asked her out."

Arta sifted through this. "He was courting her, and she confessed this to you whilst in her cups?"

"Yeah. I didn't take it well."

"You argued?"

"No, I drank my beer," Dev said, "and then I drank another. I don't remember anything after that. The next morning when I woke up, I was sitting on top of a grain silo fifteen stories off the ground. My stomach was full of turtles, and my head hurt like hell."

"You were bilious," Arta said with a wise nod. "From the drink, no doubt."

"No doubt."

She studied Dev. "You were drunk when you climbed the tower?"

"I guess. I don't remember. I almost passed out from shock when I saw the road to the Freeman farm. It was jammed with upended farm equipment. Balers, tractors, harrows, and a combine harvester, stacked on top of one another like a Jenga tower."

"I do not know this 'Jenga.'"

"It's a game," Dev said. "You make a tower out of small, wooden blocks and take turns removing the blocks, one at a time. If the tower falls, you lose. Sitting on top of the pile like the cherry on a hot fudge sundae was Mr. Freeman's truck. Farmers and emergency personnel and police were everywhere. It was a huge mess."

"And you were responsible."

"Yeah, and it gets worse. Someone shouted behind me, and I turned around. The sheriff was standing in the middle of an enormous crop circle."

"'Crop circle'?" Arta frowned. "You speak of runes?"

"More like a picture, a huge frigging picture in the middle of Clyde Freeman's cornfield."

"'Twas some demonic mischief to frighten the locals?"

"Demons weren't responsible." Dev's tone was grim. "I was. Inside this big circle was the likeness of a football player. And not just any old player, a player wearing Russ's jersey being humped by a wildcat. The words *Russ Barber Sucks* were burned in the dirt in letters a hundred feet high."

"I take it 'football' is a game?"

"More than a game, especially around here. Russ was a star player back in the day. Had scholarship offers and everything. The wildcat was our high school mascot."

Arta turned this over in her mind. "I see. You etched an image of Russ copulating with an animal into the grain to show your disdain?"

"Yeah. Told you. I was a major asshat."

"And then?"

"I climbed down." Dev stared straight ahead, as though lost in the memory. "Aunt Wee was waiting for me at the bottom of the silo. So was Livy. She'd seen the whole thing."

Arta sucked in her breath. "She betrayed you to the norms?"

"No, but she avoided me like the plague after that."

"Because you ruined her father's crop?"

"Because I scared the hell out of her. She didn't know magic existed or about my abilities."

"Then she must have been singularly foolish."

"People see what they want to see," Dev said, "and I was careful around her."

"She did not know you. You were not truly friends."

"She was the closest thing I had to one. None of the other kids in our class were supers."

"You had Winnie."

"It's not the same. Winnie's younger, and she's family. We didn't hang out back then."

"'Hang out'?"

"Do things together, stuff friends the same age do."

"I understand," Arta said. "You were not contemporaries."

"Right. She's five years younger. That's a big age difference when you're a teenager."

"And the shambles you made of the farm implements...your aunt made things right?"

He shook his head. "They called in a heavy crane from DOT to disassemble it. Afterward, though, everything worked fine. Better than fine. Livy's father used to brag that his old tractor ran like new, and he drove that pickup truck until the day he died. Never had to replace so much as a sparkplug."

"These mechanical marvels were your doing?"

"I figured it was the least I could do. That and I promised Livy I wouldn't drink. Didn't matter. She and Russ were an item, and then I..."

His voice trailed off.

"The gulf between you was too wide?"

"Yes, but I kept my promise. Haven't had a drink since...until last night. Livy was dead, it was a shit day, and there was a beer in the fridge." Color crept up his cheekbones. "I drank it. One beer, and it made me tipsy. That's my secret. I can't hold my liquor. No one knows, except Aunt Wee and now you."

"Not even Winnie?"

He shook his head. "Winnie can drink anyone under the table."

"'Tis her Dalvahni essence. The Kir and the Dal are impervious to alcohol."

"No kidding? That explains a lot."

"However," she continued, "we *are* susceptible to something called chocolate."

He threw her a startled look. "Really?"

"So I am told, though I do not speak from experience."

"You've never had chocolate?"

"I have not, although several of the Dal have imbibed."

"Yeah? Who?"

"Duncan, for one. He became inebriated on something called chocolate pie. You know him?"

"We've met."

"'Twas a terrible ruction, I am told. Demon hunters are cautioned to be vigilant and circumspect in the presence of mortals."

"*Don't alarm the norms,*" Dev said with a nod. "The Kith Council has a similar rule. What exactly did Duncan do?"

"He played a gittern—'tis similar to a lute."

"The bastard." He smacked the heel of his hand on the steering wheel. "Lock him up and throw away the key."

"You jest, but you do not understand," Arta said. "Duncan is Dal, not a mortal musician. His music is hypnotic. His song drew a large crowd of humans and supernatural folk."

"Uh-oh. This happened in Hannah?"

"Aye. The skellring was there, and Sildhjort. Your father assumed his human form, silver, horned, and naked."

"That's my pops."

"Satyrs and sylphs were with him and forest creatures of every sort," she continued. "Fairies swarmed the town square, and a clurichaun rode in on a dog. The imp, Irilmoskamoseril, was there, as well. Duncan's playing drove them into a frenzy, and a brawl ensued. 'Twas pandemonium. Illaria and Jaaka were left to make things right."

"Illaria and Jaaka?"

"Two of my sisters." She laid a hand on his muscled arm. "I tell you this for a reason, shire reeve. You, too, have regrets, I believe, especially where Livy is concerned, but think on this. When he became intoxicated on chocolate, Duncan was a warrior grown, eons old and battle-hardened, while you were scarcely more than a child. Chastise yourself no more, I beg you. You have been blessed with enormous talent. A weaker man than you would have chosen the path of destruction. Instead, you chose the path of a guardian. Methinks you have more than compensated for any youthful transgression."

Dev swore under his breath. Twisting the wheel sharply, he pulled onto the grassy embankment and yanked her close.

"Thank you, Arta." He gave her a hard, possessive kiss. "I needed to hear that."

"You are welcome." Lifting a trembling hand, she tidied an errant lock of hair. "Most assuredly."

He flashed her a smile that heated her blood, then guided the vehicle back onto the road.

Arta sat frozen in her seat, her heart fluttering against her ribs like a trapped bird. What was happening to her? She had faced legions of demons, armies of scorpion men in the crumbling tombs of Challahuk, and the giant Gogmagog on the Isle of Albion without flinching, but Dev unsettled her. She was like a greedy child sampling a tray of sweets. She wanted more. She wanted everything.

She wanted to fly and not look back.

She straightened her shoulders. Nay, she would abide. A Kirvahni huntress was not craven; a Kirvahni huntress was resolute and unwavering. She would conquer this madness, an it killed her.

'Twas a possibility, she reflected gloomily, that grew ever more likely by the hour.

They drove on past rumpled brown and yellow fields enclosed by wire-and-post fences, faded houses, and outbuildings. Shallow gullies lined the roadways, choked with tufts of blistered grass and brightly colored wildflowers. Here and there, a cylindrical tower rose from the ground like the upraised fist of some long-buried giant. Granaries, according to the Provider, similar to the one Dev had scaled in his youth. The shire reeve was a redoubtable man. The boy? Separated from others by heredity and abilities that must be kept secret, the boy, she suspected, had oft been lonely.

Loneliness—this, too, they had in common. As High Huntress, Arta knew well the cost of isolation and power.

Dev turned onto another paved road and headed south. They topped a slight rise. In the distance, Arta spied a rocky watercourse.

"Khoalisskaliss," she murmured, admiring the sparkling umber surface.

"Say what?"

"The snake goddess of Qia Leapoth," Arta said. "In the beginning, there was nothing but water and Khoa, endlessly roaming the deep. After a time, she knew the pangs of hunger and brought forth the fishes, consuming them in great numbers. The bones curdled in her belly. These she disgorged, and islands rose from the spew. On the largest of these, Onyi-ali, she took her rest, sloughing her skin in the warm sand. Animals, large and small, sprang from her discarded hide. Pleased, Khoa breathed forth the Qia, the first peoples, from her nostrils onto dry land, and they multiplied."

"That's quite a tale," Dev said. "Reminds me of the stories Aunt Wee used to tell when I was a kid."

"'Tis no tale. Together, Khoa and I routed the djegrali from the city of Qiapoth. The *morkyn* had established a stronghold there, and the battle to drive them back was brutal."

"*Morkyn*?" His voice sharpened. "Yesterday, that thing in the woods called itself *morkyn*."

"Of a certainty. The *morkyn* command the *tathul*, the rank and file of the djegrali. Together, they travel from world to world, wreaking havoc."

"Not in my county," Dev said. "Not if I can help it."

"You cannot keep them out," Arta said. "There are rifts between the worlds, and they slip through."

"Like roaches through a crack?"

"An apt description."

"Aunt Wee says there's a portal in Hannah."

"Several, more like. According to Conall, as fast as he closes one, another opens. The essence of the crater in this place draws *luthwa vonine* of every kind."

"Lootha whaty?"

"Supernatural creatures."

"You're talking about demons?"

"Nay." Arta's lip curled. "The djegrali are something altogether different. The *luthwa vonine* are creatures that mortals consider myths and legends."

"Like Trevil and that fellow Irilmoskamoseril."

"Speak not his name three times, I beg you, lest you summon him."

"Aw, come on. He didn't seem like a bad little guy."

"He is a rapscallion. The nibilanth are tricksters."

"If you say so." Dev glanced at the apparatus on his wrist. "It's ten thirty. Once we're done at R&B, we'll swing through Hannah and grab lunch at the Sweet Shop. Best food in the county." He waggled his brows at her. "They have chocolate pie. Maybe I'll get you drunk and take advantage of you."

He was outrageous.

"Need I remind you, sirrah, that I am on duty?" she said, pressing her lips together to keep from laughing. "The Behr County Policy Manual states, and I quote, 'A deputy shall avoid any intoxicant, medications, or combination thereof that might impair their ability to safely and completely perform their duties.' In my case, that means chocolate."

"When the hell did you have time to read the manual?"

"Last e'en at Winnie's before I sought you out."

"I'm surprised."

"You should not be. Am I not ever compliant?"

He laughed. "You're compliant, all right. Yesterday, I'd barely gotten the words, 'You're deputized,' out of my mouth before you took off."

"I *am* a demon hunter," she reminded him, "and Eamon needed my assistance."

"I thought you didn't like the Dal."

"Like has nothing to do with it. The Dal are vexing in the extreme, but we are plotted to the same course."

"You're family. I get that." He motioned to the weapon at her belt. "I'm glad you've read the manual, but you haven't qualified to carry a gun."

"And one does this how?"

"Practice. Winnie will take you to the range and put you through your paces."

"If you insist." The gun on Arta's hip disappeared. "But I have my bow and my knives."

"I've seen you with a bow. Are you as good with a knife?"

"Better."

"You terrify me." He pointed to a sign by the road. "This is our turn."

He guided the carriage onto a two-lane road that cut through a forest of scraggly pines. The noise from the highway faded, and the scents of resin and dry pine needles filled the Jeep. The vehicle rounded a bend, and the woods abruptly ended in a sprawling, treeless lot.

"R&B Transport," Dev announced.

Arta pointed to a neat row of large, bug-like compartments on wheels. "What might those be?"

"Tractor units," Dev said. "Basically, a towing engine for pulling large loads."

"And those?" She indicated a line of long metal rectangles.

"Dry vans. Hook one up to the tractor unit and away you go. The ones with no sides are called flatbeds. They're used for things like heavy equipment and construction materials."

"Tractor units, flatbeds, and dry vans," Arta repeated, committing the terms to memory.

"Most folks just call them semitrucks," Dev said. "Or eighteen-wheelers. Here comes one now, ready for the road."

An enormous wheeled contraption rumbled in their direction, dwarfing the shire reeve's vehicle. As the mechanical monster drew near, it emitted an earsplitting screech.

"'Strewth, it has an impressive roar."

"Truck horns come in handy," Dev said. "They warn other drivers that a truck is approaching. Wildlife, too. We have a lot of deer in Alabama."

He parked in front of a handsome building of tan brick with a slanted roof and floor-length windows. A shiny red vehicle sat in a parking space near the front door.

"I don't see Russ's truck," he said, "but that's Bootsie's Mercedes over there."

"You know every vehicle on sight?"

"No. There aren't a lot of Mercedes in Behr County, and I stopped Bootsie six or seven months ago for speeding. Seventy-five in a forty zone. That's reckless driving, but I cut her a break. She was crying and shaking and terribly upset. She was on her way to the hospital. Her dad had had a stroke." He tapped his right temple. "Knew she wasn't lying about it, and it was her first offense."

"You are too soft," Arta said. "An she broke the law, she should be punished."

"She was punished. She got a hefty fine and five points on her license. Her dad died a few days later. Bootsie's an only child." He slid out of the car. "When we get inside, let me do the talking."

"Why?"

"It's a small town, and they don't know you."

"As you wish."

Arta exited the vehicle on the other side, pausing as the hair rose on the back of her neck. She turned to scan the lot. Heat shimmered around the metal carcasses of the dry vans and trailers, and the tractor units seemed menacing—hulking beasts with watchful eyes. She inhaled and wrinkled her nose. Several acrid scents assaulted her senses, though not the rancid stench of demon. Regardless, something was amiss, though she knew not what.

A bird screeched high above them.

"Your friend is back," Dev said, squinting up at the hawk.

"Aye." Arta's gaze was on the lot. "Merta is ne'er far away."

"Shall we go inside?"

"Give me but a moment. There is something I would attend to first."

She dematerialized before he could protest and emerged on the far side of the lot near an empty trailer. She stalked around the open flatbed, her senses alert. Nothing. Disappointed, she looked around. There. The dry van parked away from the others. A jarring energy emanated from it.

She crossed the parking lot in a blip of movement. The doors in the back of the suspect van were secure. She opened them with a wave of her hand and sprang inside. The shell was empty. Letting her gaze go slightly unfocused, she perused the space once more. Dark energy zigzagged within the interior like swarms of loathsome insects. Though unpleasant, Arta knew at once the energy she sensed was not demonic residue. She inhaled. Humans in the deepest terror; the scent of their despair was palpable.

"Who are you," a harsh voice demanded behind her, "and what the hell are you doing in my van?"

Arta spun about. A large, beefy man glowered at her through the open doorway. Arta considered him. She was not adept at discerning the age of humans. Their appearance was too changeable, and a multitude of factors affected the mortal aging process—toil, climate, physical infirmities, grief, and inherited proclivities, to name a few. Children, she could quickly identify, of course, but adults were trickier to gauge. She judged this man to be in his fourth or fifth decade, if she were to hazard a guess. His hair was thinning, and his jowls and sagging belly bespoke years of overindulgence in food and drink.

"She's with me."

At the sound of Dev's deep drawl, the heavyset man whirled around, moving so quickly that he lost his balance and nearly fell.

Dev reached out and caught him, steadying the bigger man as easily as he might a toddler. "Leg still giving you trouble, is it?"

"You should know. You fucking broke it." The man clenched his fists. "You threw me thirty feet into the air."

"Now, Russ, don't start that again." Dev's tone was gentle. "You know that's not possible." He motioned to a small vehicle next to the van. "Nice UTV. I imagine it comes in handy."

"It's a big lot. I can't walk long distances, thanks to you."

Arta jumped lightly out of the van.

"Deputy Kirvahni," Dev said. "This is Russ Barber."

Arta inclined her head stiffly in greeting. But a few years separated this oaf from Devlin in age? 'Twas hard to fathom. Dev exuded the vitality of a man in his prime, whereas Russ Barber was a belligerent slug.

"This is private property," Barber said in a loud voice. "You and your deputies can't go poking around without a warrant."

"Arta's a new recruit," Dev said. "It's her first day on the job, and she's a little overzealous. I'd appreciate it if you'd take that into consideration."

"Like hell I will." Barber shoved his face in Arta's. "How'd you get in that van, girlie? I keep 'em locked."

"Draw back, you rump-fed mole wart," Arta said with a snarl, "else I will give you a lesson in manners."

Barber reddened. "What did you call me?"

"Stand down, Deputy," Dev said. "Russ, I'd advise you to move away from her." His voice held a hint of steel. "Now."

Barber stepped back. "All right," he blustered, "but I still want an answer."

"Arta?" Dev lifted a dark brow. "Kindly explain how you got inside Mr. Barber's van."

"The doors opened."

Strictly speaking, 'twas not an untruth. The doors *had* opened at her command.

Dev's eyes narrowed, but he said only, "There, you see, Barber? The doors were open."

"Bullshit. I keep my vans locked. It's an insurance issue."

"Very wise," Dev said. "You wouldn't want someone to get hurt."

Barber bristled. "What's that supposed to mean?"

"Nothing, nothing at all. The van is empty. No harm, no foul."

"Says you. You're lucky I don't sue you, Whitsun. Now, get out of here."

Barber limped back toward the cart.

"Hold on, Russ," Dev said. "We're here about Livy Freeman."

Barber halted and slowly turned. "What about her?"

"She's dead."

"Sorry to hear that, but what's it got to do with me?"

"She was wearing your bracelet when she died." Dev's voice was silky. "The one you gave her in high school."

"You're mistaken. I never gave her no bracelet."

"Come on, Russ." Dev sighed. "Everybody at BCH knew you gave Livy that bracelet. She wore it the whole time you dated."

"So what? Livy and I are ancient history. I'm a happily married man."

"Then why was she still wearing it?"

"How the hell should I know?" Barber's gaze met Dev's and skittered away. "Maybe she was still hung up on me. Some chicks are like that, you know. Can't move on. Doesn't prove I killed her."

"I said Livy was dead. I didn't say she was murdered."

Sweat popped out on Barber's forehead. "Didn't you? Guess I assumed it was foul play. Why else would you be here?"

Dev grunted. "I'd like a word with Bootsie. She around?"

"Nope. She's at her club. President-elect of the Lala Lavender League."

"I heard. Her car is parked out front. You sure she's not here?"

"She took my truck into town." Barber shifted uneasily on his bad leg. "She's having a fund-raiser at the house this weekend. Said she needed to stop by the flower shop on the way back. Didn't have room in her car for the arrangements."

"You're driving a truck now?" Dev said. "I still remember that Mustang you drove in high school."

"Big man needs a big truck. Got me a Ram 1500 Limited now. Brand new and fully loaded."

Dev whistled. "Sweet. That must've set you back a pretty penny."

"Ninety grand. More 'n you make in a year, I'll wager."

"You got me there." Dev drew a small pad from his shirt pocket and scribbled something down. "Honey of a business operation you've got here. As I remember, your dad's old place was outside of Paulsberg."

"We moved our facilities after Dad died. Bootsie thought we needed a fresh start." Barber eyed Dev nervously. "What's that you're doing?"

"Just making a few notes. Business good?"

"Business is fine."

"Glad to hear it," Dev said. "Where were you yesterday?"

"At my cabin on the river, fishing."

Dev looked up from his notes. "Fishing on a weekday?"

"I took the day off. What of it?"

"You there all day?"

"Till dark."

"Can anyone verify your whereabouts?"

"No—*yes*. Jim Stoddard at the Tackle Box. I bought bait."

Dev noted this information on the pad and slid it back in his pocket. "Deputy," he said, glancing at Arta, "do you have any questions for Mr. Barber?"

"Nay," said Arta.

"That's it, then. We'll be moving along." Dev offered Barber a bland smile. "Be sure and tell Bootsie I said hello."

Muttering under his breath, Barber limped back to the wheeled cart and climbed in. Arta followed Dev across the lot to the Jeep. Trucks rumbled past them, groaning and grinding. As they neared the patrol car, a sleek red vehicle sped away from the building. The woman behind the wheel gave them a cheerful wave as she motored past.

Arta stopped in her tracks. "Shire reeve, was that Bootsie Barber in yon carriage?"

"Yep."

"Barber lied?"

"Yep."

"Outrageous. We must track down the rascal at once and take him to task."

"Arta, if I stopped to chew out every person who lied to me, I'd never get anything done." Dev opened the driver's side door. "Besides, I got what I came for. Let's get something to eat."

Chapter Fourteen

Heat poured from the parked automobile. The inside of the SUV was roughly the temperature of hell and heat poured off the pavement in waves, but if Arta noticed, she gave no sign. Cool as a cucumber, his woman.

His woman. Dev liked the sound of that. They made a good team, he and the High Huntress. She'd asked him to come away with her. He smiled, picturing them battling demons side by side in another dimension.

He remembered his commitment to his job, and the smile faded. His predecessor, Teddy Liston, had been hopelessly norm, determined to ignore anything he labeled "wackadoo." Consequently, a lot of cases had gone unsolved...until Dev had joined the department. As a young deputy and a SNR—Super Not Registered—he'd quietly stepped in to deal with anything that smacked of the paranormal, and Liston had been happy to let him do it. Any case closed was a good case, as far as the old sheriff was concerned. Liston had eventually retired, still stubbornly in denial that strange things lived and breathed in Behr County.

If Dev left, another norm would most likely take his place. Not good. There had been an uptick in supernatural hanky-panky since he'd joined the force. A norm sheriff would be in deep water and not understand why. One day, though, Dev would have to walk away. That was the price of being immortal, but he had a few years left. So, where did that leave him and Arta? Somehow he doubted she'd hang around. The thought of losing her was unbearable, an iron fist clenched around his heart. Illogical, maybe, the intensity of his feelings for her, but undeniable.

Was it the sex? The sex was *great*—any better and he'd spontaneously combust—but his attraction to Arta went beyond the physical. Damn it, Aunt Wee was right. Arta was more than a booty call. She was the piece of himself he hadn't known was missing. She was his mate, indispensable to his happiness.

The wolf growled in agreement.

"Shire reeve?"

Dev came back to the present. "Yeah?"

"You snarled."

"I did?"

"Aye, like this." Arta gave a deep rumble, an exact imitation of his wolf.

Dev stared at her in surprise. "You speak wolf?"

"Wolf and the tongues of many other creatures. Animals are oft a demon hunter's guides and allies, especially if the locals are under the spell of the djegrali."

"Animals can't be possessed?"

"Aye, but seldom, and when they are, their forms are corrupted and easily marked."

"How so?"

"Know you many rabbits with fangs and claws and an insatiable appetite for violence?"

"Killer bunnies? Um, no."

"There you have it."

"I see," Dev said. "And humans?"

"Their eyes are as melted pitch."

"Liquid black." Dev recalled the decapitated woman lying on the floor of Sloan McCullough's store. It had been seventeen years since Winnie's grandfather had been murdered, but Dev remembered it like yesterday: the stench, the blood, the viscous goo, and the emaciated bodies of the robbers.

"Shire reeve?" Arta gave him an odd look. "What perturbs you?"

She perturbed him…in a thousand different ways. Arta Kirvahni was smart, sexy, deadly dangerous, and so beautiful she made his teeth ache. Other parts, too, if he were honest. He'd been in a constant state of arousal since they'd met. Damned awkward and unprofessional, but beyond his control. He could spend a month of Sundays in bed with Arta and still be horny as a teenager.

Maybe he was more like his father than he liked to think.

"Guess I'm surprised you speak wolf," he said, realizing he'd been standing by the Jeep without moving for several moments. "You're like an onion. You've got layers."

"And you are like a turnip—wont to hide your better self."

Dev grinned. "Touché."

They got into the Jeep with Arta riding shotgun. Cranking the engine, Dev set the AC to arctic blast and drove away from the building. On their way out, they met Russ Barber on his UTV. Heat shimmered and danced on the black asphalt, and the humidity was thick and viscous as Crisco. Red-faced and perspiring, Russ gave them a death glare as they drove by.

"That man would do you an injury, an he could," Arta remarked. "I like him not. He tried to browbeat me."

"I noticed. Why do you think I told him to step away?"

She gave an unladylike snort. "There was no need. As if such a one could daunt me."

"I wasn't worried about you. I was worried about Russ. I saw the look on your face. Poor guy didn't have a clue he was about to be gutted."

"An enticing notion, to be sure." The martial light in her eyes faded. "But I refrained. I did not think you would like it."

"Thank you," Dev said. "I'm deeply moved. You have no idea the amount of paperwork involved in an active-duty evisceration."

"Indeed?" She gave him a sharp look, and her mouth firmed. "You are roasting me."

"Maybe a little. All kidding aside, no more taking off on your own. We were at R&B to ask questions, not enter private property without a search warrant. That's a no-no, by the way, unless you have probable cause, which we don't."

"I know," she said. "'Twas in the manual."

"And you did it anyway."

She shrugged. "I am Kirvahni and unfettered by mortal strictures. I allowed the thrill of the hunt to overcome my judgment."

"Easy to do in the heat of the moment. So what did you find?"

She folded her hands and looked straight ahead. "Shire reeve, I would not for the *world* endanger your moral code."

"I appreciate the consideration, but I'll make an exception this once."

"Unthinkable. You are a man of principle."

"This is about the onion comment, isn't it?"

"A huntress does not care to be likened to a smelly, pungent bulb."

"I'm sorry, okay? No more vegetable references." He glanced at her delicate profile. "Come on. Don't make me beg."

She slid him a look so full of intimate mischief that it took his breath away. "Faith, but I already have. Last e'en, and more than once."

Dev was assailed by a stream of delicious images, Arta using her glorious body—her lips, teeth, hands, and tongue—to torture and delight him in a thousand wicked, sensual ways. Jesus H. Christ, she'd be the death of him.

He closed his eyes briefly and opened them again. "The van, Deputy. Was there evidence of demons?"

"Nay, I detected naught but human essence."

"Humans?" Dev felt a zing of surprise. "Are you certain?"

"Aye. The pall of their suffering was unmistakable."

"Good God, you think Russ is involved in human trafficking?"

"I did not say that." Arta's tone was cautious. "For aught we know, 'twas the driver's doing. Barber could be blameless."

Dev ground his teeth. "Yeah, and I'm the man in the moon."

"Shire reeve, you did it again."

"What?"

"Growled."

"Sorry." Dev took a deep breath. "I'm finding it hard to be objective about this case."

"'Tis natural. You loathe the Barber man, and Livy was your friend. Think you he lied about his whereabouts yesterday?"

"He wasn't lying when he said he went fishing," Dev said. "Though it galls me to admit it." He picked up the handheld radio. "Willa Dean, have we gotten any reports from the Feds about human trafficking?"

The receptionist's gruff, no-nonsense voice crackled back at him. "In Behr County? No way."

"I didn't think so."

"You want me to check with Monroe and Escambia?"

"No. I'm out."

Simmering with impatience, Dev disconnected.

"Lose not your focus," Arta said, sensing his agitation. "Barber will stumble. We have but to wait."

"Right," Dev said. "We'll catch the bastard."

"Of a certainty."

Fifteen minutes later they were crossing the Trammel Bridge into Hannah. Beneath them, the Devil River churned and foamed, baring its rocky teeth in a snarl.

"River's down," Dev commented. "It's been a dry summer."

He guided the SUV over the arched concrete span and onto Main Street, a tree-lined avenue of tidy storefronts, gas lampposts hung with baskets of bright flowers, and busy sidewalks. Pulling into a parking place down the block from the restaurant, Dev shut off the engine. Shoppers bustled along the walks, some pausing to exchange pleasantries with people they knew. The swinging metal and glass door of the Hannah Pharmacy opened, and a young mother with a harried expression stepped out. Clutching one child by the hand and balancing another on her hip, she hurried down the street past two gray-haired men on a bench. One old man was reading the Hannah paper, the other was smoking a pipe. Tail high, a large black hound trotted by on some mysterious doggy mission. From the brick ledge of the local bookshop, a ginger cat observed the large canine with lofty disdain. The cat stretched and jumped down, padding after the dog.

"See the flashing sign?" Dev pointed to the neon marker in the window a few doors down. The sign blinked the words *Air Conditioned*. "That's the Sweet Shop, where we're having lunch."

"Taryn and Conall have mentioned it in glowing terms," Arta said. "The viands are tasty?"

"Best meat and three around," Dev said. "Miss Vi—Viola Williams— and her husband, Delmonte, have owned and operated the Sweet Shop for more than twenty-five years. Fried chicken, meat loaf and tomato gravy, fresh vegetables, yummy desserts—those are a few things you'll find on the menu. And Del knows his way around a grill. Best barbecue in three counties. Maybe in the state." Dev pointed to the cars lining the street. "But don't take my word for it. See for yourself." He cracked open the car door. "It's early yet, but we'd better hurry. The place is always crowded."

As Arta reached for the door handle, a red Mercedes zoomed into the space beside them, and a short, pudgy woman hopped out.

"*Annnd* here's Bootsie," Dev said with a grunt of satisfaction.

Arta watched Bootsie trot down the sidewalk. "Faith, but for one so slight in stature, she moves with considerable speed."

"The Little Engine That Could," Dev said. "That's what we called her in school. Always chugging up and down the halls of the high school working on this committee or that. Bootsie is a dynamo."

Bootsie flung open the Sweet Shop door and disappeared into the restaurant.

"'Twould seem we have the same destination," said Arta.

"Yeah, how about that?"

She gave him a sharp glance. "You knew?"

"Lucky guess," Dev said. "All roads lead to the Sweet Shop in Hannah." They got out and strolled down the sidewalk.

"Gentlemen," Dev said, pausing to greet the two old men on the bench. "Anything interesting in the paper?"

Herbert Duffy, an octogenarian with a long nose and the sorrowful countenance of a moose, lowered his paper to glare at Dev. "World's gone to hell in a handbasket. You heard about the bank robbery in Robertsdale?"

"I heard."

"Robbers got clean away. Them new-fangled bank cameras didn't catch a thing." Mr. Duffy glowered at Dev. "If I've said it oncet, I've said it a hunnert times. Gadgets can't replace humans. Should've hired a guard."

"Put a sock in it, Herbert. Ain't the sheriff's fault." The old man on the bench beside him eyed Arta with interest. "You're a pretty thang. New to the area, or I'll eat my hat."

"This is Arta Kirvahni, Mr. Willis," Dev said. "She's just started with the department."

"Do not eat your hat, I beg," Arta said, gazing at the old codger with concern, "lest it make you dyspeptic."

Mr. Willis cackled. "Easy on the eyes and funny to boot."

"Enjoy your day," Dev said with a nod. "We're headed to the Sweet Shop."

Mr. Willis straightened. "Pulley bones on the menu and caramel pie. Best have Pauline bring you the pie straightaway. It gets gone in a hurry."

"Good advice," Dev said.

They continued down the sidewalk to the café. As Dev opened the door to the restaurant, a bell jangled overhead, announcing their arrival. They stepped out of the heat. The cool interior was redolent with wonderful smells: hot corn bread, the mouthwatering scents of barbecue and fried chicken and, overlying all, the rich, flavor-inducing staple of Southern cooking, fatback. The building had been a warehouse a hundred years earlier. The walls were rough plank, the high ceilings battered metal. Black and white checkerboard vinyl tile covered the floor in a honeycomb pattern. Scarred wooden booths marched along both sides of the rectangular dining area. The space in the middle contained old-fashioned round tables with laminate tops. Rusting signs on the wall proclaimed the merits of everything from cigarettes to soda. *Mountain Dew*, one sign said. *It'll tickle your innards. Put a tiger in your tank with Esso*, another declared. Squeezed between the numerous ads were quaint sayings and proverbs Dev had read hundreds of times without tiring of them.

You can get glad in the same pants you got mad in, one proclaimed.

Another warned, *You go to hell for lying same as stealing.*

A third said, *I been told it takes all kinds, and we got 'em.*

It was early, and the restaurant was half full. Conversation and the clink of glasses and silverware halted as everyone turned to stare at Dev and Arta. No, not at him, Dev admitted. Everybody was staring at Arta. Even in the drab deputy uniform, she was a sight. Seated at a table in the middle of the room, Bobby Glenn, the owner of Riverside Ford, ogled the huntress with a poleaxed expression. His eyes were wide and his mouth was agape. Whatever the poor guy had been about to say had been deleted from his hard drive by the vision in the doorway.

Dev couldn't blame him. He had a sneaking suspicion he looked the same way around Arta. He glanced at her. Tall and lithe, she held herself proudly and with confidence. She was, quite simply, stunning, radiating power and charisma, as glamorous and captivating as any star from the silver screen.

Movie star, hell. She was a goddess in their midst. The other diners knew it. And Bobby Glenn for damn sure knew it—he was practically drooling—but Arta seemed unaware of her effect. Probably used to it.

"How surpassing strange," she murmured.

Dev jerked out of his musings. "What?"

She pointed to the rear end of a turquoise automobile suspended on one wall. "'Tis an odd place to leave a carriage."

"Oh, that," Dev said. "It belonged to Delmonte's dad. Tyler wrecked it late one night playing chicken on Cat Man Road."

Arta's eyes went unfocused. "'Chicken' is a sort of joust?"

"Yep, a drag race. Two cars speed toward one another." Dev demonstrated with his hands, one approaching the other. "The first to pull aside is the chicken—or coward. Tyler was the unofficial champ until he swerved one night to avoid a young woman in the road."

"'Unofficial'?"

"Drag racing is illegal. The way Tyler told the tale, this young woman appeared out of thin air. He jerked the wheel to avoid running her over, lost control of his car, and left the road. Smashed into a tree. Lost the race, which cost him fifty dollars, but he came out the winner in the end."

"How so?"

"When Tyler got home that night, he found the young woman waiting for him on his porch swing."

"The phantom from the road?"

"None other."

"By the blood," Arta breathed. "What did he do?"

"He married her." Dev grinned. "What else? Years later, he gave the car to Del as a good-luck charm, and Del put it in the restaurant." He waved at a tall, curvaceous black woman standing at the register. "Come on. I want to introduce you to Miss Vi."

He guided Arta past the ogling customers and up to the register. "Viola, this is Arta Kirvahni, my new deputy."

"Nice to meet you," Viola Williams said, giving Arta a welcoming smile. "I've been expecting you, Sheriff. It's salmon croquette day."

"I do love your salmon patties."

"It's the Durkee's," she confided. "Makes 'em tasty." Her curious gaze rested on Arta as she spoke. "Have we met, honey? You remind me of someone."

"My sister Taryn, perhaps?" Arta suggested. "Tall with hair of flame? I am told there is a resemblance."

"That's it, sure enough," Viola said. "It's something about your eyes, I think." She shook her head. "Lands, I pity yo' daddy. He must've had to fight them boys off with a stick."

"A Kirvahni fights her own battles."

Viola chuckled. "I'll bet you do. Sheriff, will you and Arta be wanting a table or a booth?"

"A booth, if you please."

As he spoke, Dev perused the café and spotted Elizabeth Barber talking to a group of women at a table. Lala Lavender Leaguers, he'd bet. They had that polished, affluent country club set look about them.

Bootsie bade the ladies good-bye and bustled over to them. "Miss Vi, I have a favor to ask," she said, her voice soft and sweet as caramel. "Can we talk?"

"Is it life or death?" Viola asked. "'Cause if it ain't life or death, I'm too busy. Couldn't stop long enough to put out my own foot if it was on fire."

"It can wait."

"Good. Call me tonight, honey. You have my number?"

"Yes, ma'am," Elizabeth said.

Viola waved to a server across the room. "Enjoy your lunch, Sheriff," she told Dev. "Pauline will see to you."

She hurried behind the counter to tend to the line at checkout.

"Hello, Bootsie," Dev said to his former classmate. "Long time, no see."

"Hello, yourself."

Bootsie was a sturdy woman, five feet two inches tall, with heavy breasts and hips, and thick, muscular calves. Even the thick layer of makeup she wore could not disguise the freckles liberally splashed across her cheeks and turned-up nose. More freckles dotted her arms and hands. Her mousy hair, once blond, had been ruthlessly highlighted. The only child of a well-to-do pharmacist with stores in Hannah and Paulsberg, Bootsie was always dressed to the nines, even in elementary school, seldom sporting the same outfit twice. It was something Dev remembered hearing the other girls snipe about.

Today, she wore a sleeveless blue linen dress and beige sandals. A matching beige clutch was tucked beneath one arm. Dev was by no means a fashionista, but he knew Bootie's apparel was expensive. Nothing but the best for Baby Boots, her daddy had been fond of saying, and Fred Mullins had rarely denied her anything.

"I guess you heard about Livy?" Dev asked.

"Oh, my, yes." Tears sprang to Bootsie's brown eyes. "I'm sorry, Dev. I know you were close until—" She paused, reddening. "Any idea what happened?"

"We're still looking into it." Dev indicated Arta next to him. "Bootsie, this is my new deputy, Arta."

"Nice to meet you," Bootsie murmured, giving Arta the side-eye. "My goodness, you're tall. And so pretty! You could be a model."

Arta lifted one brow. "A model what?"

"Bootsie," Dev said as though on impulse, "why don't you join us for lunch? We can catch up."

"Ketchup." Arta spoke in the colorless tone of one repeating a dry tract, "a spicy sauce made chiefly from vinegar and a fruit called the *tomato*, vinegar being a sharp-tasting liquid made from sour wine."

"My goodness," Bootsie said, staring at her. "You are quite the character, aren't you?"

"Yes, she is." Dev shot Arta a warning glance. "Arta's not from around here."

"No kidding? I never would've guessed." Bootsie tapped him playfully on the arm. "I can't believe you're asking me to have lunch with you, Dev Whitsun. You never had two words to say to me in school."

"Too shy. You ran with the cool crowd."

"Baloney, a good-looking thing like you? Half the girls at BCH had a crush on you. You could've had your pick."

Dev ducked his head. "You're putting me to the blush. Here comes Pauline."

An angular waitress with graying hair and an expression that would sour paint, charged up to them. "Well," she demanded. "Don't stand there blocking the aisle. You jawing or eating?"

"Eating." Dev indicated an area at the back of the restaurant. "Over there, if you please." He smiled at Bootsie. "I really hope you'll stay."

"Stay or leave, it's all the same to me." Pauline blew a strand of gray hair out of her eyes. "I got other customers."

"I-I suppose I could grab a bite," Boostie said.

"Praise Jesus, she's made up her mind," Pauline said. "I've had BMs quicker, and my bowels stay locked."

"A boar bile enema is good for that," Arta said with perfect seriousness, "or so I have heard. Also, slippery elm."

"Just what we need around here. Another smart-ass," Pauline said, guiding them to a booth away from the other diners.

She slapped three menus on the table, took their drink orders, and flounced off.

"Boar bile, really?" Bootsie dissolved into giggles. "Did you see the look on her face? Priceless."

"I meant no harm," Arta protested. "'Tis a physic for stultification. Truly."

"In the Dark Ages, maybe." Bootsie wiped her eyes. "Serves the old crab right, talking about her bathroom business. As if anyone wants to hear about *that*. Why on earth doesn't Viola fire her?"

"She and Viola went to school together," Dev said. "Hannah High, Class of 'Seventy-Seven."

"Really?" Bootsie gave Miss Vi a thoughtful glance. "Viola looks twenty years younger, maybe more."

"Pauline's had a hard life," Dev said. "By the way, I was sorry to hear about your father."

"Yes, it was very sudden." Bootsie sighed. "Mama died three years ago. Guess that makes me an orphan now."

"I do not have parents," Arta said, "and yet, I persist."

Bootsie's expression softened in sympathy. "You're absolutely right. I need to stop feeling sorry for myself and get busy. I have a lot to do."

"Such as?" Dev asked.

"Put Mama and Daddy's house on the market, for one thing. Daddy's stores, too."

"You're selling the pharmacies?" Dev asked.

"Goodness, yes," said Bootsie. "Russ and I have our hands full running R&B."

"That's right. You're the office manager, aren't you? Business good?"

"Booming."

"Glad to hear it." Dev toyed with his fork. "Still, that's a lot for anyone to handle."

"It is. I don't mind telling you, sometimes I get overwhelmed."

"Anyone would be with all you've got going on." Dev sat back in the booth. "So, why are you starting a charitable foundation?"

"How did you—"

"FMF—the Fred Mullins Foundation for heart failure and cardiac rehabilitation," Dev said. "You're going to ask Viola to be on the board tonight. I overheard you and your friends talking about it when we came in."

Bootsie stared at him. "You heard us? We were clear across the room."

"The shire reeve has ears like a wolf," Arta said.

Bootsie looked bewildered. "The shire reeve?"

"She means me. It's…um…what they call the sheriff where she's from."

"Oh." Bootsie blinked. "Daddy and I were close, you know. He'd been in poor health for years, but it was still a shock when he passed."

"I'm sure it was," Dev said. "You were with him when he died?"

"No, visiting hours were over, and I'd gone home. I got the call a few hours later that he'd…" Her mouth quivered. "That he'd died."

"I see." Dev pulled the notepad from his shirt pocket and made notes. Flipping to the previous page, he said, "According to Russ, you're also busy with an event this weekend. Something to do with the Lala Lavender League."

"I'm the new president-elect, and I—" Bootsie faltered. "You've spoken to Russ?"

"Yes," Dev said. "We stopped by R&B on our way here." He gazed at her in sympathy. "It's all right, Bootsie. I think I know."

"Kn-know what?"

"Livy and Russ were having an affair, weren't they? She was wearing his bracelet when she died."

Bootsie's brown eyes widened in shock. "I'm sorry," she said, scooting from the booth. "I have to go."

Dev scrambled after her. "Bootsie, wait. We need to talk."

"No." Bootsie's mouth trembled. "I've got nothing to say to you, *Sheriff*."

She trotted away, steadying herself on a man's shoulder with a murmur of apology when one heel of her sandals turned. Limping toward the exit, she opened the door and hurried outside. She scurried past the plate-glass window in front of the restaurant, pausing momentarily to glance back inside, her freckled face pale with fright. Her eyes locked with Dev's. Clutching her purse to her bosom, she fled in the direction of her car.

Chapter Fifteen

Arta twisted in the booth to watch Bootsie depart. "That one is like a rabbit," she observed, turning back around. "Scampering away ere the wolf gobbles her up."

"The wolf is trying to help her," Dev said. "It's her husband she should be afraid of, not me."

"Methinks she is afraid of him," Arta said. "Did you mark how she trembled? The man should be trounced."

"Been there, done that, got the T-shirt."

"You refer to the incident from your youth?"

He nodded curtly. "Russ hurt Livy, and I lost my temper."

"You sent him hurtling into the air as he claimed?"

"Like a bird. Fortunately, the norms didn't believe him." Dev stared, unseeing, at his flatware. "It was a bad break. I can still hear him screaming."

"No doubt Livy screamed when he threw her to the djegrali."

Images of Livy's death rose in Dev's mind—stomach-churning images. "Yeah," he said, swallowing hard. "He'll pay for what he's done."

"Of a certainty. Let us seize him, here and now."

"No, we don't have the evidence. Yet."

"As you like. But I warn you—when we do have proof, he shall do more than limp. I shall break *all* his limbs."

Her eyes shone with such a savage light that Dev felt sorry for Russ. Almost.

"*If* he's responsible," he said, as much to remind himself as her. "We don't know that for sure."

"I know it, and so does the rabbit."

"People get trapped and don't know how to get out. Everyone's not as fearless as you."

"I am not fashioned of stone."

"Oh, yeah?" Dev leaned back in the booth. "Name one thing that frightens you."

"I care not for the notion of being buried beneath the crushing weight of earth and rock." She picked up her menu and scanned the contents. "Behold me alarmed. What, pray, are *baby limas*?"

"A kind of bean."

"I am immensely relieved."

Dev choked back a laugh. "Stop trying to change the subject and tell me what happened."

Lowering her menu, she gave him a stern look. "Prithee be more precise. A great many things have 'happened' in my existence."

"We were talking about a cave-in, I think."

"Were we?" Arta studied the menu as if it was the cheat sheet for a final exam. "Me, I thought we were discussing beans."

Dev reached over and snatched the laminated paper out of her hands. "Are you going to tell me or not?"

"I gather this is something you feel strongly about?" When he nodded, she folded her hands, a habit of hers, he'd noticed. "As you wish. I tracked an ogre deep into a dwarfish mine. After three days, I overtook the fiend, and we fought. I suffered a nasty blow to the head and was much diminished."

"The ogre hit you with a club?"

"Something harder—his fist. To make matters worse, our struggles brought the mountain down atop us."

Dev had a nightmarish vision of Arta crushed and bleeding beneath tons of dirt and rock. She was dying, hurt and alone, and he couldn't get to her. His heart and lungs constricted at the thought.

"Shire reeve, are you well?" Arta gazed at him in concern. "You are pale, and you have crinkled the bill of fare."

"I'm fine." Dev smoothed the wrinkles from the plastic sheet. "Go on. You were buried beneath the mountain?"

"Ah, yes. I was not myself, and the boy had been injured, as well. By a falling rock, as I recall."

"What boy?"

Plucking another menu from behind the napkin dispenser, Arta continued her perusal of the list. "I neglected to mention that the ogre had stolen the dwarf king's son?"

"Yep. Slid right past that part."

"I am remiss," she said. "The ogre held the boy for a ransom in flesh— one youngling per full moon to appease his wicked appetite."

"That's horrible."

"Ogres are not, by nature, pleasant creatures. When the king refused to comply, the foul thing snatched his son."

"And you charged to the rescue."

"A Kirvahni does not *charge*. A Kirvahni huntress uses cunning and stealth to track her quarry."

"How did you escape? Did you blast your way out?"

"Nay, I was too weak, and the prince was in extremis. I summoned the imp."

"Irilmoska—"

"Heed my warning and say not his name," she hissed, "else he will appear."

"He seems harmless to me."

"The stone-tooth mole of Nagheeri was no bigger than my thumb, yet it consumed the heart of that world, woe unto those who abided there."

"Sorry." Dev lowered his voice. "The imp saved you—then what?"

"I restored the dwarf king's son to him."

"And?"

"And what?"

"What was your reward?"

"A Kirvahni huntress seeks no reward. A Kirvahni huntress strives only for duty well-done."

"You saved the king's son. You should have gotten something…a magical talisman or an amulet or maybe a ring of power."

"Loath I am to disappoint, but they gave me none of those things."

"A dagger, then." Dev made a stabbing motion. "One forged in the heart of a mountain and inscribed with runes to make the blade strike true."

Arta's eyes danced. "Shire reeve, I had no notion you were so fanciful."

"You battled a freaking ogre, woman. *In a mine*, and you got squat."

"That is not precisely true."

"I knew it." He leaned closer. "What did they give you, a cloak of invisibility?"

"A cloak of— my dear sir, the Kir have no use for such a thing. We are quite capable of achieving invisibility on our own."

"Oh, yeah. I forgot. A pet dragon, then? A dragon would be cool." He frowned. "Unless…you're gone a lot with the job thing, aren't you?"

"The job thing?"

"Chasing demons."

"The Kir are celestial vagabonds, as it were."

"And I suppose a good dragon sitter is hard to find?"

"Nigh unto impossible. Most decent ostlers are put off by the risk of being broiled or eaten."

"So, dragons are out," Dev said, "but what about a talking steed, one made of black steel with cloven hooves? Read about a horse like that in a book once," he confided. "His name was Black, and he drank scotch."

"I did not receive a horse that talks," Arta said, "or a unicorn, or any other fantastical beast. They did, howe'er, give me this." With a flourish, she produced an emerald the size of a goose egg and placed it on the table in front of him. "'Tis the Aurora Stone."

"It's nice," Dev said, examining it, "but I'd still rather have a ring of power."

"*Nice?* This emerald was stolen from the lair of Gozz the Dread, a fire-breathing dragon with teeth like swords. 'Twas part of his hoard." Arta produced a pouch. "Mayhap this will please you, then." Opening the bag, she dumped the contents on the table. "Dwarfish gold. They gave me a wagonload of the stuff."

Dev stared at the shining heap. "A *wagonload*?"

"Aye."

"Arta?"

"Yes, shire reeve?"

"Lunch is on you."

Pauline sailed up to them with a plastic tray and plunked two quart-size tea glasses on the table. "I brung three teas. What happened to Freckle Puss?"

"Bootsie left," Dev said.

Pauline pointed a bony digit at the treasure trove on the table. "What's this mess? It ain't Mardi Gras."

"'Tis golden treasure." Arta offered her a handful of the coins. "'Tis my understanding that you have suffered much in life, hostel wench. Accept this token in appreciation for your services, an you will."

"Hostel wench, huh? Been called a lot of things in my time, but that's a new one."

"I meant no offense. Take the gold. 'Tis yours."

"No, thanks. Don't know what game you're playing, lady, but I ain't no fool."

"I assure you, the gold is real."

"Yeah, right." Disdaining the offered coins, Pauline set down the tray and whipped out a pad. "We got pulley bones, pork chops, hamburger steak with onion gravy, and salmon croquettes." The pencil hovered over the paper. "And ribs. We always got ribs."

"In truth, I cannot decide." Arta took a deep breath. "I should like one of everything, including dessert. But no chocolate, understood?"

"One of everything?" Pauline gave her a hard look. "You Dalvahni, by any chance?"

"We are related."

"Thought so." Pauline jerked her bony chin in a satisfied nod. "Them boys like to strap on the feed bag, too. You want ribs with that?"

Arta arched her brows. "But of course."

Pauline scratched something on her pad. "Hog wild, high on the hog, or whole hog?"

"Beg pardon?"

"How many ribs you want?" Pauline tapped the menu with her pencil. "Hog wild is a slab, high on the hog is two, and whole hog is four. A whole hog feeds four to six people."

"Indeed, 'tis a weighty matter." Arta looked torn. "What do you suggest?"

"A bigger table and a stomach pump, hoglet," the waitress said. "Get two slabs. You and the sheriff can share."

"Good idea," Dev said, "but bring me an order of salmon croquettes and a side of mashed potatoes. Oh, and a bowl of collards." He patted his stomach. "Got to have my greens."

Pauline spun about and headed for the kitchen to put in their orders.

Evan Beck stalked up to their booth. His expression was belligerent, and he simmered with barely suppressed anger. "How's Taryn?" he demanded.

"She is on the road to recovery," Arta said. "Kehvahn himself oversees her care."

"How long before she comes home?"

"She is home."

"Here. How long before she come back *here*? I need to see her. I'm going crazy wondering if—"

"Hello, Evan."

He whirled around. His twin, Rebekah Dalvahni, stood behind him. Evan's sister was his feminine counterpart, possessed of the same sultry good looks, dark hair, and violet eyes. Her husband, Conall, loomed protectively at her side, his flinty black gaze watchful and alert.

"Cookie. It's been a while." Evan took in her baggy sundress and swollen belly. "Marriage must agree with you. You've gotten fat."

Beck flushed. "I'm pregnant."

"No kidding? I thought you swallowed a Volkswagen."

A spasm of anger flitted across Beck's face. Controlling it with a visible effort, she offered her brother a bright smile. "Always the charmer. Daddy and Brenda tell me you've bought a house and started your own business. That's wonderful."

"Why? Oh, you mean because you thought I was a loser? Sorry to disappoint you."

"I never said—"

"The Evster is doing fine," Evan said, rolling over her sputtering protests. "I'm not dead or rotting in jail."

"Stop being a dick. I'm trying to build a bridge here."

"Sorry, sis. You blew that shit up."

Dev slid out of the booth. "People are staring. Why don't we move to a table?"

"No thanks," Evan said, stomping toward the door.

"We're having twins," Beck called after him, "and Conall and I would like you to be a godfather."

Evan stiffened and swung back around. "What happened, did hell freeze over while I wasn't looking?"

"Rebekah wishes to mend things between you," Conall said. "I told you as much a'ready."

"Fat chance of that happening with you around."

"An it makes Rebekah happy, I am amenable."

"One big, happy family, huh?" Evan's mouth twisted. "Sorry, I call bullshit."

Beck gave her husband a significant glance. "Told you he would need convincing."

Conall looked pained. "If I must, I must." Gathering himself, the powerful warrior said, "Duncan and I have spoken at length, and I have come to realize..." He ground his teeth and tried again. "Upon reflection, 'tis possible I may have rushed to judgment ere I had all the facts. 'Twould seem you are not the villain I thought."

Evan staggered and clutched his chest. "Hear that, people? Conall Dalvahni says I'm not whale shit."

"Don't be a jerk," Beck said. "We're trying to make amends."

"You suck at apologies, sis. Both of you. Just saying."

"Take it or leave it."

His eyes narrowed. "You said *a* godfather. Don't you mean *the* godfather?"

Conall folded his arms on his broad chest. "Duncan wishes to lend his patronage to one child."

"Duncan, huh?" Evan stroked his chin. "Dunky's cool, but I get dibs."

Beck's eyes flashed. "They're children, not cupcakes."

"You're the one trying to build a bridge here, Cookie," Evan said. "How did you put it? Take it or leave it."

He stormed out of the restaurant without looking back.

Beck drew a deep breath. "Well. That went better than I expected."

"Shall we leave, then?" asked Conall.

"No. I'm hungry."

"My love, you broke your fast but an hour ago."

"What's your point?"

"That we should eat again," Conall said at once. "Shire reeve, does your offer still stand?"

"Sure thing." Dev motioned to a table in the back of the restaurant. "We needed to move, anyway. Arta's ordered enough food to feed an army."

"I could not decide," Arta confessed to Conall, getting to her feet, "but I refrained from sampling the chocolate pie. Chocolate tap shackles the Dal, I am told, and while I feel certain the Kir do not suffer the same lamentable weakness, I thought it prudent to abstain."

Conall scowled. "The Kir are not superior to—"

"Very smart," Dev said, intervening, "especially since we're on duty. Arta's a deputy now."

"My condolences," Conall said.

"Ignore him," Beck said, smiling at Arta. "I'm his wife, Beck, and you must be Arta, the High Huntress." She shook Arta's hand. "Conall and Duncan have mentioned you."

"No doubt in glowing terms."

"I wouldn't say *glowing*, exactly. Unless you consider the terms *thrice cursed hag* and *ill-tempered viper* flattering?"

Arta gave Conall a look that would wither an armadillo in its shell. "I do not."

"My love," Conall protested, "an you recall, I also mentioned Arta's prowess in battle and her skill as an assassin."

"Did you?" Beck winked at Arta. "Guess I forgot."

"Why don't we sit down?" Grabbing his and Arta's drinks, Dev led them to the empty table at the rear of the room. "We'll have more privacy here."

Arta and Dev seated themselves, and Conall pulled out a chair on the opposite side.

"Rest, my love, I beseech you," he said, giving his wife a tender smile that transformed his harsh features. "'Tis as I feared—this outing was too much for you."

"Nah, I was going stir-crazy cooped up at home." Easing gratefully into the chair, she studied Arta with open interest. "How did you become the High Huntress?"

"My name was drawn from the Vessel."

"The Vessel, huh? Sounds mysterious." Beck turned her attention to Dev. "Speaking of mysterious, Sheriff, I had you pegged for a regular Joe, but Toby was right, wasn't he? You're not a norm."

"No," Dev admitted. "Where is Toby, by the way? I'd like a word with him."

"You and me both. He's been MIA for days." Beck gave him a searching look. "So, what are you? You're not kith. Don't have the purple eyes."

"It's complicated."

"Cool." She propped her chin in her hands. "I married Conall. Obviously, I like complicated."

The last thing Dev wanted to do was take a dumpster dive into his convoluted family history. Demon? Check. Human? Maybe a smidge. Other supernatural DNA? Get out your pen and paper because it was a long list.

"Forgive me, but I am puzzled," Arta said, coming to his rescue. "Your name is Rebekah, but you go by Beck. Is Beck not your family name?"

"No. My maiden name is Damian."

"Then why does your brother call himself Evan Beck?" Arta asked. "'Tis confusing."

"We were separated at birth," Beck said. "I thought Evan was dead until a few months ago."

"At which time you reunited and quarreled?"

"Yeah. Evan's a selfish ass. He doesn't care about anyone but himself."

"And yet, he chose Beck as his surname, rather than Damian, and he has the word 'Cookie' tattooed on one arm, a diminutive he used to address you," Arta pointed out. "Perhaps he is not as indifferent as he pretends to be." She shrugged. "Of a certainty, he seems enamored with my sister."

Beck sat up in her chair. "Evan's crushing on a demon hunter?" She nudged Conall. "Hear that, honey?"

"Her name is Taryn, and may she lead him a merry dance."

"You knew?" Beck's eyes flared. "Why didn't you tell me?"

"To borrow your phrase, 'Guess I forgot.'"

"Sometimes, Conall Dalvahni, you are—"

Pauline bustled up with a large tray, setting plates of fried chicken, pork chops, hamburger steak, and a huge platter of ribs in front of Arta. "Be back with the veggies and the bread."

"And the desserts?" asked Arta.

"I ain't forgot." Pauline's pad and pencil reappeared in her hands. "What about you?" She gave Beck and Conall the beady eye. "You got a hankering for everything but the kitchen sink, too? My back's done give out."

They declined, and she jotted down their more modest orders, twirling off like a wiry ballerina in sensible shoes. She returned in a twinkling with the rest of Arta's food and Dev's salmon croquettes and sides, placing a dizzying array of dishes in front of the huntress. Mashed potatoes and gravy, turnips, rutabagas, field peas, baby limas, and creamed corn crowded the table, along with cucumber salad, carrot salad with raisins, pickled beets, and pineapple casserole. She plunked fried green tomatoes and coleslaw next to steamed cabbage and arranged baskets of hot corn bread and dinner rolls beside a butter bowl. Last came the desserts: slices of coconut and butterscotch pie, a jiggling bowl of peach cobbler, sweet potato pound cake, and banana pudding with whipped cream.

Beck stared at the laden table with a queasy expression. "That's a lot of food."

"I could not decide." Selecting a pulley bone from the pile of fried chicken, Arta took a bite. "So I thought it best to sample everything."

"You didn't have to try and eat it all in one day," Dev said, much amused. "Matter of fact, you can't. The Sweet Shop is open six days a week, and the menu changes."

Arta lowered the pulley bone. "What are you saying to me?"

"I'm saying the menu changes according to the day of the week." Dev grabbed one of the plastic-covered pieces of paper and flipped it over. "See? Tomorrow is beef tips on rice, meat loaf with tomato gravy, and catfish. Friday, it's chicken and dumplings."

Beck swayed in her chair. "For the love of God, please stop talking about food."

Conall gazed at her in concern. "You are unwell?"

"Yeah, suddenly I don't feel so hot," Beck said, rising from the table.

Conall stared at the floor. "My love, you are leaking."

"What?" Beck looked down at the puddle between her feet and gave a little shriek. Her voice cut through the chatter, and everyone in the room turned to look. "Oh, no," she wailed. "The *babies.*"

"Her water has broken." Dev strode around the table. "You'd better get her home."

Mary Boston, the Presbyterian minister's wife, jumped up from her table and rushed over. She was a stylish, attractive older woman with softly waving gray hair and a trim figure. Today, she wore black pants and a deep blue top, with a matching pink and blue floral silk scarf artfully tossed around her neck à la Isadora Duncan.

"I don't think so," she said in the overbearing manner of one accustomed to being in charge. Rumor had it, Mary *was* in charge. Rumor had it she rode her husband like a rented mule, dictating the direction of his sermons and his life in general. "She should go to the hospital."

Beck shrank against her husband. "No. No hospitals."

Her reaction did not surprise Dev. Supers avoided hospitals and human doctors like the plague. Too many questions. Twins with demon blood *and* Dalvahni DNA? There'd be a media frenzy. The government might even step in.

"There's no need to be nervous, my dear," Mary said. "Hannah has an excellent hospital. I've had five babies, and Doc Dunn delivered them all. You'll be in good hands."

"No." Beck's voice rose. "I won't go. I *won't.*"

"Well," Mary said, swelling with indignation. "There's no need to screech at me."

"Never mind, Miss Mary." Dev patted her arm. "Unless I'm mistaken, Beck and Conall have made other arrangements."

"That's right." Beck smiled gratefully at Dev. "We've arranged for a midwife, Aubergine Mahon."

"A midwife?" Mary Boston clucked in disapproval. "Is that safe?"

"Perfectly safe," Dev assured her. "Lots of women use midwives these days." *Especially the kith*, he refrained from adding. "Aubergine's delivered dozens of babies."

Kith babies—the Mahons were bear shifters, but Dev kept that information to himself.

"If you're quite sure," Mary said, though she was clearly unconvinced.

"She is," Dev said. "Enjoy your lunch. I've got this."

Mary Boston turned to go, halting at Beck's gasp of dismay.

"Oh, no, I forgot," Beck cried, wringing her hands. "Aubergine's out of town. She and Ed are on a cruise."

"Be she marooned upon the far moons of Elderak, I shall find her," Conall vowed, his face grim.

"No, it's their belated honeymoon. I don't want to ruin it."

"But the babies, my love," Conall pleaded. "Be reasonable."

"Don't worry," Dev said. "I'll get word to Aunt Weoka. She delivered me and dozens of kith—" He glanced at Mary Boston and coughed. "Babies, she's delivered dozens of babies. In fact, she trained Aubergine."

Beck's eyes widened. "Oh, yes, *please* let her know. You have our address?"

"I do." Dev clapped Conall on the shoulder. "Take your wife home. Everything's going to be fine."

"Home," Conall said, latching on to the word like a lifeline. "Yes. My thanks, shire reeve."

He swept Beck into his arms and vanished.

Mary Boston let out a screech loud enough to empty a tomb. "Save us, he disappeared."

Hoping no one else had noticed Conall's vapor act, Dev glanced around the room. His heart immediately sank. People had noticed, all right. Everyone in the restaurant was staring at them. Viola Williams stood at the cash register, a flabbergasted expression on her striking face. Billy Lacey had stopped eating in mid chew, his mouth open and full of corn bread. Pauline was wiping down a booth near the door. Bent at the waist, one foot on the floor and the other cocked behind her, she gazed back at them in shock.

Dev scrambled for a plausible explanation, something to satisfy the thunderstruck norms, and came up blank. Nada. He had nothing. He'd have to bluff his way out of this one.

He gave Mary Boston a blinding smile. "Disappeared? Don't be silly, Miss Mary. You know that's not—"

He faltered when Mary Boston stared back at him without blinking. She was a stupefied, nosy parker statue of officiousness, her lips parted and her eyes cucumber slices of surprise. She was doing the jazz hand thing, palms out and fingers spread, and her scarf defied the laws of gravity, the ends outspread like the wings of a small bird captured in midflight by a taxidermist.

The other diners were petrified, too. H.C. Williams, the Hannah postmaster, sat at his favorite table by the window. Tall and gaunt with slicked-back, thinning salt-and-pepper hair, H.C. sported his signature checked bow tie. He was bent over his plate, his fork suspended above a mound of mashed potatoes. Loo Hendricks had been caught in the act of adding sugar to his tea. His spoon was tilted over his glass, a ribbon of white granules cascading from the utensil in a frozen waterfall.

Sue Bethea from the Hannah Pharmacy and Jeannine Mitchell from the Kut 'N Kurl salon stood near Viola at the register. Faces rigid, they stared at Dev, their take-out boxes clutched in their hands. Tina Lou Boatwright from Behr Insurance had been stunned while reaching for the ketchup bottle. She'd ordered the salmon croquettes, Dev noticed, staring at her plate. Tina Lou went up a few notches in his estimation based on her choice of condiment. Some folks preferred hot sauce on their fish cakes, but there was right and there was wrong, and in Dev's opinion, the *only* thing one should put on salmon croquettes was ketchup.

Ick Lovelace sat across from Tina with a bottle of pepper sauce suspended over his turnips. Pale drops of liquid hung in the air, glittering like diamonds in the sunlight pouring through the window.

No one in the restaurant moved, not a muscle, not an eyelash. The Sweet Shop was a freeze-dried slice of Southern life, a down-home display in Madame Tussaud's wax works, and it was creepy as hell.

Chapter Sixteen

The clink of flatware drew Dev's attention from the bizarre gastronomic display. Arta, friend and ally of Khoalisskaliss, snake goddess of Qia Leapoth, slayer of ogres and champion of stolen princes, skilled archer and demon hunter, heiress of a golden hoard and purloined dragon treasure, and the supreme mistress of his heart, sat at the table behind him enjoying her lunch.

"Mind telling me what's going on?" he asked.

Slicing a rib with surgical precision, she took a bite. "I am enjoying my repast."

"I was referring to the human gallery, in case you haven't noticed."

"I am not entirely obtuse." Arta chewed thoughtfully. "I care not for the pickled beets." She motioned to a small plate with her knife. "These round things, howe'er, are delightful. They are crispy and piquant."

"Fried green tomatoes."

"Pardon?"

"They're fried green tomatoes." Dev watched her delicately consume another rib. "You're supposed to get it on you. That's half the fun of eating barbecue."

"Clearly, we differ in our opinions of *fun*." She gave him a sultry look that made his blood sizzle. She wiped her fingers on a napkin. "This hostelry would benefit from the use of finger bowls."

Dev tamped down the urge to yank a certain demon hunter out of her chair and kiss her senseless. "There are hand wipes beside the napkin dispenser."

"Ah, yes. My thanks." She tore open a package and cleaned her hands. Picking up the pulley bone, she said, "Come. Let us vie for good fortune."

"You know about breaking the wishbone? Thought that was a Southern thing."

"Hardly. The Romans believed the furcula was a means of divination. An I remember correctly, the one who gets the bigger piece is granted their wish."

"We don't have time for that. We're surrounded by fossils."

"They are not fossils. They are very much alive. I suspended them in order to adjust their memories. An you recall, I told you I could."

"In the woods," Dev said. "I remember."

"You attended me? My heart sings. 'Tis one of our gifts. The Dal, as well, though they seldom use it. My sisters and I are forever tidying up after them." Her brow furrowed. "Even for a Dal, 'twas careless of Conall to vanish before a crowd of norms. I shall mention it in my report."

"Give the guy a break. His wife is having a baby."

"It seems a mortal reaction, but procreation is new to our kind, so perhaps you are right. I shall consider it." Arta waggled the pulley bone. "The furcula, sirrah. Then I shall modify the memories of these people, and all will be well."

Dev shifted uncomfortably. "I'm not okay with that. Scrambling people's brains seems wrong."

She sat back in her chair. "Of course, you are right. 'Tis a marvel I have survived this long without your moral guidance."

"You're angry."

"Nay, I am enlightened. I shall release the humans forthwith and leave you to explain."

"*Me?*"

"Aye, you may tell them that they live in a magical vortex and supernatural creatures walk among them." She waved a hand. "Pray explain also that you are immortal. Of a certainty, they will understand. Humans are famously tolerant."

"Very funny."

"To be sure, the Kith Council will applaud your honesty."

"You've made your point. No need to rub it in," Dev said. "Adjust away."

"Are you quite certain? I would not for the world do anything to offend your principles."

"Damn it, Arta. I said do it."

Her expression softened. "'Twill be a kindness, I assure you. I have seen mass hysteria, and 'tis not pretty. Humans, in my experience, are lamentably breakable."

She's right, Dev thought, remembering an incident that had occurred when he'd been a new deputy.

It had happened one starry Friday night at the BCH Homecoming game. Skipper Boone had gotten plastered to celebrate. Climbing into his truck, he'd plowed through the metal gates and onto the field, pulling a livestock trailer behind him. The first half of the football game was ending, and the marching bands had lined up, ready to take the field when Skipper had careened drunkenly onto the gridiron. Screeching to a halt at midfield, he'd staggered out of the truck.

"Release the kraken," he'd shouted, flinging wide the trailer doors.

The "kraken" was a Jersey bull named Sweetie Pie, 1,700 pounds of grain-fed mean. Snorting with fury, Sweetie had charged out of the cage and onto the green. The bull, already irritated by Skipper's rough treatment, had taken instant exception to the noise, the lights, and the red uniforms of the visiting team. More than two dozen players, cheerleaders, and band members had ended up in the ER.

Skipper had been arrested, and Sweetie Pie had gone on to fame on the rodeo circuit.

"No," Dev said. "I don't want anyone to get hurt."

"Then we are agreed." Arta wiggled the V-shaped bone again. "Shall we?"

"You're relentless, you know that?"

"A Kirvahni huntress persists."

Dev took a seat across the table and grabbed one end of the wishbone. "Ready?"

"Always."

They pulled. The bone snapped. With a cry of delight, Arta held up the longer piece. "Behold me triumphant."

"Congratulations." Dev pushed to his feet. "What did you wish for?"

"Know you nothing of wishes?" Tucking the sliver of bone in her shirt pocket, Arta stood. "Should I tell you, 'twill not come to pass."

"Sorry. My bad."

Her eyes widened. "Shire reeve, behind you."

Turning, Dev found a pair of big blue eyes staring at him from the other side of the plate-glass window. Beneath the eyes floated a black-lipped mouth. Slowly, the lips curved in a wide Cheshire cat grin, revealing square Chiclet teeth.

"Sugar?" Dev said. "What is he doing in town?"

He dashed out of the restaurant and halted in surprise. A hush so thick it was practically solid enveloped Main Street, and the cars on the street and the people on the sidewalks were unmoving. Mr. Duffy and Mr. Willis were still sitting on the bench. The smoke from Mr. Willis's pipe hung motionless in the air above his head. Mr. Duffy held his newspaper open in front of him, his wrinkled face creased in a permanent scowl. A fly landed on his nose and crawled down his cheek, but he made no move to swat it.

"My God," Dev said. "She's whammied the whole town."

Sugar materialized. "Sugar home." The bigfoot offered Dev the orb. "Dev want pretty?"

"No, Sugar," Dev said, stepping back. "You keep it."

"Sugar want Mama."

"You're homesick, I know, but hang on to it a little while longer. Please."

Boom. The earth shook, and the storefront windows rattled. *Boom, boom*.

"Bad man come," Sugar warbled, pointing toward the river bridge. "Want pretty."

Startled, Dev whirled around. A lightning-streaked shadow filled the horizon to the north. *Boom, boom*. The bridge trembled, and car horns and alarms sounded in strident protest.

"Bad man want pretty," Sugar repeated. "Dev take?"

"Dev can't take the pretty. Remember what happened to Gryffin?"

The blue eyes clouded. "Booboo?"

"That's right. The orb would hurt Dev."

"Sugar no booboo."

"Because Sugar is special."

"Good boy?"

"Sugar is a *very* good boy. If Sugar keeps the orb, everybody will be safe."

"Mama safe?"

"Yes, your mama will be safe, too." Dev flinched at another bone-rattling boom. "Run," he said. "Hide. Don't let Pratt find you."

Sugar vanished, and Dev turned back to the river. The roiling cloud was bearing down on Hannah, pulling up the trees in its path like weeds. Bright orange flashes detonated within the murky expanse. Treetops boiled to the surface like broccoli crowns and were swallowed up. The effluvium neared the embankment, and everything in its path—shrubs, trees, and vegetation—withered and turned to ash. The paved road leading into Hannah cracked and burst open, spewing dirt and concrete into the air.

Quickly, Dev summoned a shield on the far side of the river to block Pratt's approach. The thunderhead rolled up to the barrier and stopped. Sickening tendrils slithered from the mass, touched Dev's shield, and recoiled.

"That's done it," Dev said with a zing of satisfaction. "The shield has stopped him."

Bolts of lightning smashed into the spell wall, dispelling his elation. Sparks shot into the air, and the shield trembled.

"Oh, no, you don't," Dev muttered.

Concentrating, he poured every ounce of his will and strength into the barrier. Sweat ran down his face and soaked his shirt, and his head pounded from the effort. He ignored the discomfort and bore down harder; gradually, the shield steadied.

"Thank God," Dev said, gasping for breath.

Without warning, an enormous fist emerged from the cloud and slammed into Dev's barricade with the force of a battering ram. The blow knocked Dev to his knees. The huge fist smashed into the magical wall a second time and a third; the shield clanged in protest. Cracks formed in the glistening surface and spread. Dev cried out and clutched his throbbing head. The pressure was too much. The shield would not hold. He would fly apart.

He felt a light touch on his shoulder, and the pain was gone. Power flooded through him. He got to his feet, his body singing with renewed vitality and strength.

And purpose.

Thrusting his hands out with a shout, he sent a beam of energy into the wavering shield. The magical wall solidified, and the fissures in the sparkling skin closed.

Pratt's roar of frustration shook the river bridge and shattered the pharmacy display window a few doors down, showering Dev with broken glass. He scarcely noticed. His gaze was on the shield.

Would it hold?

The titanic hand lifted again, as though to strike the shield, then abruptly withdrew. The thunderhead swelled with frustrated fury, then dissipated, streaming back to the north like smoke up a chimney.

"Thanks for the boost." Dev grinned at Verbena. "We did it. Pratt's leaving."

"Pratt ain't leaving on account o' us." Verbena was barefoot. Her hair was uncombed, and she still wore Winnie's shorts and T-shirt. She pointed to a blazing figure on the bridge. Springing from arch to arch, the fiery creature bounded after the fleeing god. "Pratt's running from Gryffin."

"That's Gryffin?" Dev was shocked. "What happened to him?"

"Pratt and the orb done changed him," Verbena said. "Gryffin means to kill Pratt." She made a face. "Leastways, he means to try."

"With your help, no doubt. Don't go with him, Verbena." Grabbing her by the shoulders, Dev gave her a little shake. "It's too dangerous."

Verbena chuckled. "'Preciate the thought, big brother, but I been taking care o' myself a long time now."

Shocked, Dev released her. "You know? Who told you?"

"Daddy Deer. Tole me on the hillside when we found Gryffin." She tapped her forehead. "Heard him in my noggin, clear as frogs on a rainy summer night."

"Why didn't you say something?"

"No time. 'Sides, I didn't want to sour your stomach."

"I'm not ashamed of you. I'm *proud* of you."

She blushed. "Thankee, Sheriff. I'm proud o' you, too."

"Dev. Call me Dev."

She wrinkled her nose. "Dev don't seem respectful."

"To hell with that. I'm your brother."

There was an enraged bellow from across the river.

"Gotta go," Verbena said, jerking like a puppet on a string. "Gryffin's in a taking on account o' Pratt's done give him the slip."

Dev reached for her, but she darted away like a startled deer. Crossing the bridge, she ran up to the glowing warrior. He enfolded her in his arms, and they disappeared.

The bell on the restaurant door jangled, and Arta stepped outside. "The adjustments have been made," she announced. "Your friends will be groggy for a few hours, but they will have no memory of Conall's precipitous departure." She noticed the unmoving tableau and halted. "What mischief is this?"

"You mean, you didn't do it?" said Dev.

"Nay, 'twas not I."

"Then who is responsible?"

"In truth, I cannot say." She gazed in horror across the river. "Shire reeve, the land! 'Tis ruined."

"Pratt had a temper tantrum. He was after Sugar and the orb. I told Sugar to hide, and Verbena and I raised a shield to keep Pratt out of town. Surprised you didn't hear the noise."

"I heard a rumbling, but I thought it was a storm. Verbena was here? 'Strewth, what else have I missed?"

"Gryffin was here, too. He's morphed. You wouldn't recognize him."

"Morphed, how?"

"Picture a star," Dev said. "An *angry* star. With legs."

Arta stared at him. "Truly? Then Kehvahn must be informed at—"

She broke off as the air grew heavy with the aroma of apples and spices, a cloying scent that climbed up Dev's sensitive nose and made him sneeze.

"What the—" he said, sneezing again as a man in a wrinkled robe and leather sandals appeared.

Arta bowed low. "Master, you honor us with your presence."

Dev studied Kehvahn in surprise. He'd envisioned someone more impressive, a towering, awe-inspiring figure, not this nebbish with a befuddled expression and flyaway brown hair. Silver spectacles rested on the bridge of his long nose, and his clean-shaven cheeks were ruddy. A large white bird with jeweled eyes and a sweeping plumed tail perched on one shoulder.

Kehvahn stroked the bird's velvet feathers with ink-stained fingers. "I am responsible for the tableau you see before you. I quelled the mortals to protect them from my brother's wrath."

"You didn't protect them," Dev said. "You trapped them and left them to die."

Arta gasped. "Forgive him, Master. He is distraught."

"Hush, child. He speaks the truth."

Kehvahn's eyes were brown...or were they blue or green? Regardless of the color, they were old eyes, filled with understanding and a vast, incomprehensible knowledge.

"Long have I watched you, son of Sildhjort," Kehvahn said in a voice rich as warm caramel, the kind of voice that could recite the tax code and make it fascinating. "I had every confidence you would rise to the occasion and keep the humans safe. I hoped also that Pratt would shrink from Gryffin's fury. Both came to pass."

"Master, you know of Gryffin's alteration?" Arta said.

"My child, the very Universe trembled when the child of the forest healed Gryffin with the orb. Certainly, I knew."

"Pratt's your brother," Dev said. "Why didn't you stop him?"

"I dare not thwart him, lest there be war among the gods."

"Politics." Dev was disgusted. "Bottom line—Pratt does what he likes, including *murder*, and you do nothing."

"Not nothing, my dear boy." Kehvahn's eyes twinkled. "I am counting on *you* to bring him to account."

"Hate to break it to you, but Pratt's stronger than I am."

"At present, but your powers will equal his in time."

"In time, huh? How much time?"

"Ten millennia? A score? I cannot say."

"Ten thousand years? Who lives that long?"

"The Kir and the Dal." Kehvahn paused, adding gently, "And you, son of Sildhjort."

"Me?"

"You are immortal. Surely you know this?"

"I've never given it much thought."

"You are young, and the young always think themselves immortal."

"We don't have thousands of years," Dev said. "Pratt has to be stopped now. How do I defeat him?"

"Use his weakness against him," Kehvahn advised, "and combine your resources."

"Thanks. That's a *big* help."

"I do what I can." Kehvahn gave Arta a fond smile. "Farewell, my daughter—son of Sildhjort. My blessings upon you both."

He vanished in an apple-cinnamon funk, and the cars and people on the street began to move again. Across the river, the wasteland shimmered, and trees and lush greenery appeared.

"Kehvahn has removed the blight," Arta said. "Is he not beneficent?"

"Oh, yeah, he's a pip. Are you really thousands of years old?"

"Yes."

"Shit."

"Why do you curse?"

"Because I'm... You're—" Dev gestured helplessly. "Older. A lot older."

"What of it? Our master is older than the stars."

"It's different. I'm not...you're— Never mind." He cocked his head at a high-pitched whine, a sound too shrill for the human ear to detect. "Bank alarm's going off," he said. "Guess your peach of a god didn't fix everything."

The automatic bank doors swung open, and the big black dog Dev had noticed earlier padded out carrying a large duffel bag strapped to his back. The ginger cat followed him with a smaller canvas tote. Trotting down the sidewalk, the odd couple turned right on Church Street.

"Follow that cat and dog," Dev said, striding after them.

Arta accepted this strange statement without comment. Cool, calm, and collected, that was the High Huntress. Dev liked that about her. He liked a lot of things about her. Too many things for his own peace of mind. The question was, what did she see in him?

She was thousands of years old. *Dayum.* The secret hope he'd nourished that she would stay with him vanished.

They passed the pharmacy and the hardware store, turned right at the Greater Fair, and halted at the corner of the Kut 'N Kurl.

"There's a parking lot behind the stores on Main Street," Dev said. "Dollars to donuts that's where they went."

He glanced at Arta when she remained silent. Her expression was tight with anticipation. The huntress was on the prowl.

They eased around the brick building and made their way silently across the asphalt.

Dev pointed to a green Chevy truck in the middle of the lot. "There," he said in a low voice.

The dog and cat stood next to the vehicle, the bags they'd been carrying on the ground beside them.

"Sheriff," Dev said in a loud voice. "Don't move."

The cat hissed and darted behind a wheel of the truck. Dev waved a hand and fashioned a shield around the bottom of the Chevy, trapping the cat underneath.

"I've got this one," he told Arta. The dog rolled a startled eye at him and bounded away. "Dog's making a run for it."

"He will not get far," Arta said.

She motioned, and a battered van spun out of a parking space and in front of the fleeing animal. *Thwack!* The hound slammed into the van and bounced off. The dog's form rippled, and a man with a black beard and hair appeared. He staggered to his feet and took off running again.

Arta materialized in his path. "'Tis a game we play? What are the rules?"

The man swore and swerved around her, darting between rows of cars. Again, Arta materialized in front of him, but this time, she grabbed him by the shirt.

"Freaky bitch," the man screamed. "Leggo of me. Leggo!"

She lifted him, one-handed, into the air. "Me, I would happily oblige, but the shire reeve has plans for you, methinks." She glanced back at Dev. "What would you have me do with the steaming lump of goat excrement?"

"Restrain him."

She nodded and tossed the man into the air. Shrieking in terror, he hurtled toward the ground and came to an abrupt stop in midair, the breath exiting his lungs in a loud whoosh. Arta motioned, and a length of black chain appeared. Snaking around the man, the chain bound him tight. Another flick of her fingers, and her prisoner clanked to the pavement.

"'Tis done," she announced. "The lout is restrained."

"Nice job," said Dev, "but next time use the cuffs."

She frowned and nudged the man with the toe of her boot. "You mislike the chain?"

"It's a little much, doncha think? The norms are bound to notice."

"'Strewth, you are right. I had not thought of that." The chain vanished, and she removed the handcuffs from her belt. "Flee, varlet, to your everlasting regret."

"Go to hell," he wheezed as she put the cuffs on him. "You almost broke my neck, throwing me around like a goddamn ball. I should sue your ass." He craned his head to look at Dev. "I want a lawyer, Sheriff."

"Why am I not surprised?" Hunkering down, Dev peered under the truck. "I've lowered the shield, so you can come out now," he said to the cat, adding when she growled, "That's not a suggestion."

Twitching with fury, the cat slunk from beneath the vehicle.

"That's better," Dev said. "Show yourself."

The animal's sleek form wavered, and a petite young woman appeared wearing cut-offs, a tank top, and a pair of dirty Keds. Her bright orange hair was shorn close above her ears with long bangs swept to one side.

"You ain't no norm," she said with a scowl.

"Sharp as a warm gummy bear, aren't you?" Dev bound her hands behind her back. "Unless I miss my guess, you're a Leon. Does your daddy know you're messing with a Shaw?"

"Avery and me ain't *messing*. We're engaged."

"That right? Bank robbery is a federal offense. Hope you like long-distance relationships because you and Prince Charming are headed to prison."

"Whatever." She tossed her head defiantly. "Can't no jail hold us for long."

"I'm sorry to hear you say that because escape would be a mistake." Dev dropped his mask, giving her a glimpse of the wolf, and she recoiled in fright. "I'd have to come after you, and that would make me cranky. Believe me, you do *not* want to make me cranky." He hit the button on his radio with his free hand. "Willa Dean? We've apprehended the suspects in the Robinsonville bank job. Let Sheriff Huie in Baldwin County know."

"Hold on," Bad Kitty protested. "You ain't got no proof we done that job."

"We'll have all the proof we need once Avery flips."

"Avery won't flip. He loves me."

"Sweetheart, Avery would throw his own mother under the bus to save his sorry hide."

"That's a lie."

"Is it?" Dev gave her a pitying look. "You know Lorraine Davis?"

"Fat heifer went to jail? What about her?"

"Once upon a time, she and Avery were engaged. The 'fat heifer' and Avery got caught stealing cars, and Avery sold her out."

"I don't believe you."

Dev shrugged. "Love is blind. You got your story worked out?"

"What story?"

"For the Feds. They'll want to know how you two pulled off these heists. In detail. You can't tell them you and Avery are shifters." She gaped at him, and he said gently, "What's the first rule of kith?"

"D-don't excite the norms."

"Exactly. You tell the norms what you are, and you won't last a hot second. The Kith Council has people on the inside." Dev slashed a finger across his throat. "And they know how to deal with blabbermouths."

Bad Kitty began to shake. "Avery? We need a story, baby." She twisted around, facing him. "Avery? What we gonna do?"

Avery gave her a sullen glare and turned away.

"Told you," Dev said. "Avery's all about Avery."

"What do I tell them?" Twisting her head, Bad Kitty gazed at Dev in panic. "The norms, I mean."

"No idea, but I'm sure you'll think of something. You'd better."

"I wanna talk to my daddy," Bad Kitty yowled. "You hear me, Sheriff?"

"Pretty sure folks in the next county heard you." Dev frog-marched her across the parking lot. "You'll get your phone call, though I suspect 'daddy' won't be happy with you. Cats and dogs, working together? Doubt he will approve."

"Times are changing."

"Not that much," said Dev.

Chapter Seventeen

The next morning at dawn, Dev awakened with Arta in his arms. She was naked, her silken, lithe body pressed close to his. Her head rested on his shoulder, and one slender arm was draped possessively across his chest.

She arched against him. "Devlin, my Devlin," she murmured.

It was *shire reeve* this and *shire reeve* that when they were with anyone else, but *Devlin* when they were alone. Dev loved the sound of his name on her lips, an intimate, husky rhapsody she played only for him.

He loved—

His thoughts fled as her hand drifted down his belly and curled around his erection.

"I see you are awake…in all respects." Her hand moved, stroking him, measuring him. "How magnificent you are."

Dev rolled over to face her and pulled her close. "I'm glad you approve." He nuzzled her throat, breathing in her delectable floral scent. "God, you smell good." He traced the tip of one full breast with his tongue. "Taste good, too. If I had my way, we'd have breakfast in bed." His voice deepened. "And you'd be the main course."

He gave her a slow, lingering kiss meant to satisfy them both, but it had the opposite effect. Kissing Arta always left him longing for more. He couldn't get enough.

He lifted his head with a sigh of resignation. "We have to stop. It's six thirty. Winnie will be here any minute. You're riding with her today."

"To the Pit with Winnie." Arta slid one knee over his hip, rubbing against his hardness in open invitation. "Raise a shield and keep her out. Lower it not until we are sated."

Dev smiled at her. "That could take hours." *Or forever*, he thought, given his insatiable craving for her. "Do you really want to keep Winnie kicking her heels at the end of the driveway? You know how she is."

"I care not. I want you, my Devlin. *Now*. Do not deny me. No true knight could be so cruel or discourteous to a damsel in need."

"You're the farthest thing from a damsel in distress I've ever met, and I'm no knight."

"I beg to differ. You are stalwart and honorable, courageous and just, a paragon of all good things."

"High Huntress of the Kirvahni, are you trying to turn my head with flattery?"

"Aye." She pressed her body closer to his. "'Tis working?"

"Hell, yeah, it's working," Dev said, entering her silken wetness in one, swift stroke. "Like a charm."

An hour and a half later, they had showered and dressed and were sitting at the kitchen table enjoying breakfast when Winnie stomped in.

"What the hell, Dev?" One look at her face, and Dev knew she was hopping mad. "I've been twiddling my thumbs out there for more than an hour. What's with the stupid shield?"

Arta took a bite of bacon. "The shire reeve and I were…occupied."

"I know good and damn well what you and the *shire reeve* have been doing." Winnie gave him a seething look. "It's after eight. Your radio is off. While you two have been monkeying around, I've been fielding calls from dispatch."

Dev pushed his chair back and got to his feet. "My radio was off?" He checked the device on his belt. "Seems to be working fine now. Probably a glitch."

"I silenced the device," Arta said with cool indifference. "It squawks in a most annoying fashion, and I desired the shire reeve's full attention."

"You desired—" Winnie slammed her hand on the table. "Damn it, Dev. Do something with her."

Arta raised her brows. "He has been 'doing something' with me. Were you not attending?"

"That's it," Winnie said. "I'm not riding with her."

"Bah," Arta said. "I do not need your offices."

"The two of you are riding together," Dev said flatly. "The matter is not negotiable."

"But, *Dev*—"

"Shire reeve," Arta protested.

"Together," Dev said. "And Winnie? Teach Arta how to handle a gun. I want her proficient with it."

"I do not—" Arta began.

"Yes, you do," Dev said, cutting her off. "A gun is not a plaything." He set his plate and cup in the sink. "Your first assignment is to find Toby Littleton."

"The shifter?" Arta said.

"Yep," Dev said. "Round him up and bring him to the station. And, for God's sake, the two of you get along."

"But of course, shire reeve." Arta folded her hands on the table, her expression demure. "I will be the soul of affability. You will be all astonishment. This I vow."

"Jesus, give me strength," Winnie said. "I'm going to kill her."

* * * *

Three weeks later

"You've brought me the wrong guy." Dev frowned at the deputies standing beside his desk. "This can't be him."

The man lounging in a chair in front of his desk was tall and fit, with thick, wavy brown hair that hung below his broad shoulders. His long, lean legs were encased in jeans, and he wore scuffed boots and a faded Buckingham Nicks T-shirt. He was handsome and young—in his late twenties, if Dev had to guess.

Much too young to be Toby Littleton.

"I've met the man," Dev said. "Toby Littleton's seventy years old, if he's a day."

The man propped one booted ankle on his knee. "A hunnert and sixty-three come November twenty-fifth, according to the family Bible," he drawled. "Granny Eller raised me, but she couldn't write. Cleotha—that was Granny Eller's sister—didn't record my birth in the Bible until years later." He scratched his head. "Never was sure Cleo got the year right."

"You see?" Arta's eyes held a challenging glint. "This is the shifter you seek."

The man's white teeth flashed in an easy smile. "Don't know why you're looking for me, Sheriff, but I'm sure enough Toby Littleton."

"Prove it," Dev said.

"I already showed these nice deputies my driver's license."

"Driver's licenses can be faked," Dev said. "And it's not just your age. You don't look a thing like Littleton. You're too..."

"Comely?" Arta suggested. "Handsome and winsome? Of an aspect most fair and pleasing?"

Dev shot her a glance of annoyance. "Beefy. Toby Littleton is whiteleather and gristle."

The man chuckled. "Conall didn't tell you what happened to me?"

"Conall and I are not what you'd call close."

Arta made a derisive noise. "You would get aught from him in any case. The captain is besotted with his wife and twins. Faith, I cannot understand the appeal. Babies mewl and cry and soil themselves. What is more, they require constant care."

"They're trouble, but they're worth it," the man said. "Can't wait to hold my new grandbabies. 'Course, Beck ain't really mine, but might as well be. I brung her up from a little scrap. You know her daddy, Jason? He owns the Burger Doodle in Hannah."

"I know him," Dev said. "He makes a mean hamburger."

"Beck's father is the creator of the Party Burger?" Arta's eyes shone. "The man is an artist and his special sauce"—she kissed her fingers—"divine. Winnie, we must pay the Burger Doodle another visit, and soon."

"You're worse than a teenage boy," Winnie grumbled. "Always thinking about food."

"I think of many things—one in particular, but you do not like me to speak of it."

"Damn straight. Keep that mess to yourself."

"'Tis not *mess*. 'Strewth, I do not understand your aversion," Arta said. "Coitus is—"

"Zip it," Winnie said. "Not one word about *coitus* or *swiving* or *coupling*. It's gross."

"'Tis not gross," Arta said. "Copulation is enjoyable and highly beneficial to mind and body." She gave Dev a smoldering look that made his heart jerk. "Do you not agree, shire reeve?"

Three pairs of eyes regarded him with interest. Dev's neck and ears burned. He glanced at Arta. Her luscious mouth was curved in a secret smile. She knew her effect on him. The she-devil was taunting his weakness.

"Shire reeve?"

Dev cleared his throat. "You were saying?" he said to the man sitting across his desk.

"I was telling you about Beck," he said. "Me and Jason were partners back in the day. His wife got possessed and ran off. Showed up months later with a baby girl."

"Beck?" Dev asked.

"Yup. Jason's a norm through and through. Couldn't wrap his head around the idea of a kith baby. Didn't know what to make of her. Mind you, he did his best, but he'd pretty much turnt Becky over to me by the time she was four."

"He knew you were kith?"

"He knew I wasn't human. Caught me shifting once." He laughed. "That was a fun day. Almost ended our friendship, but then Becky started doing things and..." He shrugged. "Jason asked for my help, and I obliged. Best thing ever happened to me. I gave Becky away at her wedding, you know."

Dev did know. Details of Beck and Conall's nuptials had passed through the kith community like wildfire, reaching him. Toby Littleton had given Beck Damian away at her wedding with the Dalvahni in attendance.

Another bead on Dev's mental abacus clicked into place.

"Okay," he said. "You walk like a duck, and you quack like a duck, so we'll assume you're a duck."

"What have ducks to do with anything?" Arta demanded.

"It's an expression, nimrod," Winnie said. "Try to keep up."

"'Tis a stupid expression."

"So are *'strewth* and *forsooth* and *mayhap* and half the other shit you say."

"Fie on you, benighted rube," said Arta.

"There, you see? I don't know what that means."

"And thus you embody the epithet."

Toby gazed at Dev with sympathy. "They go at it like this often?"

"All the time," Dev said. "How do you explain your appearance? Are you a chameleon?"

"Nah, my shifter form is a dog," Toby said. "You know Cassie Ferguson? The norms call her the witch of Devil River, but Cassie ain't no witch. She's one of us."

Dev knew Cassie. He'd been at her place on the river the first time he'd seen Jeb Hannah, the walking, talking bronze statue. Dev had seen a lot of strange things, but that one had come as a shock.

Jeb. Good God, what was he going to do about Jeb? He couldn't keep an animated statue at Aunt Wee's forever.

"Cassie and I have met," he said, pushing aside his worry about Jeb. "Go on."

"Me and Cassie go way back. Several weeks ago, she asked me to deliver a message to Zeb Randall. He was the pack alpha at the time. Zeb turned out to be a whack job. Real paranoid piece of work. Obsessed with something called the orb."

"I'm familiar with it."

Sugar had the orb. The worry worm in Dev's brain started wiggling again. Was Sugar all right? He'd told him to hide. And, in true Sugar-good-boy fashion, the bigfoot had outdone himself. No one had seen the sasquatch in weeks. Pratt, either, but he was out there, somewhere. Dev sensed the god's malignant presence like a gathering storm. Pratt knew that Sugar could wield the orb. The bigfoot had used it to free Gryffin. Pratt would be more eager than ever to capture Sugar and bend him—and the orb—to his will. Dev couldn't let that happen.

"Go on," he said, forcing his focus back to the present conversation.

"Zeb and his weres jumped me. Tore me up bad. Would've died if Duncan hadn't healed me." The man's mismatched eyes, one purple, the other hazel, studied Dev. "Verbena helped. Gave him a little boost, if you know what I mean. You remember Verbena? Skinny thang. Smart as a whip. You met her at Beck's Bar a few days before it burned down." His handsome face creased in a scowl. "Earl Skinner done that, the low-down buzzard. Know you ain't supposed to speak ill of the dead, but he was a trifling piece of trash."

"Earl Skinner is dead?" Dev straightened in his chair. "I've had a BOLO on him for months. What happened to him?"

"Got his sorry ass et by a dragon, that's what."

"A drag—" Dev caught himself. "Never mind, I don't want to know. As for Verbena, of course I remember her." He hesitated and decided, what the hell? He'd told Arta and Winnie about Verbena weeks ago. Aunt Wee, too. What was one more person? "As a matter of fact, we're related."

"What, like cousins?"

"No. She's my sister—half-sister, to be exact."

"That right?" Toby's easygoing expression hardened into an unforgiving mask. "If Verbena's kin, how come you didn't help her? That gal's been through hell backwards."

"I didn't know," Dev said. "Had I known, I would've done something about it, but I didn't find out about the Skinners or that Verbena and I were siblings until last month."

"That right?" Toby sat back with a grunt. "Reckon you ain't to blame, then. You an enhancer, too?"

"No," Dev said. "Not even close."

"The shire reeve is too modest," Arta said. "He is a demigod, the son of Sildhjort."

"Phila who?"

"*Sil*-dhjort," Arta said, repeating the name with emphasis, "one of the lesser gods."

"Don't know him."

"You would not. He is seldom seen and keeps mostly to the woods."

A slow grin spread across Toby's face. "The sheriff is a dimmy?" He smacked his palm on the arm of the chair. "I *told* Beck you weren't no norm. A dimmy—if that don't take the rag off the bush."

"Yes, well…you were saying?" Dev asked, embarrassed. "The weres attacked you, and then what?"

"That's pretty much it, except that Verbena gave Duncan a little push," Toby said. "Faster 'n you can say Lash LaRue, I was good as new. Better, in fact."

"Lash LaRue?" Winnie said. "Who's that?"

"Western film star from the nineteen forties."

"Word of advice, bro," she advised. "Twentysomethings don't talk about old dead people. It's a tell."

"Lash ain't dead," Toby said. "He's one of us. Lives on a slough in Bon Secour. Charters fishing boats these days."

Dev sat back in his chair. His internal lie detector rarely failed him, and this man was not lying.

"He's telling the truth," he said at last. "He really is Toby Littleton."

"Dadnabbit, I *told* you I was," Toby said. "Why would I make up a whopper like 'at?"

"People lie," Dev said. "They lie about big things and little things. They lie to save their skins or to keep from hurting someone else. Sometimes people lie for the pure-t fun of it."

"Well, I ain't lying."

"Be not perplexed, good sir," Arta said in her dulcet voice. "The shire reeve believes you, and so do I. Your story matches Duncan's account."

Slowly, Dev turned his head to look at her. "Duncan's account?"

"Duncan and Verbena mended someone named Toby Littleton, a demonoid savaged by werewolves and left to die." Her lips tightened in disapproval. "Indeed, they did more than heal the stricken shifter. They fundamentally *changed* him."

"That's right." Toby opened his arms wide. "I'm a new man, Sheriff. Done been youth-a-nized and Dalvahni-ized."

"You knew about this?" Dev demanded, staring at Arta. "How?"

"I was present when Duncan confessed the deed to Kehvahn." She opened her eyes wide. "Surely I have mentioned it?"

"No," Dev said. "You have not."

"How surpassing strange." Her brow creased. "'Tis not like me to forget such a salient fact."

"Hold on." Winnie's eyes were bright with anger. "Are you saying— You *knew* about this and didn't tell me?"

"I did not conceal the matter a-purpose, if that is what you mean." Arta shrugged. "What does it matter? We found him."

"What does it—" Winnie sputtered. "We've been looking for some old wrinkle bag for *weeks*, not Stud Lee McMuffin here." She glanced at Toby in apology. "No offense."

"None taken."

"*You* may have been looking for an old man," Arta said, unruffled, "but I have not."

"Why you—" Winnie looked ready to blow a gasket. "You…you—"

"It's done. Let it go." Dev turned to Toby. "What the deputies say is true. They've been looking for you the past three weeks. Where have you been?"

"Winston County," Toby said. "The change come as a shock, as you can imagine. Skedaddled up there to clear my head. Got me a cabin not far from Nauvoo. Peaceful and quiet. Good place to think, and I know a feller in Double Springs makes IDs, so it was a twofer."

"He knows a feller," Dev muttered. "Wonderful."

"What else could I do?" Toby made a helpless gesture. "Time was a person could stay off the grid. Slide in and out of the same town every fifty years or so without causing a fuss, but not no more. The Man, you know?"

"What man?" Arta asked.

"He means the government," Dev explained. "Paperwork and proof of identity."

"Got a new body, needed new IDs," Toby said, "so I took care of things legal and proper."

"With fake papers," Dev said. "Jesus wept."

"Dadgummit, what other kind of papers you 'spect me to get?" Toby said. "I can't go around with a driver's license issued in 1953."

Arta lifted a brow. "An you wished a new beginning, why not change your name?"

"Did," Toby said. "I go by Tobias James *Aloysius* Littleton, now. Added the Aloysius, see?"

"Oh, yeah," Winnie said. "The Aloysius makes a huge difference."

"Different enough," Toby said. "If anyone asks, the old me was my uncle."

"I am my own grandpa," said Winnie brightly.

"Done that, too, after the Great War," Toby said. "Poodled around Europe for a few years and come back to the States as my own grandson."

"Good God," Dev said.

"What about her?" Toby jerked a thumb at Arta. "She got papers?"

"Funny you should ask." Winnie smirked. "Deputy Kirvahni's paperwork keeps getting mysteriously lost."

"Thank you, Winnie," Dev said. "I'm sure Mr. Littleton isn't interested in an administrative snafu."

"Snafu my—"

"No doubt you're wondering why you're here," Dev said, giving her a repressive frown. "I need a tracker, and I hear you're the best."

"Depends on the quarry. I can smell supers." Toby tapped his nose. "Power's like pepper in my snout. Being in the room with the three of you, it's a blue wonder I ain't sneezing my head off."

"You knew we weren't norms from the get-go?" Winnie asked.

"'Course I knew," Toby said. "Same as I knew the sheriff wasn't no norm the first time I seed him."

There was a knock on the door, and Willa Dean, the receptionist, stepped into the room. A tall, dignified matron with a tussock of lacquered gray hair piled high as the Tower of Pisa, Willa Dean had been a fixture at the Sheriff's Department since before Dev had joined. No one knew Willa Dean's age. No one dared ask.

She wore her usual uniform, a neatly ironed, pleated cotton dress belted at the waist and low-heeled shoes.

"Mayor Tunstall is on the phone." Her flinty eyes snapped with irritation. "He insists on speaking with you."

"I'm busy," Dev said. "Tell him I'll get back to him."

"He's called ten times this week. I have more important things to do than mollify that sawed-off possum toter."

"That's a good one." Toby grinned at Willa Dean. "On account of the mayor has a pet possum."

Willa Dean did not return his smile. "I don't recall asking your opinion."

"No, ma'am, you sure didn't." Toby made a quick, twisting motion at one corner of his mouth. "Shutting my mouth. Not another word from me. No sirree."

"Thank you, Willa Dean," Dev said. "Tell the mayor there are no updates on the missing statue, and I'll get back to him when I have news."

"Humph." Willa Dean fixed Toby with her steely glare. "You've changed."

"Yes, ma'am."

"Humph," she said again and stalked from the room.

Dev gazed at Toby in surprise. "She recognized you?"

"Yep."

"How?"

"Nothing much gets past Willa Dean." Toby chuckled. "Crabby old coot, but that's the way with the echidna. They ain't known for sweetness and light."

Dev's jaw sagged. "What did you—are you saying Willa Dean is a-a..."

"Gorgon," Toby said. "Offspring of Echidna, the mother of monsters."

"Are you *sure*?"

"'Course I'm sure. I'm on the Kith Council, and she's registered." He gave Dev an appraising look. "Which is more 'n I can say for you."

"I'm not kith."

"Neither is old Snake Dome."

"My aunt didn't add my name to the register when I was born. She wanted me to decide for myself."

"When you were older," Toby said, nodding in understanding, "and oncet you become sheriff, you decided to stay under the radar. Smart. You can slide in and out with nobody none the wiser, be they kith or norm."

"That's the idea," Dev said. "The less people know about me, the better."

"A man of mystery," Toby said. "Sheriff, you got more layers than an onion."

"The shire reeve is not an onion," Arta said. "He is a turnip."

Toby's brows shot up. "'Scuse me?"

"Nothing," Dev said. "It's a private joke."

There was another knock on the door, and Jim Parks came in. The graying deputy turned beet red when he saw Arta.

"S-sorry, didn't realize you were busy, Sheriff," he stammered. "I can come back."

"No, what is it, Parks?" Dev asked.

"We got the forensics back on the fibers found at the Freeman scene. It was from a cotton dress shirt, high-end and expensive."

"A man's dress shirt?"

"Yes, sir."

Russ, Dev thought. Russ liked expensive clothes.

"What about the tire prints?" he asked.

"Tires were Goodrich, nineteen fives."

"That's a big help," Winnie said. "Every redneck in Behr County with a trailer and a load has a truck with nineteen fives."

"The right back print was altered," Parks said. "Believed to be caused by a deficiency in the tire tread."

"I do not understand," Arta said. "Deficiency in the tread?"

Parks glanced at her. His color deepened, and he jerked his attention back to Dev.

"There's a small chunk missing in the rubber, about the size of a coin," he said. "Should make it easier to narrow down the owner."

"Continue," Dev said. "What else?"

Parks stared at the piece of paper in his hand as if he'd forgotten how to read. "Forensics also notes that the tire tread looks new," he managed at last. "Want me to have Willa Dean call some of the local tire places, see who's bought new tires recently?"

"*No*," Dev and Toby said sharply in chorus.

"Jeez, there's no need to shout," Parks said. "She won't eat me."

"She might do worse," Dev said. "Mayor Tunstall's been pecking her to death about Jeb Hannah's statue, and she's in a mood."

"Oh," Parks said. "*Oh*. Thanks for the warning. I'll make the calls myself."

"Excellent idea."

Parks darted another flustered glance at Arta and hurried out.

"What ails the man?" Arta asked when he'd gone. "Is he addled?"

"Stupefyin' Jones," Toby said. "She was a character in the funnies. You done rooted him to the spot."

"I know not what you mean."

"Comic strips," Dev said. "A form of entertainment."

"Yes, the Provider has explained," Arta said. "What has this to do with Parks?"

"Stupefyin' Jones was so gorgeous, she froze hapless males with her feminine wiles," Toby said. "Like you. You done stupefied Parks."

"Hapless males? Feminine wiles?" Arta's eyes narrowed. "Methinks you are not the ignorant bumpkin you pretend to be."

"I talk slow, but that don't mean I'm stupid," Toby said. "Got three undergraduate degrees and an MBA from the University of Alabama. First degree was in the eighteen seventies," he said, ticking the items off on his fingers, "the second was after World War I, and the last 'un I got in the sixties." He smiled wistfully. "The sixties were fun, man. I was a hippie."

"Really?" Winnie murmured. "Who would've thought?"

"But that ain't neither here nor there." Toby looked at Dev. "You're interested in my nose, not my education. What kind of super are you looking for?"

"I'm looking for several, actually," Dev said. "A sasquatch, a god, a Dalvahni warrior named Gryffin, and Verbena."

Toby chuckled. "Is that all? Piece of cake."

"I'm serious."

Toby sobered. "Well, now, Sheriff, if this here swamp ape you're looking for is Sugar, I'm gonna pass. Sugar saved my life. Found me in the woods and toted me back to Cassie's place, or I wouldn't be sitting here."

"Sugar's not in trouble with the law," Dev said. "He has something called the orb, and a crazy god is after it."

"This here crazy god got a name?"

"Pratt," Dev said, "and he's extremely dangerous."

Arta frowned at Dev. "Hold. You neglected to mention Korth."

"I'm not worried about Korth," Dev said. "He's the least of my problems."

"You may be unconcerned, but Korth is a priority with me." Arta turned to Toby. "You are familiar with thralls?"

"Know what they are," Toby said. "Met one oncet, a real looker named Lenora. This Korth gal a looker, too?"

"Korth is not a woman," Arta said. "He is an incubus, a male demon. He followed me here and must be returned to the proper plane."

"Why, what's he done?"

"Nothing that we know of," Winnie said. "She's afraid Korth will screw someone to death. He's a sex vampire, only he gets his jollies from emotion, not blood." She met Dev's gaze. Her expression was innocent. "What? That's what Arta said."

"Screw someone to death." Toby chuckled. "If that don't beat all. What does he look like?"

"Muscular build, around my height," Dev said. "Long blond hair. Weighs maybe two hundred and fifty pounds. Last seen wearing a leather kilt."

"That should narrow it down." Toby's eyes crinkled at the corners. "Can't be too many sexed-up Thor types running around in a skirt, even in Behr County."

"So you would think," Arta said, "but my sisters Illaria and Jakka have sought Korth a fortnight and more, to no avail. He has proven elusive."

"I told you, but you won't listen," Winnie said. "Korth probably went back to Horny Town, or wherever it is thralls hang out."

"They reside in the House of Eternal Bliss, and he is not there," Arta said, giving her a severe look. "Illaria has checked."

Toby coughed. "Five supers. That it?"

"Yes," Dev said. "Report back to me when you find them, but don't go near them."

"Same go for Sugar?"

"Yes," Dev said, "and Verbena and Gryffin. I want to know where they are. Nothing more."

Toby tilted his chair back. "You up to sumpin, Sheriff. What is it?"

"I've got an idea. It might not work. Don't want to jinx it."

"Didn't figure you for the superstitious sort."

"I prefer to think of it as being cautious. A smart player doesn't tip his hand," Dev said. "What I need from you is information, plain and simple. You in or out? I can pay you from the discretionary fund."

"Money, I got. Made a few investments here and there, so I'm comfortable. Tell you what I would like, though."

"What's that?"

"Got me a hankering to be a deputy."

Dev stared at him in surprise. "You're interested in law enforcement?"

"Gotta find something to do with my time." Toby shrugged. "Latrisse is managing the restaurant for Becky and doing a fine job, so I ain't needed there. Been cogitating on it, and I reckon you could use my nose around here." He grinned. "Behr County ain't short on supernatural criminals."

"Entry-level deputy position doesn't pay much. Thirty-five thou to start, plus benefits."

"That's fine. Ain't in it for the money."

"You'd be arresting your own kind," Dev said. "You okay with that?"

"Don't expect it will keep me up at night. You?"

"No, but I'm not kith. Even if I were, I'd bring them in. Someone—anyone—breaks the law in my county, they answer for it."

"I can respect that," Toby said. "As for family, I ain't got no one but Beck, and I don't see her getting sideways with the law."

"You'll have to resign from the Kith Council," Dev said. "It would be a conflict of interest."

"Planning to do that anyway, what with the new face and all," Toby said. "Did a lot of thinking while I was at the cabin and come to a conclusion. The less I say about 'the change,' the better it'll be for Verbena. The Council gets wind of her abilities, they'll try to use her. Politics." He shook his head. "Some bastard is always trying to get the upper hand. Know what I mean?"

"As a matter of fact, I do," Dev said, thinking of the County Commission. "Do you have any law enforcement experience?"

"Yup, but it's been a while."

"How long a while?"

Toby tugged on his ear. "Lemme see...hunnert years or so, best I can recall. Hightailed it out of Alabama in my twenties and went to Texas. Granny Eller's brother was with the Rangers, and I joined up. We worked the mining towns for a spell. Tracked down robbers and cattle thieves, that kind o' thing." Toby's eyes were bright. "Uncle Caleb was a pistol, sure nuff. Them were wild and wooly days."

"The *Texas* Rangers?"

"Yup."

"How long were you with them?"

"Couple of decades, if 'n I remember right. I signed up in eighteen eighty-six and got out before the Great War."

"You'll do," Dev said. "I'll start you out as a reserve officer. If things work out and you decide to make it permanent, you'll attend the Academy."

"Right." Toby rose and shook Dev's hand. His grip was firm, his fingers lean and strong. "'Preciate the opportunity, Sheriff. You won't regret it. You want me to start tracking them supers right away?"

"Yes," Dev said. "Locate and report. Nothing more."

"Got it."

"Be careful," Dev said. "Pratt's a psycho, and Gryffin..." He recalled the flaming figure on the bridge. "I'm not sure what Gryffin is, but he could be more dangerous than Pratt."

"Begging your pardon, but if he's such a bad 'un, why are you letting your sister run around with him?"

"Not much I can do about it."

"The hell there ain't. You tried talking to her?"

"Yes. Verbena has a mind of her own. She's convinced Gryffin needs her."

"Maybe he does," Toby said. "Stranger things have happened, but I don't like it. Fond of Verbena. Don't want to see her hurt."

"Neither do I," said Dev.

Toby strolled for the door. He paused and looked back at Arta. "You're a demon hunter. Been around the block a time or two."

"I am a seasoned warrior." Arta folded her arms on her chest. "What of it?"

"Piece of advice. Willa Dean's a vegetarian. A basket of fresh fruit or a nice salad would be appreciated. Partial to figs and local honey, too."

"What are Willa Dean's caprices to me?"

"Local honey helps with the sniffles." Toby tapped the end of his nose. "You ever gotten sideways with a gorgon with seasonal allergies?"

"I cannot say that I have."

"Didn't think so." Toby flashed them the peace sign. "Ladies...Sheriff. It's been groovy."

He ambled out the door and was gone.

Chapter Eighteen

"No, like this." Winnie leveled the Glock .22 at the target on the tree and fired, hitting the man-shaped silhouette squarely in the chest. "See?"

Arta eyed the neat holes in the paper. "My vision is unimpaired. What is your point?"

"You're supposed to aim the gun, not use magic. Bullets don't leave sparkly trails in the air or zoom around a tree before they hit the target."

"You mislike pink? I will gladly change the color."

"Forget the color. No glitter and no zooming. It's physics not a cartoon show."

"Bah." Arta indicated the holes peppering the center of the bright yellow outline. "The result is the same."

"You used magic. Bet you can't hit the side of a barn without it."

Arta raised her brows. "You doubt my marksmanship?"

"Yeah." Winnie attached a fresh target to the tree trunk and stepped back. "Fire again, and no cheating."

Arta discharged her weapon at the human form. "There, 'tis done," she said. "Regard you the—what did you call them?—perfectly executed kill shots to the head and chest."

"Nice," Winnie said. "There's just one problem. You aimed the gun, but you didn't pull the trigger."

"I directed the weapon to fire. It complied."

"You *directed* the gun to fire?" Winnie smacked her forehead with her palm. "Listen to what you're saying. That's cuckoo for Cocoa Puffs. What if you're working with Parks or some other norm? You can't fire your weapon without pulling the trigger. Someone is bound to notice."

"Should that happen, I will adjust their memories."

Winnie threw her hands up in disgust. "Fine. Shoot daisies out of the damn thing, for all I care."

"You are overwrought."

"I'm *pissed*. We've been at it an hour, and you haven't made any progress. This was a waste of time."

"I cannot agree." Arta looked around with a sense of satisfaction. The wind sighed through the trees, and a nearby stream chuckled and sang. "Me, I am enjoying myself vastly. These woods are unspoiled and idyllic."

"This is Dev's land."

"Indeed? 'Twas thoughtful of him to send us here."

"He wasn't being thoughtful," Winnie said. "He told me to bring you where it's safe."

Arta raised her brows. "We are in danger?"

"Not us—the norms. Dev doesn't want you at the practice range."

"Why not?"

"Because, Madam Mim, he's afraid you'll pull some freaky shit and wig people out."

"Madam Mim?"

"Ugly witch with purple hair."

"I am neither a witch nor ugly. I am a demon hunter."

"Lighten up. It was a joke."

"Ah, camaraderie. We are having fun, are we not?"

"Look at my face." Winnie glowered. "Do I look like I'm having fun?"

"In truth, you seem slightly dyspeptic. Something you ate has disagreed with you, a bit of fish, perhaps?"

"It's nothing I ate. It's you. You annoy the ever-living shit out of me."

"What have I done to earn your censure?"

"Everything."

"That is not helpful. Strive to be more specific."

"I can't train you. You're hopeless. I'd have better luck training a squirrel."

"Bah, you exaggerate."

"A squirrel, Arta, a frigging pea-brained squirrel."

"A squirrel's brain is not the size of a pea. A squirrel's brain is the same size as that of a crocodile, a large predatory reptile found—"

"I know what a crocodile is, for God's sake. I don't need a dissertation."

"Patience, little sister," Arta said. "Or do you enjoy acting like a wild ass in a field of barley?"

"I'm an ass? You've got a lot of—" She stopped short and frowned. "What did you call me?"

"Little sister," Arta said. "I told you before that you are one of us. Anger is an unproductive emotion. Control it or find a healthier means of release. Something less destructive."

"I swear to God, Arta, if you tell me to get laid one more time, I'll—"

"You'll what?"

"I don't know, but it won't be pretty."

Arta shrugged. "Regardless, your comparison is inept. I am not a squirrel. A squirrel could not possibly wield a Gluck—"

"Glock," Winnie said through her teeth. "It's called a *Glock*."

"—or wear this uniform."

"What?"

"It could not be altered to fit so small an animal."

"That's it. I'm done."

Arta regarded her thoughtfully. "You yield too easily. A Dalvahni warrior knows patience in the pursuit of a goal."

"I'm not Dalvahni."

"Neither are you human. You have the essence of a Dalvahni warrior, thanks to Eamon. But for his intercession, you would be dead."

"I didn't ask him to save me. If Aunt Wee and Dev hadn't been around to explain things, I'd have been royally screwed." Winnie sent a pine cone sailing with her foot. "Your boy Eamon left a time bomb ticking and split."

"Split?"

"Left. Took the phantom train. Exited the building with Elvis. Vamoosed."

"You're saying that he quit this sphere?"

"Yeah, like his leather britches were on fire."

"Demon hunters are not maternal," Arta said. "Death is our constant companion, indifference our armor. And yet, something about you appealed to Eamon. Appealed to him so much that he defied our laws to spare you. 'Tis extraordinary."

"Yay. Remind me to send him a bouquet."

"You are tense."

Winnie rolled her neck and shoulders. "I'm antsy as hell. Something's coming. Something bad. I feel it."

"Is it the djegrali?"

"Maybe. I dunno." Winnie picked up a stick and broke it against a tree. "It's probably nothing. I've been on edge since Bucky showed up."

"Bucky?"

"Eamon. He reminds me of Captain America's sidekick."

"I fear I do not—"

"You wouldn't."

"What does Eamon have to do with your ill humor?"

"Everything. He drives me up the wall."

Arta nodded in understanding. "The Dal can be galling." She motioned, and the used target was replaced with a clean one. "Shall we continue?"

"Magic, again?" Winnie looked at her in disgust. "I could have changed the target, you know."

"My way is faster. Have you consulted the Provider as I suggested? 'Tis time you honed your skills."

"I've been busy. Haven't had time."

"You must make time. 'Tis important."

"For God's sake, don't nag."

"Enough, Winifred. Let us be done with strife," Arta said. "'Tis too glorious a day for brangling."

Winnie scowled. "Don't call me Winifred."

"You dislike it?"

"Yeah. I got teased about it something awful in school. Winifred Sanderson is a bucktoothed witch in a Disney film. A real meanie who preys on children."

"Another crone? 'Strewth, you are preoccupied with maleficent beings today."

"When you're a kid, you watch movies."

"You are no longer a child. Set aside the cruel japes you endured and embrace your name. 'Tis lovely."

"It's not just that. It's..."

"'Tis what?"

"Winfred was my grandfather's middle name, all right? I'm named after him."

"A signal honor."

"Yeah? You don't get it." Winnie clenched her hands. "I don't *deserve* to be named after him. They murdered him while I stood there like a dope."

"You were a child confronted by unspeakable evil," Arta said. "There is naught you could have done."

"I don't care. I still should have tried." Winnie hunched her shoulders. "Forget it. You wouldn't understand."

"You feel guilt, because you are alive and he is not," Arta said, "and regret for the moments not cherished. There is anger also and sorrow, a vast sea of it, and a thirst for revenge that cannot be quenched."

Winnie stared at her. "You lost someone?"

"A most beloved sister." Arta gazed at the target on the tree, unseeing. "Our wise and noble leader, Valla. She was the High Huntress afore me."

"I thought demon hunters were indestructible."

"We are a hardy race, but our life force ebbs when we are beheaded. Valla was slain by the giant Urq in battle."

"A giant? Cool."

Arta frowned. "You and the shire reeve share a foolish obsession with dangerous creatures. Giants are not 'cool'."

"Don't be a joy suck. What did the giant look like?"

"As giants go, Urg was not large—perhaps thrice the height of a man with thews of iron and shoulders wide as an oxcart. He had a large, craggy nose, and a forehead that bulged like an overstuffed grain sack. His hair was long and matted with animal fat and debris, and he was unclad but for a sheepskin loincloth." Arta wrinkled her nose. "The stench of him I remember still. 'Twas a horrible malodor of sweat, excrement, and dead things."

"Yuck. He killed Valla?"

"Aye. She confronted him whilst I led the charge against his goblin army. I took an arrow to the thigh and shoulder. The rakka I rode was—"

"The what?"

"An armored rabbit, the mount favored in that demesne."

"You rode a bunny into battle?"

"The rakka are huge, the size of a warhorse, and possessed of enormous stamina. Moreover, they are easily trained."

"If you say so. You charged in on Peter Cottontail—then what?"

Peter Cottontail? An image of a fictional rabbit flashed through Arta's mind.

"You speak of a whimsical creature," she said sternly. "The rakka are majestic mounts."

"With fluffy white tails."

"My steed was pierced by a spear and went down," she continued, ignoring Winnie. "Valla heard the animal scream and looked back. Urq seized upon her distraction and struck her head from her neck with an axe. So, you see, I know something of loss and regret. Valla died because of me."

"What happened to the giant?"

"I killed him and mounted his head on a pike for the crows."

"I thought you were injured?"

"The Kir heal in an instant but for beheading."

"And now you're High Huntress. Awkward."

"The irony was not lost on me when I was chosen to be the High Huntress," Arta confessed. "My inclination was to decline, but I thought better of it." She gave Winnie a steady look. "A mewling sob-gut, Valla would dub me, should I wallow in self-pity and loathing and neglect my duty."

"I can't help the way I feel."

"You can and you must, or else be shackled to the past. Do not forget what happened—learn from it."

"Thanks, Obi Wan," Winnie muttered. "I'll tape that to my mirror."

Arta paid her no heed. "Carry your grandsire's name proudly. Live well and be happy. 'Tis how you may honor him best." She adjusted her stance. Placing one foot in front of the other, she turned her shoulders to face the target. "Enough. Attend you me."

Gripping the pistol firmly, she focused her eyes on the front sight and squeezed the trigger smoothly and evenly. *Crack, crack, crack,* three holes appeared in the center of the target.

Arta lowered her weapon. "Behold. I aimed the weapon and pulled the trigger as instructed. I trust you are gratified?"

Winnie walked over to the tree to inspect the target and spun around. "You heifer. You've been messing with me."

Arta grinned. "I have, I confess."

"You didn't need training." Winnie's eyes were bright with anger. "You already knew how to handle a gun."

"I am a demon hunter. We have a natural affinity for weapons of every ilk."

"Damn it, Arta, why didn't you say so?"

"In truth, I do not know. Some imp of mischief seized me, and I could not seem to help myself. Levity is quite enjoyable, is it not?"

"Yeah, I've been having a swell time. Who taught you to shoot—Dev?"

"Nay, I consulted the Provider and read the Academy instruction on gun safety. I also memorized the gunsmith's guidebook. Did you know that Gaston Glock, the inventor of the gun we carry, first constructed something called a curtain rod ere he turned to weaponry?"

"Gaston—so the 'Gluck' thing was a joke, too?" Winnie groaned. "I should've known. Why, Arta? Why not save us the time and trouble?"

"What is time to a demon hunter? In truth, I have enjoyed our outings, and it seemed important to the shire reeve."

"You traipsed into the woods to please Dev?"

"Why not?" Arta shrugged. "'Tis a small thing."

"Lurve." Winnie shook her head. "You got it bad."

Arta's earlier amusement evaporated, and her head felt strangely light. "You are mistaken. I am not in love with the shire reeve."

"Oh, please. Sell that shit to someone else. Dev's eat up with it, too."

The world seemed to tip and then right itself. "You believe the shire reeve has feelings for me?"

"Oh my God, girl. *Yes.* I've seen the way he looks at you. Like he could eat you up with a spoon. It's nauseating."

"If this is true, he has not spoken of it."

"He won't. That's your move. Dev would never pressure you to stay, especially if you don't feel the same way."

"He is an honorable man."

"Yeah. Dev's the best. Break his heart, and I'll kick your ass."

"I believe there is another reason for his silence," Arta said, brushing aside Winnie's threat. "The difference in our ages seems to chafe him."

"So, you're a few years older. Big deal."

"'Tis considerably more than a few. The shire reeve, I believe, is thirty-four in Earth years?"

"Yeah."

"I am ten thousand."

"Ten thousand—good God Almighty." An expression of mingled astonishment and dismay flitted across Winnie's face. "What about Bucky? Is he older than dirt, too?"

"The Kir and the Dal are of an age."

"Wow. That's a shit ton of parties."

"The Kir and the Dal do not celebrate the passing of the years."

"You're ten thousand years old, and you've never had a frigging birthday cake?" Winnie shook her head. "That stinks out loud."

"The shire reeve..." Arta hesitated. "You think the gulf between us too great?"

"Not necessarily, but I guess it doesn't matter since you're not in love with him."

"True." Arta heaved a sigh. "The Kir are not susceptible to emotion."

"Bullshit. If the Kir are so all-fired hard ass, why has your girl Taryn hooked up with an ogre?"

Arta frowned. "'Tis perplexing, I admit. Howe'er, it does not follow that *I* suffer from the same condition."

"It's love, Arta, not acid reflux. If you're not in love with Dev, prove it. Leave."

"Leave?" Panic sliced through Arta. "Now?"

"Wolves mate for life. The longer you hang around, the harder it's going to be for Dev to get over you."

"Get over me?"

"Move on to someone else."

A fist closed around Arta's heart. Devlin—*her* Devlin—with another? No.

"Holy cow, you should see your face," Winnie said. "You're jealous."

"I am not—"

"Are, too."

"I refuse to discuss this any further," Arta said. "As it happens, I cannot leave. The shire reeve and I are partners in this investigation. There is also the matter of Korth."

"I see. You're staying out of duty?"

"Of a certainty."

Winnie rolled her eyes. "What a crock."

The radio on her belt crackled, and a feminine voice droned, "BR-Eighteen, come in."

"This is BR-Eighteen." Winnie spoke into the device. "Cedrica, that you? What are you doing on dispatch?"

"Filling in for Willa Dean. There's a Ten-Ninety-seven-D on Peterson Mill Road outside of Hannah."

"Out where the old mill used to be, the one that burned down?"

"Ten-four. Scuffle at a pickle contest. Sheriff's requesting backup. What's your twenty?"

"Kirvahni and I are twenty miles away."

"Report to location. Proceed with caution."

"Copy." Winnie snatched up the stack of extra targets and strode off through the woods. "A fight at a pickle contest. I told you something bad was coming."

"A fight is nothing. At least 'tis not the djegrali."

"Rednecks are a different kind of demon."

They reached the patrol car, and Winnie tossed the paper targets in the trunk and got behind the wheel.

Arta climbed in on the passenger side. "When will I be allowed to operate this—what is it called again?"

"It's a Dodge Charger, and the answer is when hell freezes over and the devil sells ice cream."

She turned on the siren and sped down the dirt road, the vehicle kicking up dust and grit as she drove. Winnie gripped the wheel and stared straight ahead. Tension radiated from her. Her mood was contagious, and by the time they had reached the highway, Arta's nerves were stretched tight. Winnie turned onto the highway and headed south toward Hannah. With the narrow dirt road safely behind them, she drove faster, and the gray pavement sped by.

She rounded a wide bend in the road and slammed on the brakes. "Damn."

Arta leaned forward in her seat. "Why do we slow?"

"Combine harvester," Winnie said, motioning to the rumbling metal engine chugging down the road in front of them. "Three of them, in fact, with a tractor in the lead. We've got ourselves a convoy."

"Drive past. We must hasten."

"Can't. This is a no-passing zone." Winnie pointed to the double yellow line down the middle of the road. "See that sign on the berm, the one that looks like a snake?"

"What of it?"

"There are curves ahead. We could hit someone head-on if we try to go around these slowpokes."

"Then we shall go over them, not around them."

Arta made a sharp lifting motion with her hands, and the patrol car rose twenty feet in the air.

"Arta, what the hell are you—" Winnie clutched the steering wheel. "We're flying. Arta, *we're flying.*"

The vehicle sailed over the ponderous machines and landed with a gentle thump.

"What are you, nuts?" Winnie demanded. "Cars don't fly."

"'Tis not flying, precisely. 'Tis more like jumping."

"Cars don't jump, either."

"Our carriage is a Charger. A charger is a powerful warhorse. Warhorses jump."

"Patrol cars don't—forget it. What about those poor farmers? What are they going to think?"

"I care not. Drive, Winifred." Arta lifted a hand, palm up. "Or do we soar?"

Winnie let out a blistering string of profanities and pressed the pedal beneath her foot. The Charger raced down the highway, leaving the farm machines behind.

They were traveling quickly now, but not fast enough to suit Arta. Winnie was right. Something was amiss. Her unease increased with each passing mile. Devlin was in danger. She could feel it in her bones.

He needed her.

"Too slow," Arta said between clenched teeth. "We go too slowly."

"I'm going ninety on a two-lane road."

"Bah." Arta reached for the Provider. *Know you the location of a mill on Peterson Mill Road near the town called Hannah?*

The Provider's dry voice spoke in her mind. *The mill no longer exists.*

That is the place, Arta said. *Show me.*

An image appeared in her mind's eye. She oriented herself on the map.

"I go," she said. "You may join me anon."

"Go?" Winnie gave her a startled glance. "You can't go. We're partners."
"I go."
Arta allowed the Void to take her and disappeared.

Chapter Nineteen

Dev sped down Peterson Mill Road. It was more of a logging trail than a true road, really, a wide dirt track surrounded by scrub pine, hardwoods, wild honeysuckle, wisteria, kudzu, and privet hedge. A huge dog with wiry hair bounded out of the woods and halted in front of the Jeep.

Dev screeched to a stop in a flurry of red dust. He slammed the car into park and climbed out of the SUV. "That was a damn fool thing to do," he said, striding up to the panting hound. "You want to wind up a hood ornament?"

The dog's form blurred, and Toby Littleton appeared, wearing his deputy's uniform and a duty belt. His mismatched eyes shone with excitement. "Pratt's coming."

"You sure about this?"

"Oh, yeah, he's hard to miss." Toby's nose twitched with elation. "Headed for the festival."

The pickle festival was being held on the site of the old Peterson mill, where the new pickle factory would be. The remote location suited Dev's purposes to a T. Everything was finally coming together.

Unless something went wrong.

Dev shoved the worry aside. "Sugar?"

"Already here."

"You've seen him?"

"Eventually. Smelled him before I saw him," Toby said. "That bigfoot's a pickle thief. Snagging baby gherkins left and right. Saw them jars floating through the air and put two and two together. Sugar's made himself invisible. Did you know he can do that?"

"Yes." Dev remembered the disembodied mouth and eyeballs he'd seen floating outside the Sweet Shop window. "Where is he now?"

"Safe. Put him in a refrigerated truck with a case of pickles."

"That should keep him happy for a while."

"That was my thinking."

"And the others?"

Toby frowned. "I lost Verbena and that rogue feller this morning. Had 'em in my peepers, and they disappeared."

"Damn. I was counting on Verbena's help."

"You having second thoughts?"

"No, we're in too deep."

"Pratt follows Sugar, and the rogue follows Pratt," Toby said. "Verbena could still show up."

"Let's hope so." Dev opened the driver's side door of the Jeep. "Get in, unless you want to dog foot it the rest of the way?"

"I wouldn't mind a ride."

Dev got behind the wheel. Toby climbed in beside him, and they continued down the road in companionable silence.

"Got a call from dispatch on my way here," Dev said as the SUV bumped over a rut. "There's a Ten-Ninety-seven at the festival. I've called for backup."

"We don't need backup for no fight."

"Not for the fight." Dev paused significantly. "For the other thing."

"Oh. That."

"I've requested McCullough and Kirvahni."

"Good thinking. Parks and Johnson are swell, but they can't help with this."

"Nope," Dev said. "Teats on a boar hog."

"Forgot to tell you," Toby said. "Willa Dean's here. Saw her."

"She took the day off." Dev avoided a pothole. "She's entered a pickle contest. Been talking about it for weeks."

"It's a big deal. The category winners get their pickles added to the Jerkins' product line."

"Oh ho, she didn't tell me that part," Dev said. "Willa Dean is a shoo-in to win. She knows her way around a cucumber. Gives me a variety pack of pickles every Christmas."

Toby sat up straight. "She give 'em to the rest of the staff, too?"

"Yep. Hands them out at our annual Christmas party."

"Hot diggity dog." Toby rubbed his hands together. "Why didn't you say something before?"

Dev glanced at him in amusement. "Should I add it to our benefit package?"

"Sweetens the pot for sure."

Dev chuckled. He liked his new deputy. Toby was laid-back and amiable, and proving to be a damn good deputy. Plus, he was a super, which meant Dev didn't have to watch what he said around him. All in all, Toby was a good addition to the department.

"Bring me up to speed on this festival."

"They've gone all out," Toby said, his deep voice warming with enthusiasm. "There's a pickle eating contest and a pickle juice drink-off, and music, and line dancing. You can even get your picture took with the Pickle Princess."

"The what?"

"Sassy Peterson, the Pickle Princess," Toby said. "Her mama's Eleanor Jerkins, one of *the* Jerkinses. Peterson on one side, Jerkins on the other. Reckon that makes her a double heiress. Closest thing to royalty we got in these parts."

"We've met," Dev said. "She's Sassy Dalvahni now. Married a demon hunter a while back."

"Did she? Ain't that sumpin?" Toby said. "Demonoids, the Petersons, and rich as all get-out."

"Sassy's something else besides kith," Dev said. "Something... sparkly. Fairy, rumor has it."

"That so? Didn't know the Jerkins had fae blood."

"They don't. I'm told Sassy had an unpleasant encounter with a witch and had an accident. Best I can tell, she suffered a fairy infusion of some sort."

"Huh." Toby sounded impressed. "That's a new one on me, but I can't say as I'm surprised. She'd have to be forty kinds of magical to pull this shindig together in just a few months. Word is, they plan to make the festival an annual thing. Planning a pickle parade next year through downtown Hannah—in the fall so it won't interfere with the Peanut Festival."

"Another parade?" Dev made a note on his mental calendar to consult with Chief Davis at the Hannah PD. Parades meant stress and extra work for both departments. "Where'd you hear that?"

"Miss Vi, where else? She hears all the scuttlebutt."

That was true. The Sweet Shop was a hotbed of gossip and chatter. Dev glanced at his newest officer. Department regs required short hair, neatly trimmed.

"How are you adjusting to the new haircut?" he asked.

Toby shrugged. "It's hair, not a kidney. 'Sides, it grows back overnight."

"Over*night*?"

"Yup."

"Is that a demon hunter thing?"

"Yes, and no. Dalvahni hair grows fast, but not like mine. Duncan reckons it's on account of the boost your sister give me. Bought me some clippers and a pair of scissors, so's I can cut my hair every day."

"Every day?" Dev glanced at him, startled.

"Yup. Bound to get tongues a-wagging if 'n I showed up with my hair growed past my shoulders from one day to the next."

"You could rotate barbers. Cutting your own hair must get old."

"Ain't enough barbers in Behr County not to cause talk. I don't mind. I let it grow out on weekends. Duncan reckons things will calm down in a century or two." Toby paused. "Apparently, I'm going through a stage."

Dev chuckled. "You're a teenager, a *hormonal* Dalvahni teenager."

"Very funny. Been through that once, and it weren't no fun. You know how a teenage boy will get a woody? Imagine being a teenage *shifter*. Popped a shift oncet at a church social. Caused no end o' ruckus."

Dev laughed. "I'll bet. What happened?"

"Your aunt Weoka smoothed things over. She's got a way about her, your aunt."

"Yes, she does. I didn't realize you knew Aunt Wee."

"Lord, yes. Wee and I go way back."

"She never told me."

"Your aunt had a life before you, you know. Reckon there's a lot she ain't told you." Toby leaned forward and pointed to the line of cars and trucks parked along both sides of the road. "Better slow down. Ain't far now, maybe a mile."

Ahead of them, people streamed in and out of the entrance to the old mill. Dev eased the Jeep past the clutter of vehicles and festival attendees and stopped at the gates. A dark-skinned man in a canvas apron with the word TICKETS stamped on it walked up to the car.

Dev rolled down the window. "Hello, Leroy. I didn't expect to see you here. You sign on to work at the new pickle factory?"

"Hell, no. I'm a timberman, through and through," Leroy said. "Manage the Peterson properties, now the mill is gone. Miss Sassy asked me to help out today." He looked vaguely puzzled. "Can't say no to her, for some reason."

"She does have a way about her." Dev observed the mob of people. "Looks like somebody kicked over an anthill."

"I know, right?" Leroy waved at the people flowing in and out of the gates. "I'd rather take a poke in the eye with a sharp stick than be in this mess. What brings you here, Sheriff?"

"We got a call about a fight."

Leroy snorted. "That? Ain't what I call a fight. Claudine Kearley's bread and butters took third prize, and Duke got into it with the judges. You know how he is. Big as a grizzly and a temper to match. Tempest in a teapot."

Dev took his foot off the brake. "Thanks, Leroy. We'll check it out anyway, long as we're here."

Leroy shrugged. "Suit yourself. Food's good if you ain't interested in gee gaws."

Dev drove slowly through the gates. A two-lane dirt road ran through the festival. All traces of the burned lumber mill were gone, and the site had been bulldozed and cleared. Booths and tents mushroomed in the open space, and a large crowd milled around the multitude of vendors.

"Good God." Dev ran a quick mental tally. "There must be eight thousand people here and seventy or eighty merchants."

"The Jerkins family has influence," Toby said. "People have turned out in support."

Dev nodded and eased the Jeep through the throng of folks, waving at people he recognized. A variety of merchandise was on display in booths and tents, including jewelry, healing crystals, candles, pottery, gourd art, monogrammed items, and more.

"T-shirts. Get your T-shirts," a man shouted from behind a stack of folded garments. He held up a lime-green shirt with the words FIRST ANNUAL PICKLE FEST on it. "We got your size, from baby to buffalo."

"Needs to work on his sales pitch, if you ask me," Toby said. "Don't nobody wanna be a buffalo."

Dev locked eyes with a luscious redhead in one of the booths. She gave him a nervous smile and went back to the huddle of customers waiting to buy her specialty line of lotions, shampoos, and soaps. A tall man with long white-blond hair and the perfect face and muscular physique of the Dal stood near her in the booth. Dressed in jeans and a snug T-shirt, he seemed unaware of the lascivious interest directed at him by the women waiting their turn.

Toby nodded at the blond man. "Ansgar Dalvahni and his wife, Evie. She's a shy thing."

"We've met," Dev said. "Evie was a suspect in Meredith Peterson's murder last year. She was exonerated, but I don't think she's ever quite forgiven me."

Toby chuckled. "Making friends wherever you go."

"Part of the job."

Bing. Meredith appeared on the hood of the Jeep. The ghost wore a flirty white tie-waist jumpsuit with pickle-green trim and beige ankle strap sandals. Tucking her legs gracefully to one side, she gave a passing couple a homecoming wave. The woman seemed oblivious, but the man shot her a startled look.

She glanced coyly over her shoulder and batted her eyelashes at Dev. "Did somebody say my name?"

Dev jerked to a halt. "Meredith. Get off the car. *Now.*"

"So commanding." The ghost shivered in delight. "Me likey."

She vanished and reappeared in Toby's lap.

Toby yelped and jerked his hips in surprise. "Gawd a'mighty. Feels like somebody dumped a twenty-pound bag of ice in my lap."

"Ectoplasm spasm." Wrapping her slender arms around his neck, Meredith gave him a reptilian smile. "What's your name, scrumptious?"

"Uh...Toby, ma'am."

"Toby?" Her pert nose wrinkled. "That sounds familiar. Have we met?"

"Yes, ma'am, this past Thanksgiving. You crashed the family feed at Jason Damian's house."

"Did I?" Meredith pressed closer to Toby, making him shiver. "How naughty of me. Still, you'd think I'd remember a tasty dish like you."

"Reckon you had other things on your mind."

"Reckon?" Meredith giggled and sat back. "Aren't you adorable?"

"Meredith," Dev said. "What are you doing here?"

"If you must know, Sheriff, I'm looking for my husband."

"Your husband is dead."

"Muh duh, I know. Trey haunts this place, the stupid mutt, or he did before the mill burned down." Meredith's lips thinned. "He's spending his afterlife as a dog. It's super annoying."

Toby perked up. "A ghost dog? What kind?"

"Dalmatian," Meredith said. "This gathering of the Great Unwashed was his sister's brainchild, and I thought he might show up to lend his support." She pouted. "Everybody *loves* the Fairy Fart, including Trey. Personally, *I* don't see the appeal."

"The Fairy Fart?" Toby gave Dev a quizzical look.

"I think she means Sassy Peterson," Dev told him. "Part fairy, remember?"

"Oh, yeah. Got it."

Dev returned his attention to the ghost. "Sorry, Mrs. Peterson. We haven't seen your husband."

"Trey's not the only reason I came to this hillbilly hoedown." She leaned closer, smothering him in her lemony perfume. "I came to warn you, Sheriff. You're barking up the wrong tree."

"How so?"

"Stork Legs and her sidekick have been poking around Bailey's Tires." She sat back. "I heard them ask Marvin for a list of customers. Customers who've purchased a certain size and brand of truck tire in the past six months." She pursed her crayoned mouth. "I forget the specifics. Tires are boring."

"Goodrich nineteen fives."

"Yes, that's it." Meredith wagged a finger at Dev. "I know what you're up to, naughty boy. You're trying to connect Russ Barber with the tire print found near Livy's body." Her eyes gleamed with spite. "But you won't."

"Why not?"

Her eyelashes fluttered. "Tell me I'm pretty."

"What?"

"Tell me I'm pretty if you want to know."

"You're pretty. Why won't I connect the tire print to Russ?"

"Because, silly, it wasn't Russ's truck."

Dev stared at her. "It wasn't? Then, whose truck was it?"

Meredith tossed her head. "Really, Sheriff, you can't expect me to do *everything*. Try mulling it over if you want to know."

Dev clenched his jaws. "If you know something, you—"

"Yoo-hoo, Sheriff." Elizabeth Barber waved at him from a nearby booth. "The Lalas need your support. We've got cheese straws and petit fours with pickle-green fondant. Or maybe you'd rather have a pickle ornament for your Christmas tree?"

Meredith's neck corkscrewed, her head swiveling one-hundred-and-eighty degrees on the twisted stump. "Bootsie Barber and Trish and Blair," she hissed. "I'm going to cool sculpt those treacherous bitches."

"No, you're not," Dev said. "There'll be all kinds of commotion, and that would mess up my sting."

Meredith's head snapped back into place. "A sting?" Her expression tightened with excitement. "What kind of sting? Is it drugs? Moonshine? Is the Fairy Fart running an illegal operation and using the festival as a cover? Ooh, wouldn't I *love* to see her bedazzled little ass in jail."

"This has nothing to do with Sassy Peterson, other than the fact that it's happening on her property," Dev said. "This is something else." He hesitated. "And I could use your help."

"What's in it for me?"

"The satisfaction of doing your civic duty."

"Aren't you precious. Do I *look* like a chump?"

"Aw, let it go, Sheriff," Toby drawled. "Doubt she'd be much help, anyhow."

Meredith straightened in his lap. "I beg your pardon, Deputy Dickwad. I ran the Lala Lavender League Nails and Hairathon three years in a row. Have you ever dealt with a group of cosmetologists?"

"No, can't say as I have. Hard, is it?"

"Try impossible. It is *not* for the weak. What's the job, Sheriff?"

"When this thing goes down—"

"Hold on," Meredith said. "*What* thing?"

"I'd rather not go into specifics. When things start to happen, I need you to lead the norms away from the river and through the gates."

"Why should I help a bunch of breathers?"

"That's the job. Are you in or out?"

"I'm thinking, I'm thinking." She drummed her nails on the dash. "Okay, but I want to be listed as a consultant for the Sheriff's Department."

"I'm afraid I can't do that," Dev said. "How would I explain it to the norms?"

"Not on your site, shit-for-brains. On the Dead Net. It will be good for business. I need the street cred."

"Oh." Dev thought about it. "I guess that would be okay."

"Oh, goody." Meredith bounced happily, making Toby wince. "What's the signal?"

"The signal?"

"When do I get to scare the bejeezus out of the breathers?"

"You're supposed to lead them to safety, Meredith, not scare them."

She waved a hand. "Semantics. How will I know when it's time?"

"You'll know."

Her eyes narrowed. "Why do I get the feeling you're about to do something stupid?"

"I don't consider doing my job stupid."

"Schmuck," she said. "If it gets you killed, it's way stupid."

"Why, Meredith, I didn't know you cared."

"I don't. How can I use you as a reference for Bitchin' Banshee Services if you're dead?"

She disappeared in a whiff of burnt citrus.

"Lordy, what a stench." Toby lowered his window to let in some fresh air. "Did you see that thing she did with her neck? Give me the willies." He shifted uncomfortably in his seat. "Dadblame spectrally nuisance done froze my gonads."

"She said if I want to connect the tire print with the suspect, I should mull it over. What do you think she meant?" Dev asked.

"No idee."

Shrieks drew their attention to the Lala League booth. Bootsie and two more stylishly coiffed and dressed women came running out with Meredith hard on their heels. The ghost's face was twisted in a ghoulish mask.

"Thought you told her not to mess with the Lalas."

"I did." Dev shrugged. "She didn't listen."

"Should we go after her?"

"And do what?"

"Danged if I know."

"Me, either," said Dev.

They abandoned the Lalas to their fate and drove on, passing tables loaded with baked goods, local honey, roasted peanuts, pumpkin seeds, kettle corn, and homemade candy. The food vans selling Conecuh sausage, elephant ears, pretzels, and cotton candy were doing a brisk business, and there were scads of pickle-themed items to choose from, including fried pickles, pickle corn, pickle pops and slushies, pickle smoothies, and pickle ice cream, to name a few.

Toby pointed to a man spinning liquified sugar in a machine. "Good Lord, is that what I think it is?"

"I believe it is," Dev said. "Dill pickles wrapped in cotton candy."

"That's just wrong," Toby said. "Looks like there's a long line at the Trinity Episcopal Church table." He stuck his head out the window and inhaled, breathing in the smoky, sweet scent of grilled meat. "Pork smells good."

"Yep," Dev said. "The Butt Brothers make a mean barbecue, and their camp stew is nothing to sneeze at."

They cruised past the Pint-Sized Pickle Pageant where a group of boys and girls ages four to six sang, tumbled, and danced on a runway before a cheering crowd.

"Cute little tadpoles, ain't they?" Toby chuckled. "That little girl with the dark hair turning cartwheels reminds me of Becky when she was a young 'un. She was a pepper pot, and no lie. Still is, think on."

They rolled beyond the pageant and approached a dirt arena marked off with plastic cones and ribbons of tape. A wide banner with the words PICKLES FOR PAWS CONTEST in bright green letters fluttered in the October breeze. Inside the ring, costumed dogs of all sizes and pedigrees paraded in a circle. Dev spied a Great Dane wearing a lion suit with a rainbow mane, a beagle dressed as a lobster, and a trio of Westies dressed as an ewok, Darth Vader, and a storm trooper.

"Stop," Toby yelled.

Startled, Dev laid on the brakes. "What's wrong?"

"That." Toby pointed to the dogs in their regalia. "It ain't dignified."

"The dogs don't seem to mind," Dev said, "and it's for a good cause."

Toby glared at Dev. "You got a shifter form, don't you?"

"Who told you that?"

"Winnie might've mentioned it."

"Winnie talks too much."

"I'll take that as a yes. How would you like to be dressed up like a bumblebee or Donald frigging Duck?"

"I wouldn't like it at all," Dev conceded, "and neither would my wolf."

"Didn't think so."

Toby stuck his broad shoulders out of the window and let out a shivering howl. The cry was echoed by the other dogs, much to the confusion of their owners. A small dog in a Gandalf costume with a cloak, staff, and tall felt hat leapt onto the judges' table and shredded the pile of scorecards to bits. The dog had a double row of teeth and glowing red eyes. The judges took one look at the furry four-legged barracuda and fled.

A short, plump woman with a wealth of brown curls hurried over to the snarling dog. She wore a hooded black cape, a gray tunic minidress, knee-high faux leather boots, and plastic gauntlets on both wrists. The front of the dress laced up, displaying her ample bosom. Snatching the dog close, she planted a kiss on the animal's ugly head. "No, no, Frodo," she scolded. "Don't eat paper. It gives you the poops. Mama will buy you a pretzel instead."

She hurried off with the dog in her arms.

"Did you see the choppers on that thang?" Toby's nose worked. "That weren't no ordinary pooch."

"You're right," Dev said, easing the car forward once more. "That woman was Nicole Eubanks. She works at the flower shop in Hannah and is dating Dan Curtis."

"Hannah police officer?"

"That's the one," Dev said. "According to Dan, Nicole's dog is an Allihuahua, whatever the heck that is."

"Allis are demon dogs."

"Demon—" Dev whipped his head around in surprise. "Nicole is a norm. Should I do something?"

"What fer? She ain't in no danger," Toby said. "Can't say the same about anyone who tries to mess with her, though. Allis are extremely loyal and protective."

"I detect the voice of experience."

"An Alli took up with us oncet when I was a boy, maybe nine or ten," Toby said. "Spent the winter under my granny's porch. Wouldn't let nobody near it, but we made sure it had food and water. Gang of riffraff wandered up early one morning looking for mischief. Tried to hurt my granny. Me, too, when I objected. That Alli come out from under the house and swallowed 'em whole."

"Whole?"

"Whole," Toby said.

"What became of it?"

"Dunno. Spring came, and the Allihuahua lit out. Never saw it again."

Dev drove down to the river. A large stage had been erected on a broad slope overlooking the river, and a band was playing country music for an enthusiastic crowd. The band launched into a rousing rendition of "I Got a Bad Case of You," and the audience whistled and clapped in appreciation.

"Beelzebubba." Toby's eyes lit up. "Ain't seen them boys in an age. They used to play at Beck's."

"They're shifters?"

"What else? Can't book a norm band at a shifter bar. Hardly a night went by at Beck's that some customer didn't get drunk and bust a shape," Toby said. "You know the Orams?"

"Snake shifters?" Dev said.

"Yep. Whole passel of Orams got liquored up one Saturday, and *wham.* We had us a dadburn rattlesnake rodeo. Becky and I were running around snatching up snakes and throwing 'em in croaker sacks for the better part of an hour." Toby sighed. "Lordy, those were the days."

"The restaurant's doing a good business, I hear."

"Yeah, but it ain't the same." Toby sounded glum. "That's why I joined the Department. Only so much navel-gazing a feller can do."

Dev parked the Jeep near the bandstand. To the right of the stage was a line of high-peaked canopies marked JERKINS PICKLE-OFF. There were ten tents in all, one per pickle category, plus a huge pavilion at the far end of the row that said HOSPITALITY TENT. People of all ages wandered around the Pickle-Off and concert areas. Dev and Toby exited the vehicle and weaved their way through the throng. The crowd parted, and Dev spied Willa Dean's tall, regal form. She stood in front of the pickled fruit tent, a vision of dignified severity in a belted cotton dress printed with dancing green pickles. A matching green bow rested in her tower of gray hair. At her side was a gaunt older man dressed in unrelieved black with flowing white hair, prominent cheekbones, and skin the color of mozzarella. His emaciated features were hidden beneath a round, wide-brimmed black hat.

"Jehoshaphat," Toby breathed. "Samael Reaper's here."

"Don't know him. Is that a bad thing?"

"It is for somebody. Sam's an Ankou."

"A what?"

"A soul-gatherer," Toby said. "Sam usually keeps to himself. Lives out County Road 5 by the old cemetery. When he shows up, it means death's a-coming." He glanced around with an uneasy expression. "You ain't seen a wooden cart and a skeletal horse, have you?"

"No."

Toby exhaled. "Good. He and Willa Dean are an item. Maybe he's here to show support and not to...you know."

"Willa Dean has a *boyfriend*?" Dev said, his mind boggled.

"Lord, yes. Willa Dean and Sam been sparking for years."

"I had no idea."

"Didn't know she's a gorgon, either," Toby pointed out. "Willa Dean don't shout her b'ness to the world, anymore 'n you do."

Dev had a sudden, uncomfortable thought. "Do you think she knows I'm a super?"

"Don't think it, know it. Gorgons use their peepers for more 'n petrifying folks. Canny critters, gorgons. Take me, for instance. Willa Dean knew who I was the minute she clapped eyes on me, and the change be damned."

"You're right." Dev thought back to the day Toby had come into the office with Arta and Winnie. "She did recognize you."

"Yup." Toby straightened. "Hush. Here they come."

Willa Dean and her beau strolled up to them. "Sheriff. What brings you here?"

"We received a call about a fight."

"A tempest in a teapot." There was a militant sparkle in Willa Dean's obsidian eyes. "I won three categories—bread and butter, dill, and baby gherkin—and Claudine Kearley got her panties in a bunch." Her lips tightened. "That boorish husband of hers accused the judges of bias."

"Bull feathers." Sam pointed a skeletal finger at the blue ribbons hanging around Willa Dean's neck. "You won fair and square. Your pickles are cucumbery bites of heaven, and everybody knows it." His hollow eyes gleamed beneath the deep brim of his hat. "Claudine's pickles are soggy, and that's a fact."

"She picks her cucumbers too late and too big," Willa Dean confided. "Early morning, that's the best time to pick cucumbers, and you go for the small, firm ones. You can use black tea and ice water all day long, but if a cuke's too big, you're going to wind up with a mushy pickle."

"Ain't nobody likes a mushy pickle, but Duke wouldn't see reason." Sam shook his head. "He started bellowing and pushing the judges around."

"He got physical with the judges?" Dev said.

"Sure did." Sam assumed a boxer's stance. "So I socked him."

"I'm impressed. Duke's a big man." Dev eyed the elderly man. "Must outweigh you by a hundred and fifty pounds."

"I'm slim, but I'm wiry."

"Sam defended my honor." Willa Dean smiled at him. "Gave that blowhard a pip of a shiner."

"Weren't nothing," Sam said, but he looked pleased nevertheless. "I'd had enough of his guff."

"Where's Duke now?" asked Dev.

"In the hospitality tent," Willa Dean said. "He's a sawdust cowboy. Nothing but swagger and big talk. As for his wife, well..." Her mouth flattened. "She's a shrew, and that's the nicest thing I can say about her."

Dev and Toby found Duke Kearley seated in a chair inside the hospitality tent. The big man held an ice pack to one eye. His wife, Claudine, a heavyset woman in her fifties with a graying bun and a dour expression, stood next to her husband. Sassy Peterson Dalvahni flitted around them, a petite, maddened butterfly in a sparkly, pale green ball gown with puff sleeves, and sprinkles of crystal pickles on the wide hoop skirt. A tall, glittering crown rested on her shining blond head. In one hand, she clutched a pickle wand.

A group of judges and curious onlookers hovered near the doorway. Murmuring uneasily, they gawked at Duke and his wife.

"All right, folks," Dev said, herding the spectators out the door of the tent. "Move along. Show's over."

"Sheriff," Sassy said with a nod of thanks. "What brings you here?"

"Heard there was a scuffle."

"Oh, pooh, nothing of the kind. It's all been sorted out." Sassy turned her glowing smile on Duke. "Isn't that right, Mr. Kearley?"

He opened his mouth to reply, but his wife cut him off.

"No, it ain't," Claudine said. "Sam Reaper assaulted my husband. Show him, Duke."

"Aww, Claud."

"You heard me."

Duke reluctantly lowered the compress. His left eye was swollen and an ugly shade of purple.

Toby let out a whistle of surprise. "Willa Dean was right. That's a pip of a shiner."

"Willa Dean?" Claudine bristled. "That woman may find this amusing, but *I* don't. I want that hooligan arrested."

"Oh, *no*." Sassy turned her limpid gaze on Duke. "You don't want Mr. Reaper arrested, do you?"

"You hush up." Folding her fleshy arms, Claudine glared at Sassy. "You ain't fooling me with that sugar-won't-melt-in-my-mouth act. You're trying to smooth things over because you don't want folks to find out your contests are fixed."

"Our pickle contests are not—" Sassy vibrated with indignation. "Oh, bunny rabbits. I don't have time for this." She flourished her pickle wand at Claudine Kearley. "Be *nice*."

A puff of green sparkles smacked Mrs. Kearley in the face, and her plump cheeks sagged.

"Gluck," she said, her hostility instantly vanishing.

"That's better." Sassy straightened her crown. "Picklefest will be an annual event, Mrs. Kearley. Take my advice and consider cinnamon pickles next year."

"Cinnamon pickles." Claudine repeated Sassy's advice with a woozy grin.

"Oh, my, *yes*. Cinnamon pickles are a crowd favorite, and much more forgiving than some of the other categories." Sassy aimed the force of her effervescence at Duke. "I'm sorry about your eye, Mr. Kearley, but, really, you shouldn't have shoved poor Mavis Godwin into the display table. *So* ungentlemanly of you. And then you threatened to tear off Joe Frazier's head and—" She shook her head. "Well, I won't repeat the rest because I'm a lady, but my goodness, what were you thinking?"

Duke hung his head in shame. "Sorry."

"I know you are." Sassy's tone was kindly. "And I *know* you want to make up for it."

"Make up for it," he promised.

"Amazeballs," Sassy said. "Here's what you're going to do. Starting today, you're a new man, a *kind* man, positively a prince of pleasant. No more bullying. No more mean, grumpy, *nasty* Duke Kearley." Sassy tapped him with her wand. "From now on, you're going to be *Darling* Duke Kearley, the man who's super nice to everybody."

"Super nice," Duke repeated, gazing at her in helpless adoration.

"And you won't press charges against Mr. Reaper?" she said. "After all, Mavis isn't pressing charges against *you*."

Duke blinked his good eye. "No charges."

"Sparkalicious," Sassy said, clapping her hands.

"Claudine—"

"Will be sweet as pie from now on," Sassy assured Duke. "The two of you are going to be happy as clams." She turned to the dazed matron. "Mrs. Kearley, I think it's time you and Duke went home."

Claudine stirred. Tugging her Duke to his feet, she gave him a wet kiss. "Come on, sugar. Let's go."

She led her bemused husband out of the pavilion.

"Be sure and stop by the Trinity table on your way out and pick yourself up some barbecue," Sassy called after them. "Compliments of Picklefest." She dimpled at Dev. "There, you see, Sheriff? Everything is awesomesauce."

"Mrs. Dalvahni," Dev said, trying his best to sound stern, "what did you do to Claudine Kearley?"

She widened her eyes at him. "Do to her, Sheriff?"

"You whacked her with your wand. I saw you."

"This old thing?" Sassy held up the green baton. Her expression was innocent. "It's just a prop."

"It is not just a prop. Something glittery shot out of it and hit Claudine in the kisser, and she's suddenly sweetness and light. I've known Claudine Kearley since I was a kid. She's an ornery old badger."

"Oh, pooh," Sassy said. "I was nice to her, is all, and niceness is contagious." She glanced at her watch. "Marshmallows, look at the time! I really must be going. The children are waiting to have their pictures taken with me. I'm the Pickle Princess, you know."

She whirled to leave, halting in surprise when an attractive older woman with stylishly cropped silver hair and an elegant figure appeared in the doorway. At her side was a tall, well-dressed man, a muscular gallant with long blond hair and perfect masculine features.

"Aunt Susan," Sassy squeaked. "Bunny rabbits, what are you doing here? And who's this with you?"

Arta materialized. "All is well, shire reeve?" the huntress said. "I sensed a disturbance and came as quickly as I—" She noticed the attractive grand dame and her handsome companion and broke off. "Korth? What is the meaning of this?"

"Greetings, Sol' Vanna." The thrall bowed. "We meet again."

Chapter Twenty

"Sol' Vanna?" A surge of raw, unreasoning jealousy washed over Dev. He did not like the thrall. He did not like him one little bit. As far as he was concerned, Korth could have stayed lost. Forever. "What's that supposed to mean?"

"'Tis a term of respect," Korth said in his deep, mesmeric voice. "It means most noble and revered one."

"Lull me not with flattery, thou honey-tongued adder," Arta said. "Where have you been? Long have I searched for you in vain."

"Don't know why she's so riled," Toby muttered to Dev. "She ain't the onliest one been looking fer him. I done run my paws sore trying to find the blasted feller. Searched the river from Hannah all the way to Paulsberg with nary a sign. Reckon I know now why I couldn't find him." He cut his eyes at the woman with Korth. "He's been shacked up with her. Peterson, you know, and a demonoid." He rubbed the end of his nose. "Leastways, I know my snoot ain't broke. Happens, sometimes—the scent of one powerful super will mask the scent of another."

Dev nodded, though he was barely listening. His attention was on Arta. How did she feel about Korth being with another woman? Was she jealous? God, did she want him back? The thought made Dev want to howl.

Korth raised a languid brow. "You seem wroth, Sol' Vanna. You have need of me?"

"I do not require your services," Arta said in a voice of barely suppressed fury. "You are my responsibility. 'Tis my duty to take you"—she glanced at his companion and checked herself—"home," she finished awkwardly.

"No need to be flustered... Arta, isn't it?" the silver-haired beauty said in a syrupy drawl. "*I* won't turn you in for violating the Directive Against

Conspicuousness, if that's what worries you. Why would I? We're all supers here." She gave Dev and Toby a look of carnal interest. "Including these two strapping officers of the law."

Dev was startled. "How do you—"

"Know that you and that long, tall drink of water you call a deputy aren't human?" She gave him a wicked smile. "Darling, please. You're both fragrant with power. I can practically *taste* you."

"You got the nose, too?" Toby said. "Ain't that sumpin."

"It's a mixed blessing, as I'm sure you know, especially when one is inundated by a profusion of smells." The woman produced a small sachet from one sleeve and held it to her nose. "Which is why I always carry one of these." She shuddered. "I simply *loathe* the smell of corndogs."

"Nose drunk, are you?" Toby said with sympathy. "This here festival's a regular smell-o-thon. Whatchoo got in the bag, cloves?"

"Yes, as a matter of fact."

"Cloves numb the nose. Me, I prefer orange peel."

"Fascinating, to be sure," Arta said, favoring Toby with a scathing look, "but I would know how this...this *person* learned of the Directive."

"Korth told me," the woman said. "We share everything." Her voice dropped to a sensuous purr. "And I do mean *everything*."

"Indeed?" Arta's lips flattened. "Who are you, madam?"

"She's my aunt," Sassy said with a little bounce of excitement. "Actually, my *great*-aunt. She's Susan Grace Peterson Gordan Cherry Woody Harwood."

"Gordan *Gordan* Cherry Woody Harwood," the woman corrected. "I married the same man twice, but I don't expect anyone to remember all that. God knows, I barely do. Call me Susan." The woman stroked the thrall like a beloved pet. "As for Korth's whereabouts, we've been together. I was driving home from the club one night in September and found him wandering along the side of the road, alone and half-naked. I took him home with me."

"He was lost and alone and you took him in?" Sassy's eyes shone. "Bunny rabbits, that was awfully sweet of you, Aunt Susan."

"Sweet had nothing to do with it, my dear. This glorious creature is my consolation prize—you got the mill." Susan leaned against the thrall's muscular form. "I got Korth. We have an arrangement, don't we, darling?"

Korth smiled down at her. "I am your devoted servant."

"Impossible," Arta said. "Korth cannot remain here. He is Thralvahni and not of this world."

"*You* are not of this world, High Huntress." Susan Harwood laid a possessive hand on one of the thrall's muscular arms. "And yet, *you* remain."

"That is different. I am Kirvahni, and duty binds me here."

"Duty?" Susan Harwood threw back her head with a throaty laugh. "Is that what they're calling it these days?" She surveyed Dev from beneath heavy lids. "My goodness, you must simply *adore* your work."

To Dev's surprise, Arta flushed. "The Directive—" she began.

"Has naught to do with me," Korth said. "The Directive is a covenant between you and your maker. The Thralvahni are not bound by your rules."

"The Thralvahni serve the Kir and the Dal."

"That life no longer serves me." Korth lifted Susan's hand to his lips and kissed her palm. "I am sorry, Sol' Vanna, but I cannot go back. I will not."

"Kehvahn may disagree."

"I think not. By my count, half a dozen Dalvahni warriors dwell here with Lord Kehvahn's blessing. One of the Thralvahni, as well, I am told. 'Tis my hope and belief that he will afford me the same lenience." He straightened his broad shoulders. "No matter. My mind is made up."

The barometric pressure dropped, and there was a threatening rumble far in the distance.

"Goodness, is that thunder?" Sassy's eyes widened in dismay. "It's not supposed to rain today. I triple-checked."

Heat lightning illuminated the fabric walls of the tent, and the music from the bandstand ground to a halt. "Storm's coming, folks," the lead singer of Beelzebubba announced over the microphone on the stage. "Band's taking a break."

Sassy snatched up her voluminous skirts and ran outside. "Oh, no, people are starting to leave," she cried. "They're gathering their things and heading for the gate. This is terrible. The weatherman said no rain. He *promised.*"

Dev strode from the pavilion and looked around. The sky across the river was the color of an overripe plum. A darker mass stained the horizon.

"Um…Sheriff?" Toby joined him, his worried gaze on the approaching storm.

"I know. I see it," Dev said. "Where did you say you put our pickle thief?"

"In the Conecuh sausage truck." He pointed to a van parked under a large, shady tree. "It's got a cooling unit. Didn't want the big furball to overheat."

"Good thinking. Time?"

"Dunno." Toby eyed the lowering sky. "Thirty minutes, maybe? That storm's moving fast."

"Time?" Arta's voice was sharp. "What mean you?"

Dev met her gaze. Adrenaline sizzled through his veins. His wolf was awake and eager for blood. "Reckoning day."

"'Tis Pratt?" She inhaled sharply, her lovely face alight with dreadful eagerness. "At last, we shall make him pay for his deeds."

"That's the plan."

"My heart rejoices, but what of the norms? Their numbers are many, and he will give them no quarter. 'Tis wise, you think, this locus for a battle?"

"Battle?" Sassy's voice rose and people turned to look. "You can't have a battle here. This is Picklefest. It's…it's *dilly-icious*, the perky personification of pickle perfection. I won't allow it. I won't!"

"I'm sorry." Taking her by the arm, Dev guided Sassy back into the tent. *More than one storm coming*, he thought. The Pickle Princess was going to have a conniption when she found out what he'd done. "I never expected the festival to be this big. I chose this location because it's remote, and because I was trying to attract a certain…er…pickle lover."

"Pickle lover?" Sassy stared at him like he had three heads. "This is a pickle festival, Sheriff. Everybody here loves pickles."

Arta strode back into the pavilion with Toby. "He speaks not of a human," she said. "The shire reeve refers to the skellring."

"The *what*?"

"A bigfoot," Dev explained. "His name is Sugar, and he loves baby gherkins. I was counting on the festival to attract him, and it did."

"If he's such a love bunny, why are you having a brawl with him?" Bright spots of color stained Sassy's cheeks. "Brawls are *horrid*."

"Oh, we're not fighting Sugar. Sugar wouldn't hurt a fly. We're after someone else, someone we hoped would follow him here."

Thunder boomed in the distance, and a howling wind whipped the fabric walls of the pavilion. The hardware holding the hospitality placard in place over the door snapped, and the banner fluttered to the ground. A gust of wind caught the flimsy vinyl, and it skittered away.

"A trap?" Sassy's petite form shimmered and pulsed with violet light. "You've used my darling festival to set a *trap*?" To Dev's shock, her sunny voice deepened to a shivery growl. "How *dare* you, Sheriff."

"I'm sorry," Dev said, "but the…er…person we're after is dangerous and must be stopped. It's a matter of public safety."

"I don't care." Sassy stamped her foot. "You could have picked anywhere in the county for your nasty little ambush, but *noooo*. You had to have it at *my* event. Do you have any idea—the tiniest *inkling*—how much effort goes into a festival of this size?"

"No," Dev admitted. "I can't say I do."

"*Months* of planning and preparation." Sassy's bosom swelled. "Favors called in, and favors owed. Friends and family involved. Tickets and publicity and licensing, and permission from the county for I-don't-know-what-all. Merchants and food vendors lined up, and garbage and waste disposal and cleanup, not to mention the old mill bulldozed and cleared away." Her skin darkened to a dusky purple, and vicious black claws sprouted from her fingertips. "And you think you can waltz in here and ruin everything without so much as a by-your-leave? I don't think so, Sheriff. I DON'T THINK SO."

Arta's bow appeared in her hands. Stepping in front of Dev, she nocked an arrow and aimed it at Sassy. "Have a care, shire reeve. Methinks she is possessed. 'Tis the djegrali?"

"She's not possessed," Dev said. "She's part—"

Sassy snarled something guttural and waved her wand. The bow in Arta's hand writhed, transforming into a purple and green snake with feathery pink ears.

Arta dropped the snake with an oath. The reptile reared, glaring at Arta with eyes like chips of emeralds. With an irritated trill, the creature slithered out the door.

"—fairy," Dev said.

The air shimmered, and Grim appeared. "The others will be here anon," the big warrior said. He spied Sassy, and his stern demeanor eased. "Ah, there you are, my heart." If he was startled by the change in his vivacious wife's appearance, he did not show it. "A storm approaches, bringing with it a battle of monumental proportions. I am come to take you home."

"You knew." Sassy's eyes turned black as pitch. "That's why you wouldn't come with me today. You were planning a horrid fight."

"Sassy, my sweetest love." Grim made a helpless gesture. "Conall summoned a war council. I am Dalvahni and must needs attend."

"Ooh," Sassy shrieked. The back of her gossamer gown ripped, and a pair of glistening wings, raven-black and huge, sprouted from her slender shoulders. "You are on my list, Grim Dalvahni." She rounded on Dev. "You, too, Sheriff Whitsun. I thought you were a nice man, but you're not. You are not nice at *all*."

Unfurling her wings with a thunderous clap, she shot through the roof and exploded in a peony burst of stars.

"Mercy." Susan Harwood gazed up at the bright streak in the sky, all that remained of her niece. "There's more to sweet little Sassy than meets the eye." She looked thoughtful. "Much more."

"She is wroth." Grim's expression was troubled. "I must after her. Try to make her understand."

"Don't do it, mister," Toby pleaded "You saw them claws. She'll have your gonads for a necklace. Best leave her alone for a spell. Let her cool off."

"I cannot. She is in distress. She has expended much energy on this affair and is weary and overwrought."

Dev shook his head. "And I came along and upset the apple cart."

"My wife is a blithe spirit. She is never angry for long," Grim said. "I will seek her out and return forthwith."

He vanished in Sassy's wake.

"Well, this has all been very interesting, I'm sure, but I'd like to go home now," Susan Harwood announced. "I want no part of a free-for-all."

"At once, my love." Korth bowed to Arta. "Sol' Vanna. I will see her to safety and return to lend mine aid."

"Don't bother," Dev said. "We don't need your help."

"I do not recall asking your permission," Korth said. "This is my home now, and I must needs defend it."

He wrapped his arms around Susan, and they disappeared.

"That guy can't take a hint," Dev said.

"You were discourteous." Arta's voice held a hint of reproach. "'Tis not like you."

"I don't like him."

"That much is obvious. Why?"

Dev muttered something under his breath.

"Beg pardon?" Arta said. "I did not hear you."

"I said, I don't trust him. He's too good-looking."

"What does his appearance have to do with it? 'Tis irrational. Moreover, *you* are extremely handsome, and I trust you implicitly."

"You do?"

"But of course. This you should know a'ready."

"Extremely handsome, huh?" Dev rubbed his jaw to hide his smile. "Thanks. Does Korth even know how to fight?"

"In truth, I cannot say. In my experience, the Thralvahni serve but one purpose."

Dev's momentary enjoyment vanished, and the demon of jealousy raised its head again. Thralls had one purpose, and he knew what it was. He tamped his possessiveness back down.

"Guess we'll find out," he said. "That is, if he comes back."

Bing! Meredith materialized inside the big tent.

"'Tis the shade." Arta eyed the ghost with dislike. "What brings you here, adder harpy?"

"The sheriff asked for my help, not that it's any of your bees wax." Meredith aimed an oozing smile at Dev. "You said there'd be a sign. The sky looks like the Wrath of God. I'm guessing that's it?"

"Yes."

"Shire reeve, is this wise?" Arta protested. "The phantom cannot be trusted."

"Shut it, you," Meredith said. "The *shire reeve* and I have a deal." She simpered at Dev. "Don't we, Devy Wevy?"

"That's right," Dev said. "Meredith and Sildhjort are going to lead the norms to safety."

"Sil-dah-who?" Meredith's face tightened with suspicion. "Hold the phone. You didn't say anything about a partner."

"Sildhjort is not a *partner*. He is a god." Arta gave Dev a searching look. "Things are well between you?"

"We're not best buddies, but he's agreed to lend a hand. Or a hoof, as it were," Dev corrected.

Shouts and cries of excitement drew them outside the tent. On the far shore, a huge silver stag pranced on glowing hooves. Exclaiming and pointing, people rushed to the water's edge to get a closer look at the fabulous beast.

"Lookee here," Meredith said in a singsong voice. "It's a big, shiny deer."

"'Tis Sildhjort, the shire reeve's sire."

Meredith gave Dev the side-eye. "Deerzilla is your *daddy*?"

"Yup," said Dev.

"That's seriously messed up. Who's the little creep with him?"

"Creep? I don't—" Dev did a double take and saw a small figure in a yellow tunic, patched stockings, blue slippers, and an orange skullcap astride the stag. "Aw, hell."

"'Tis the nibilanth," Arta said. "You did not expect him?"

"No."

"Nibba what?" Meredith asked.

"Capricious, troublesome creatures," Arta said. "Half fairy, half imp." She studied the ghost. "You two have much in common. You should deal famously."

"Ha-ha," Meredith said. "So Bambo and Rumplestilskin are our reinforcements, which leaves one question." She stabbed a finger at the angry cloud barreling toward them. "Who's riding the Sauron Express?"

"His name is Pratt."

"Pratt?" The ghost flickered in alarm. "Are you out of your tree? That guy is the worst—batshit *and* scary powerful."

"You do your job and let me worry about that."

"You bet your sweet tookus I will. Mer Bear wants nothing to do with that psycho."

Arta looked down her nose at her. "Pudding heart. I do not fear him."

"Then you're an idiot," Meredith said. "He shredded a pack of weres faster than you can say Jack Robinson."

"I know not Jack Robinson," Arta said, "nor do I have any intention of invoking his name."

"It's an expression, micro-brain."

Arta's eyes narrowed. "You try my patience, shade. Methinks I should school you in manners."

"Oh, yeah?" Meredith swelled. "You and what—"

A loud snort interrupted them. Wisps of fog curled from Sildhjort's nostrils, and the shining nimbus around him pulsed outward in radiant bands. The stag lowered his head, and light beamed from his antlers to form a glowing bridge across the river.

"*Fág an bealach,*" the imp cried, brandishing a miniature war hammer over his misshapen head.

Sildhjort reared and galloped across the gleaming arch, each strike of his hooves ringing like a bell on the shining surface. Thundering down the slope, he bunched his massive hindquarters and sprang over the clamoring people. He flew over their heads and landed on the other side in a shower of sparks. With a snort, he turned and tossed his magnificent head at the crowd.

"You heard him, you noisome dalcops," Irilmoskamoseril shouted, waving his hammer. "Follow the shiny bastard!"

Sildhjort leapt away, and the mesmerized throng swept after him. People poured out of tents, booths, and alleyways, stampeding after the stag in the direction of the main gates.

"Suckers." Meredith's upper lip curled in contempt. "On the plus side, Big Daddy seems to have everything under control, so it looks like I'm not needed." Her form thinned and began to dissipate. "Catch you on the flipside, losers."

"Not so fast," Dev said, lifting a hand.

A golden thread shot from his palm and wrapped around Meredith, halting the ghost in mid-fade.

"*Hey.*" Meredith struggled to free herself from the spell line. "What's happening?"

"I've tethered you to this plane until you complete your assignment."

"You placed an onus on her?" Arta's eyes were warm with admiration. "How marvelous, shire reeve!"

"It's no big deal." Dev's tone was light, but he was secretly pleased. "She's not my first haint. All shield work involves channeling energy. A tether's just another form."

"You are too modest," Arta said. "Me, I think you very clever."

"Oh my God, stop fawning over one another before I ectopuke," Meredith howled. Her face distended grotesquely, and her eyes grew large as dinner plates. "Let me goooo!"

"No." Dev folded his arms. "You've offered your services more than once, and I'm holding you to it."

"Bully," Meredith wailed. "Why is everyone so *mean* to me?"

"Mayhap because you are a foul-mouthed, vile, and hag-ridden shrew?" Arta suggested sweetly.

"You say that like it's a bad thing." Meredith stretched against the tether. Her body elongated like a rubber band and snapped back to its former shape. "Ooh," she growled in frustration. "Fine. I refuse to break a nail over this shit. What do I have to do?"

"Round up any stray norms that didn't follow Sildhjort out of the park." Dev waved a hand at a clump of dazed men and women standing in the middle of the dirt avenue that ran between the tents. "Those folks, too. They're kith. I recognize some of them. Apparently, Sildhjort and his happy hormones don't affect them."

"Hate to break it to you, asshole, but I'm not kith," Meredith said. "The weirdos won't pay any attention to me."

"Lucky for you, I'm a weirdo, too. They'll pay attention to me," Toby said, shifting into dog form with a crack of bone and sinew.

"Great, just what I need." Meredith's expression was sour. "Another goddamn stinking dog."

Dev ignored her grousing. "Check every nook and cranny, every tent, booth, and wagon, and chase them out of here. This is ground zero. I don't want anyone but our team within a mile of this place."

Toby barked in affirmation.

"And Toby?" Dev glanced at the gloom beyond the river. Pratt was drawing closer. "Hurry."

The dog barked again and bounded off.

"You'll be sorry for this." Meredith shot Dev a look of smoldering resentment. "Nobody puts Mer-Mer on a leash."

She swooped away, trailing the glowing tether behind her.

Dev watched the ghost dart behind the grandstand. "I think she's ticked. Sassy, too."

"'Strewth, 'tis a rare talent you have with women, shire reeve, and no lie," Arta said.

"Tell me about it," Dev muttered. "And the day's not over yet."

A startled shriek drew their attention. Fifty yards away, a man burst out of a tent with Meredith in pursuit. Cackling like a deranged hen, she chased him, screaming, toward the exit.

"Yeah, buddy, that's what I'm talking about," the ghost shrieked. "Hot damn, I'd pay for this. Tormenting breathers is *fun*."

Warming to her work, she zoomed into display stands and behind booths, routing dawdlers before her. Toby was not far behind. With a chilling growl, he charged the kith, his shaggy form expanding with every bound. He was the size of a pony, then a horse, then a Clydesdale. The startled kith scattered, some of them so frightened that they shifted on the spot and streaked into the woods.

In the blink of an eye, the park was empty. An eerie silence settled over the tents and grandstand, but the quiet did not last long. Lights flashing and siren wailing, a county patrol car turned out of the midway and sped toward Dev and Arta.

"Behold," Arta announced. "Winnie thunders into battle upon her glorious steed."

The car screeched to a stop, and Winnie sprang out.

"What the hell, Dev?" Red-faced, she stalked up to them. "This isn't a fight. It's crazy town. I like to never got my unit through. People running down the road like their drawers were on fire. Animals, too. All kinds—coyotes and possums and raccoons, and I don't know what-all. A bobcat jumped on the hood of my car and kept going, and I swear to granny I saw a giant-ass dog." She spread her hands wide. "Damn thing was the size of a van. Bigger, even."

"'Twas Toby, in his shifter form," Arta said. "Quite impressive, is he not?"

"I'm not talking to you," Winnie said, turning on her. "You left me. Not cool, Arta. Definitely not cool."

"Swallow your spleen, my sister, and rejoice, for battle is nigh," Arta said. "See the approaching storm?" As if in reply, there was an earsplitting boom of thunder, and lightning struck a tree across the river. "Pratt lies within yon foul vapor. Today, we challenge him and bring him to task."

"*Awesome*." Winnie rubbed her hands together, her eyes bright with anticipation. "After training you for the past few weeks, I need to kill something."

"I thank you," Arta said. "You are a delight, as well. And, I might add, you did not 'train' me atall."

"Whatever," Winnie said. "What's the plan, Dev?"

"Simple," he said. "Step one, we get Pratt to follow Sugar to a location of my choice. That part is done. Step two, we take him into custody."

Winnie frowned. "Like...put him in cuffs?"

"Yes, in the supernatural sense."

"Earth to Dev. He's a god. We're going to need help."

"Relax. I've recruited an army."

"What army?" Winnie looked around. "I don't see an army."

The temperature plummeted, and Conall arrived on a blast of cold air. He was dressed in leathers and flanked by a score of burly, ferocious warriors. Most of them were strangers to Dev, but he recognized Brand Dalvahni, who'd married Addy Corwin, a local florist, and Ansgar.

Grim reappeared, along with a warrior with bloodred hair.

"My brother Rafe," Grim said, introducing the redhead. "You know Bunny Raines?"

"The Hannah librarian?" Dev said. "Yeah."

"She and Rafe are married."

"Congratulations. Nice to meet you." Dev shook the red-haired warrior's hand. It was like voluntarily closing his hand in a vise. "Thanks for coming to our little...er...gathering."

Rafe inclined his head. "We are Dalvahni. We ever relish a fight."

"It could get ugly," Dev warned him. "We may be outnumbered and outgunned."

"The Dalvahni are not easily daunted."

"Where's Duncan?" Dev asked, looking around. "I sent him to find Evan."

Conall glanced at the angry black cloud that was almost upon them. Dark shapes moved within the sickening mass. "With any luck, they will be here anon. Methinks we shall have need of the ogre."

The air shimmered, and Eamon appeared.

"What are you doing here?" Winnie glared at him in loathing. "Isn't it more your style to cut and run?"

"Cut and run?"

"Leave, vamoose, skedaddle," Winnie said. "That's what you're good at."

"I am come to lend my sword arm against Pratt and his villainy," Eamon said through his teeth. "Mine lifeblood, if need be. Why are *you* here?"

"It's my job," Winnie said. "I'm Dev's backup."

"A scruff of a girl, rash and untutored in the art of war?" Eamon scoffed. "Then surely our cause is doomed."

An angry flush crept up Winnie's cheeks. "Tell him to leave, Dev. I won't fight with him. I refuse."

"You won't have to—" Dev began.

"Ha." Winnie pumped a fist in the air. "Hear that, asshat?"

"—fight with him, because you and Arta will be in the van protecting Sugar."

Dev braced for the explosion, which he fully expected to be huge.

"*What?*" Winnie said.

"WHAT?" Arta roared.

Her voice shattered the windows and both windshields in the Charger, flattened the row of tents, and crumpled the folding chairs in front of the stage like so much tinfoil.

Yep, her reaction was huge, all right. Seismic, in fact.

Chapter Twenty-One

Arms folded and one shoulder propped against the wall, Arta watched Winnie pace back and forth inside the rectangular metal box. The interior of the conveyance humans called a "truck" was cool, the ceiling height half again as tall as a Dalvahni warrior and thrice the length. Crates marked CONECUH SAUSAGE in bold script filled one end of the delivery carriage. The labels on the containers portrayed a leering pig seated before a burning brazier. Dressed in a skimpy white shirt that exposed a mound of plump, pink belly and a pair of red trousers, the hog held a fat sausage on a skewer in one cloven hoof. Arta found the look of lascivious and cannibalistic glee on the animal's face disturbing.

Lounging on a stack of these boxes was their charge, Sugar. The skellring was enjoying a jar of pickles—his eighth, judging from the discards at his wide, hairy feet.

Winnie sent an empty jar skittering across the metal floor with the toe of her boot. "How can you stand there, calm as a boiled egg, with everything that's going on?" she demanded of Arta.

"I am not calm. Verily, my blood sings for battle, but we have not the space for both of us to parade about."

"Verily, my ass. I don't get it, Arta. Dev *needs* us. He's about to go toe-to-toe with a god, and you act like you don't care. I've met mailboxes with more feeling."

Arta straightened. "You think me cold? Allow me to disabuse you."

Dropping her cloak of indifference, she blasted Winnie with the sickening mix of frustrated battle lust, anger, and gnawing worry for Devlin that she'd been holding tightly leashed. The surge knocked Winnie to one knee and flattened the fur on the skellring's face.

Sugar trilled in surprise. Reaching up, he smoothed his facial fur with a large paw. "Tickles, Arr," he said, his limpid blue eyes swimming with reproach.

"I beg your pardon." Shaking with reaction, Arta drew a ragged breath. "'Tis unseemly for a Kirvahni huntress to lose her temper, but, by the gods, Winnie, you push me too far. I am not insensible to the shire reeve's danger, no matter what you say."

Winnie climbed to her feet. "Then why did you cave? Any of those meatheads could have stayed with Sugar."

"Meatheads?"

Winnie waved her hands in the air. "The Dalvahni."

"As I have stated afore, the blood and essence of the Dalvahni courses through your veins, thanks to Eamon's meddling. An they are 'meatheads,' you are one, as well."

"I don't want to talk about Eamon. *Ever.* My point is, some other supernatural duo could have stayed with Sugar. It didn't have to be us."

"The Dal are not the shire reeve's to command. We are. I could not refuse him before Conall and the Dal. 'Twould have pricked his pride."

"Give me a break. You disobey Dev all the time."

"Not all the time. Only when I disagree with him, or he is being unreasonable."

"Like I said, all the time." Winnie's mouth twisted bitterly. "But not today. Today, it was, 'Yes, shire reeve,' and 'An you will, shire reeve.' Next thing you know, we're cooling our heels in this bucket. It sucks."

"'Tis highly unsatisfactory, I agree," Arta said. "Once, in the mountains of Varsoom, I was pinned beneath a dead runderblasken for three days ere I cut my way out. The stench of the decaying creature lingered in my nostrils for moons afterward. Still, 'twas more to my liking than this."

"Runderblasken? Of all the—" Winnie spluttered. "You and Dev are two of a kind. You're both pains in the ass."

Arta listened to these grumblings with half an ear, a faint *skree* from above having announced Merta's arrival. Opening her mind, Arta merged with the hawk and got a clear view of the scene outside the truck. Though it was early afternoon, the sun had dimmed, and the sky was dark and brooding. The Dalvahni were heavily armed and braced for battle. Toby had returned from routing the kith. Still in dog form, the huge hound padded back and forth, hackles raised and teeth bared, but where was the shire reeve? The hawk made another sweep and Arta spotted him, her blood quickening at the sight of Dev. She would know his tall, lean form anywhere. His image, she realized, had been burned in her mind from the start. What strange and wondrous thing was this between them?

Love, or so Winnie would have it, though Arta's practical mind balked at the notion. Love was a human foible. She was attracted to the shire reeve. That much she would admit, but 'twas nothing to marvel at. The Kirvahni were highly sexual, and coitus with Dev was satisfying. Transporting, even, leaving her spent and sated after.

But not for long. Never for very long.

She was like a greedy child when it came to Dev Whitsun, and he was a platter of sweetmeats. She could not get enough.

Still, the attraction went beyond the merely physical. Arta *enjoyed* his company more than anyone else's. That, in and of itself, was shocking. The Kir were a tightly knit sisterhood bound together by purpose, a grim, violent history, loyalty to their kind, and service to their god, but with Dev, she was...

Faith, dared she say it? She was happy. Dev Whitsun was a pleasing man in substance and form. Strong, sinewy body. Firm, mobile mouth and handsome face. She liked, too, his slow, thoughtful manner of speaking and his deep, masculine voice. He had a way of lingering over certain words and phrases, lazily caressing the syllables, that was devastating to the senses. His eyes were likewise compelling. Hooded and gray, they were set beneath slashing dark brows. They crinkled at the corners when he was amused, and the shire reeve was frequently amused. Humor and levity were not qualities valued among her kind, but since getting to know Dev, Arta was learning to savor them.

'Strewth, in the long drought of her existence, Dev's quiet intelligence and gentle wit were an oasis, a balm to her weary soul, but love? She did not know. Indeed, how could she?

'Twas not in her nature to love.

Merta made a third pass, giving Arta another glimpse of the object of her musings. Dev stood in conference with Conall. His aura flared red and white, a warrior preparing for combat. Preparing? Nay, Dev relished the prospect, foolish man. He radiated determination and purpose, but Pratt was no human criminal or kith miscreant. Pratt was a powerful deity.

Winnie had the right of it. The shire reeve needed them.

Faith, he needed *her*. She was Kirvahni, honed by eons of combat with the djegrali. She was the swift, unerring arrow that found its mark in the darkness, the dagger of justice, the bulwark that had stood between mortals and evil for thousands of years. He should not face Pratt without—

"Hey!" Winnie snapped her fingers in Arta's face. "Pay attention when I insult you."

Arta blinked. "An I smote you for every insolence, you would be a smoking ruin."

"Very funny." Winnie resumed her pacing. "Shit's happening, and I'm stuck in this tin can babysitting an overgrown rabbit. Unbelievable."

Sugar looked up from his snack, his nose wrinkling in surprise. "Arr wabbit?"

"Not her, fuzz ball, *you*." Winnie poked him in his broad chest. "I'm talking about you."

"Sugar not wabbit. Sugar squatch." He tilted his head curiously at Arta and held out the pickle jar. "Arr want gherk? Wish-us."

"I thank you, no."

"Win?" His expression was hopeful. "Treat?"

"For God's sake, Sugar, give it a rest," Winnie said. "Nobody wants your stupid pickles."

Sugar pursed his lips in disapproval. "Win say uggie word."

"What, stupid? I've said worse. Now, shut up and eat your pickles."

"Shut up bad—"

Winnie glared at Sugar, and he shrugged and drained the brine from the glass. Slurping the slick, green-skinned fruit into his mouth, he chewed and dropped the empty jar to the floor with a clatter.

"Dang it, Sugar," Winnie said, jumping at the noise. "Stop messing around. My nerves are worked."

"Sugar no mess. Sugar *good* boy."

"Toby had no business giving you an entire case of pickles. If you get sick, I am *not* cleaning up your honk."

"Sugar not—"

"Zip it, Sugar. I mean it." A thunderous *boom* rocked the truck, tossing Winnie into the wall. "Ouch." Rubbing her bruised elbow, she regained her balance. "What the hell?"

A high, shivering wailing sounded on the heels of the thunder. "Pratt," Arta said. "He draws nigh, and he brings the djegrali with him."

Sugar trilled in alarm. "Bad man come? Sugar hide."

The skellring disappeared.

"What the—" Winnie turned full circle. "Where did he go?"

"Judging from the evidence, I would surmise that Sugar has made himself invisible."

"He can do that? How did I not know he can do that?"

"The wealth of your ignorance is vast and unending."

"Smart-ass. If he can make himself invisible, why does he need us?"

"To mask his presence from Pratt, as the shire reeve explained. It matters not whether Sugar can be seen. He possesses the orb, and Pratt is drawn to it as a moth to flame."

"If that's the case, Pratt should've found Sugar weeks ago."

"I do not think the orb wants to be found. Not by Pratt, in any case." Arta frowned in thought. "Mayhap the orb conceals the skellring from Pratt. 'Tis unimaginably powerful."

Winnie growled in frustration. "I repeat—if the orb can conceal Sugar, *why do we need to be here?*" She resumed her jerky pacing. "Any way you look at it, this doesn't make sense. Why not move Sugar and the orb someplace safe? Pratt could blast the whole area, take the truck out and us with it."

"I am Kirvahni. I would survive, and so would you."

"Yeah, but what about Sugar? What about the orb? Pratt could grab it and run."

"Pratt's heart is black as the Pit. The touch of the orb would be unbearable to him."

"He's a god, Arta. I'm sure he's thought of a way around that."

Winnie was right. Again. Indeed, Pratt had used Gryffin for exactly that purpose.

"You make a salient point. I had not thought..." Arta shook her head. "There was no time to discuss things with the shire reeve."

Winnie snorted. "Dev's not big on discussion. It's the whole Lone Wolf thing."

"Ere you arrived, Dev remarked that he chose this site for its isolated location. Think you he has had this scheme in mind for some time now?"

"You can bet on it. Knowing Dev, he's had this planned down to the tiniest detail for *weeks.* Dev doesn't like surprises."

Arta's lips thinned. "Nor do I. And yet he made no mention of his intentions to me."

In the distance, there was an earsplitting bellow. Something was out there, something huge.

"What was that?" Winnie demanded.

"Pratt." Arta allowed her gaze to go unfocused. "He is concealed within a dark vapor. The shire reeve and my brothers cannot see him."

Winnie slammed her fist into the wall. "And we're stuck in a sausage truck and can't help them. This sucks."

"An observation you have made a'ready. Endeavor not to repeat yourself. 'Tis tiresome."

"Wait a minute." Winnie's eyes narrowed. "If Dev can't see Pratt, how can you?"

"Merta and I are connected. The hawk's eyes are sharp, and they have pierced Pratt's disguise."

"Merta?"

"My hawk."

"Your *hawk*? You've got a seeing-eye hawk and didn't tell me?"

Ding. Two huntresses appeared inside the delivery carriage on a breath of jasmine and lemongrass.

Winnie's hand went to her gun. "Who the hell are you?"

The taller of the two huntresses, an elegant, brown-skinned woman with fine, dark eyes, looked her up and down. "I am Illaria. Who are you?"

"The chick who's fixing to whip your ass."

Illaria raised her brows at Arta. "This is the one you spoke of?"

"Yes."

"She is as you described, an impudent firebrand."

Winnie stiffened. "What did you—"

Arta laid a hand on her shoulder. "Peace, Winnie. They are here at my behest." She nodded at the petite brunette with Illaria. "Greetings, Jaaka. Where are the others?"

Jaaka bowed. "On their way, High Huntress."

"Others?" Winnie scowled. "What others?"

"I have summoned a number of the Kir to lend their aid to our cause." Arta paused, adding, "Illaria and Jaaka will guard Sugar in our stead."

Winnie's expression tightened with eagerness. "So we can fight?"

"Yes, Winnie. So that we may fight."

Snatching Arta close, she planted a noisy buss on her cheek. "I *knew* my partner couldn't be such a wimp. I knew it! It was a trick, right? You never intended to sit this one out."

"A Kirvahni huntress does not"—Arta glanced at her sisters and flushed. They were staring at her in astonishment, clearly baffled by Winnie's familiar manner—"shrink from battle," she finished.

"Damn straight, and neither does a McCullough." Winnie grinned. "You lied. Dev's going to be pissed."

Arta lifted her chin. "The shire reeve may wallow in his spleen. He has been less than forthcoming with me. And I did not *lie*. I said I would stay with the skellring, and so I have. I did not say how long I would abide."

"Semantics," Winnie said. "That tune won't play with Dev."

"Stay, then, an you are so exacting."

"Not if you nail my fricking feet to the floor."

"Indeed, you must not go, friend Winnie." Illaria's tone was kindly. "Your pluck is admirable, but you are human and will surely perish."

"Winnie is not human," Arta said without further comment. She had not divulged Winnie's peculiar lineage to her sisters. They would be shocked. They would marvel and mutter and ask innumerable questions, questions she had neither the time nor the inclination to answer. "She does, howe'er, require a suitable weapon."

"No, I don't," Winnie said. "I've got my gun."

"A gun will not avail you in this instance."

"The hell it won't." Winnie patted the gun at her hip. "This baby packs a punch."

Arta closed her eyes and opened them again. "You would try the patience of a Kikudosi monk, Winnie McCullough. Mortal weapons are useless against the djegrali. Have you forgotten the monsters in the wood?"

"Oh, yeah." Chagrin, followed by alarm, flitted across Winnie's expressive face. "Don't even *think* of telling me to stay here because I won't. I mean it, Arta."

"'Twould be a waste of breath." With a flourish, Arta produced a battle axe and a war hammer, one in each hand. "Allow me to present you with a weapon of your choosing from my personal store. Forged in dragon fire by the dwarf king of Hedeel Zor and etched with runes of power, either will serve you well. Which would you have, the hammer or the axe?"

"The axe," Winnie said without hesitation.

"An excellent choice." Arta returned the hammer to the nothingness and handed the axe to Winnie. "The edge of the blade stays ever sharp."

"Thanks, Arta." Winnie hefted the weapon. Turning it over, she admired the deadly curved blade and stout handle. "It's a beaut."

"You are most welcome. An you speak its name, 'twill return to your hand. Demon Cleaver, I named it."

"Too cheesy. I'm going to call him Bob."

"*Bob*? Preposterous."

"Is it my axe or not?"

Arta sighed. "Very well. Bob it is."

Illaria gave a deprecatory cough. "Pardon, High Huntress, but where is our charge? We have yet to see the skellring."

"Pratt's arrival startled him," Arta said. "Show yourself, Sugar. There is naught to fear. Illaria and Jaaka are my sisters."

A large pair of anxious blue eyes appeared, followed by a trembling, black-lipped mouth. Slowly, the rest of the skellring came into view. "Fam?"

"Yes, they are my family."

Jaaka gasped. "By the Vessel, he is white as the snows of Meldad."

Thrusting his paw into his thick belly fur, Sugar produced a dull brown globe and offered it to her. "Pretty?" he asked the huntress with a blinding smile.

"Is that—" Jaaka said, much startled.

"The orb." Arta considered Sugar thoughtfully. "A primordial pouch. So that's where you have been keeping it. I wondered... Clever, Sugar. Very clever."

The skellring beamed and held out his paw. "Arr want pretty?"

"No, Arr does not want the pretty. Put it away, an you please." Sugar reluctantly obeyed, and Arta gave him a nod of approval. "Good boy. Go with Illaria and Jaaka. They will keep you safe."

"Go, High Huntress?" Illaria looked confused. "I thought we were to tarry here."

"Winnie has noted certain weaknesses in that arrangement," Arta said, "and, upon reflection, I agree. You will remove Sugar to a safer locale."

Winnie whistled. "Dev's going to be pissed."

"So you keep saying, but I, too, chart my own course." Arta turned to her sisters. "Take the skellring someplace secret, someplace where he cannot be found."

Illaria and Jaaka bowed. "We will guard him with our lives, High Huntress."

Taking Sugar by the arm, they disappeared. Arta turned and strode to the back of the truck. She waved her hand and the truck doors swung open. The clangor of battle assailed them and the thick, suffocating odor of putrefaction.

Coming up behind her, Winnie coughed and spat. "Lord a-mercy, what is that smell?"

"The djegrali." Arta summoned her spare bow and quiver from the ether. "Disgusting, is it not?"

"Like roadkill soup. You know, Arta, that's a handy little trick."

"What?"

"Being able to pull shit out of thin air. One day, you're going to show me how you do it."

"One day, perhaps, but not this day. This day, we fight, little sister." Slinging the quiver over one shoulder, Arta leapt lightly from the truck. "Come. Let us to war."

* * * *

Dev stood between Conall and Ansgar on the sandy shore of the Devil River. Toby had returned. Still in dog form, he restlessly paced the water's edge. Snarling, the huge canine watched the sickly mass of clouds gather on the opposite bank. Within that darkness, shadows spasmed.

Dev eyed the ragged shapes uneasily. "Demons?"

"Aye, Pratt's minions," Conall said. "Sent to spring our trap, no doubt."

"You think he suspects us?"

"I do not doubt it. Pratt is sly." The grim-faced captain ran a loving cloth down the blade of his sword, a plain but serviceable weapon with a wood and leather grip and rounded pommel. "But we will destroy his evil army, and his machinations will be for naught." He slid Dev a curious look. "You are a swordsman, shire reeve?"

"Um...no."

"You have skill with the bow?"

"Not really, but I have a gun."

"A gun is worthless against the djegrali."

"The shire reeve has another weapon at his disposal." Ansgar checked the shaft of one of his arrows. "He reduced one of the *morkyn* with his bare hands, to hear Eamon tell it."

"Reverse spell work." Dev shrugged. "Even diamonds crack under enough pressure."

"A rare gift, but of little use in close quarters and against so many," Ansgar said, shaking his head. "Why do you not call upon the wolf?"

"The wolf?" Conall asked sharply.

"The shire reeve's other form. Together, the wolf and I fought the djegrali in league with Blake Peterson. The wolf is a fearsome creature."

"I remember," Dev said. "But the wolf can't do certain things."

"Ah, you mean shield work," Conall said. "Every form has its limitations, does it not? An you are to fight beside us, you require a vorpal weapon." He tossed the cleaning cloth into the air. It vanished, and a spiked metal ball mounted on a sturdy shaft appeared in his hand. "Take my morning star," he said, handing the weapon to Dev. "Little skill is required other than a strong arm and good aim."

"Hell's version of a baseball bat?" Dev gave the morning star an experimental flourish. "I like it. Thanks. I'll give it back when this is over."

"Nay, keep it. It has been gathering dust this eon and more."

"I promise to put it to good use. Any advice?"

"Mind your aim," Conall said. "I used it once against an armored kissu, and it bounced back and smacked me in the skull. I saw spots for weeks."

"Kissu?"

"Body of a lion, head and tail of a lizard, and a shell harder than stone. As the djegrali are amorphous, that should not be a problem. Like all Dalvahni weapons, the touch of the morning star is death to a demon."

"How many demons are we talking?"

"Five hundred, by my count."

"Five hundred?" Dev was taken aback. "Good God."

"Good sport, methinks. The Dalvahni have prevailed against far greater odds." Conall's mouth twisted in a rare smile. "'Tis not the djegrali that should worry you. I would rather face a thousand demon hordes than Arta in a rage."

Dev glanced at the truck beneath the spreading oak. The vehicle was parked more than a hundred yards away. Yet, even at a distance, Arta's anger beat at him in waves. "Yeah, I don't think she's very happy with me right now."

"You give yourself too little credit," Conall said. "Ne'er have I seen the High Huntress in such high dudgeon."

And no wonder, Dev thought. *You humiliated her in front of the Dalvahni.*

An unforgiveable sin. Long legs braced, she'd glared at him, hurt and rage shimmering in her glorious eyes. Jesus, even her *hair* had looked angry. When on duty, she wore her silvery tresses in a tight chignon, but it had come loose. Floating around her shoulders, it had writhed and twisted, too furious to be contained.

He'd stepped in it for sure, but he'd do it again in a heartbeat. Anything to keep her safe.

"How long do you think she'll stay mad at me?" he asked.

"Who can say? A thousand years…mayhap more?" Conall said. "No matter. 'Tis a battle for another day." He raised his voice for the benefit of the Dalvahni warriors on the strand. "Today is a good day, my brothers. Today, we fight the djegrali."

The Dalvahni rumbled in answer. Their numbers had swelled to more than two dozen, and they were an impressive lot. Black-, brown-, white-, or golden-skinned, to a man they were fiercely handsome, tall, and heavily muscled.

They were also armed to the teeth, though their weapons, like their physical appearance, varied. Most carried swords, but Dev saw bows, axes, war hammers, and several other weapons he did not recognize. Grim and Eamon stood among them. Grim carried a blade, a long, two-handed affair with a curved cross guard. Eamon, like Conall, favored a shorter weapon. He stood beside a black warrior with a strong jaw, prominent cheekbones, eyes the color of jade, and long, thick curly hair. The warrior carried a halberd, a wicked combination of pole and axe. A mace hung at his hip, and a big knife was strapped to each bulging thigh.

Dev did a double take when a warrior stepped from the crowd to speak to Grim. The man was armed with a horseman's pick and bluer than Papa Smurf.

"Our brother Malothan," Ansgar said, noticing Dev's startled expression. "Cursed by Ena for slaying one of the djegrali in her temple."

"Ena?"

"Enallalual, a goddess. Kehvahn's sister."

"Wasn't he just doing his job?"

"Of a certainty, but this particular demon happened to occupy the body of Ena's favorite lover at the time, a human male named Varad," Ansgar said. "She demanded Mal's head on a platter for the offense, but Kehvahn interceded on his behalf."

"Did he, now?" Bitterly, Dev recalled his conversation with Kehvahn outside the Sweet Shop. "He wouldn't lift a finger to help me stop Pratt."

"The gods seldom hinder one another," Ansgar said, "lest there be dissension among them."

"Yeah, that's pretty much the party line."

"He offered you no further counsel?" Ansgar asked.

"Only to combine my resources."

"And so you have." Conall motioned to the assembled warriors. "The Dal have your back."

"Aye, we do," Ansgar said. "I would speak to Mal. Long has it been since last we met."

The blond warrior strolled over and grabbed the blue fellow around the neck. They tussled briefly and embraced.

"Ansgar and Malothan fought together in the siege of Ospar," Conall said, watching them. "They are very close." He turned his black gaze on Dev. "I am curious, shire reeve. How do you mean to deal with Pratt?"

"I'm going to bind him with a shield."

"You can do this?"

"Maybe. Hope so, anyway." Dev made a face. "I was counting on Verbena's help."

"Ah, the Enhancer... But she is not here."

"Nope."

"And still, you mean to try this binding?"

Dev's jaw hardened. "Yep."

"And should you succeed?"

"Pratt will be brought up before the Kith Council and tried for his crimes."

"And if he is found guilty, what then?"

"I have a special jail for violent supernaturals."

Conall grunted in surprise. "You devised this prison?"

"No, my great-grandfather."

"This prison is strong enough to confine a god?"

"Should be. It was made by one," Dev said. "His name is Selvans. Aunt Wee says I got my knack for shield work from him."

"Impressive," Conall said, "but in my experience, even the most carefully devised campaign encounters setbacks. You have an alternative plan should things go awry with Pratt?"

Dev hefted the morning star. "Whack him upside the head?"

Conall chuckled. "I admire your spirit, though I have my doubts about your chances of success." Toby barked in warning, and the captain's face tightened with anticipation. "Hark, our friend sounds the alarm. The moment of reckoning is upon us."

The djegrali boiled out of the thundercloud on the opposite shore. Screeching like a thousand bad fan belts at once, they swept across the river.

Lifting his sword, Conall shouted, "What say you, my brothers? Shall we fight?"

The Dalvahni roared in defiance and rushed to meet the demons. Dev got a fleeting glimpse of black wings, claws, and teeth, and then the demons were upon them. The stench of the djegrali was incredible, solid enough to chew. Dev coughed and swung the morning star in a wide arc. The weapon struck a group of wraiths, and they howled and dissolved into smelly powder. Dev kept swinging, annihilating demons left and right, but for each one he slew, three more took its place. Shoulders aching, he paused to wipe his eyes and looked around. Conall, Ansgar, and Malothan fought side by side. Hacking and hewing, they attacked the noxious mass. Ansgar was singing, and Conall's eyes were alight.

By God, they were enjoying themselves.

A blob of demons attacked Dev from behind. They shredded his uniform shirt and duty belt and left burning trails and bite marks on his skin. Yelping in pain, Dev tried to pluck them off, but they stuck to him like blobs of tar. He rolled on the ground, dislodging them, and sprang to his feet. Five demons hissed up at him from the ground, hideous, squirming things with shrunken chiropteran faces. He shuddered and reduced them to dust with his morning star.

Screeching in outrage, a second clump of demons dived at him. Dev gripped his weapon and braced for the impact, but the attack never came. Arrows twanged, piercing the demons and reducing them to whiffs of smelly smoke.

He turned to thank his rescuer, the words dying on his tongue when he saw the avenging fury striding toward him. Light pulsed from her in golden waves, and warriors and wraiths alike parted before her shining form. Hissing, a swarm of demons threw themselves at her, only to be washed away like flotsam on the tide.

Her glowing nimbus enclosed Dev, and the sounds and smells of combat faded.

Little stars danced before Dev's eyes. "Kissu," he murmured in stunned amazement. This, then, was how Conall must have felt when he'd bonked himself in the head with the morning star. With an effort, he shook off the spell. "Arta, I thought you were with Sugar. What are you doing here?"

"Saving you, 'twould seem." Her eyes blazed in her pale face, and all hint of softness in her had burned away. She was a fiery nemesis, retribution in glorious female form. She looked him up and down, taking in his injuries and tattered, bloody uniform. "You are hurt."

"It's nothing, just a few scratches. I've never fought a demon army before."

"Obviously."

Dev clenched his teeth. "Where's Sugar?"

"Whisked to safety in the company of two of my sisters. The orb, also."

"That's not what I told you to do," Dev said. "You and Winnie were supposed to stay with him in the truck."

"And you are a demigod. You are *supposed* to be able to defend yourself."

"I am defending myself." Dev held up his mace. His hands were grimy with dust. "I have Conall's morning star."

"Much good it will do you. You have no training."

Dev's temper flared. "And you can't follow orders to save your life. You're nothing but trouble. I never should have made you a deputy."

Arta went white around the mouth. "Then allow me to remedy your mistake." She flung her badge at his feet. Her form blurred and her uniform disappeared, leaving her clad once more in her huntress garb. "I would say the experience has been a pleasure, but that would be a lie, and I know your aversion to untruths."

She spun on her heel and stalked away, taking the light with her.

"Arta, wait. I'm sorry. I didn't mean—"

With Arta's shining aura gone, Dev was exposed, fresh meat for the enjoyment of the djegrali. A cluster of shrieking demons attacked. He cursed and swung the mace, turning the demons to ash. A bell gonged, and a score of Kirvahni materialized beside Arta. Winnie was with her, too, Dev saw. Her eyes were shining, and she held a sturdy axe. The blade of the axe glowed with a greenish light.

Vorpal blade, Dev thought.

Arta threw her head back and screamed, a cry not of fear, but a chilling, ululating call to battle. The sound shook Dev to the core. Arta was going to war and Winnie with her, the thing he'd hoped to avoid. They could be hurt or—

Shrieking like banshees, Arta, Winnie, and the Kir charged into the horde of demons and were swallowed up.

"Arta," Dev shouted, lunging after her.

A demon dived at his head. Raking him with its claws, the fiend left a burning trail from Dev's forehead to his chin. As he raised his morning star to strike, a huge gray shape leapt between him and the wraith. It was Toby. Snatching the demon out of the air, the dog tore it to pieces.

Panting, Toby growled something at Dev.

"It's nothing. A few scratches," Dev said, understanding the dog's snarling. He wiped the blood from his eyes and pointed to the swarming djegrali. "Arta and Winnie are in there."

Toby growled again.

"You're right." Grabbing a handful of the giant dog's thick, wiry fur, Dev sprang onto Toby's back. "Let's go get them."

Chapter Twenty-Two

The dog bounded across the narrow beach and plunged into the thick cloud of darkness with Dev astride him. Wraiths swarmed them like ravenous overgrown mosquitoes. Toby snarled and shredded them with his sharp teeth. The stench of the djegrali was overpowering. It stole Dev's breath and clung to his skin, burning the scratches on his face, arms, and chest, and coating his throat. He coughed and spat. Yelling in defiance, he swung his mace, and demons shrieked and fell.

They fought their way to the heart of the reeking mass. The demons parted, and Dev caught a glimpse of Arta. She was surrounded by the Kir. Brandishing her weapon, Winnie stalked outside the ring of huntresses, keeping the djegrali at bay. Cords of electricity ran down her arms, and the axe in her hand blazed with light. The axe hummed as it connected with a knot of demons. They died, shrieking, but more took their place.

There were always more. Their numbers seemed endless.

Every fiber of Dev's being was focused on Arta, on reaching her, protecting her. If she were hurt...if something happened to her—

In the center of the circle, she doubled over.

"Arta," he cried, terror painfully squeezing his heart.

A dazzling luminescence pulsed beneath her ribs, bright as the burning heart of a star. Straightening with a shout, Arta threw her arms wide. Light poured from her and spread in broad, shining bands like the rays of a rising sun. The pale tide washed harmlessly over the Kir and their allies, but it destroyed the djegrali. Pulverized demons drifted to the ground like flakes of dirty snow.

Conall materialized beside Dev and Toby. "I commend your choice of mount, shire reeve. The tribes of the Durngesi plains also ride their dogs into battle."

Toby growled and showed his teeth.

"Toby says he ain't nobody's dawg," Dev said.

"So I understood." Conall executed an exaggerated bow. "I meant no offense, oh most noble of hounds."

Dev stared at him in surprise. "You speak dog?"

"Of a certainty. Kehvahn gifted us with the ability to communicate with animals to aid in our appointed task." Conall surveyed the ash-covered battlefield. "The High Huntress has summoned the *scaldscar*. Take your rest, my brothers," he said, raising his voice to address the other warriors. "The demons are routed."

The Dalvahni looked sullen but lowered their weapons.

"Their blood runs high," Conall explained, gazing at his men with pride. "Such is our nature."

"This *scaldscar* thing you mentioned. What's that?"

"A gift granted the High Huntress. Arta is the Vessel."

My name was drawn from the Vessel. That's what Arta had told Beck when they'd had lunch at the Sweet Shop. Had it only been a few weeks ago? It seemed as if he'd known Arta forever. She was part of him now, integral to his happiness and well-being. Life without her was unfathomable. She was his weakness, his Achilles' heel. He'd never been in love, but he'd fallen hard for the High Huntress.

"Shire reeve?"

Dev shifted uneasily on Toby's back. "I thought the Vessel was a cup," he said.

"'Tis both," Conall said. "As High Huntress, Arta is connected to her sisters and granted a small measure of their individual powers. She calls upon their collective source in times of need. To my knowledge, Arta has summoned the *scaldscar* but twice ere today, and ne'er with such ferocity."

"I might have had something to do with that," Dev admitted. "Arta and I had a disagreement. I...um...lost my temper and said some things."

Hurtful things, things he regretted. *You're nothing but trouble... I never should have made you a deputy.*

"Ah." Strands of crushed djegrali floated by Conall like tissue paper. Toby pounced on a flimsy strip and shook it. "No doubt the burning was fueled by her ire. Impressive, is it not?"

"Very." Dev tightened his hands in Toby's fur. "She practically took out Pratt's demon army by her lonesome."

Conall gave him a sharp look. "You were worried for her? 'Tis why you relegated her and Winnie to the sausage truck?"

"Yeah. Pratt's an ugly customer, and Arta is, well..."—Dev shrugged—"*Arta*, and Winnie's a hothead."

"Do not berate yourself, shire reeve. Love is a strange and bewildering affliction."

"That obvious, huh?"

"Only to those who suffer the same malady. I wish you happy."

"Don't congratulate me yet. I'm not sure Arta feels the same way."

"Have you confessed your feelings?"

"No, I've been waiting for the right time." Dev made a helpless gesture. "Hell, I'm not even sure she *can* return my feelings. She says love is a human weakness."

"I, too, believed myself inviolable, but I was wrong. Rebekah assaulted my defenses and sundered them. Arta is displeased with you?"

"Apoplectic."

"A propitious sign, methinks." Conall clapped him on the shoulder. "An she felt nothing for you, she would not be splenetic."

"Thanks," Dev said, much cheered. "I hadn't thought of it that way."

"Conversely, her gall could be rooted in extreme dislike," Conall added, dashing Dev's brief hopes. "In any event, I recommend you declare yourself swiftly and ardently, given her present distemper. Tell her how you truly feel and hide not behind the shield of pride."

"Good advice," Dev said. "Thanks."

"Moreover, a little groveling would not be amiss," Conall said, his black eyes twinkling.

Korth appeared on a shiver of music. The thrall eyed the wafting demon orts curiously for a moment, then plucked a morsel out of the air and stuck it in his mouth. His eyes widened. With a low moan of pleasure, he unhinged his lower jaw and sucked the rest of the djegrali fragments down his throat like a monstrous, industrial vacuum cleaner. He burped and glanced around, reminding Dev for all the world of a kid caught with his hand in the cookie jar.

"By the sword." Conall stared at Korth, thunderstruck. "The thrall *ate* the djegrali."

Brand strode up to them. "Unsettling, is it not? The thrall Lenora once ingested the remains of a *morkyn* in my presence, else I would not have credited it."

"'Tis disgusting," Conall said with feeling. "Perverted."

"That's a little strong, don't you think?" Dev said. "Some people like peanut butter and pickles. Different strokes for different folks. If thralls have a taste for demon, it can only make your job easier."

Conall gave him a black look. "*Easy* is not the aim of the Dalvahni. We hunt the djegrali. 'Tis our privilege and appointed task."

"*Was* your appointed task." Dev was beginning to enjoy the tough-as-nails captain of the Dalvahni's discomfort. "Kehvahn may have other ideas."

Conall opened his mouth to retort, but Toby's rumbled warning cut him off.

"I see him, Toby, thanks," Dev said. "North side of the river, Conall. Twelve o'clock."

Pratt had abandoned his cloud and glowered at them from the far bank. He was not what Dev had expected. Like Kehvahn, he wore a robe, but there, any resemblance to his dweebish brother ended. Pratt was fair of face and form. In fact, he more closely resembled the Dalvahni than their maker, with his broad shoulders and flowing dusky hair. Dark energy vibrated from him in sickening bands, and a warning bell clanged in Dev's head. He'd busted up enough meth labs to know psychosis when he saw it.

Pratt was off his rocker.

Off his rocker? Pratt was off the porch and upside down in the flower bed.

Arta stepped away from her sisters and strode to the water's edge, head high and pale hair whipping around her shoulders. "Begone, foul demiurge of destruction," she said in a ringing voice. "Your demon army is destroyed."

"Good God," Dev said. "Is she *trying* to give me a heart attack?" He pressed his knees against Toby's flanks, and the dog loped up to Arta. Dismounting, Dev grabbed her by the arm. "What's the matter with you?" he said, meeting her furious gaze. "Don't you know better than to poke the bear?"

She jerked away from him. "Curb me not. By the Vessel and the blood, *this* bear shall pay for his iniquities."

"Absolutely," Dev said, "but it's my job as sheriff to bring him in, not yours."

"Bring me in? What nonsense is this?" Pratt's stentorian voice rippled with amusement. "I am not bound by human law."

Dev stepped in front of Arta. "You are in this county. Name's Dev Whitsun, and I'm the sheriff. You're under arrest on charges of murder and attempted murder."

Pratt laughed. "I am a god. You cannot constrain me."

"Maybe not, but I sure as hell mean to try."

"Presumptuous flea." Dismissing Dev with a sneer, Pratt turned his appreciative gaze on Arta. "Your beauty and spirit please me, High Huntress." He gestured imperiously. "Come. I would make you my queen."

"Tempting, but no," Arta said.

"Think carefully, fair one, ere you deny me. Once I regain the orb, my dominion shall be complete. Together, we could rule the many worlds, you and I."

"I think not." Arta folded her arms. "You have tried to master the orb for thousands of years and failed."

Pratt scowled. "The fault was not mine. I chose the wrong bearer. E'en bound and broken, Gryffin was far from tractable. The skellring has the mind of a child and is easily led."

"Withal, Sugar and the orb are gone."

"You lie," Pratt shouted. "I tracked them to this very place."

"'Twas a trick to lure you here," Arta shouted back. "The skellring is gone, I tell you, and the orb with him."

Pratt howled in fury and shattered the trees along the bank.

"That's it." Dev tossed Arta unceremoniously on Toby's back. "You can call me ten kinds of sumbitch later, if you like, but we're out of here."

He leapt up behind her and slid his arms around her, shielding her in place when she tried to wriggle down.

"How dare you imprison me?" she said, flushed and panting with fury. "I do not answer to you."

"The hell you don't. My county, my rules, remember?"

Dev nudged Toby, and the dog raced away.

"I shall have the orb," Pratt howled after them. Pulling up a tree by the roots, he threw it at them like a spear. It hit the riverbank a few feet behind them with the force of a bomb, sending plumes of sand, rock, and driftwood shooting into the air. Toby swerved and ran faster. "I shall not be denied," the maddened god screamed. "'Tis mine, *mine*."

The dog darted through the line of warriors and skidded to a halt in front of Conall. Lifting his shaggy head, he growled at the captain.

"You have the right of it, my friend," Conall said to Toby. "Pratt has, indeed, 'lost his marbles,' as you so aptly put it."

The dog growled something else.

"Aye, I saw him throw a tree at you." Conall shook the grit from his black hair. "My brothers and I also wear the evidence of Pratt's ire."

With a sound of impatience, Arta shoved her hands against Dev's wrists. "Release me. I find your interference insupportable."

"Then don't act like a harebrained idiot," Dev said. "You do something stupid like that again, and I will interfere. Every. Damn. Time."

She stiffened. "Let me go."

Dev lowered his shield, and Arta flung herself off the dog, stalking away from him without a backward glance.

"'Harebrained idiot'?" Conall raised his brows. "This is your idea of ardor, shire reeve?"

"I can't help it," Dev said, jumping off Toby's back. "The damn woman makes me crazy."

There was another angry howl from the opposite bank of the river.

"Fools, you think to best me so easily?" Pratt bellowed. The god's eyes were wild, and spittle clung to his bottom lip. "I will teach you what a god can do."

Lightning shot from his hands and struck the earth. Gaping chasms opened, and hundreds of giant centipedes, millipedes, spiders, and scorpions boiled out.

"Bugs," Dev said in disgust. "Why does it always have to be bugs?"

"It matters not what form the enemy takes," Conall said, decapitating a monstrous fire ant with a single blow, "only that we fight. To me, Dalvahni! Once more into the fray."

Roaring in exaltation, the Dalvahni threw themselves at the monstrous insects.

Dev spun around at a loud hiss. A mammoth centipede was bearing down on him with mandibles clacking. He yelped in surprise and slammed his war hammer into the oval shield that protected the thing's bulbous head. The shield split and grayish-green ichor splashed Dev in the face. Blinded, he staggered back. Scraping the goo from his eyes, he looked up. The wounded centipede teetered above him like a drunken sailor on shore leave. He scrambled out of the way, narrowly avoiding being crushed as the bug crashed to the ground with a meaty thud.

Dev blinked the last of the ichor out of his eyes and glanced around. The Dalvahni and the Kir had spread out along the river to engage the enemy. Rafe, the warrior with the bloodred hair, was battling an enormous antlion. At his side, Conall and Ansgar fought a scorpion the size of a railroad car. Conall sliced off the creature's wicked barb with his sword, and Ansgar slew it with a golden arrow. Dev's gaze moved to Toby. The giant dog was worrying the back legs of a huge spider as Grim attacked the creature from the front.

A droning noise made Dev look up. Buzzing like a low-flying crop duster, an enormous wasp dove at a fierce, dark-skinned beauty. With a flick of her wrists, the huntress sent a stream of throwing stars into the wasp's compound eyes. The insect screeched and hit the ground, leaving a deep trench in the earth. The huntress trotted over and decapitated the wasp with a blow of her short sword.

"Well done, Tylisia," Arta shouted.

"My thanks, sister," the huntress shouted back.

Avoiding an assassin bug's needle-like beak, Arta scaled one of the insect's zebra-striped legs and skewered it with an arrow through the head. The creature bawled and collapsed. Arta jumped free and threw herself at a wood louse the size of a Humvee.

Dev whirled at a loud clicking sound. A gigantic tiger beetle was sizing Korth up like a particularly tasty snack. Lowering its head, the beetle charged.

"Korth, look out," Dev yelled.

If the thrall heard, he gave no sign, remaining motionless as the huge bug barreled toward him. At the last second, Korth stepped smoothly aside. Catching one of the beetle's wings, the thrall sprang onto the beast and flattened his palms on the bug's bony thorax. The insect shrieked and thrummed, vibrating faster and faster. The hard exoskeleton split with an audible *crack*, and the beetle dissolved in a mound of jelly. Korth landed on his feet, then quickly dispatched a black blister beetle in the same fashion.

A defiant scream drew Dev's attention from the thrall. Winnie was riding a huge crawdad. She slammed her axe into the lobster's armored carapace. The shell cracked, and blue blood jetted out. Whistling in pain, the monster bucked and threw Winnie to the ground. She hit her head on a rock and was still. Hissing in triumph, the crawdad pounced.

"Winnie," Dev shouted, lunging toward her.

Eamon got there first. Materializing in the monster's path, the warrior sliced off the lobster's waving antennae. The slender feelers toppled to the ground, and the crawdad screamed and attacked him. Eamon's sword flashed again, severing the creature's segmented front legs. The crawdad's heavy body buckled, and Eamon moved in for the kill.

Dodging a whirring green lacewing, Dev ran up to Winnie. "Wake up," he said, patting her cheek. "Come on, brat. Open your eyes."

Her eyelids fluttered. "Who are you calling a brat?"

"You, punk. You scared me into next week." Dev helped her to her feet. "Take it easy. You hit your head."

"I did?" She swayed. "I don't—" She noticed Eamon staring at her and scowled. "What are you doing here?"

"Delivering you from the jaws of death."

"Yeah?" Her scowl deepened. "Who asked you to, buster?"

"No one. I fear it has become something of a habit." Swaggering over, Eamon picked up her axe and handed it to her. "A word of caution, whelp. In future, strive not to dash your head against a rock in the heat of battle. 'Tis a remarkably hard pate, to be sure, but hardly good fighting form."

He vanished, leaving Winnie red-faced and sputtering, and reappeared on the riverbank. A towering praying mantis struck at him. Darting between the insect's spiked legs, Eamon stabbed it in the abdomen. The huge bug jerked horribly and died.

"Whelp? *Whelp?*" Winnie glared at Dev. "Did you hear what that jackass called me?"

"That jackass saved your life," Dev pointed out. "You'd be bug food if not for him."

"I was doing *fine*. I certainly don't need—"

A gray shadow streaked between them, knocking them aside. Startled, Dev whirled to face the danger. Two humongous stink bugs had sneaked up on him and Winnie while they argued. Toby threw himself at one of the bugs and tore it to pieces.

Dev smashed the other one with his hammer. "Thanks, Tobe," he said.

Winnie wiped her streaming eyes. "Gah, stink bugs stink."

"Thus, the name," Dev pointed out. Rolling an eye at Dev, Toby hacked and growled. Dev chuckled. "Toby says they taste nasty, too."

"You can understand him?" Winnie frowned. "Why can't I?"

"I dunno. Ask Eamon."

"I wouldn't ask that jerk a damn—"

A bugle blared in the distance, and Jeb Hannah clanked out of the woods with a familiar gray-haired figure on one shoulder.

"It's Aunt Wee." Winnie's eyes opened wide. "What's she doing here?"

"Lending a hand, I hope," Dev said, adding under his breath, "And about damn time."

Conall materialized, covered in mud and bug funk. "'Tis a good skirmish, no?" Grinning at Dev, he jabbed the point of his sword at the new arrivals. "The Lady Weoka and the metal giant are more of the resources you mentioned, shire reeve?"

"Yep."

"The behemoth seems a doughty fighter."

"He packs a mean peanut," Dev agreed, watching Jeb whack a tremendous grasshopper between the eyes with his club.

Daisy, Daisy, give me your answer, do, Jeb boomed, clomping down to the river.

I'm half crazy,
All for the love of you.

Gently, he set Weoka down.

"Thank you, Jeb." Straightening the strap of her overalls, she immobilized the swarm of enormous bugs with a wave of her hand and turned to face the god on the opposite bank. "You responsible for this goat rodeo?"

"What if I am?" Pratt thundered. "Begone. I do not answer to the likes of you."

"You're the one who needs to skedaddle," she said. "I'm the goddess of this river, and this is *my* home."

The veins in Pratt's neck bulged. "Nay, I will not."

"Have it your way, mister," Weoka said, raising her hands.

"Uh-oh." Dev scrambled back in alarm. "*Run.*"

Water surged over the banks and roared toward them. Grabbing Winnie by the arm, Dev pulled her away from the thundering flood and up the slope. Toby tugged the ragged sleeve of his uniform, growling something low in his throat.

"You're right." Dev threw Winnie on the dog's back. "Four legs are faster than two."

He clambered up behind her, and Toby raced away, the river licking hungrily at the dog's heels. They reached the dirt road at the top of the ridge and looked back. The water rolled over Pratt like a miniature tsunami, soaking his robe and washing away those bugs closest to the banks. Still, the river kept rising.

The Dal and the Kir materialized on the hill beside Dev.

"Where's Arta?" Dev asked, quickly scanning their ranks.

Conall pointed at something down the slope. "In yon carriage with the thrall."

Arta and Korth were seated in the back of a white 1960 Cadillac convertible. Korth was slumped against the cushioned red leather upholstery, his face gray and drawn.

"The thrall seems unwell," Conall said.

Dev grunted. "Too many demons. Probably has a bellyache."

"Please." Conall shuddered. "Do not remind me."

Samael Reaper was at the wheel of the Caddy, a gleaming vehicle with razor-sharp tailfins, fender skirts, and a front hood painted to resemble the ghoulish head of a skeletal steed. Flames shot from the tapered headlights, and sparks flew from the tires.

Toby tipped his head back with a mournful howl. "*Ankouuuuu.* Somebody's gonna die."

A shiver of apprehension shot down Dev's spine. He was responsible for this mess. If someone died, it would be on his head.

Willa Dean sat beside Samael in the shining Caddy. Back stiff and hands folded in her lap, the elderly receptionist stared straight ahead, her stony expression firmly in place.

Sam glanced in the rearview mirror. The brown wall of water was inches from the back bumper. "Faster, Dolly, faster," the reaper shouted, slapping the palm of his hand against the steering wheel.

The Cadillac screamed in response and sped up the incline to the road, spewing rocks and sand in its wake. The river reached the top of the rise and washed back down, sweeping away the last of Pratt's insects.

"You shall pay for this affront," Pratt bellowed, plucking at his sodden robes. "I shall… I shall—"

"What, throw another temper tantrum?" Aunt Weoka chuckled. "Thought a good dunking might calm you down, but I guess not."

Willa Dean exited the car with the brisk energy of a much younger woman and strode up to Dev, a martial glint in her eyes. "Sheriff Whitsun, who is that awful creature hollering at Weoka? He needs to learn some manners."

"I couldn't agree more, Miz Willa," Dev said. "'Scuse me."

He trotted down the hill to Weoka's side. "It's over, Pratt," he told the fuming god. "The orb is safe, and your armies are defeated."

"Insolent worm, I do not need the orb to best you or this puny Earth goddess," Pratt shouted, his body expanding and growing taller and taller until he towered over the trees. Lumbering across the river, he lifted a giant foot to crush them. "I shall grind you both beneath my heel."

Jeb Hannah blew his horn and slammed his peanut club into Pratt's right shin. The god howled in pain and hopped up and down on one foot.

"Now, boy," Aunt Wee said to Dev. "Best do it now while he's distracted."

"Yessum."

Summoning a golden rope, Dev lassoed Pratt around the ankles. A second rope followed, and a third. Bracing his feet in the sand, Dev yanked hard on the sturdy magical cords, but Pratt did not budge. A gray shape went by him. It was Toby with Winnie on his back. Snarling, Toby nipped at Pratt's calves, and Winnie hit him with the butt of her axe. Red-faced with fury, the god kicked them into the river.

Ain't nobody like a bully, Jeb sang, clanking over to lend Dev a hand.
Ain't nobody studying you,
Ain't nobody like a meanie,
Kicked a dawg and a purdy girl, too.

Ping. Conall, Arta, and Eamon materialized. They grabbed the ends of the ropes and pulled, adding their superhuman strength to Dev's, but Pratt shook them off like rag dolls. Dev flew into a pine tree, sliding to the ground in a shower of cones and bark. Dazed, he looked around. A few feet away from him, Conall sat up with a groan. Jeb and Eamon had landed in a heap on a sandy shoal in the middle of the river. The behemoth's bugle was twisted and bent. A spasm of sheer terror ripped through Dev. Arta? *Where was Arta?*

He looked around frantically and found her sitting at the top of a tall hickory on the far side of the river. She glared back at him.

Annoyed but unharmed, thank God, Dev thought, slumping with relief.

Pratt shrank back to his former size, his eyes bulging with fury. "You dare lay hands on me?" Lightning formed at his fingertips. "I shall smite you for this blasphemy," he said, raising his hands to end them. "Aye, you and this place. I will wipe you from all memory."

The Cadillac zoomed down the hill and screeched to a stop. "That's enough of your nonsense," Willa Dean said briskly. Climbing out of the car, she marched up to Pratt. "Nobody—but *nobody*—threatens my home and my friends."

A snarl of snakes sprang from the teased gray hammock of Willa Dean's hair. Red beams shot from her eyes, pinning Pratt where he stood. The god went rigid, his mouth slightly open in surprise, and his handsome face hardened and turned chalky white. Slowly, the leprous contagion crept down his neck to his arms and chest. In moments, his entire body had turned to stone. With a sibilant hiss, the snakes disappeared once more into Willa Dean's nest of hair.

Dev got to his feet. "Is he...dead?"

"Petrified," Sam said, getting out of the car. "Nice work, honeybunch."

"Thank you, Sam-I-Am." Willa Dean patted her hairdo back into place. "Maybe standing around with bird poop on his head for a few hundred years will teach him a lesson, but I doubt it."

Aunt Weoka coalesced from a puddle of water. "Gracious, that was exciting."

"'Tis not often one contends with a god," Ansgar said, materializing beside Conall. "You are uninjured, Captain?"

Conall slapped the sand from his leather breeches. "My pride has suffered a blow, 'tis all."

Blip. Arta vanished from the tree branch and reappeared beside Weoka.

Dev strode eagerly toward her. "Arta, I'm glad you're..."—he paused at her frosty glare—"okay," he finished.

"I am perfectly well, thank you," she said with all the warmth of a glacier. "An you will excuse me, I must confer with my sisters."

She blinked from view and reappeared at the top of the rise. She said something to the Kir, and they vanished. Arta's lithe form wavered, and she vanished, too.

Without a word.

Without so much as a single backward glance.

Dev's chest felt hollow, as if someone had taken a giant spoon and scooped out his insides, including his heart. Was this it? Was she done with him?

A knowing chuckle drew his gaze from the spot where Arta had been standing.

"That was some look she gave you," Aunt Weoka said, watching him in amusement. "Don't look so hangdog, boy. She'll be back."

"I'm not so sure. We had a fight."

"Figures. What did you do?"

"Me?" Dev protested. "What makes you think it was me? You're supposed to be on my side."

"Am on your side," she said, "but you could make a Mennonite cuss." She gave him her patented I-will-get-to-the-bottom-of-this look. "Well?"

"I might have told her she was nothing but trouble," Dev muttered.

"Cut your throat with your own tongue. Go on."

"And I might have said it was a mistake to make her a deputy."

"I'll say one thing for you, my boy. You don't do things by half. Stepping in it wasn't enough. You had to lie down and roll."

"I know, I know," Dev said. "I really screwed the pooch."

"Yup. I'd say you're in for a rare bear jawing."

"She can chew me up and spit me out as long as she comes back."

"Oh, she'll be back," Weoka said. "Arta ain't the type to run away."

Korth groaned and sat up in the back seat of the Cadillac. "What happened?"

"You ate a shit ton of demons and killed a few giant bugs," Dev said. "Oh, and Pratt's been petrified."

"The demons and the bugs I remember." The thrall belched. "I fear I am unwell. As you no longer need me, I will be on my way."

"Sure, go ahead," Dev said, "and thanks for your help."

Korth's form glimmered, and he was gone.

Conall turned to Ansgar. "Thank our brothers for their service, also, and give them leave to depart. You may leave, as well." He glanced at Eamon, who was arguing with Winnie on the sandbar. "Eamon, it seems, is otherwise occupied and will abide here for the nonce."

Ansgar nodded and disappeared. A moment later, he and rest of the Dalvahni were gone.

"*No.*" Dripping wet from her dip in the river, Winnie glared at Eamon. "I didn't ask you to pull me out of the river," she shouted. "Get it through your thick skull. I don't need or *want* your help!"

Eamon shook his fist at the heavens and vanished.

"Good riddance," Winnie said, a little shakily.

She dived in the water and swam for shore. Emerging from the river, she pushed her sodden hair out of her face. "Where's Toby?"

"Right here." Toby climbed slowly out of the water. Though he'd returned to human form, he was obviously in pain. "Sumbitch cracked a couple of ribs, but they'll heal. Can't say the same for Jeb's horn."

The animated statue was sitting on the sandbar gazing forlornly at his crumpled bugle.

So long, Mary, he sang,
Mary, we will miss you so!
So long, Mary,
How I hate to see you go.

Toby shook his head. "Breaks your heart, don't it?"

"We'll get him another bugle," Dev said. "Go home, Toby, and let those ribs heal. Winnie will give you a ride."

"But, Dev—" Winnie said.

"That's an order."

Muttering to herself, Winnie slogged up the hill with Toby. A moment later, Dev heard the engine start and the car drive away.

"Winnie likes to be in the middle of every dogfight," Weoka said. "Can't stand the thought of missing something."

"Tell me about it." Dev stared at his aunt. "You vaporized. Pratt almost squished me, and you vaporized."

"Oh, pooh, you were never in any danger," Weoka said. "Why didn't you put up a shield?"

"I forgot," Dev said. "Everything happened too fast."

"You've gotten rusty, boy. Shield work takes practice, and you've come to depend on your gun," she scolded. "It's a darn good thing Willa Dean was here. She put that bully Pratt in his place."

Willa Dean sniffed. "Somebody had to. I can't abide rudeness."

There was a loud rumbling across the river to the northwest. The trees parted, and a huge granite-skinned creature shambled out of the woods. The goliath's legs were thick as tree trunks. Duncan trotted at the brute's side. Lifting his head, the warrior said something to the ogre.

Willa Dean's coiffure trembled ominously. "What's this, more trouble?"

"It's okay, Willa Dean," Dev said quickly. "He's with me. I sent for him."

"Sent for him? Far be it from me to tell you how to do your job, Sheriff, but ogres are notoriously stupid and unpredictable."

Dev swallowed a snort. Willa Dean Mooneyham had been bossing him around since he'd been in high school.

"His name is Evan Beck," Dev said. "I thought he might come in handy—"

"Pratt." The ogre roared, breaking into a clumsy run. "Ebban smash Pratt."

"—in dealing with Pratt." Dev paused as the ogre let out another ear-shattering yowl. "For obvious reasons."

"I see." Willa Dean's flinty eyes narrowed. "He seems a mite testy."

"He only turns into the ogre when he's upset."

"That right? He certainly seems upset right now."

"Pratt blighted a Kirvahni huntress named Taryn and left her for dead," Dev said.

"And Evan's dotty about her," Aunt Weoka added.

"How sweet." Willa Dean pointed to the horizon. "And that?"

Dev squinted at the bright patch of light bearing down on them. "That'll be Gryffin and Verbena. They were supposed to be here earlier, but they're late, too."

"Pratt," the ogre boomed, splashing across the river. He reached the sandy shore and looked around. "Where Pratt?"

Duncan materialized beside Dev. "I have brought the ogre, as requested."

"Thanks, but you're too late," Dev said. "The fight's over."

"Over?" Duncan's face fell. "My apologies, but Evan could not be found in any of his usual haunts. After much searching, I located him in a part of Hannah known as Froggy Bottom."

"I know Froggy Bottom," Dev said. "Bunch of dilapidated trailers in a slough. Been there several times looking for suspects. What was he doing there?"

"Sulking," Duncan said. "He misses Taryn."

"Told you." Aunt Weoka winked at Willa Dean. "Dotty about the gal."

"Pratt." The ogre stamped his blockish feet. "Where Pratt?"

"Oh, for heaven's sake, cool your jets, boy." Striding up to the monster, Aunt Wee motioned toward the statue. "Pratt's been petrified."

"Pratt?" The ogre fixed his wobbly, myopic gaze on the calcified god, and his brutish face darkened. "*Pratt? Ebban smash.*"

"No, Evan, don't," Dev cried.

The ogre brought his fist down on Pratt's head, shattering it. He howled and hit the statue again. Pratt's torso cracked in two and tumbled to the ground. The ogre kept pounding until the god's marble body lay in tiny pieces.

"Hurt Red." Chest heaving, the ogre glared down at the god's dusty remains. "Ebban smash. Smash good."

"*Noooo.*" Gryffin appeared. His muscular body was limned with light, and his eyes shone like headlights. "Pratt was mine. Vengeance was *mine.*"

Raising his arm, he hurled a white-hot ball of light at the ogre. The monster howled in pain. His huge form wavered, and Evan appeared. He swayed and crumpled to the sand beside Pratt's powdered remains.

"Mine, and you took it from me," Gryffin roared, raising his hand to strike Evan again.

A slim figure darted from behind the rogue to stand over Evan. "No, Gryffin, no!"

"Move, Verbena," Gryffin said through his teeth.

"I won't. I *won't,* I tell you." Verbena clutched a small ginger dog in her arms. "I ain't a-gonna let you hurt Mr. Evan. It weren't his fault."

"Nay, 'twas your doing," Gryffin shouted. "Had we not paused to rescue that miserable cur, I would have reached Pratt in time."

"In time fer what, to kill him yourself? Pratt's dead, ain't that what you wanted?"

"*I* wanted to kill him," Gryffin shouted. "I needed to kill him. 'Twas my right. The thought of vengeance and vengeance alone has kept me sane these many years." He glared at her with unspeakable fury. "You have robbed me of that sweetest of pleasures, and I shall never forgive you. *Never.*"

Raising his arms, Gryffin shot into the sky like a rocket, the force of his departure sending shock waves rippling around them. His glowing figure hung suspended in the air for a long moment, and then Gryffin streaked away with a huge thunderclap and was gone.

Chapter Twenty-Three

Duncan strode quickly over to Verbena. "You are unharmed?" he asked. "Cassandra and I have been concerned for you."

"Indeed," said Conall. "We all have."

"That's the truth," Aunt Weoka added. "Where you been keeping yourself the past few weeks, girl?"

"Me and Gryffin been staying in an empty cabin on the river," Verbena said. "Gryffin wanted to stay close on account o' he was a-feared Pratt might give him the slip." She buried her face in the dog's patchy fur. "Now Pratt's dead, I won't never see Gryffin again."

Dev put his arm around her thin shoulders. "You don't know that."

"Reckon I do." Verbena lifted her head. Her expression was so woebegone that it made Dev's heart ache. "You seen his face. He hates me."

"He doesn't hate you. He's angry. Give him time. He'll cool off."

Arta would cool off, too, Dev hoped, but he didn't give a hill of beans about her mood. She could be mad as fire. She could call him everything but a child of God. Hell, she could go full-blown nuclear weapon on him. He didn't care, so long as she came back.

"Where'd you get the dog?" he asked.

She squeezed the mutt in her arms, a pitiful specimen, malnourished and obviously abused. "This here's Bobo."

The dog whined and licked her chin at the sound of his name.

"I thought Joby Ray killed Bobo," Dev said.

"He lied, the no-good skunk." Verbena scowled. "Done it to spite me, I reckon. He always was a mean 'un."

"I'm glad Bobo's alive," Dev said, though *alive* was a relative term. He'd seen better-looking roadkill. "How'd you find him?"

"Me and Gryffin was chasing Pratt through the woods, and Bobo must've got a whiff o' me, 'cause he set up a howl. Gryffin didn't wanna stop, but I set up a howl o' my own. Me and Bobo, we's a team. Ain't that right, boy?" She planted a kiss on the scrawny dog's head. "We found him tied up and half-starved in the Skinner caravan."

Rage at Joby Ray's deliberate cruelty filled Dev. As far as he was concerned, people who abused animals deserved a special place in hell. He wanted to find Joby Ray and strangle him.

Slowly.

He took a deep breath. "Did Joby Ray try to stop you and Gryffin from taking Bobo?"

"Nah." Verbena gave a deep chuckle. "Joby Ray took one look at Gryffin and wet his britches. He's all gums and no teeth."

"He won't be bothering you or Bobo again," Dev promised. "When I'm done with him, Joby Ray will be cooling his heels in county lockup on charges of kidnapping and animal abuse."

"You won't find him. Gryffin's done sent him to some place called the Pit."

"Demon jail?" Dev frowned. "I don't like it when folks take the law into their own hands. That's not how it's supposed to work."

"Gryffin don't give a rose-scented toot about how it's supposed to work."

Evan groaned and tried to sit up.

"Hold, my friend," Duncan said, hurrying over to the injured shifter. "You have been dealt a grievous blow."

Evan stared at him without recognition and slumped back to the ground, unconscious.

"How is he?" Dev asked, joining Duncan.

Duncan shook his head. "Alas, I fear he is in sore distress."

"Here, let me look." Aunt Weoka knelt beside Evan and gave him a cursory examination. "Broken ribs and likely a concussion, judging from the knot on his head." She sat back on her heels. "Bruises and a few burns, but he'll live."

Conall exhaled in relief. "Thank the gods."

"'Strewth, I am surprised by your solicitude, Captain." Duncan got to his feet. "I thought you misliked Evan."

"'Tis no secret that Evan and I do not agree, but I love my wife to distraction, and he is her brother," Conall said. "She is determined to reconcile with him, and that she cannot do an he is dead."

Aunt Weoka stood. "He needs rest and some of my special soup— chicken stock with ginger, chaga mushrooms, and milkvetch. I'll see to him until he mends."

Conall's harsh expression lightened. "Thank you, milady. Rebekah and I are much in your debt. First, you deliver the twins, and now you would succor her brother."

"It's no trouble."

"Thank you, I am most grateful," Conall said. "I confess Rebekah and I are sorely distracted at present with the twins."

"Babies have a way of doing that."

"Aye," Conall said, "and Evan is hardly manageable under the best of circumstances."

"Ornery as a crocodile on a good day," Weoka agreed cheerfully, "but Verbena and I will handle his crochets."

"Huh?" Verbena said.

"You're coming home with me, gal."

"I am?"

"What, you thought I'd let you keep traipsing around the woods like a varmint? Not while I draw breath. You're family."

Verbena's eyes rounded in surprise. "You know about me and the sheriff...that we have the same pappy?"

"Always known Sildhjort was Dev's father, but you were a surprise."

"What is this?" Conall started in astonishment. "The shire reeve and Verbena are siblings?"

"Yup. Different mamas, same daddy."

"That explains a good deal." Conall looked thoughtful. "I have always known that Verbena is something quite out of the ordinary."

"Yes, she is," Dev said, smiling at her, "and I want everybody to know she's my little sister."

Verbena colored. "Got one o' them a'ready, I reckon."

"You mean Winnie?" Aunt Weoka shook her head. "Winnie's part of the family, but she and Dev aren't related. Winnie's folks are norms to the bone."

"They is? But ain't she a—" Verbena began.

"Super? Yup," Aunt Weoka said. "It's a long story. I'll tell you all about it over a nice hot supper." She looked the scrawny young woman up and down. "You could use a bath and good meal...or seven. You're skin and bones. Don't know who needs fattening up worse, you or that mutt. That shift you're wearing is miles too big."

Verbena plucked at her cotton dress, a baggy garment of sprigged cotton that swallowed her. "Found it in a rag bag in the closet where me and Gryffin was staying."

"Disgraceful," Aunt Weoka said, clucking in disapproval. "If that fire-eater were still here, I'd give him a piece of my mind. What in tarnation was he thinking, dragging you from pillar to post? Least he could do was find you some decent clothes."

"Told you." Verbena's mouth trembled. "Alls Gryffin cares about is Pratt, and he's dead now."

"Oh, I don't think that's all he cares about. Some people are slow on the uptake, is all." Aunt Weoka gave Dev a speaking glance. "Reckon he'll figure it out before long. In the meantime, we'll find you some clothes that fit."

"I got clothes. Left most of my things with Miz Beck and the captain when I run off."

"I will send them to you at once," Conall said. "Unless you would rather come home with me?" His stern expression softened into a surprisingly fond smile. "Unlike my ill-tempered brother-in-law, I would welcome you and gladly. Rebekah and I have missed your bright presence."

"Or you may stay with me and Cassandra," Duncan put in. "We have missed you, too, and there is room to spare."

"Hey, she's *my* sister," Dev objected. "Got an extra bedroom with your name on it, if you want it, Verbena."

Verbena's blush deepened. "Thankee kindly, all of you. I don't know what to say."

"Tell 'em to go suck an egg," Aunt Weoka said. "You're living with me, and that's final." She held up a finger when Verbena started to argue. "For now, anyway."

"Best say 'yes, ma'am,' and do what she says." Dev grinned at Verbena. "I can tell you from experience it makes life a whole lot easier."

"Yes, ma'am," Verbena said, meekly folding her hands.

"Good. It's settled, then." Aunt Weoka cocked her head. "Company coming."

A column of light shot from the heavens, and Kehvahn stepped out. The god's robe was rumpled, and his fine hair was tousled, giving him the appearance of a startled chick.

"Hush, Bobo, hush," Verbena said as the dog erupted in a frenzy of barking. "He's all right."

"Indeed, I do not mean you or your mistress any harm." Producing a piece of jerky from his pocket, Kehvahn offered it to the dog. Bobo sniffed the treat and wolfed it down. "There," the god said, stroking Bobo's head. "Let us cry peace."

Conall stepped forward and bowed. "Master, I bear sad news. Pratt is dead."

"I know." Kehvahn sighed. "We felt his passing."

"We?" Dev said.

"My brothers and sisters," Kehvahn replied. "They will be here anon. Pratt was troublesome," he said, gazing at Dev with a hint of reproof. "Imprisonment I anticipated, but was it necessary to slay him?"

"It was an accident," Dev said. "He...uh...got broken."

"Broken? How—" Kehvahn's gaze fell on Willa Dean. "Ah, I begin to understand. When I suggested you gather your resources, shire reeve, I had no notion you were in league with a gorgon."

"It was a surprise to me, as well."

Willa Dean bristled. "Don't blame the sheriff. Your brother refused to cooperate. Threatened to wipe us all out. I wasn't about to let that happen."

Kehvahn's long face creased with sadness. "Pratt was ever querulous. How did he come to be sundered?"

"He ticked off an ogre," Dev said.

"An ogre?" The lines in Kehvahn's face deepened into disapproval. "Really, shire reeve, you surprise me. Ogres are notoriously dense and erratic."

"That's what I told him," Willa Dean declared. "Brains of a gnat, ogres."

Dev met Kehvahn's gaze with a shrug. "You told me to work with what I had. The ogre's gone now, at any rate."

He resisted the urge to glance at Evan. Strictly speaking, it was true.

"And the orb?" Kehvahn asked.

"Here, master."

Arta materialized with Sugar, and Dev's heart skipped a beat, his worry and tension dissolving at the sight of her. She'd come back.

"Illaria and Jaaka took the skellring to the In-Between where Pratt could not find him," Arta said.

"The In-Between?" Dev asked.

"The empty space between the various planes," Conall explained. "The Void, some call it. 'Tis everywhere and nowhere, all at once."

"You took Sugar there at great risk," Kehvahn said to Arta with a touch of severity. "The In-Between is vast and unending. Many have lost their way forever in that nothingness. How did you locate him?"

"I did not. Sugar found me," Arta said. "'Tis my belief the orb communicates with him. He knew of Pratt's demise."

"Bad man dead." Reaching in his pouch, Sugar pulled out the orb. "Pretty?"

"Astonishing. Observe that the orb does not pain him atall." Kehvahn took a hasty step back. "No, no, my dear fellow, you must keep it. I flatter myself that I am not a bad sort, as gods go, but I am far too old to be innocent."

"Sugar can't keep it," Dev said. "I promised him he could go home."

"Mama," Sugar chirped. "Home."

"Dev's right," Aunt Weoka said. "Sugar's an only child, and his mama is pining something awful for him."

Kehvahn's eyes gleamed with interest behind his spectacles. "I am Kehvahn. And you are...?"

"Weoka Waters."

"Weoka Waters." Kehvahn rolled the name around in his mouth as though committing it to memory. "Delighted to make your acquaintance, Weoka, but the orb must have a keeper and one who is pure of heart. If not Sugar, then who?"

"Got an idea about that." Aunt Wee put her fingers to her lips and whistled. "Jeb, quit moping and get your butt over here. Got somebody I want you to meet."

The animate statue obediently creaked to his feet. Wading from the sandbar to the shore, he clomped up to them.

I gave you rings for your fingers, he sang, gazing mournfully at his dented horn,

I gave you rings for your toes.
You sold 'em, you bold one,
For what they would bring
And that's why, my darlin',
We can't have nice things.

"A metal man and most marvelously made," Kehvahn cried, "and he *sings*."

"All the dad-blame time," Verbena said. "But nothing you ever heared of. Old, dead-people music—that's all he knows."

"I think him delightful," Kehvahn said. "Do not grieve, my metal friend. This misfortune is soon mended."

He clapped his hands, and Jeb's bugle was good as new. Jeb's burnished cheeks parted in a delighted grin.

Sweetheart, I have grown so sad and dreary, he warbled, holding the shining bugle aloft,

Thinking of my life without you,
For I love you, oh, so dearly,
And I've been so very blue.

"Delighted to be of assistance," Kehvahn said. "I am Kehvahn. Have you a name, oh noble bronze giant?"

"This is Jebediah Gordan Hannah," Aunt Weoka said. "They don't come any nobler or more heroic than Jeb. He'll keep your orb safe."

"And the orb will neither tempt nor burn him." Kehvahn beamed at her. "The perfect solution. Weoka, you are splendid!"

"Oh, pshaw," Aunt Wee said, turning pink.

"It really is splendid, Aunt Wee," Dev agreed. "I've been racking my brain for weeks trying to figure out what to do with Jeb."

"Maybe Jeb don't wanna keep the orb." Verbena glared at them stubbornly. "Maybe he wants to stay here."

"He's a soldier, gal, and a soldier needs a purpose," Aunt Weoka said. "Jeb will be happier on duty, but don't take my word for it. Let's ask him. How 'bout it, Jeb?" she asked, gazing up at the statue. "You up for this mission?"

Old Jeb Hannah took the orb, Jeb sang to the tune of "Yankee Doodle Dandy,"

And kept it ever safely.
Guarded it from everyone
And stood his post most bravely.

"See?" Weoka said. "He wants to do it."

"Give him the orb, Sugar," Dev told the sasquatch.

"Pretty?" Sugar warbled, holding the brown globe aloft.

Jeb accepted the orb and dropped it in a pouch on his uniform belt.

A bell gonged.

"There, you see?" Kehvahn smiled. "The Universe approves."

"Can Jeb stay here with the orb?" Verbena asked.

"I'm afraid not," Dev said. "It's a miracle some norm hasn't seen him already, and what if some super stole the orb?"

"'Twould drive them mad," Duncan said. "The werewolf Zeb Randall possessed the orb and lost all reason."

Kehvahn adjusted his spectacles. "Duncan and the shire reeve have the right of it. The orb cannot remain on the earthly plane."

"The Hall of Warriors, then," Conall suggested. "The Dal would guard it well."

"I would not have the orb within my purview, nor, indeed, the purview of any god," Kehvahn said. "'Tis too seductive." He looked sadly down at Pratt's dusty remains. "As my poor brother could attest, were he still with us."

"The In-Between," Arta said. "Jeb could keep the orb there."

"No, it ain't safe," Verbena cried. "You done said so. What if Jeb gets lost?"

"Methinks he cannot lose his way whilst in possession of the orb," Arta said.

"But I won't never get to see him, and he'll be lonely." Verbena's voice trembled. "I don't want him to go."

"He doesn't have to stay in the In-Between all the time," Dev said. "He can come and go, right, Kehvahn?"

"But of course," Kehvahn said. "Jeb can pay the occasional visit, so long as he is discreet, and the sojourn is not prolonged. 'Tis better for all if the orb is largely secluded." He turned his bespectacled gaze on the statue. "Ready to assume your post, my stalwart?"

Jeb nodded and reached down, gently stroking the top of Verbena's head.

Don't cry, darlin', he crooned,
Everything will be okay,
Farewell for now, I'll soon return,
We'll meet again someday.

Lifting the bugle to his lips, Jeb blew a last note and disappeared.

Tears rolled down Verbena's cheeks. "How will Jeb know where to go?"

"The orb, dear child," Kehvahn said. "'Twill guide your friend to the In-Between."

"Sugar good boy." The sasquatch gazed hopefully at Dev. "Mama?"

"Yes, Sugar," Dev said. "You can go home now."

The sasquatch trilled happily and loped into the woods.

"Everybody's leaving." Verbena angrily swiped at her wet cheeks. "I hate it."

"Not everybody," Dev said. "We're still here, and you've got Bobo."

Producing a handkerchief from another pocket, Kehvahn handed it to her. "You have had a trying day, but the shire reeve is right. You are not alone. Dry your tears."

"Thankee." Verbena blew her nose loudly into the hankie. "I ain't usually such a watering pot."

Bobo started barking again.

"Quite right, my furry friend," Kehvahn said. "The others draw near."

The air shimmered with power, and five glowing figures appeared, three females, a male, and a gender-fluid deity with a slender, graceful body, breasts, and a thick beard braided with precious jewels.

"Oolira, Garlene, and Enallalual," Kehvahn said, solemnly addressing the three goddesses. He inclined his head to the two remaining deities. "Ystus and Imis, I bid you greeting. Our brother Pratt is no more."

A goddess with dark skin and red eyes stepped forward. "Who is responsible for this travesty?" she demanded. "They must be punished."

"Of a certainty," another goddess agreed, a matronly figure with a complexion like newly minted gold and hair the color of autumn leaves. "'Tis an affront to the order of the Universe."

"Enallalual and Garlene are right. Gods cannot be arbitrarily slain," said the god with the sparkly beard.

The remaining goddess, a whippet-thin figure with gray skin and a shock of white hair, crackled with raw energy. "I agree with Imis," she said, nodding at the god with the bedazzled beard. "What is to become of us should mortals realize their gods can die?"

"Events have left you shaken, sister, and small wonder, but your grief and confusion will dim with time," Kehvahn said. "Meanwhile, let us withdraw to mourn our brother's passing."

A brawny god with a mushroom-shaped nose and skin like bark rumbled in protest. "What of the culprit? Surely this cannot be allowed to pass."

The other gods murmured in agreement.

Kehvahn held up his hand, silencing them. "The lone culprit in Pratt's death is Pratt, my dear Ystus," he said. "His greed and obsession with the orb led to his demise."

"Greed and obsession did not turn him to stone or lay him waste," the goddess with the white hair retorted.

"All will be explained to your satisfaction, Oolira. On this, you have my word." Kehvahn turned to Samael. "Reaper, you would do the honors?"

"Glad to."

Samael motioned, and the trunk of the Caddy popped open. A large earthenware vessel floated out and settled on the ground next to the pulverized statue. Samael lifted his hand, and the shattered pieces of the dead god flew into the urn.

The lid clattered onto the jar and sealed itself. Sam retrieved the urn and offered it to Kehvahn. "The remains," he said. "I'll see the soul gets delivered, right and proper."

"You are kindness itself." Kehvahn clutched the urn with ink-stained fingers, his gaze anxious behind his wire-rimmed glasses. "'Tis your first occasion to render the essence of a god?"

Willa Dean's eyes flashed. "No such thing. Sam's a professional. You ever heard of Baldur? Dionysus? Osiris?"

"No," Kehvahn admitted. "I fear I am woefully ignorant of the gods of this plane." He gazed at Weoka, his eyes warm with interest. "Though 'tis an omission I would rectify forthwith."

Sam cleared his throat. "Willa Dean's right. I've had some experience with deities."

"Then I will leave the matter in your capable hands." Turning to the other gods, Kehvahn said, "Come, beloved. Let us repair to the Shores of Ilden and release our brother's ashes upon the foam."

The gods shimmered and were gone, taking with them the oppressive sense of power.

Sam kissed the palm of Willa Dean's hand. "Miz Mooneyham, you is my champeen."

"Humph," Willa Dean said, looking nonetheless pleased. "Somebody had to explain it to him."

He opened the car door. "Climb in, and I'll take you home."

"Are you sure, Samael? I don't want to keep you from the job."

"The boss will understand if I take a short detour." Sam tipped his broad-brimmed black hat at Weoka. "Goddess."

"Reaper," Aunt Weoka said, inclining her gray head.

Sam slammed the door and vaulted behind the wheel. Lifting his hand in farewell, he punched the gas, and the Cadillac roared up the hill and disappeared in a shower of dust.

"Well," Dev said. "They get my vote for weirdest couple."

"I've seen weirder." Weoka straightened. "Past time we got Evan home and tucked in bed. Duncan, you bring him to the house. Conall will show you the way."

Conall bowed. "With pleasure, milady."

"Good," Weoka said, "'cause I'm counting on you to see Verbena gets home, too."

"I don't need no—" Verbena said.

"Hesh up, gal," Weoka said. "You'll hurt Conall's feelings."

"Bull feathers." Verbena eyed the black-eyed warrior uncertainly. "Mr. Conall don't set no store by me."

"To the contrary, I set a great deal of 'store' by you," Conall said. "An you do not allow me to escort you home, fair lady, I will be crushed."

"I ain't no lady, and I fer dang sure ain't fair."

"You are whatsoever you choose to be, my dear." Conall held out his hand. "May I?"

"I reckon, but I'm a-telling you I knows the way," Verbena grumbled, slipping her hand into his.

"Ah, but the Dalvahni way is faster." He gave Duncan a hard look, and something passed between them. "You have the location fixed in your mind?"

"Aye, Captain."

"Excellent."

Conall and Verbena wavered and disappeared.

Duncan lifted Evan over one shoulder. "What of you, milady?" he asked Weoka. "I would happily transport you as well."

"No need. Got my own ride."

Striding to the water's edge, Weoka stepped into the shallows. She glanced back at Dev. "Take my advice and make it right. Regret will choke you same as gristle."

Her body dissolved and merged with the river. A sparkling form flitted beneath the water's surface and darted upstream.

"A handy mode of transport," Duncan remarked.

"Anywhere water can go, Aunt Wee can go," Dev said. "One time, the Baptist preacher showed up at the house without an invite, and she went down the kitchen sink."

Duncan laughed and vanished, leaving Dev alone with Arta.

He shoved his hands into his pockets. "Hell of a day, huh?"

"'Twas eventful."

She met his gaze, but there was a wall between them, an impenetrable layer of detachment that made Dev's stomach clench. Aunt Wee was right. Regret sucked.

"Listen, Arta," he said, "about what I said earlier—"

She held up her hand. "Spare me the recitation. You have made your opinion of me abundantly clear."

Turning on her heel, she stalked up the hill.

Dev caught up with her. "Wait a minute, damn it," he said. "Listen to me."

She stopped. "Why? What is there to say?"

"Plenty. I'm trying to apologize. Those things I said...I didn't mean them. I was angry, and I lashed out. I was terrified that you'd get hurt."

"Your agitation was unwarranted. I am not a delicate flower bruised by the merest passing touch."

"I know, I know." Dev raked his hands through his hair until it stood on end. "I just get crazy when I think about..."

Her brows rose. "About?"

"About losing you, goddammit."

"What am I, a button? You never had me, Devlin. I am a Kirvahni huntress, not a thing to be owned."

"Maybe not, but I'm yours, lock, stock, and barrel," Dev shot back. "Have been since the moment I laid eyes on you."

"Nonsense. You confuse emotion with lust."

"It's a hell of a lot more than that. I'm a wolf, and you're my mate. I love you, Arta."

Her eyes blazed. "You do not love me, Devlin. You do not *know* me, else you would never have put me in that sausage truck."

Her form flickered. "Arta, wait," Dev said, reaching for her. "Don't—"

His hand closed around thin air. She was gone.

* * * *

Arta paced back and forth in the living room of Winnie's home, a small house on a two-hundred-acre farm roughly ten miles outside of Hannah. She had borrowed clothes from Winnie, something Winnie called "shorts" and a baggy T-shirt. Her body hummed with adrenaline as it did on the eve of a battle, and her nerves sang with outrage and something else, something she could not quite name.

"And then he had the effrontery, the utter unmitigated gall to profess his feelings for me. What a…a…"

"Assbag?" Winnie suggested. "Douche potato? Dicknoob?"

"Totally *Devlin* thing to do." Arta marched from the open living and dining rooms into the kitchen, wheeled, and marched back again. "After the things he said. After mortifying me before the Dalvahni. He thinks he can tell me that he loves me, and all is forgiven? Nay, I say. Nay and nay again."

"Yeah, I know," Winnie said. "You've made the same speech, like, a million times. You're righteously indignant. Steamed to the max. Majorly cheesed. I get it. For the record, I don't appreciate being patronized, either."

"Patronized! Yes, yes, that it is exactly. I am a Kirvahni huntress. I have lived a hundred of his lifetimes, seen things you would not believe, fought countless battles, and won. 'Tis infuriating."

"Uh-huh. You need to sit down. You're making me nervous, and you're wearing a hole in my carpet."

"I cannot. I am too disordered. I feel like I am flying apart."

"You need a drink."

Arta dismissed the offer with a wave of her hand. "Alcohol does not affect me."

"No shit? Me, either. Tell you what *does* get me totally hammered." Winnie got up and went into the kitchen. Opening the pantry door, she produced a large, brightly colored bag and shook it. The bag rattled. "M&-freaking-M'S. A tablespoon of these bite-sized chocolate orgasms after a ballbuster day, and I'm relaxed. A couple of handfuls and I'm slizzard."

Arta paused. "Slizzard?"

"Drunk."

"I do not wish to be drunk. The idea is repellent."

"So, don't get drunk. Get chill."

"I am chill." Arta resumed her agitated pacing. "Icy rage fills me to the marrow of my bones."

"Not that kind of chill. Mellow." Winnie stepped in front of her and shoved the bag in her hands. "For the love of God, have some fucking M&M'S. One of us has got to have a break."

"An you insist."

"I do." Winnie pushed Arta into an oversized chair and stood over her, hands on hips. "I insist the shit out of it."

"You curse too much," Arta said. "It shows a lack of restraint."

"Yeah, wanna know how much I care? I give zero fucks. Do the math."

Arta ignored this bit of nonsense and examined the top of the bag. "'Tis a zip block, no?"

"Ziploc, and yeah." Taking the bag from Arta, Winnie opened it and grabbed a few M&M'S for herself. She slipped them in her mouth and plopped the open bag in Arta's lap. "Can't have you drinking alone. Chick code."

"Strictly speaking, 'tis not drinking."

"Shut up, Arta, and eat the damn chocolate."

"Very well." Taking some of the candy, Arta spread the round pieces on the palm of her hand. "They are quite pretty. What do the different colors signify?"

"Dick all, except for the green. The green ones make you horny."

"Truly?"

"Nah, but listen up, 'cause this is important. There is a right way and a wrong way to eat M&M'S. Some folks divide them up by color—get your yellows mixed up with your blues or your reds, and there'll be total anarchy, or so they believe."

"You frighten me."

"Now me," Winnie said, ignoring her, "I hold with the theory that M&M'S are meant to be savored, eaten slowly and allowed to melt in your mouth."

"An interesting premise."

"The purists among the melt-in-your-mouth faction maintain you should eat M&M'S one at a time. Two at a time in a pinch. Some people take it a step further and insist you should only eat M&M'S on the *left* side of your mouth."

"An alarming number of strictures. My apprehension mounts."

"It's total baloney. The optimum number of M&M'S is *four* at a time, as anyone with the brains God gave a goose can attest."

"Four?"

"Four," Winnie said firmly. "No more, no less. Four gives you that rush of chocolatey goodness when the candy coating dissolves on your tongue and—"

Arta tossed a fistful of candy in her mouth and chewed.

"—she slams 'em back like a shot of bad whiskey." Winnie shook her head. "Sacrilege. Give me that." She snatched the bag back from Arta and sat down on the couch beside Arta's chair. "The idea is to take the edge off, not get schnockered, remember?"

"Hmm." Arta smacked her lips. "I like M&M'S. They are most tasty. The frangible crunch of the outer shell reminds me of the bones of the garacooza bird."

"The what?"

"A delicacy among the Ashua people of the Yesken marshland."

"Oh, the *Ashua*." Winnie rolled her eyes. "Everybody knows about the Ashua."

"Verily?"

"No, Arta. Nobody knows, and nobody cares."

"You should care. You may venture there someday in pursuit of the djegrali."

"Me, travel to another plane? Seriously?"

"With training. You are Dalvahni." Arta frowned. "Now, what was I saying? Ah, yes, the garacooza bird. In truth, 'tis not a bird atall, but a large, winged insect. They roast them whole in clay ovens and roll them in honey."

"I'm not eating bugs."

"You will an you desire the Ashuas' help. The Yesken marshland is rife with hidden dangers."

"God almighty," Winnie said. Tilting her head back, she poured a rainbow stream of candy into her mouth.

"What happened to the theory of four?"

"It went out the window with the gazooky bird."

"Garacooza."

"Whatever." Winnie dumped a small mound of M&M'S in Arta's hand. "So are you staying or what?"

"'Twas my hope you would allow me to abide with you for a time. If not, I can always make camp in the woods."

"I don't mean *here*." Winnie jabbed a finger at the floor. "Of course, you can stay with me. I mean in Behr County."

Arta straightened in her chair. "The demons who killed Livy Freeman remain at large. I am sworn to their capture."

"Uh-huh." Winnie passed Arta the bag of M&M'S and watched, her eyes narrowed, as Arta ate another mouthful of the candy. "And this lofty mission has nothing to do with Dev?"

"Certainly not."

"Liar," Winnie said. "I mean that in the nicest possible way, but you are a big old fat liar, Arta Kirvahni."

"You would impugn my honor? I have killed men for less."

"Give me a break. We both know why you're staying, and don't give me any crap about duty and the Kirvahni way." Winnie shook her head. "Don't get me wrong, I'm glad you're not leaving. You're a major pain, but I've gotten used to you. Kind of like a carbuncle."

Arta blinked, suddenly and unaccountably misty-eyed. "Thank you, Winifred. I have grown accustomed to you, as well."

"As long as you're hanging around, you can show me the ropes." Winnie gave her a woozy grin. "Teach me some demon hunter shit. Can't go bouncing from plane to plane if I'm a total igno. And don't start singing about Eamon, 'cause we've already been down that road, and it's closed."

There was a mournful howl from the trees beyond the barn. Winnie jumped to her feet and went to the window.

"It's Dev," she said, peering through the curtains. "He's watching the house from the woods like a giant creeper. Pah-thetic."

"Let me see." Arta joined her. She parted the flowing drapes and peered into the darkness. In the shadow of the woods, a pair of golden eyes gleamed. "'Tis Devlin, right enough. He is in wolf form."

"No shit, Sherlock. The wolf howl was your first clue."

"How did he know I was here?"

"He probably followed Myrtle."

"Merta. The hawk's name is *Merta*."

"Okay, okay, *Merta*. Sheesh."

Arta was half-listening. "I do not understand. I gave no indication where I was going when we parted."

"I might have mentioned you were here when I talked to him on the phone."

"*What?*"

"You were in the shower, and he asked. What was I supposed to do, *lie?* It's Dev. He's a walking, talking lie detector."

Arta said something extremely foul in Sakaath.

"I don't know what you just said, but I have a feeling it wasn't nice." Winnie jumped as the wolf let out another mournful howl. "He'd better stay out of my chickens, damn it."

She grabbed a long-barreled firearm from the rack on the wall and slammed out the front door.

Arta followed her onto the porch. "What are you doing?"

Boom. Winnie fired the gun into the air. "Get on," she shouted, brandishing the gun. "You're not wanted here."

The golden eyes blinked and disappeared.

Arta's stomach pitched in a most peculiar fashion. "He is gone."

"Damn straight," Winnie said. "That's what you wanted, isn't it?"

"Of a certainty."

It was the truth...wasn't it?

"Come on." Winnie slapped her on the back. "Let's go back inside and hit the bag. There's an M&M in there with your name on it."

"Really?"

"No, Arta. It's an expression."

"Oh."

Glancing back over her shoulder at the darkness, Arta followed Winnie into the house.

Chapter Twenty-Four

Arta glanced at the pendulum clock on the wall. It was near midnight, and the wolf was calling.

Arta. Arta...come to me. The whispered entreaty was a relentless, electric tug that set her nerve endings on fire. *I need you... I want you...*

Damn the man. They were miles apart, but her awareness of Dev grew stronger by the minute, his persistence softening her mood and dissipating the worst of the chocolate fumes from her brain.

Winnie was unaware of her struggles. Winnie was too busy eating M&M'S and singing.

Winnie had a voice like a rusty gate.

"Gone?" Winnie shook the empty M&M'S bag and threw it aside. "Theresh another bash in the cabinesh." She tried to push herself off the couch and collapsed against the cushions. "I'll fesh it as soon ash the room stops spinning."

"Nay, yoosh—" Arta's tongue felt stiff and unwieldy. She tried again. "We both have. "Comsh...*Come* the morrow, our heads will be sore, methinks."

"How do you know?" Winnie peered at her suspiciously. "I thought thish wash your first toot?"

It took Arta a moment to decipher this gibberish. "Yoosh..." she slurred, then scowled as she heard herself. "Fiend seize my clumsy tongue! You refer to a drunken spree? Humans love to tipple—elves and other species, as well. 'Tis not my first time seeing someone in their cups." She rose and slung Winnie over one shoulder. "High time you were abed."

"Hey, put me down," Winnie protested. "I'm gonna throw up."

"You will not throw up. I forbid it."

Winnie giggled, dangling over Arta's shoulder. "Bossy. Doesh Dev like that?"

"You will have to ask him."

"I bet he doesh. I bet he likes it a lot."

Winnie launched into an inane ditty about a couple sitting in a tree, k-i-s-s-i-n-g. Arta ignored her and staggered down the hall. The Kir were exceptionally strong, and Arta could lift a fully laden oxcart with ease, but there seemed to be something amiss with her legs. They kept bumping her into the walls and pitching her about like a boat on a rough sea.

"Arta ish a loushee driver, loushee driver, loushee driver," Winnie chanted, trailing her fingers along the wall.

"Winifred Rose, you are foxed."

"So are you."

"Aye, but I am not completely owled. I cannot say the same for you, baggage."

"Baggage." Winnie giggled. "I like the way you talk."

"Behold me gratified."

Lurching into Winnie's room, Arta dumped her on the bed and covered her with a blanket. "Go to sleep."

Winnie sighed and rolled over.

Arta reeled back down the hall. Opening the front door, she stepped onto the porch. The evening was cool and shrouded in a dusky cloak.

Arta... Arta...

"Oh, be quiet," Arta muttered crossly. "I will not go to you. I will not." She brought her fist down on the porch rail. "I will conquer this."

The moon winked down at her. *Why?*

"Because I must." She peered up at the glowing orb. "I am the High Huntress."

Can you not be both the High Huntress and a woman in love?

"What do you know of love, moon?"

Much, child. I have watched the Earth for a long time, and wooings and courtships happen with some frequency.

"*Human* courtships. I am Kirvahni. The shire reeve and I are too different. He will try to cosset and protect me. It will not work."

Some things are worth fighting for. But perhaps you are afraid. There is safety in isolation—this I know—but also great loneliness.

"Afraid, am I?" Arta glared at the moon. "Come down here and say that to my face, you great gabbling glob of light."

But the moon had scudded behind a cloud. Muttering in indignation, Arta transported herself to Dev's, though if she'd been asked, she could not have said why.

Of a certainty, she did not long for him with a ferocity that left her shaken. Nay.

Nor did she have the slightest desire to gaze upon his pleasing features and strong, hard body or hear the deep, sexy timbre of his voice.

Most assuredly not.

And she had *not* come here at the moon's behest, stupid shiny ball.

She was here to rectify certain misconceptions Dev seemed to have. Yes, that was it. Nothing more.

She breathed in the pine-scented air. The trip through the Void had sobered her somewhat, though she still felt a certain delicious lassitude. In the woods around her small animals stirred, and the traitorous moon peeped at her through the tops of the trees.

A subtle shift in energy made her skin tingle and the hair on her arms stand on end.

Dev was nearby. She sensed him.

She padded softly to the edge of the thicket and looked out. The house was quiet. No lights shone inside or out, but she had excellent night vision.

There. Her heart thudded like a Ruthari lizard drum. He was sitting on the porch in the shadows, waiting for her. Arrogant man.

She started from the copse, pausing as a shaft of moonlight shot through the tree branches.

Hold, the moon said. *You would go into battle clad like that?*

"I am not going into battle. The shire reeve seems to think he has but to beckon, and I will come. I mean to disabuse him of the notion."

But you did come.

"To remedy his presumption."

As you say. The moon sounded unconvinced. *Still, I would see you properly armed.*

Radiance swirled around Arta, and Winnie's borrowed clothes disappeared, leaving her garbed in a gossamer-light tunic. Pale as starlight, the gauzy material shimmered and sparkled, clinging to Arta's breasts, and showing her long legs to advantage.

The moon chuckled. *There. That should set him on his heels.*

"'Tis lovely." Arta was touched. She traced the delicate fabric with the tips of her fingers. "Thank you."

But the moon had gone, slipping once more behind the clouds. Arta took her hair down, allowing the silvery mass to tumble about her shoulders and down her back.

She stepped from the woods and crossed the green in front of the house. Dev rose and strode down the steps to meet her.

Arta's mouth went dry at the sight of him. Gods, but he moved like a young lion. He was half-dressed, his muscular chest bare and his powerful legs clad in loose trousers for repose. There was a term for the garment he wore...

Sleep pants, she thought hazily. Yes, that was the name for them.

He stopped a few paces from her, and her gaze moved from the hard ridges of his abdomen to the dark marks on his face, chest, and arms. "Your wounds," she said with a frown, the tongue-lashing she'd prepared forgotten. "They are not healed."

"It's nothing. They'll be gone by morning." His deep, slow baritone sent a shaft of desire through her. 'Strewth, but she loved to hear him talk. His voice was a slow melody that played upon her senses. "I'm glad you're here," he said. "I figured you'd still be angry with me."

"I am still angry with you." She lifted her chin. "Exceedingly."

"But you still came. I'm glad."

"Do not be. I came because the moon dared me." She paused, swaying a little, and added with scrupulous honesty, "And because I have eaten too many M&M'S."

His mouth twitched. "M&M'S? Arta, did Winnie get you drunk?"

"A little, perhaps, but Winnie, I fear, is quite tippled. I left her to sleep it off."

"I see." He eased closer, enveloping her in his warm, woodsy scent. "I like your dress."

"'Tis not a dress." She tried to sound stern and utterly failed. "'Tis an *elutabi*, the traditional garb of the Kir. 'Twas a gift from the moon."

"The moon, huh? The moon's been busy."

"You do not like it?"

"I like it very much." The husky note in his voice made her pulse flutter. "It's beautiful. *You're* beautiful." He lifted a lock of her long hair. "I love your hair...like moonlight on water."

"A pretty speech, sir, but 'twill take more than flattery to overcome my spleen."

"How about this, then. I meant what I said this afternoon, Arta. I love you." Taking a deep breath, he rushed on. "I know I screwed up, but I was trying to keep you safe."

"You shamed me."

"I know, and I'm sorry. I was wrong. You can take care of yourself."

"Yes, I can, and I have no desire to be coddled."

"I know. I was a fool ever to doubt you."

"Yes."

"I acted like an ass."

"Yes, you did."

"It won't happen again, I promise."

"Liar."

He stared at her in shock. "What?"

"You lie, Devlin Theodulf Whitsun. 'Tis your nature to guard and protect. At the first inkling of danger, you will bully me without compunction...or try to." She gave him a tremulous smile. "This I know because I love you, too."

"*Arta*." He reached for her and stopped. "Don't play with me. This is too important. Do you mean it?"

"You are the one with the talent for detecting untruths. You tell me, oh shrewdest of shire reeves. Am I lying when I say I love you?"

His gaze searched her face. With a muffled curse, he yanked her close. "Arta, sweet Jesus, I hoped, but I—"

He buried his face in her hair, unable to continue.

He was trembling. Arta slid her arms around his neck and pressed her body against his. The moon dress was insubstantial as a spiderweb, and the heat of his skin through the diaphanous cloth made her fierce with longing. She wanted him with feverish desperation, wanted his mouth on her and the hard length of him inside her.

Never had she wanted anything more. A hundred thralls could not satisfy this strange yearning ache. Only him.

At long last, she was home.

He lifted his head. "Arta? What is it?"

"Nothing," she said. "Everything," she murmured against his firm, sensuous mouth. "Take me to bed, my Devlin. I need you. I need you now."

His eyes gleamed in the dark. "Yes, ma'am. Anything you say."

Swinging her into his arms, he strode up the steps. Arta looked back. The moon was smiling down at them.

Dev carried her inside and shut the door.

* * * *

The radio on the table beside the bed beeped. Dev rolled over and looked at the clock. It was five thirty in the morning.

The radio chirped again.

Beside him, Arta stirred. "Make it stop," she said with a groan. "My head aches like the very devil."

"It's called a hangover," Dev said. "That's what you get for chugging M&M'S."

"They seemed harmless. Pretty morsels of sweetness and nothing more."

"Duncan probably thought the same thing when he ate that chocolate pie."

"'Tis Winnie's fault. She led me astray."

The radio sounded a third time.

"Devlin, for the love of the gods."

Dev chuckled and picked up the device. "Go ahead," he said.

"There's a Ten-Fifty-four on Goblin Road," Frankie the dispatcher said. "That's near your place, isn't it, Sheriff?"

"Yeah, less than five miles away."

"Shall I send another unit, or are you on it?"

"I'm on it."

Dev signed off and returned his attention to the naked woman in his bed. She was temptation itself, a delectable, irresistible mess, her hair a pale tangle across the pillow and her lips still swollen from his kisses. She lay on her side facing him, one bare shoulder peeking from the covers. The hollow of her collarbone was a valley he longed to explore. She was mysterious, alluring. Perfect. If he had his way, they'd stay in bed all day, and he'd kiss her from head to toe and then start all over again, but he had a job to do.

"I have to go." Sliding his hand under the covers, he caressed the silken curve of her hip. "I'll see you later at the office?"

She opened one bleary eye. "You will not. I renounced my post."

"You mean this?" Rising from the bed, he crossed the room to his five-drawer chest and retrieved her badge. He lobbed it onto the pillow beside her. "Found it by the river yesterday. I'm giving it back to you."

"I do not want it."

"Too bad. You can't quit. We haven't found Livy's killer."

She glared at him. "I will help you find Livy's killer, but not as your deputy. According to departmental policy, and I quote, 'No member of the Behr County Sheriff's Department may report to a higher-ranking member of the BCSD to whom he/she is related, married, or with whom he/she is engaged in a romantic relationship.'"

"Are we in a romantic relationship?" He feigned surprise. "Personally, I'm just in it for the sex."

"Do not tease, Devlin. 'Tis a wonder no one has turned us in a'ready. Strictly speaking, I should have relinquished my badge weeks ago."

"You're a demon hunter, and this case involves demons. I'm usually not one to bend the rules, but I need your expertise. Once we're married, you'll have to resign, but for now—"

"*What?*"

She bolted upright and the covers tumbled below her waist, baring her full breasts to his appreciative gaze. Desire sizzled through Dev, hot and hard.

To hell with the cows, he thought, wanting to chuck duty out the window.

It took every ounce of his considerable willpower to resist.

"I guess I could resign," he said with a shrug, "but I figure you'll have plenty to keep you busy as High Huntress."

"You know perfectly well I would not allow you to resign your position as shire reeve."

"Then what are you yelling about?"

"I am not—" She pressed her lips together, something she did when he annoyed her. It made him want to kiss her senseless. "You have not asked me to marry you."

"Haven't I? I seem to recall telling you last night that I adore you and want to be with you forever." He grinned at her. "Literally forever, in our case."

"That does not count. You were inside me at the time, and all the blood was in your nether regions."

"That's my normal state around you," he said, dressing quickly. "I'd like nothing better than to be inside you right now, but the damn cows won't catch themselves." He strapped on his gun and the radio and strode back to the bed. Sitting down beside her, he took her face in his hands. "Marry me, Arta," he murmured against her mouth. "I can't live without you, and even if I could, I damn sure don't want to."

"Sheriff?" Frankie's voice sounded from the radio.

Dev straightened with a sigh and clicked the device. "Go ahead."

"We got more cattle in the road. You en route?"

"Yeah, headed there now." He gave Arta a hard, possessive kiss and got to his feet. "You can give me your answer later."

"And if the answer is no?"

"Then I'll change your mind. I warn you, I'm not giving up, not if it takes a thousand years."

"Tyrant."

He smiled down at her. "Pot meet kettle."

She gave him a haughty look. "I am not a tyrant. I am strong-willed."

"R-i-i-ght. There are chocolate bars in the pantry if you need a little hair of the dog."

She shuddered. "An you truly loved me, you would not speak to me of chocolate."

He laughed. "See you at the station."

"Later, mayhap." Arta pulled the pillow over her head. "Much later."

Dev reached Goblin Road in no time and spotted the cows. A section of fence was down, and two dozen Red Angus blocked the two-lane highway and wandered along the berm. The farmer, James Harms, was doing his best to round them up, but the cattle weren't cooperating. A man in a brown 2003 Ford Conversion van didn't help matters when he honked his horn, scattering the animals.

Dev parked his vehicle sideways across the middle line and turned on his lights. He got out and approached the van. The driver, a fellow with a face like a pit bull, rolled down his window. "This process will go a lot faster if you don't blow your horn," Dev said. "You're scaring the cows."

The man grumbled something, and Dev went to help the farmer. Fifteen minutes later, the herd was back in the right pasture, and the grumpy man in the van was gone.

"Here's your problem, Jimmy," Dev said, picking up a fallen post. "Your posts aren't deep enough."

"Yeah, I know." Jimmy, a man in his late fifties, removed his hat and swiped a hand through his thinning hair. His face was bronzed from years in the sun, and his forehead was fish-belly white. A farmer's tan, the locals called it. "My youngest boy put this line of fence up and did a half-ass job."

"Teenager?"

"Yup. Senior at BCH."

"Go Wildcats," Dev said. "Don't be too hard on him. Teenage boys are hepped up on hormones."

"Pecker led," Jimmy said. "I got three boys, so I should know."

"It's a common ailment," Dev said, thinking of the tantalizing woman he'd left in his bed.

It was early. If he hurried, he still had time to make love to Arta before work. His body tightened at the thought.

Jerk, she has a hangover, remember?

Oh, yeah. Breakfast, then, followed by some serious cajoling. One way or another, he'd convince Arta to marry him. Feeding her was a start. Arta loved her chow, and he wasn't above a little pancakes-and-Conecuh sausage bribery to get what he wanted.

And he wanted Arta. He wanted her with every fiber of his being. She was stubborn and fearless and tenacious in the pursuit of her goals, altogether impossible, in fact, and she'd ruined him for other women.

He strode back to the Jeep and opened the door. The crackle of the radio greeted him.

"Sheriff, you there?"

"Damn," Dev muttered, climbing behind the wheel. He picked up the scanner mic. "This is the sheriff. Go ahead."

"Parks, here." The deputy's voice vibrated with excitement. "I think I finally got a lead on those Goodrich nineteen-fives."

Dev's gut clenched with anticipation. This was it, what he'd been waiting for. He could feel it. "Call me on the link."

Parks signed off. A moment later, Dev's link phone beeped.

"Whatcha got?" he asked, answering the private line.

"So, you know my mom lives in Hannah?"

"No," Dev said, girding his impatience. "Can't say I did."

"Yeah, on Magnolia Street. Old part of town. Big lots with mature trees."

"I'm familiar."

Magnolia Street was in the historic part of Hannah, an architectural mishmash of arts-and-crafts-style homes, two-story Victorians with gingerbread trim, and the random Tudor dwelling. The long, narrow lots were shaded by hundred-year-old oaks and glossy magnolia trees, and in spring, the yards were starbursts of dogwoods, redbuds, and azaleas in bloom.

"Right," Parks said. "Mom had a knee replacement, and I've been staying with her. Since Dad died, there's no one else. My sister lives in Baltimore, you know, and—"

"Parks."

"Yeah, okay," Parks said, recognizing the warning in Dev's voice. "Mom has a miniature poodle, Short Stuff. Damn dog has a bladder the size of a peanut. Woke me up this morning whining to go out. Shorty ran into the neighbor's yard, and I had to chase after her. My mom is nuts about that dog. Anyway, that's when I saw it."

"What?" Dev was rapidly losing patience.

"The truck with the Goodrich nineteen-fives. It's parked in the carriage house behind the Mullinses' house."

Dev sat up. "The Mullinses' house?"

"Yeah, Fred Mullins is my mom's neighbor. Or was, I should say," Parks added. "He's dead, and the house is empty. His daughter is putting it up for sale. Fred was a pharmacist."

"Try mulling it over, if you want to know," Dev muttered.

"Huh?"

"Nothing. Something someone said to me. Makes sense now."

"I checked the tires," Parks said. "The right back tire has a missing plug in the rubber. Whatchoo wanna bet that divot matches the tire tracks we found near Livy Freeman's body?"

"That's how he did it," Dev said. "Russ borrowed his father-in-law's truck."

"You want me to question him, Sheriff?"

"No."

A burst of adrenaline shot through Dev. He had Russ. He had him now. His wolf rumbled with predatory eagerness.

"What was that?" Parks said. "Sounded like a big dog."

"Never mind," Dev said. "Good work, Parks. I'll handle this one myself."

Thirty minutes later, Dev pulled into Bootsie and Russ's driveway. The Barbers lived in River Ridge, a gated community that was, ironically, nowhere near the river, with brick homes, small lots, a clubhouse with a pool, and a HOA that could give the Gestapo lessons in autocracy. Not Dev's cuppa, but then different strokes for different folks. Bootsie's Mercedes was parked in the driveway, but Russ's truck was gone.

"Damn." Dev drummed his fingers on the steering wheel. He'd really been hoping Russ would be here. He and the wolf had business with that son of a bitch.

Calm down, Whitsun. Nice and easy. Don't blow it.

Might as well talk to Bootsie. She could tell him where to find Russ.

Reining in his impatience, he slid out of the Jeep and strode up the front steps. He rang the bell and waited.

Bootsie answered the door. She had a serious case of bedhead, and she wore bubblegum-pink silk pajamas and a matching robe. Her feet were bare, and she wasn't wearing any makeup. She looked younger and more vulnerable without it, the freckles on her nose and cheeks clearly visible.

She blinked at him in surprise and tucked a strand of hair behind one ear. "Goodness me, Sheriff. It's barely seven o'clock. What brings you here?"

"Sorry to bother you, Bootsie," he said. "I'm looking for Russ. Is he in?"

"No, he ran to the gas station to grab some eggs. I was making a frittata for breakfast and realized we were slap out. I declare, I am forever running out of milk and eggs and bread."

"It's a problem," Dev agreed.

Bootsie opened the door wide. "Come in and have a cup of coffee while you wait. He should be back any moment."

Dev wiped his boots on the mat and stepped inside. The Barber house looked like something out of a magazine, everything new and perfectly coordinated. Floral arrangements and expensive-looking knickknacks were scattered about, and the living room couch contained an alarming number of throw pillows. None of the furniture looked as if it had ever been sat on.

He followed Bootsie through the foyer and living room to the kitchen at the back of the house. It was large, boasting white cabinets, granite countertops, an island you could land a small plane on, and stainless-steel appliances. Dev spotted the swanky refrigerator.

"Nice fridge," he said, taking a seat at the enormous island. "You buy it in Hannah?"

"Gracious no, that's a Miele."

"Beg pardon, ma'am, but I'm a country boy. What in tarnation's a Miele?"

She laughed. "It's a sixteen-thousand-dollar refrigerator, that's what it is. Bought it in Mobile." Bootsie pulled a mug out of one of the cabinets and poured Dev some coffee. "Cream? Sugar?"

"Black's fine," Dev said, taking the cup.

She tilted her head, reminding Dev of a plump sparrow. "What did you want with Russ?"

"I've got some questions about your daddy's truck," Dev said. "Does Russ ever drive it?"

Bootsie's brow furrowed. "We both do. Don't want the seals to rot or the tires to go flat. Why?"

Dev hesitated. He didn't want to hurt Bootsie. None of this was her fault, but he was about to turn her world upside down. He took a sip of his coffee to buy time, and his eyes almost rolled back in his head. It was the best damn coffee he'd ever tasted, a complex mixture of sweet citrus, milk chocolate, and caramel. The stuff he'd been drinking all his life was pig wash compared to this elixir of the gods.

He set the cup down with regret. It didn't feel right drinking Bootsie's primo coffee under the circumstances. Best to get it over with.

"We have reason to believe that the tire prints on that truck match the ones found near Livy Freeman's body," he said. "I'm afraid Russ is a murder suspect."

Her eyes flared wide, though not with shock. With something else. Excitement? Triumph?

The wolf raised his hackles in warning too late.

Something slammed into the back of Dev's head, and everything went dark.

Chapter Twenty-Five

"Get up."

Arta flung open the curtains in Winnie's room and let the midday light pour in.

Winnie bolted upright in the bed. "Arta, what the hell? I'm off duty today." She scrubbed her eyes and face with her hands. "God, my head."

"Cropsick," Arta said briskly. "I, too, have a head this morning, but there is no time to languish. Dev is missing."

Winnie peered at her, red-eyed. "How do you know? You stayed with me last night."

"I confess I did not. I went to Dev at the behest of the moon."

"You what?"

"'Tis not important. Regard me. Dev left at daybreak to see to some wandering cattle. Whilst there, he received a call from Parks with information pertaining to the murder of Livy Freeman. This I know from Parks himself. Willa Dean sent Parks to Dev's house looking for him when he did not answer his radio."

"And you were there?"

"I have told you so a'ready."

"Please tell me you didn't answer the door naked."

"Of course not. I donned one of Devlin's shirts."

"You were wearing his shirt? Jeez, Arta. Parks is a good guy, but he can't keep a secret to save his life."

"As I did not confide in him, I do not see the problem."

"Oh, you confided in him, all right. You as good as announced that Dev took a ride on the Hootie Train with one of his deputies. If the county commission gets wind of this, you'll get canned, and Dev will be in serious trouble for fraternizing."

"As it happens, I no longer work for the department, and so I told Parks."

"Whadda you mean, you don't—" Winnie looked her up and down, taking in her deerskin tunic and leggings. "Why aren't you in uniform?"

Arta clenched her fists. "Have you not been attending? Bah, I am done with you."

Spinning on her heel, Arta stalked for the door.

"Hold on. *Hold on.*" Winnie scrambled out of the bed. "I'm going with you. Give me ten minutes." Her mouth worked. "My tongue is covered in fur, and I have sweaters on my teeth." Wadding her dark hair on top of her head, Winnie looked back at Arta from the doorway to the bathing chamber. "Grab a pair of my jeans and a shirt. You can't wear that elf costume into town. People will notice."

"'Tis not a—" Arta pressed her lips together. "I will be in the car." Worry gnawed at her. "And Winnie, make haste."

Ten minutes and thirty-seven seconds later, Winnie opened the driver's door and slid behind the wheel in a swirl of lemon and honeysuckle scent.

"You are late." Arta scowled at her. "And you abluted."

Winnie started the car. "Calm down, Doris Thesaurus, I took a quick bird bath. Brushed my teeth in the shower to save time." She glanced at Arta. "My jeans fit you. I'm surprised. You're taller, and your legs are longer than mine."

"I adjusted them."

"Woo-woo tailoring? That is freaking *awesome*. Any details on the lead Parks gave Dev?"

"Parks found a tire that matched the prints at the murder scene."

"No kidding? Where?"

"At the abode of a Fred Mullins, now deceased. The truck with the tire was parked behind the man's residence."

Winnie smacked the heel of her hand on the steering wheel. "Elizabeth Barber's father. Dev was right. Russ is in this thing up to his eyeballs."

"His wife, too, I suspect," Arta said. "She seems a puling thing to me—no doubt browbeaten into wickedness by her blockish husband—but Dev seems to like her well enough."

"Bootsie and Dev went to school together."

"So I understand. In his last communication with Parks, Dev announced his intention to speak with Russ Barber."

The car crunched down the driveway. "Then our first stop is the Barber residence." Winnie reached for the radio. "I'll get the address from Willa Dean."

"No need," Arta said. "I have been there a'ready."

"To the Barber house? How did you—"

"I got the location from the Provider and teleported, as you like to call it. No one was home."

Winnie pulled onto the highway and turned toward Hannah. "How can you be certain?"

"I blew the door off the hinges and searched the abode most thoroughly."

"Well, that's one way to go about it," Winnie said. "A highly illegal way, but still, a way. The Jeep?"

"Not there."

"Barber's trucking business. Did you check it?"

"Of course. I am not a complete fool."

"Okay, okay, don't bite my head off. You should have gotten me up sooner. I would've gone with you."

"You are with me now." Arta met Winnie's gaze. "I am afraid, Winnie. For the first time in my life, I am afraid. Dev is in danger, and I—" She covered her face with her hands. "I fear the worst."

"Hey, hey, none of that." Winnie reached over and squeezed Arta's shoulder. "We'll find him."

The radio crackled. "We got a twenty on that missing Jeep," Willa Dean said. "It's been located at the quarry. No sign of the Ten-Eighty-six."

A 10-86. Missing person.

Arta stared out the window, her chest and brain on fire. Dev had been reduced to a number. He was not a number. He was *all* the numbers, the sum of her happiness. Her world. How had she lived a small eternity without him? Looking back, life before Dev seemed a pale thing, an endless drudgery of duty, warfare, and pursuit. With Dev there was color, laughter, and joy.

The panic she'd been fighting since Parks had arrived on Dev's doorstep fluttered to the surface like a flock of startled sparrows. Dev had asked her to marry him, and she had not answered. Fear and regret clawed at her. What if she never got the chance? What if he—

Nay, she would not think it. She could not. That way lay madness.

Emotions. By the gods, how did mortals deal with them?

According to certain mental health sources, the Provider intoned, *you should identify your feelings and accept them.*

"Easily done," Arta said. "I am near frantic with worry."

"What?" said Winnie.

"I was not speaking to you. The Provider is giving me counsel."

"What about?"

"Feelings." Pausing to listen to the dry voice in her head, Arta said, "He suggests I journal."

"Somehow, I don't think you're the journaling type."

"I confess, it does not appeal."

The temperature inside the Charger dipped, and Meredith appeared on a gust of lemon scent. "You should try my therapist, Leonard Swink," she said from the backseat. "He mostly deals with deathnesia and PTDD—Post-Traumatic Death Disorder—but he's done *wonders* for me. I was a real bitch before I started seeing him."

Winnie let out a loud screech and wrenched the car onto the side of the road. "Who the hell are you?" she demanded, turning to stare at Meredith.

"Meredith Peterson." The ghost produced a card from thin air and handed it to Winnie. "Bitchin' Banshee Services. I work with the sheriff."

Winnie opened her mouth, but no sound came out. "You do?" she finally managed to say. "Since when?"

"Recently."

"But you're—"

"Dead?" Meredith said. "Nothing gets past you, does it?"

"Desist," Arta ordered, losing patience. "Why are you here?"

"I heard about Devy Wevy." Producing a small, shell-shaped case, Meredith opened it and admired herself in the mirror. "It's all over the deadnet that he's been kidnapped."

"You know where he is?" Arta's voice was dangerously quiet.

Winnie shifted uneasily. "Um…Arta."

"Not now, Winnie."

"'Course I know where he is. I'm a specter detective." She closed the container with a snap. "Knowing things is my business."

"Then you will tell me at once."

"*Arta.*"

"What?" Arta snapped, glaring at Winnie.

"You're lit up like the Griswolds' at Christmas. If you detonate in the car, you'll blow us to kingdom come."

Arta became aware of the glowing nimbus surrounding her. She closed her eyes and opened them again. "The location," she said to the ghost through her teeth.

"*Sooo* grumpy," Meredith replied. "You know the abandoned grain silo on Butcher Road?"

"I do," Winnie said. "It's an old brick building. Majorly creepy."

"That's where she's keeping them."

"She?" Arta said.

"Bootsie Barber. She and that troglodyte hubby of hers have been selling people to the demons." Meredith wrinkled her nose. "Although, to be fair, I think it's mostly been Bootsie. I *told* you she's a heifer."

"Bootsie is involved in human trafficking?" Winnie's expression was incredulous. "But...why?"

"Money," Arta said. "Dev suspects they are under the hatches."

"Huh?"

"Without funds."

Meredith rolled her eyes. "God, Storky, they're in debt. Just say it."

"Storky?" Winnie asked, raising her brows.

"For reasons I cannot fathom, it amuses the shade to jape about my legs." Arta narrowed her eyes at Meredith. "How many people do the Barbers have?"

"Six, including the sheriff," Meredith said. "Tell Devy I said you're welcome. He can pay me back some other time...and he will." She began to fade, then solidified again. "Oh, and I'd get a move on, if I were you. That Bootsie is half a loaf shy if you know what I mean. No telling what she might do."

She gave them a little finger wave and disappeared.

Winnie checked her mirrors and did a one-eighty in the road. She turned on the flashing lights and punched the pedal to the floor. The car raced down the highway. "Butcher Road is less than twenty miles from here," she said. "Don't worry. We'll get there in time."

Urgency rode Arta with whip and spur. "I cannot wait. I have the location from the Provider."

"Damn it, Arta, don't you dare leave me here like a sack of turds."

"I go," Arta said and vanished.

* * * *

Dev awoke to searing pain. It felt like someone had driven a hot piece of rebar through his skull. He fumbled for his gun. Gone. So was his radio. He tried to sit up, but his arms and legs didn't work, and his muscles seemed to have turned to jelly.

"Easy, not too fast," a smooth, masculine voice said.

Strong arms grasped Dev by the shoulders and helped him to a sitting position. He looked for the exit, but the room swam, the dark walls shuffling around him like so many cards.

"Thanks," Dev gasped.

He leaned over and was violently sick.

"Concussion," the man said, hunkering down beside him. "Combined with an excess of alcohol. Not a good mix."

Dev focused on the speaker with an effort. His law enforcement training automatically kicked in, and he noted the man's characteristics. Black male, late twenties or early thirties. Six feet tall, athletic build. Short hair and neatly trimmed beard. No piercings or visible tats. Jeans and a gray Bama T-shirt. Brown Timberlands.

The room was spinning like a merry-go-round, and Dev pressed his forehead against his knees to keep from throwing up again. "I don't drink."

His words were slurred. Blurred vision, difficulty speaking, impaired cognitive function. He might not drink, but he was sure as shooting drunk, he realized with a sense of shock.

"Me, either," the man said. "My dad was an alcoholic, so I avoid the stuff like the plague. They bonged you. Stuck a tube down your throat and emptied a fifth of vodka into your stomach. I told them to stop, but they wouldn't listen."

Dev lifted his head. "The Barbers?" he asked with difficulty.

It was hard to speak, much less think through the alcohol fog.

"Yup."

Bootsie's round, freckled face swam in Dev's mind's eye. *Everyone has secrets*—hadn't Aunt Wee always said that?—and Bootsie had a doozy. She wasn't a victim. She was the villain...or one of them.

He'd allowed his hatred for Russ to keep him from seeing the truth. He could kick himself for being stupid.

"You took quite a blow to the head," the man continued, regarding him thoughtfully. "Between that and the booze, you should be dead."

"The jury's still out on that one." Dev touched his aching head and winced. He had a knot on his scalp the size of a goose egg. "Where are we?"

"In a grain silo."

"Silo?" The room dipped, and Dev planted both hands on the floor to keep from falling over. There was something he needed to ask, something important. "Where...Barbers?"

"Gone, but they'll be back soon."

"We need..." Dev tried to get to his knees and face planted. "Get out...before...return."

"Can't." Once more, the man helped him to sit up. "Bootsie and Russ have guns, and they keep the access door locked at all times. Only one way in or out."

"Damn." Dev closed his eyes at a fresh wave of dizziness. "Name's Dev. Local sheriff."

"I know who you are, but I'm not surprised you don't recognize me. I was in middle school the last time you saw me. I'm Jax Freeman."

"Livy's younger brother. I've been looking for you." Opening his eyes, Dev focused his blurry gaze on him. "You have...same eyes."

"Yeah, there's a definite resemblance."

"Hard to find..." Dev's mouth was mushy, and he spoke slowly to keep from slurring. "Tried to reach you for weeks."

"I was hiking the Appalachian Trail and decided to go old school. After being tied to a pager for the past three years, I left my phone behind. Wanted to disconnect, you know?"

"Doctor? 'Member now. Looked you up after..." Dev swallowed and shook his head. "After she died."

A spasm of pain crossed Jax's face. "I still find it hard to believe Livy's gone."

A fresh wave of grief and regret pinched Dev's heart. "Me, too."

"She was excited I was moving back this way," Jax said. "I've been working in Ohio, but I accepted a position at the hospital in Hannah. Less money, but Livy's my only family. I wanted to be close to her, and I hated the snow. I was supposed to start the new job in November. Took a few months off to hike the Trail." He rose and began to pace. "Figured there'd be plenty of time for me and Livy to catch up once I moved back home. How was I to guess that pasty-faced bitch would kill her?"

Vertigo assailed Dev. "Bootsie killed Livy?" he mumbled, trying hard not to pass out. "She confessed?"

Jax laughed bitterly. "Bragged about it. She's obsessed with the idea that Livy and Russ were having an affair."

"Were they?" Dev managed to ask.

"Hell no. Sis was done with that jackass years ago. It was Russ who wouldn't leave her alone." He paused to squint at Dev. "Say, you don't look so good."

"Sick," Dev said, and vomited again. He wiped his mouth with the back of his hand. "Sorry."

"Don't worry about me. I've seen it all in the ER. Speaking of hospitals, you should be in one."

"Nah, I'm feeling better."

It was true. With some of the alcohol out of his stomach, Dev's head felt clearer, and he found it easier to think. "Russ gave Livy a charm bracelet in high school," he said. "If they weren't having an affair, why was she wearing the bracelet when she died?"

"I'll tell you why—because that crazy bitch Bootsie made her wear it. Turns out, she stole that charm bracelet. Lifted it off Livy one night at a party while Livy and Russ were still dating."

"She told you this?"

"Oh, yeah, *raved* about it. Apparently, she wanted Russ for herself even way back then, and she hated Livy for dating him."

"She was jealous?"

"Eat up with it."

"Then why make Livy wear the bracelet?"

"To taunt her, maybe? Who knows? Bootsie is certifiable." Jax resumed his pacing. "Sis planned to start college in the fall, did you know that?"

"No."

But you would have known if you'd made more of an effort to mend your friendship, Dev thought with another twinge of remorse.

"She always wanted to be a teacher, but she put her plans on hold to help me through medical school," Jax said. "That's why she took the job at the plant."

"She was a good sister." Dev was still woozy and sick, but it was getting easier to talk without mumbling. "She always took care of you, even when we were kids."

"Yeah." Jax kicked a low stool out of his way. "It was supposed to be my turn to help her. She registered at South Alabama in the spring."

The stool skittered into an oak coffee table and came to a stop. Dev blinked, taking in their surroundings. The space had been turned into a makeshift living room with a large three-cushion pink and blue floral sofa and a recliner. A small end table and a vase of artificial pink daisies with blank, grinning faces completed the décor. On the far side of the sofa marched a line of neatly made single beds, complete with white coverlets and plump pillows. A stuffed animal had been carefully arranged on each of the beds like an offering to a puerile god.

Dev's gaze moved past the furnishings to the rounded brick walls. He tipped his head back, wincing at the slight movement. His head was splitting. The walls of their prison soared upward ninety feet or more and had no windows. At the top of the brick cylinder was a circular opening, the only light in the dark tube other than the glow from a couple of battery-operated lanterns.

"I know this place," Dev murmured. "We're in the Butcher."

"Yep." Jax dropped to the floor beside him. "My friends and I used to party here when we were in high school."

"I thought you didn't drink."

Jax flashed him a grin. "Who said anything about drinking? This was our hideout. We could raise all kinds of hell in here without our parents or the cops finding us. No offense."

"None taken." Dev rubbed his aching temples. "How long…"

"Have I been here?" Jax stretched his legs out and crossed his ankles. "A week, I think. Not sure. I went nuts when I found out about Livy and stormed into Russ's office to confront him. Somebody knocked me out, and I woke up in this lovely little bungalow." He grimaced. "So my knowledge of concussions is firsthand, not merely textbook."

"I'm surprised they didn't kill you."

"Oh, Bootsie wanted to, but Russ convinced her I could be of use with the kids."

"Kids?"

"Teenagers," Jax said. "Runaways, mostly."

"How many?" Dev asked, counting the row of beds.

"As many as a dozen in the past, from what they've said, but this is a small haul. Only four this time."

Dev shifted on the hard stone. The throbbing in his head had spread, radiating down his spine. "What can you tell me about the victims?"

"Nothing, really," Jax said. "They keep them drugged, so I haven't been able to get much out of them. Best I can tell, the Barbers are running a prostitution ring, and they're mixed up with some rough customers. *Djegrali*, they call them. Some kind of syndicate, I guess. Italian, maybe, or Albanian? I dunno." He frowned. "I can tell you this, though. These kids were in bad shape when the Barbers snagged them—malnutrition, skin wounds, bronchitis, STDs." He pointed to a stack of boxes against the wall. "Bootsie makes sure I have whatever I need—antibiotics, vitamins, supplements. You name it, she's got it."

"Her dad ran a pharmacy."

"That explains it. She feeds 'em good, too. Keeps fussing that they're too skinny. Says she wants them in good shape for her 'clients'."

"Fattening them up for the oven," Dev said, "like the witch in 'Hansel and Gretel.' Where are the kids now?"

"The Barbers took them to her dad's house to shower," Jax said. "There's no toilet or running water here. We've been using a chamber pot and taking spit baths."

"Lovely," Dev muttered. "Let me guess—the clients arrive tonight?"

"Yep." Jax met Dev's gaze and there was fear in his eyes. "They've got something awful planned for you. I heard them whispering about it." He took a deep breath and exhaled. "Me, too."

"Don't worry, we'll get out of this," Dev said. "I promise."

"How?"

"I don't know, but I'll think of something."

Jax flinched at a screech of metal from outside the silo portal. "Better make it fast. They're back."

A square of light opened in one of the brick walls, and three girls and a boy stumbled inside. The boy wore new jeans and a polo shirt, and the girls reminded Dev of a bouquet of flowers in their printed, puff-sleeved dresses. The teens looked groggy and confused. Clearly, he wasn't the only one under the influence.

Bootsie bustled into the silo with her usual take-charge verve. She was stylishly clad in a sleeveless, abstract-print shirtdress and bronze flats. Her pinched mouth was painted bright coral to match one of the blobs of color on her dress, and her hair was teased and styled. A small handbag hung from one shoulder by a gold chain. She was a model of country club affluence and chic, except for the gun in her hand.

"There, now." She shooed the teens over to the couch, speaking in the same perky voice she'd used at pep rallies back in high school. "You've been fluffed and fed, and we're ready for the party. This is going to be *such* fun."

A party? More like lambs to the slaughter.

Bootsie glanced back. "Russ? Hurry up, Pudgeums, and don't forget to lock the door."

"Calm your tits." Russ lumbered inside carrying a large cooler. "I'm right behind you."

The door clanged shut, and he limped past with the ice chest. A Colt .45 pistol protruded from the back of his trousers.

"Don't say *tits*," Bootsie scolded. "It's vulgar. Put the cooler with the ice over by the snacks."

"I know the drill." Russ trudged over to a large, shrouded shape along one wall and dropped the heavy cooler with a grunt. "How many of these shindigs have we done now, seven or eight?"

"Today makes ten," Bootsie said, "and I want everything to be just right."

Hurrying over, she whipped off the covering, revealing a long, rectangular table draped in a pristine white tablecloth, the kind Aunt Wee saved for Christmas and Easter dinners. The table was laden with junk food of every description, as well as plastic goblets, pale blue paper plates with tiny yellow and pink flowers, and matching napkins. Bottles of liquor and wine were carefully arranged on one end.

She picked up one of the plates and examined it. "The Floating Garden pattern is too summery," she said, frowning, "but, between the Lala Lavender League and Picklefest, I've been too busy to run to the Vera Bradley store in Mobile." She sighed and returned the plate to the stack. "Oh, well. It will just have to do."

"For Christ's sake, Bootsie, nobody gives a rat's ass about the frigging plates."

"Russ, your language, please!" She looked around the space with a tiny smile of satisfaction. "You know I like things done a certain way. That's why I had you move Mama's old furniture in here and bought those darling little beds for the kiddos."

"Like to broke my damn back," Russ grumbled. "And for what?"

"For our *guests*. As president of the LLL, I have my reputation to think of, and our clients are paying good money." She gave him a fond pat. "*So much money. Our troubles are over. Isn't it wonderful?*"

"Hunky-dory, so long as you keep them satisfied," Russ muttered.

"Don't worry," Bootsie said in a girlishly saccharine voice, "I won't let those nasty old demons hurt my Pudgy Wudgy."

Jax got to his feet. "Demons? What the hell are you talking about?"

Bootsie spun about. "Dr. Freeman, you startled me." She spied Dev, and her eyes widened. "Dev, you're awake."

"Awake?" Jax said. "It's a miracle he's alive, considering the amount of alcohol you gave him."

"We didn't have a choice." Lumbering over, Russ glowered at Dev. "He's one of *them*."

Jax looked confused. "Them?"

"A freak," Russ said. "You mean you ain't figured it out, Mr. Fancy Pants Doctor? The sheriff ain't human."

"At least I'm not a piece of shit," Dev said, "which is more than I can say for you."

"Shut up, you," Russ said and kicked Dev in the face.

The blow knocked Dev flat on his back and broke his nose. The pain in his head was white-hot and agonizing. He groaned and rolled over.

"Jesus, Barber, what the hell?" Jax cried, kneeling beside Dev. "The man already has a concussion!"

"Don't worry about it." Dev sat up and wiped the blood from his face. "It's not the first time he's broken my nose."

"Keep running your mouth, Whitsun, and you'll get worse," Russ growled.

"Calm down, sweetie." Bootsie trotted over to her husband with her gun. "You have high blood pressure, and the doctor said you shouldn't get upset." She noticed the pool of vomit on the floor beside Dev. "Oh, dear, you've made a mess, and our guests will be here any moment."

"Guests?" Dev staggered to his feet. "That's a pretty name for some ugly customers, Bootsie."

"They're *rich*. That's all I care about."

"No matter how much they're giving you, the money's not worth it. Let me help you before it's too late."

She tittered. "Too late? Too late for what, pray tell?"

"You and Russ." Dev could hardly see for the pain in his head. "You won't get away with this. I've got backup."

"You ain't got dick." Russ pointed his gun at Dev. "Nobody knows where you are, Whitsun. We took your radio and your gun and dumped your car. You're our prisoner, and that means we can do anything we like with you. So, go on. Give me an excuse to kill you. Please. I ain't forgot you broke my leg."

"No, no, Pudgy. You can't kill him." Bootsie shoved the muzzle of Russ's gun aside. "We have other plans for the sheriff, remember?"

"Oh, yeah, I forgot." Russ gave Dev a grin that made his skin crawl. "Kagrek."

"Kagrek?" Dev echoed.

"Our most important client," Bootsie said. "One of the *morkyn*...not that I expect you to know what that is."

"I know you're in way over your head, Bootsie."

"I *was* in over my head. Russ is not the businessman his daddy was—he's run R&B Trucking into the ground."

"Hey," Russ protested, "it wasn't just me. You spend money hand over fist. Who the hell pays sixteen grand for a frigging refrigerator?"

Bootsie gave him a pout. "You know I like nice things, Pudgy, and we have to keep up appearances."

"By selling people to demons?" Dev asked.

"Why not?" Bootsie shrugged. "The way I see it, we're doing the world a service by getting rid of the riffraff...homeless people and runaways and the like."

"You're a regular hero. You should run for office on that ticket."

"I know, right?" Bootsie's eyes sparkled. "It's a sweet deal, and Kagrek has been very generous."

"Until he turns on you."

"He won't. I'll make sure of it."

"Don't give me to Kagrek, Bootsie," Dev warned. "It would be a mistake."

"Afraid, Sheriff?"

"For you, not me."

Jax made a sound of frustration. "I think you've all lost your minds."

"I know it's hard to believe," Bootsie said to Jax, "but Behr County is *crawling* with supernaturals, and the sheriff is one of them." She arched a feathery brow at Dev. "That's right, I know your little secret. Livy sang like a songbird before she died. She told me *everything*, including the fact that you can't hold your liquor."

"Livy wasn't your first victim, though, was she?" Dev said, a memory clicking into place. "You killed your father, too."

"Why, yes. How did you guess?"

"That day in the Sweet Shop, I asked if you were with your father when he died, and you said no. I knew you were lying. What happened, did he catch you stealing drugs from the pharmacy?"

"Yes, but not for me—for the kiddoes," Bootsie said. "Gracious me, he was *so* upset. He actually threatened to turn me in. Can you believe it?" She shook her head. "He got so worked up that he wound up in the hospital. Bad heart, you know. I slipped into his room after visiting hours and injected him with lidocaine. Easy-peasy lemon squeezy. No more Daddy."

Any sympathy Dev might have felt for his old classmate withered and died. She was cold and calculating, and utterly evil, and she had to be stopped.

"And Livy? Why did you kill her?"

Bootsie's eyes glittered. "Because that skank was messing with my husband."

"No, she wasn't," Jax said. "That was all Russ. He came sniffing around, but she told him to take a hike."

"Liar!" Bootsie shouted. "She tried to take Russ away from me, and no one messes with my Pudgeums. So, I killed her, and I enjoyed it, too." Her orange mouth curved in a sickly smile. "You should've heard her scream when I fed her to the demons. Too bad I didn't record it. Makes me hot just to think about it."

"Crazy bitch," Jax said, lunging at her.

Bootsie shot Jax in the chest, and he fell to the floor. She aimed the gun at the doctor and pulled the trigger again, but the bullet hit something and ricocheted.

"*Shit*." Russ ducked as the bullet whizzed by his head and buried itself in a wall. "What the hell, Boots? You nearly got me."

"I'm sorry, Pudgy." Bootsie shook the gun. "I don't understand. How could I miss at such close range?"

"It was him." Russ leveled his .45 at Dev. "The freak did something. His hands are glowing."

"I put up a shield," Dev said, "but I won't be able to protect you from the demons. My head hurts and the alcohol…makes it hard to think."

Bootsie laughed. "We don't need your protection. I know how to keep our clients happy."

"I wouldn't be so sure," Dev said, swaying. "While we've been talking, your hors d'oevres have escaped."

"*What?*" Bootsie whirled around. The silo portal stood open, and the teens were gone. "Russ," she wailed. "I told you to lock the door!"

"I had my hands full with the cooler," Russ said. "You should've locked it."

"Well, don't just stand there," Bootsie shrieked. "Go after them! They can't have gone far. They're too doped up."

There came a high-pitched wail from above.

"Too late." Dev looked up and nearly lost his balance. "Your guests have arrived."

A cluster of smoky shapes flew through the crack in the silo roof. *Kraa, kraa, kraa,* the demons shrieked, circling the downward spiral of the silo like a drain.

"Oh, no," Bootsie cried. "Find those kids, Russ. Quick, before it's too late!"

"You find 'em," Russ said. "I'm out of here."

"Russ, come back," Bootsie squeaked as he made a beeline for the door. "Don't leave me!"

The heavy metal door slammed shut, and Russ halted, cursing as a misty, malformed shape materialized to bar his way. The demon was enormous, twenty feet tall and hideous, with a toothy, gaping mouth, scales like a dragon, glowing red eyes, and a multitude of clawed feet and hands. A ghastly stench poured off the fiend, a miasma of evil mixed with the choking smell of rotten meat that made it hard to breathe.

"Kagrek." Bootsie's round face was pale as the inside of a biscuit. "H-how nice to see you. We've been waiting for you."

The demon's dreadful gaze fastened on the injured man on the floor. Jax was unconscious but still breathing. "What is this?" The raspy voice sent a shiver of revulsion down Dev's spine. "This meat is spoiled."

"Oh, *that*," Bootsie said. "That's nothing, your worship. Pay no attention to him." She pointed a shaking finger at Dev. "This is the treat I promised you."

The demon's burning gaze fastened on Dev, taking in his bloodied appearance. "This vessel also appears damaged."

"A broken nose," Bootsie said quickly. "Nothing major. You're going to be pleased with him, I swear."

"Let us hope so for your sake. The last two humans you provided me were paltry. They scarcely lasted a few moons."

"B-because Kagrek is n-no ordinary demon," Bootsie said, tripping over her words in her haste to placate the demon. "This time, I've brought you someone more worthy, someone young and strong and handsome. A-a person of consequence."

"So you say. And the others...the morsels for my pets?" The djegrali shrieked and rubbed against Kagrek like a clowder of affectionate cats. "Where are they?"

"W-we were only able to get four this time," Bootsie stuttered. "They're waiting outside. Russ was just about to fetch them, weren't you, Russ?"

"You bet," Russ said, sidling toward the door.

"Hold," Kagrek growled, freezing Russ in his tracks. "First, I would inspect my offering. If I find the vessel to my liking, then you may present the others." Reaching down, he lifted Dev in a huge, clawed hand and gave him a lingering sniff. "There is something strange about this one, something I cannot quite name..." The demon opened his maw and lapped at the blood on Dev's face with a long, slimy tongue. He stiffened and flung Dev aside. "This is no human. He is *unluath*."

Dev flew twenty feet through the air and slammed into a wall. His head hit the unforgiving bricks, and he slid to the floor in a daze. Bleary-eyed, he watched Bootsie try to placate the demon.

"*U-unluath*?" she said, faltering. "Forgive me, great Kagrek, but I-I don't know what that—"

"He is a lesser god and part demon," Kagrek roared. "His blood stinks of it."

"He's powerful. I thought you'd be pleased."

"Imbecile." Kagrek's hideous face twisted with fury. "The djegrali cannot possess such a one, not even the *morkyn*."

"I'm sorry." Bootsie was sobbing with fright. "I didn't know."

With a piercing shriek, another wraith flew into the silo to circle Kagrek's grotesque head.

"What is this?" Kagrek thundered. "Sargath tells me the vessels have escaped. Deceivers! You shall be punished."

Russ yelped and made a dash for the door. Kagrek snarled and snatched him up, kicking and screaming.

"No, Kagrek, don't hurt him," Bootsie pleaded. "Please, don't—"

Kagrek bit Russ in two and tossed his lower body aside.

"Russ, *nooo*," she cried, falling to her knees beside what was left of her dead husband.

"Bootsie, get up." Dev struggled to his knees. "*Run*."

Kagrek barked a guttural command, and the wraiths swarmed Bootsie. She screamed in anguish and tottered to her feet, plucking desperately at the demons clinging to her head, face, and body. When she stumbled and fell, the wraiths settled on top of her like vultures, their black forms heaving and shifting as they fed. Her cries grew gradually weaker and weaker and finally stopped. The demons scuttled aside. Bootsie's body was a shriveled husk, her mouth open in a soundless scream.

Jax moaned and stirred in pain.

The slight motion drew Kagrek's attention. "Still hungry, my pets?" The demon chuckled wickedly. "Feast upon him, if you will."

"No," Dev said. "Leave him alone."

Crawling across the floor, he shielded the injured man with his body.

Kagrek laughed. "You cannot stop me, *unluath*. Your strength is spent, and you are too weak."

"Maybe I am, but *she's* not," Dev said, the wolf's ears pricking at a noise in the distance.

The ominous rumbling grew nearer, the drumbeat of an avenging horde bearing down upon the enemy.

Or one extremely pissed-off Kirvahni huntress.

The earth shook, and the silo wall exploded in a shower of bricks. A shining form appeared in the opening, terrible in its beauty and awful to behold. Shrieking and cawing, the wraiths streamed out of the gaping hole and fled in terror.

Kagrek's monstrous form wavered in alarm. "What is that?" he demanded.

With the last of his strength, Dev lifted his head. Black spots danced at the edge of his vision. "That?" He gave the demon a woozy grin. "That's my girlfriend, and you're in big trouble, asshole."

He collapsed on top of Jax and let the blackness claim him.

Chapter Twenty-Six

Two weeks later

Dev guided Arta through the crowded restaurant, one hand on her narrow waist. It was a mild November night, and Chez Beck's was a wonderland of light, sound, and smell. The air was atremble with music and the murmur of conversation, and a bevy of intoxicating scents tickled the wolf's keen nose. The building faced the water, and floor-to-ceiling windows gave breathtaking views of the surrounding woods and the Devil River. A large garden sloped down to the riverbank. The lush greenery twinkled with tiny lights. Glimmering dots fluttered into the air, forming the initials *H* and *O*, in honor of Beck and Conall's newborns, then settled back down again.

"Fairies?" Dev said, halting in surprise.

Conall strode up to them. "'Tis Evie's doing. Ansgar's mate has a way with the fairy folk." He shook Dev's hand. "Thank you both for coming."

"Wouldn't miss it," Dev said. "Congratulations on being a dad, by the way."

Conall's harsh features softened. "'Tis a strange thing, is it not? I confess I have never been enamored with human babes—mewling things, in my experience, leaking from both ends—but 'tis altogether different when they are your own. Oft, I look upon the twins and am so overcome with emotion that—" He stopped himself. "But I digress. Allow me to say that you are in exceptionally good looks tonight, High Huntress."

Dev wholeheartedly agreed. Everyone was dressed to the nines, the men in tuxes and the women in gowns, but Arta left them all in the shade, a vision in a skintight chainmail evening dress with a belted waist and short sleeves. A slit in the back of the gown allowed her freedom of movement and gave all and sundry a peek at her shapely calves. Her pale hair was worn in a long ponytail with a hint of curl, and diamonds sparkled in her earlobes.

She was exquisite, a deadly beauty equally capable of slaying demons or capturing hearts, depending upon her mood.

God knows she had captured his.

"Thank you, Captain," Arta said. "You cut a dashing figure yourself." She handed him a small, beribboned box. "A token of our esteem. The shire reeve and I share in your joy."

"Many thanks." Conall looked up at the sound of a husky voice. "Ah, Rebekah summons us. Come. She is with the babes and would bid you welcome."

They followed the captain, weaving their way through the guests. Heads together, Evan and Beck were admiring the infant in Evan's arms. The brother and sister made a striking pair with their gleaming raven's-wing hair and sensuous good looks. Evan—usually surly at best—gazed upon the dark-eyed infant in his care with surprising tenderness. Duncan stood next to him with the other twin, a round-cheeked baby with a thatch of dark hair and purple eyes. Duncan's mate, Cassie, magnificent in a pale blue gown with a V-neck and a plunging back, was entertaining Bunny and Rafe Dalvahni's toddler, a red-haired cherub, with a spirited game of peekaboo under the doting gazes of his parents.

"Sheriff...Arta," Evan said, hailing them as they approached. "Come take a look at the brats. They're perfect."

"Evan is besotted," Conall said, "but at last we agree. My son and daughter are perfect."

"Have you decided on names?" Dev asked.

"Yes." Conall's black eyes gleamed with paternal satisfaction. "Hélène for our daughter, and Oran for our son."

"Good names, both, and blessed," Arta said. "May the favor of the gods shine upon them and you."

"And you." Conall bowed. "I understand you and the shire reeve are handfasted?"

"Yes." Arta colored with a delightfully unexpected touch of shyness that made Dev want to snatch her into his arms and kiss her senseless. "Kehvahn has given us his blessing, and we have placed our names in the Great Book."

In the Great Book, in the Temple of Calm, on another astral plane, Dev thought with a touch of amusement. Kehvahn had presided over the ceremony, with the Kir in attendance. The Temple of Calm, like the

Kirvahni, was elegant and beautiful, a serene, airy manse of white marble, spiraling columns, soaring ceilings open to the stars, and secret pools with feathery waterfalls. Enchanting, peaceful, and restorative—the last of Dev's hurts had healed in his brief time there. Under Kehvahn's indulgent eyes and the slightly disapproving gazes of the Kir, he and Arta had signed their names in the enormous leatherbound tome. The quill had been bronze, and the letters had burst into flame and burned away, leaving their signatures shining on the page. Somewhere deep in the temple, a bell had gonged.

"'Tis done," Kehvahn had said. "You are one."

With that, the temple had disappeared, and he and Arta had found themselves back home.

"Rebekah and I, too, signed our names in the Great Book." Conall broke off as Beck left Evan and joined them. "Ah, here you are, my heart. I was felicitating the shire reeve and Arta on their recent union."

"Congratulations," Beck said, smiling at them. "Conall and I were married twice, once in the Hall of the Warriors and again in the spring." She sighed. "It was lovely."

"Arta and I are planning a spring wedding, too," Dev said. "Aunt Wee insists. She and Winnie and Verbena weren't included in the temple thingamabob, and their feelings were hurt."

Arta gave him a look that would have daunted a weaker man. "'Thingamabob'? You refer to the sacred ceremony wherein we were bound, heart and soul, for all eternity?"

"Yep," Dev said, unabashed. "Aunt Wee gave Kehvahn a piece of her mind after we signed the Great Book, and he spent a few days in the doghouse."

Conall seemed puzzled. "The doghouse?"

"Kehvahn fell out of the Lady Weoka's good graces, much to his dismay," Arta explained. "He is smitten with her."

They lingered a few more minutes, oohing and ahhing over the babies and admiring Rafe and Bunny's sturdy little boy, then withdrew to make room for a line of well-wishers that included Addy and Brand, Evie and Ansgar, and Sassy and Grim. Drawing Arta aside, Dev nuzzled her neck, breathing in her jasmine and rose perfume.

"Conall's right," he murmured in her ear. "You look amazing tonight, and you smell as good as you look. Slip back out to the car, and I'll let you take advantage of me."

"Coitus in the car?" Arta's fine eyes gleamed with interest. "This is done, truly?"

"You've never had sex in a car?"

"Nay, thralls do not have cars, and you and I have not coupled in one." Her expression grew thoughtful. "Though now I think on it, we might have done so on one occasion, had a certain shade not interrupted us."

Meredith appeared as if on cue, wearing a bronze lace gown with a fitted bodice and spaghetti straps. "It's called a cock block," she said, "and it was my civic duty. Shame on the two of you, dry humping on the side of the road like a couple of horny teenagers." She eyed Dev up and down. "Sheriff, you are positively a snack. I do love a man in a tuxedo."

"Then you are in luck," Arta said. "An you would observe, all the warriors in attendance are similarly garbed."

"So they are," Meredith said, gazing around the room at the Dalvahni in admiration. "Have either of you seen my husband?"

"Trey?" Dev shook his head. "No, we just got here and—"

"Never mind." Meredith's raptor gaze fastened on the man at the piano across the room. "I see my father-in-law. I'll ask him."

She flounced over and said something to the pianist. He gave her a startled look and disappeared.

"The musician is a ghost?" Arta asked in surprise.

"Yeah, haven't you noticed? Everyone here is a supernatural, with a few exceptions," Winnie said, strolling up to them, beautiful in a dramatic strapless ruby red gown with a cascading ruffle down one side. "Jason and Brenda Damian were invited." She waved her drink at a middle-aged man and his wife. The woman stood uncertainly near the door wearing the frozen expression of someone in extreme social discomfort. "Grandparents, you know, and Muddy and Amasa Collier. Everyone else is kith or a super, including the bartenders and the waiters."

"Should Brenda and Jason be here?" Dev asked, frowning in concern. "Things have a way of happening when you get supers together...and what about the fairies?"

Toby sauntered up, resplendent in a tux. "Jason knows shit goes off the grid around here—his young'uns are demonoids, after all—but Brenda is a horse of a different color. She's a norm through and through."

"No worries," Winnie said. "Kev says to leave our badges at the door and enjoy ourselves. Says it's all under control. Something about a mindwipe."

"Kev?" Arta said.

"The nerdy dude with the flyaway hair and the old-timey glasses." Winnie motioned toward the windows. "He and Aunt Wee went for a stroll in the gardens. Aren't old people the cutest?"

"His name is Kehvahn," Arta said, giving her a stern look, "not 'Kev.'"

"Okay, okay. No need to poker up." Winnie offered her glass to Arta. "Drink?"

Arta eyed the brown concoction with misgiving. "That depends. What is it?"

"Chocolate martini."

Arta shuddered. "I thank you, but no. I have yet to fully recover from our last revel."

Winnie snorted. "Some revel. We sat on the couch and knocked back some M&M'S. We had fun, though, didn't we?"

"We did," Arta said, "and paid the piper after. I prefer to keep a clear head."

"Boring," Winnie pronounced.

"Be that as it may, I do not enjoy the aftereffects."

Eamon and Malothan materialized at Winnie's elbow, dashing in formal attire.

Eamon bowed to Winnie. "Greetings, fair one. You are a vision, a beauty to pierce the heart of any warrior, and no doubt."

Winnie scowled at him. "What a load of horse—"

"And a tongue to cut him with, should he survive the initial blow," Eamon concluded smoothly. Giving Winnie a mocking smile, he turned to Arta. "Well met, High Huntress. Mal has been telling me how you bested the *morkyn.*"

"Mal was there?" Dev turned to the blue warrior. "Then I wish you'd tell me what happened, because I passed out, and Arta won't talk about it."

"There is nothing to tell," Arta said with lofty indifference. "I killed the *morkyn*, and you are safe."

Winnie's eyes narrowed. "Uh-huh. You don't remember, do you?"

"What? Of course, I—" Arta bit her lip. "'Strewth, I am loath to admit it, but 'tis a blur."

"Really?" Dev said. "What part?"

"I recall approaching the tower where you were being held and nothing more."

Dev stared at her in surprise. "Why didn't you tell me?"

"Because such a thing has ne'er happened to me, and I am not proud of it."

"It's nothing to be ashamed of, love," he said, tugging her close. "People do a lot of things when they're under stress. It happens."

"I am not 'people,' and it does not happen to *me*."

"As a rule, the Kir and the Dal are not metamorphic," Mal said, not unkindly. "Doubtless, your alteration in form resulted in your memory lapse."

"Alteration?" Arta went still. "What do you mean?"

Winnie held up her hand. "First things first. Half the law enforcement in Behr County were looking for the Barbers and Dev. How on earth did you find them, Mal?"

"As it happens, a dog told me."

"Not me," Toby said when Winnie gave him a startled look. "Mal was telling me about it earlier. From his description, the dog he's talking about was Trey Peterson."

"Trey Peterson?" Winnie said. "But he's..."

"Dead as a doorknob," Toby said. "Likes to run around as a Dalmatian."

"If this be so, then we speak of the same creature," Mal said. "I was hunting in the woods when a spotted hound approached me. I knew at once the dog was phantasmic by its wavering form. Naturally, I was leery at first, but the shade persisted, and I followed him some three leagues distant. A golden hawk led me the rest of the way."

"Merta," Arta murmured.

"The very same," said Mal. "She was circling a masonry spire in some distress. I sensed the presence of the djegrali—their foul stench is unmistakable—and knew at once the cause of the bird's unease. I readied my sword and pick, prepared to do battle, but ere I could engage the enemy, the wolf arrived."

"Wolf?" Dev said, much interested. "What wolf?"

"A huge, fearsome beast"—Mal spread his arms wide to indicate the creature's size—"silver and shining as the sun." He glanced at Arta and quickly away again. "A female, my hunter's instincts told me."

"Oh ho," said Winnie. "I see where this is going."

"Your perspicacity is a marvel," Eamon murmured, earning a scowl from her. "Do go on, Mal. You near the finish."

"Beams of light shot from the she-wolf's eyes," Mal continued, warming to his story, "and one of the walls crumbled. A scourge of wraiths flew from the opening, and the she-wolf opened her dreadful jaws and swallowed them whole. Thrusting her head and shoulders into the granary, the wolf snatched a demon in her jaws." His eyes shone at the memory. "'Twas one of the *morkyn*, huge and hideous of aspect. She shook the fiend like a rat, snapping him in two. The remnants, she savaged."

Winnie slapped Arta on the shoulder. "That's my girl. When did you realize the wolf was Arta, Mal?"

"Not until she resumed her natural form," Mal said. "The wolf disappeared, and Arta was standing there. 'Twas a shock, to be sure. She strode inside and returned, carrying the shire reeve over one shoulder and a human male by the waist."

"Jax Freeman," Dev said. "Bootsie shot him."

"That must be when I arrived," Winnie said. "I pulled up and almost had a heart attack. Dev was so jacked up, I thought he was dead, for sure."

"Three licks to the head and a fifth of hooch will do that to you," Dev said. "Good thing I've got a thick skull and a fast metabolism."

"How's the doctor doing?" Toby asked.

"Jax will recover," Dev said. "Should be able to start work in a few weeks. Fortunately for his peace of mind, he won't remember anything. Bootsie shot him before the demons arrived."

Toby chuckled. "Which is more 'n I can say for Brenda Damian, bless her heart. Poor woman looks like she's swallowed a toad."

Dev glanced across the room. Brenda had noticed Malothan and was staring at the blue warrior in shock.

"If she asks, Mal, tell her you're an actor," Dev suggested, "and you've dyed your skin for a part."

"A clever ruse," Mal said. "Thank you, shire reeve."

"Wait, you haven't always been blue?" Winnie gazed at him in rapt fascination. "I assumed it was your natural color."

Mal flashed her a grin. "'Tis a tale of woe, to be sure."

"Fascinating," Winnie said, her voice dripping honey. "I'd *love* to hear it."

Mal took the empty glass from her hand. "Then allow me to replenish your drink, and I will recount the yarn in full."

"Wonderful." Smiling, Winnie linked arms with the striking warrior, and the two of them strolled away in the direction of the bar.

Eamon watched them leave with a frown. "'Tis stuffy in here," he announced abruptly. "Methinks I am in need of air."

He disappeared.

"Trouble brewing," Toby said, shaking his head. "Our Winnie's playing with fire."

"She's a big girl," Dev said. "She'll figure it out."

"Hope so." Toby looked worried. "Word's out about your kidnapping, Sheriff. Town's buzzing. The Barbers were muckety-mucks, and folks are asking questions."

"I can imagine," Dev said. "Finding out the president of the Lala Lavender League and her husband were running a criminal operation must have come as a shock."

"The norms don't know about the demons, of course," Toby said, "but they wanna know where the Barbers are and what happened to them. I been telling anyone who asks that you escaped, and we don't know where the Sam Hill the Barbers are. Seems to satisfy 'em, and folks assume the Barbers made a run for it."

"That works," Dev said. "The less said, the better. Still no sign of the kids the Barbers were holding hostage?"

"Nope. My guess is, they hightailed it."

"Can't say as I blame them," said Dev. "They're damn lucky, though I'm sure they don't see it that way."

"Guess the Barbers' business will eventually be put up for auction?"

"I guess," Dev murmured, gazing at Arta. "A wolf, huh?"

"Why not?" Toby said. "She's your mate. Like to like, you know."

"I confess, 'tis surprising and more than a little disconcerting," Arta said. "As Mal pointed out, demon hunters are not wont to shift."

"Folks don't always fit the box assigned to 'em, and that ain't a bad thing," Toby said. "'Scuse me. Think I'll meander over and dandle one of them babies."

He wandered away, leaving Dev and Arta alone.

"I'm glad it was a wolf," Dev said, brushing the back of his fingers across Arta's silken cheek. "It's a sign we were meant to be together."

She smiled up at him. "Had you any doubt?"

"Nope, but the wolf settles it, as far as I'm concerned."

"*I* chose the form of the wolf, my Devlin, not the other way around."

"Because you're my mate. Chicken or the egg."

"'Tis a silly argument and circular."

"Exactly."

She frowned, as though tempted to disagree, but was distracted when a party came through the door. Following the direction of her gaze, Dev saw Aunt Wee and Kehvahn enter the restaurant. A pretty blonde in a three-quarter-length champagne gown with a fitted bodice and draped short sleeves was with them.

"Verbena!" Taking Arta by the hand, Dev strode over to his sister. "You look like a million bucks."

Verbena blushed. "Thanks, big brother. You clean up nice, too." She smiled shyly at Arta. "Ma'am."

"Please, we are family now," Arta said, taking her hands. "You must call me Arta."

"Arta, then," Verbena said, her smile widening. "You's purty as a picture and glowing like a star."

"Hmm." Weoka looked Arta up and down. "You're right, child. I'm thinking April for the wedding, at the latest. Wouldn't push the date much past that on account of the baby."

"*Baby?*" Arta swayed. "What baby?"

"Easy, love," Dev said, steadying her. "Our baby, of course. You're pregnant."

"What?" She stared at him, dazed. "How?"

Aunt Weoka chuckled. "Reckon you know the cause, right enough. Don't know why you act so surprised. Dev's father is a stag."

"I had no notion I could conceive a child." Arta's gaze narrowed on Dev. "You seem remarkably unruffled, sirrah. Explain yourself."

"I suspected," Dev admitted, "or I should say the wolf suspected. Your scent has changed, but not in a bad way," he added, seeing her stiffen. "In a good way. It's sexy as hell."

Weoka chuckled. "Like I said, like father, like son."

"I do not know what to think." Arta pressed her fingertips to her temples. "My mind is awhirl."

Dev pulled her close. "Whirl away. We have plenty of time to adjust."

"I wouldn't be so sure," Weoka said. "Arta's not human, and every super is different. We don't know how long her gestation period may be."

Arta's eyes widened. "Faith, Dev, she is right. What shall we do?"

"Whatever we need to do," Dev said. "I love you, and I already love our baby."

"Or *babies*," Weoka put in.

"Not helping, Aunt Wee."

The energy in the room shifted, and a dazzling redhead in a green gown materialized.

"*Red.*" Bulldozing his way through the crowd, Evan charged up to her. He swallowed hard, his chest heaving. "You..." He devoured her with his gaze. "You look well."

"By the Vessel, you are a dullard," Taryn said. "Is that the best you can do?"

With a muffled curse, Evan jerked her into his arms and kissed her.

"*Han-nah-alah*, my beloved." Spreading his arms wide, Kehvahn beamed. "Blessings upon you all!"

Arta looked much puzzled. "But, Master, does not *Han-nah-alah* mean the end of things?"

"Indeed, it does, beloved daughter," Kehvahn said, smiling fondly at her, "but it also signifies renewal, and with every ending comes a new beginning." His doting gaze moved around the room. "Love is in the air, and my children are fruitful and multiply. Is it not wonderful?"

"To love," Conall shouted.

"To love." Sliding her arms around Dev's neck, Arta whispered in his ear, "And to car sex."

Dev smiled down at her. "Right now?"

She gave him a smile so full of sensual promise that it took his breath away. "Yes, my Devlin, this very moment. What say you?"

"Hell, yeah," Dev said, and pulled her toward the door.

Printed in the United States
by Baker & Taylor Publisher Services